THE INTERPRETATION OF
MURDER

THE INTERPRETATION OF
MURDER

A NOVEL

JED RUBENFELD

HENRY HOLT AND COMPANY
New York

Henry Holt and Company, LLC
Publishers since 1866
175 Fifth Avenue
New York, New York 10010

Henry Holt® and are registered trademarks of Henry Holt and Company, LLC.
Copyright © 2006 by Jed Rubenfeld
All rights reserved.

ISBN-13: 978-0-7394-7969-8

Designed by Meryl Sussman Levavi

Printed in the United States of America

To Amy,

only, always

and to

Sophia and Louisa

THE INTERPRETATION OF
MURDER

In 1909, Sigmund Freud, accompanied by his then disciple Carl Jung, made his one and only visit to the United States, to deliver a series of lectures on psychoanalysis at Clark University, in Worcester, Massachusetts. The honorary doctoral degree that Clark awarded him was the first public recognition Freud had ever received for his work. Despite the great success of this visit, Freud always spoke, in later years, as if some trauma had befallen him in the United States. He called Americans "savages" and blamed his sojourn there for physical ailments that afflicted him well before 1909. Freud's biographers have long puzzled over this mystery, speculating whether some unknown event could have led to his otherwise inexplicable reaction.

PART

1

THERE IS NO mystery to happiness.

Unhappy men are all alike. Some wound they suffered long ago, some wish denied, some blow to pride, some kindling spark of love put out by scorn—or worse, indifference—cleaves to them, or they to it, and so they live each day within a shroud of yesterdays. The happy man does not look back. He doesn't look ahead. He lives in the present.

But there's the rub. The present can never deliver one thing: meaning. The ways of happiness and meaning are not the same. To find happiness, a man need only live in the moment; he need only live *for* the moment. But if he wants meaning—the meaning of his dreams, his secrets, his life—a man must reinhabit his past, however dark, and live for the future, however uncertain. Thus nature dangles happiness and meaning before us all, insisting only that we choose between them.

For myself, I have always chosen meaning. Which, I suppose, is how I came to be waiting in the swelter and mob of Hoboken Harbor on Sunday evening, August 29, 1909, for the arrival of the Norddeutsche Lloyd steamship *George Washington,* bound from Bremen, carrying to our shores the one man in the world I wanted most to meet.

At 7 P.M. there was still no sign of the ship. Abraham Brill, my friend and fellow physician, was waiting at the harbor for the same reason as I. He could hardly contain himself, fidgeting and smoking incessantly. The heat was murderous, the air thick with the reek of fish. An unnatural fog rose from the water, as if the sea were steaming. Horns sounded heavily out in the deeper water, their sources invisible. Even the keening gulls could be only heard, not seen. A ridiculous premonition came to me that the *George Washington* had run aground in the fog, her twenty-five hundred European passengers drowning at the foot of the Statue of Liberty. Twilight came, but the temperature did not abate. We waited.

All at once, the vast white ship appeared—not as a dot on the horizon, but mammoth, emerging from the mist full-blown before our eyes. The entire pier, with a collective gasp, drew back at the apparition. But the spell was broken by the outbreak of harbormen's cries, the flinging and catching of rope, the bustle and jostle that followed. Within minutes, a hundred stevedores were unloading freight.

Brill, yelling at me to follow, shouldered through to the gangway. His entreaties to board were rebuffed; no one was being let on or off the ship. It was another hour before Brill yanked at my sleeve and pointed to three passengers descending the bridge. The first of the trio was a distinguished, immaculately groomed, gray-haired, and gray-bearded gentleman whom I knew at once to be the Viennese psychiatrist Dr. Sigmund Freud.

❧

AT THE BEGINNING of the twentieth century, an architectural paroxysm shook New York City. Gigantic towers called skyscrapers soared up one after the other, higher than anything built by the hand of man before. At a ribbon-cutting on Liberty Street in 1908, the top hats applauded as Mayor McClellan declared the forty-seven-story redbrick and bluestone Singer Building the world's tallest structure. Eighteen months later, the mayor had to repeat the same ceremony at the fifty-story Metropolitan Life tower on Twenty-fourth Street. But even then, they were already breaking ground for Mr. Woolworth's staggering fifty-eight-story ziggurat back downtown.

On every block, enormous steel-beam skeletons appeared where empty lots had been the day before. The smash and scream of steam shovels never ceased. The only comparison was with Haussmann's transformation of Paris a half century earlier, but in New York there was no single vision behind the scenes, no unifying plan, no disciplining authority. Capital and speculation drove everything, releasing fantastic energies, distinctly American and individualistic.

The masculinity of it all was undeniable. On the ground, the implacable Manhattan grid, with its two hundred numbered east-west streets and twelve north-south avenues, gave the city a stamp of abstract rectilinear order. Above this, in the immensity of the towering structures, with their peacock-like embellishments, it was all ambition, speculation, competition, domination, even lust—for height, size, and always money.

The Balmoral, on the Boulevard—New Yorkers at the time referred to Broadway from Fifty-ninth to 155th Street as the Boulevard—was one of the grand new edifices. Its very existence was a gamble. In 1909, the very rich still lived in houses, not apartments. They "kept" apartments for short or seasonal stays in the city, but they failed to comprehend how anybody could actually live in one. The Balmoral was a bet: that the rich could be induced to change their minds if the accommodations were sufficiently opulent.

The Balmoral rose seventeen stories, higher and grander than any apartment building—any residential building—had ever climbed before. Its four wings occupied an entire city block. Its lobby, where seals cavorted in a Roman fountain, shone with white Carrara marble. Chandeliers in every apartment sparkled with Murano glass. The smallest dwelling had eight rooms; the largest boasted fourteen bedrooms, seven baths, a grand ballroom with a twenty-foot ceiling, and full maid's service. This rented for the appalling sum of $495 a month.

The owner of the Balmoral, Mr. George Banwell, enjoyed the enviable position of being unable to lose money on it. His investors had advanced $6,000,000 toward its construction, of which he had kept not a penny, scrupulously remitting the entire amount to the builder, the American Steel and Fabrication Company. The owner of this firm, however, was also Mr. George Banwell, and the actual construction cost was $4,200,000. On January 1, 1909, six months before the Balmoral was to open, Mr. Banwell announced that all but two of the apartments were already let. The announcement was pure invention, but it was believed, and therefore within three weeks it was so. Mr. Banwell had mastered the great truth that truth itself, like buildings, can be manufactured.

The Balmoral's exterior belonged to the Beaux-Arts school at its most flamboyant. Crowning the roofline were a quartet of thirteen-foot floor-to-ceiling glass-paned concrete arches, one at each corner of the property. Because these great arched windows gave off the top floor's four master bedrooms, someone standing outside them could have had a very compromising view inside. On Sunday night, August 29, the view from outside the Alabaster Wing would have been shocking indeed. A slender young woman was standing within, lit by a dozen flickering candles, barely clothed, exquisitely proportioned, her wrists tied together over her head, and her throat embraced by another binding, a man's white silk tie, which a strong hand was making tight, exceedingly tight, causing her to choke.

Her entire body glistened in the unbearable August heat. Her long legs were bare, as were her arms. Her elegant shoulders were nearly bare as well. The girl's consciousness was fading. She tried to speak. There was a question she had to ask. It was there; it was gone. Then she had it again. "My name," she whispered. "What is my name?"

*

DR. FREUD, I was relieved to see, did not look like a madman at all. His countenance was authoritative, his head well formed, his beard pointed, neat, professional. He was about five-foot-eight, roundish, but quite fit and solid for a man of fifty-three. His suit was of excellent cloth, with a watch chain and cravat in the continental style. Altogether, he looked remarkably sound for a man just off a week's voyage at sea.

His eyes were another matter. Brill had warned me about them. As Freud descended the ship's ramp, his eyes were fearsome, as if he were in a towering temper. Perhaps the calumny he had long endured in Europe had worked a permanent scowl into his brow. Or perhaps he was unhappy to be in America. Six months ago, when President Hall of Clark University—my employer—first invited Freud to the United States, he turned us down. We were not sure why. Hall persisted, explaining that Clark wished to confer on Freud the university's highest academic honor, to make him the center-piece of our twentieth-anniversary celebrations, and to have him deliver a series of lectures on psychoanalysis, the first ever to be given in America. In the end Freud accepted. Was he now regretting his decision?

All these speculations, I soon saw, were unfounded. As he stepped off the gangway, Freud lit a cigar—his first act on American soil—and the moment he did so the scowl vanished, a smile came to his face, and all the seeming choler drained away. He inhaled deeply and looked about him, taking in the harbor's size and chaos with what looked like amusement.

Brill greeted Freud warmly. They knew each other from Europe; Brill had even been to Freud's home in Vienna. He had described that evening to me—the charming Viennese house filled with antiquities, the doting and doted-on children, the hours of electrifying conversation—so often I knew his stories by heart.

From nowhere a knot of reporters appeared; they gathered around Freud and yelled out questions, mostly in German. He answered with good humor but seemed baffled that an interview should be conducted in so haphazard a fashion. At last Brill shooed them away and pulled me forward.

"Allow me," Brill said to Freud, "to present Dr. Stratham Younger, a recent graduate of Harvard University, now teaching at Clark, and sent down by Hall specially to take care of you during your week in New York. Younger is without question the most talented American psychoanalyst. Of course, he is also the *only* American psychoanalyst."

"What," said Freud to Brill, "you don't call yourself an analyst, Abraham?"

"I don't call myself American," Brill replied. "I am one of Mr. Roosevelt's 'hyphenated Americans,' for which, as he says, there is no room in this country."

Freud addressed me. "I am always delighted," he said in excellent English, "to meet a new member of our little movement, but especially here in America, for which I have such hopes." He begged me to thank President Hall for the honor Clark had bestowed on him.

"The honor is ours, sir," I replied, "but I'm afraid I hardly qualify as a psychoanalyst."

"Don't be a fool," said Brill, "of course you do." He then introduced me to Freud's two traveling companions. "Younger, meet the eminent Sándor Ferenczi of Budapest, whose name is synonymous throughout Europe with mental disorder. And here is the still more eminent Carl Jung of Zurich, whose *Dementia* will one day be known all over the civilized world."

"Most happy," said Ferenczi in a strong Hungarian accent, "most happy. But please to ignore Brill; everyone does, I assure you." Ferenczi was an affable sandy-haired fellow in his late thirties, brightly attired in a white suit. You could see that he and Brill were genuine friends. Physically, they made a nice contrast. Brill was among the shortest men I knew, with close-set eyes and a wide flat-topped head. Ferenczi, although not tall, had long arms, long fingers, and a receding hairline that elongated his face as well.

I liked Ferenczi at once, but I had never before shaken a hand that offered no resistance whatsoever, less than a joint of meat at the butcher's. It was embarrassing: he let out a yelp and yanked his fingers away as if they had been crushed. I apologized profusely, but he insisted he was glad to "start learning right away American walls," a remark at which I could only nod in polite agreement.

Jung, who was about thirty-five, made a markedly different impression. He was better than six feet tall, unsmiling, blue-eyed, dark-haired, with an aquiline nose, a pencil-thin mustache, and a great expanse of forehead—quite attractive to women, I should have thought, although he lacked Freud's ease. His hand was firm and cold as steel. Standing ramrod straight, he might have been a lieutenant in the Swiss Guard, except for his little round scholarly spectacles. The affection Brill clearly felt for Freud and Ferenczi was nowhere in evidence when he shook Jung's hand.

"How was your passage, gentlemen?" asked Brill. We could not go anywhere; our guests' trunks had to be collected. "Not too wearisome?"

"Capital," said Freud. "You won't believe it: I found a steward reading my *Psychopathology of Everyday Life*."

"No!" Brill replied. "Ferenczi must have put him up to it."

"Put him up?" Ferenczi cried out. "I did no such—"

Freud took no notice of Brill's comment. "It may have been the most gratifying moment of my professional life, which does not perhaps reflect too well on my professional life. Recognition is coming to us, my friends: recognition, slowly but surely."

"Did the crossing take long, sir?" I inquired idiotically.

"A week," Freud answered, "and we spent it in the most productive way possible: we analyzed each other's dreams."

"Good God," said Brill. "I wish I had been there. What were the results, in the name of heaven?"

"Well, you know," Ferenczi returned, "analysis is rather like being undressed in public. After you overcome initial humiliation, is quite refreshing."

"That's what I tell all my patients," said Brill, "especially the women. And what about you, Jung? Did you also find the humiliation refreshing?"

Jung, almost a foot taller than Brill, looked down on him as if at a laboratory specimen. "It is not quite accurate," he replied, "to say the three of us analyzed each other."

"True," Ferenczi confirmed. "Freud rather analyzed us, while Jung and I crossed interpretative swords with each other."

"What?" Brill exclaimed. "You mean no one dared to analyze the Master?"

"No one was permitted to," said Jung, betraying no affect.

"Yes, yes," said Freud, with a knowing smile, "but you all analyze me to death as soon as my back is turned, don't you, Abraham?"

"We do indeed," Brill replied, "because we are all good sons, and we know our Oedipal duty."

⟲

IN THE APARTMENT high above the city, a set of instruments lay on the bed behind the bound girl. From left to right, there were: a man's right-angled razor, with a bone handle; a black leather riding crop about two feet in length; three surgical knives, in ascending order of size; and a small vial half full of a clear fluid. The assailant considered and picked up one of these instruments.

Seeing the shadow of the man's razor flickering on the far wall, the girl shook her head. Again she tried to cry out, but the constriction of her throat reduced her plea to a whisper.

From behind her came a low voice: "You want me to wait?"

She nodded.

"I can't." The victim's wrists, crossed and suspended together over her head, were so slight, her fingers so graceful, her long legs so demure. "I can't wait." The girl winced as the gentlest possible stroke was administered to one of her bare thighs. A stroke, that is, of the razor, which left a vivid scarlet wake as it traced her skin. She cried out, her back curved in exactly the same arch as the great windows, her raven hair flowing down her back. A second stroke, to the other thigh, and the girl cried out again, more sharply.

"No," the voice admonished calmly. "No screaming."

The girl could only shake her head, uncomprehending.

"You must make a different sound."

The girl shook her head again. She wanted to speak but couldn't.

"Yes. You must. I know you can. I told you how. Don't you remember?" The razor was now replaced on the bed. On the far wall, in the wavering candlelight, the girl saw the shadow of the leather crop rising up instead. "You want it. Sound as if you want it. You must make that kind of sound." Gently but implacably, the silk tie around the girl's throat drew tighter. "Make it."

She tried to do as she was bid, moaning softly—a woman's moan, a supplicating moan, which she had never made before.

"Good. Like that."

Holding the end of the white tie in one hand and the leather crop in the other, the assailant brought the latter down upon the girl's back. She made the sound again. Another lash, harder. The sting caused the girl to cry out, but she caught herself and made the other sound instead.

"Better." The next blow landed not on her back but just below it. She opened her mouth, but at the same moment the tie was drawn still tighter, choking her. Her choking, in turn, made her moan seem more genuine, more broken, an effect her tormentor evidently liked. Another blow, and another and another, louder and faster, fell on all the softest parts of her body, rending her garments, leaving glowing marks on her white skin. With every lash, despite the searing pain, the girl moaned as she had been told to do, her cries coming louder and faster too.

The rain of blows stopped. She would have collapsed long before, but the rope from the ceiling, tied to her wrists, kept her upright. Her body was now scored with lacerations. Blood ran down in one or two places. For a moment all went dark for her; then the flickering light returned. A shiver passed through her.

Her eyes opened. Her lips moved. "Tell me my name," she tried to whisper, but no one heard.

The assailant, studying the girl's lovely neck, loosened the silk binding around it. For one instant she breathed freely, her head still flung back, the waves of black hair flowing to her waist. Then the tie around her throat went taut again.

The girl could no longer see distinctly. She felt a hand on her mouth, its fingers running lightly over her lips. Then those fingers drew the silk tie yet tighter, so that even her choking stopped. The candlelight went out for her again. This time it did not return.

❧

"THERE IS TRAIN *below* river?" asked Sándor Ferenczi incredulously.

Not only did such a train exist, Brill and I assured him, but we were going to ride it. In addition to the new tunnel across the Hudson River, the Hoboken tube boasted another innovation: full baggage service. All a voyager arriving in the United States had to do was mark his luggage with the name of his hotel in Manhattan. Porters stowed the trunks in the train's baggage car, and handlers on the other end did the rest. Taking advantage of this amenity, we walked out onto the platform, which overlooked the river. With the setting of the sun, the fog had lifted, revealing the jagged Manhattan skyline, studded with electric lights. Our guests stared in wonder: at the sheer expanse of it, and at the spires piercing the clouds.

"It's the center of the world," said Brill.

"I dreamt of Rome last night," Freud replied.

We waited on pins and needles—at least I did—for him to go on.

Freud drew on his cigar. "I was walking, alone," he said. "Night had just fallen, as it has now. I came upon a shop window with a jewelry box. That of course means a woman. I looked around. To my embarrassment, I had wandered into an entire neighborhood of bordellos."

A debate ensued on whether Freud's teachings dictated defiance of conventional sexual morality. Jung held that they did; indeed, he maintained that anyone who failed to see this implication had not understood Freud. The whole point of psychoanalysis, he said, was that society's prohibitions were ignorant and unhealthy. Only cowardice would make men submit to civilized morality once they had understood Freud's discoveries.

Brill and Ferenczi vigorously disagreed. Psychoanalysis demanded that a man be conscious of his true sexual wishes, not that he succumb to them. "When we hear a patient's dream," said Brill, "we interpret it. We don't tell the patient to fulfill the wishes he is unconsciously expressing. I don't, at any rate. Do you, Jung?"

I noticed both Brill and Ferenczi sneaking glances at Freud as they elaborated his ideas—hoping, I supposed, to find endorsement. Jung never did. He either had, or affected having, perfect confidence in his position. As for Freud, he intervened on neither side, apparently content to watch the debate unfold.

"Some dreams do not require interpretation," Jung said; "they require action. Consider Herr Professor Freud's dream last night of prostitutes. The meaning is not in doubt: suppressed libido, stimulated by our anticipated arrival in a new world. There is no point talking about such a dream." Here Jung turned to Freud. "Why not act on it? We are in America; we can do what we like."

For the first time, Freud broke in: "I am a married man, Jung."

"So am I," Jung replied.

Freud raised an eyebrow, nodding, but made no reply. I informed our party that it was time to board the train. Freud took a last look over the railing. A stiff wind blew in our faces. As we all gazed at the lights of Manhattan, he smiled. "If they only knew what we are bringing them."

CHAPTER TWO

IN 1909, A small device had begun to spread widely in New York City, accelerating communication and forever changing the nature of human interaction: the telephone. At 8 A.M. on Monday morning, August 30, the manager of the Balmoral lifted his mother-of-pearl receiver from its brass base and placed a hushed and hurried call to the building's owner.

Mr. George Banwell answered the call sixteen stories above the manager's head, in the telephone closet of the Travertine Wing's penthouse apartment, which Mr. Banwell had kept for himself. He was informed that Miss Riverford from the Alabaster Wing was dead in her room, the victim of murder and perhaps worse. A maid had found her.

Banwell did not immediately respond. The line was silent for so long the head manager said, "Are you there, sir?"

Banwell replied with gravel in his voice: "Get everyone out. Lock the door. No one enters. And tell your people to keep quiet if they value their jobs." Then he called an old friend, the mayor of New York City. At the conclusion of their conversation, Banwell said, "I can't afford any police in the building, McClellan. Not one uniform. I'll tell the family myself. I went to school with Riverford. That's right: the father, poor bastard."

❧

"MRS. NEVILLE," THE MAYOR called out to his secretary as he rang off. "Get me Hugel. At once."

Charles Hugel was coroner of the City of New York. It was his duty to see to the corpse in any case of suspected homicide. Mrs. Neville informed the mayor that Mr. Hugel had been waiting in the mayor's antechamber all morning.

McClellan closed his eyes and nodded, but said, "Excellent. Send him in."

Before the door had even closed behind him, Coroner Hugel launched into an indignant tirade against the conditions at the city morgue. The mayor, who had heard this litany of complaints before, cut him off. He described the situation at the Balmoral and ordered the coroner to take an unmarked vehicle uptown. Residents of the building must not be made aware of any police presence. A detective would follow later.

"I?" said the coroner. "O'Hanlon from my office can do it."

"No," replied the mayor, "I want you to go yourself. George Banwell is an old friend of mine. I need a man with experience—and a man whose discretion I can count on. You are one of the few I have left."

The coroner grumbled but in the end gave way. "I have two conditions. First, whoever is in charge at the building must be told immediately that nothing is to be touched. Nothing. I cannot be expected to solve a murder if the evidence is trampled and tampered with before I arrive."

"Eminently sensible," replied the mayor. "What else?"

"I am to have full authority over the investigation, including the choice of detective."

"Done," said the mayor. "You can have the most seasoned man on the force."

"Exactly what I don't want," replied the coroner. "It would be gratifying for once to have a detective who won't sell out the case after I have solved it. There's a new fellow—Littlemore. He's the one I want."

"Littlemore? Excellent," said the mayor, turning his attention to the stack of papers on his large desk. "Bingham used to say he's one of the brightest youngsters we have."

"Brightest? He's a perfect idiot."

The mayor was startled: "If you think so, Hugel, why do you want him?"

"Because he can't be bought—at least not yet."

WHEN CORONER HUGEL arrived at the Balmoral, he was told to wait for Mr. Banwell. Hugel hated being made to wait. He was fifty-nine years old, the last thirty of which had been spent in municipal service, much of it in the unhealthy confines of city morgues, which had lent his face a grayish cast. He wore thick glasses and an over-sized mustache between his hollow cheeks. He was altogether bald except for a wiry tuft sprouting from behind each ear. Hugel was an excitable man. Even in repose, a swelling in his temples gave the impression of incipient apoplexia.

The position of coroner in New York City was in 1909 a peculiar one, an irregularity in the chain of command. Part medical examiner, part forensic investigator, part prosecutor, the coroner reported directly to the mayor. He did not answer to anyone on the police force, not even the commissioner; but neither did anyone on the force answer to him, not even the lowliest beat patrolman. Hugel had little but scorn for the police department, which he viewed, with some justification, as largely inept and thoroughly crooked. He objected to the mayor's handling of the retirement of Chief Inspector Byrnes, who had obviously grown rich on bribes. He objected to the new commissioner, who did not appear to have the slightest appreciation of the art or importance of a properly held inquest. In fact, he objected to every departmental decision he ever heard of, unless it had been made by himself. But he knew his job. Although not technically a doctor, he had attended a full three years of medical school and could perform a more expert autopsy than the physicians who served as his assistants.

After fifteen infuriating minutes, Mr. Banwell at last appeared. He wasn't, in fact, much taller than Hugel but seemed to tower over him. "And you are?" he asked.

"The coroner of the City of New York," said Hugel, trying to express condescension. "I alone touch the deceased. Any disturbance of evidence will be prosecuted as obstruction. Am I understood?"

George Banwell was—and plainly knew it—taller, handsomer, better dressed, and much, much richer than the coroner. "Rubbish," he said. "Follow me. And keep your voice down while you're in my building."

Banwell led the way to the top floor of the Alabaster Wing. Coroner Hugel, grinding his teeth, followed. Not a word was spoken in the elevator. Hugel, staring resolutely at the floor, observed Mr. Banwell's perfectly creased pin-striped trousers and gleaming oxfords, which doubtless cost more than the coroner's suit, vest, tie, hat, and shoes put together. A manservant, standing guard outside Miss Riverford's apartment, opened the door for them. Silently, Banwell led Hugel, the head manager, and the servant down a long corridor to the girl's bedroom.

The nearly naked body lay on the floor, livid, eyes closed, luxurious dark hair strewn across the intricate design of an Oriental carpet. She was still exquisitely beautiful—her arms and legs still graceful—but her neck had an ugly redness around it, and her figure was scored with the marks of a lash. Her wrists remained bound, thrown back over her head. The coroner walked briskly to the body and placed a thumb to those wrists, where a pulse would have been.

"How was she—how did she die?" Banwell asked in his gravelly voice, arms folded.

"You can't tell?" replied the coroner.

"Would I have asked if I could tell?"

Hugel looked under the bed. He stood and gazed at the body from several angles. "I would say she was strangled to death. Very slowly."

"Was she—?" Banwell did not complete the question.

"Possibly," said the coroner. "I won't be certain until I've examined her."

With a piece of red chalk, Hugel roughed a circle seven or eight feet in diameter around the girl's body and declared that no one was to intrude within it. He surveyed the room. All was in perfect order; even the expensive bed linens were scrupulously tucked and squared. The coroner opened the girl's closets, her bureau, her jewelry boxes. Nothing appeared to be amiss. Sequined dresses hung straight in the wardrobe. Lace underthings were folded neatly in drawers. A diamond tiara, with matching earrings and necklace, lay in harmonious composition inside a midnight-blue velvet case on top of the bureau.

Hugel asked who had been in the room. Only the maid who had found the body, the manager answered. Since then, the apartment had been locked, and no one had entered. The coroner sent for the maid, who at first refused to come past the bedroom door. She was a pretty Italian girl of nineteen, in a long skirt and a full-length white apron. "Young lady," said Hugel, "did you disturb anything in this room?"

The maid shook her head.

Despite the body on the floor and her employer looking on, the maid held herself straight and met her interrogator's eyes. "No, sir," she said.

"Did you bring anything in, take anything out?"

"I'm no thief," she said.

"Did you move any article of furniture or clothing?"

"No."

"Very good," said Coroner Hugel.

The maid looked to Mr. Banwell, who did not dismiss her. Instead, he addressed the coroner: "Get it over with."

Hugel cocked an eye at the owner of the Balmoral. He took out a pen and paper. "Name?"

"Whose name?" said Banwell, with a growl that made the manager cower. "My name?"

"Name of deceased."

"Elizabeth Riverford," Banwell replied.

"Age?" asked Coroner Hugel.

"How do I know?"

"I understood you were acquainted with the family."

"I know her father," said Banwell. "Chicago man. Banker."

"I see. You wouldn't have his address, by any chance?" asked the coroner.

"Of course I have his address."

The two men stared at each other.

"Would you be so good," asked Hugel, "as to provide me the address?"

"I'll provide it to McClellan," said Banwell.

Hugel began grinding his molars again. "I am in charge of this investigation, not the mayor."

"We'll see how long you're in charge of this investigation," answered Banwell, who ordered the coroner for a second time to bring his business to a close. The Riverford family, Banwell explained, wanted the girl's body sent home, a duty he would be seeing to immediately.

The coroner said he could by no means allow it: in cases of

homicide, the decedent's body must by law be taken into custody for an autopsy.

"Not this body," answered Banwell. He instructed the coroner to ring the mayor if he required clarification of his orders.

Hugel responded that he would take no orders except from a judge. If anyone tried to stop him from taking Miss Riverford's body downtown for an autopsy, he would see that they were prosecuted to the fullest extent of the law. When this admonition failed appreciably to move Mr. Banwell, the coroner added that he knew a reporter for the *Herald* who found murder and obstruction of justice highly newsworthy. Reluctantly, Banwell yielded.

The coroner had brought his old, bulky box camera with him. This he now put to use, replacing the exposed plate with a fresh one after each smoky detonation of his flash-light. Banwell remarked that if the pictures made their way to the *Herald,* the coroner could be sure he would never be employed in New York or anywhere else again. Hugel did not reply; at that moment a strange whine began to fill the room, like the quiet cry of a violin stretched to its highest note. It seemed to have no source, coming from everywhere and nowhere at once. It rose louder and louder, until it became almost a wail. The maid screamed. When she finished, there was no sound in the room at all.

Mr. Banwell broke the silence. "What the devil was that?" he asked the manager.

"I don't know, sir," replied the manager. "It's not the first time. Perhaps some settling in the walls?"

"Well, find out," said Banwell.

When the coroner finished his photography, he announced he was leaving and taking the body with him. He had no intention of questioning the help or the neighboring residents—which was not his job—or of waiting for Detective Littlemore. In this heat, he explained, decomposition would rapidly set in if the corpse was not refrigerated at once. With the assistance of two elevator men, the girl's body was taken down to the basement in a freight elevator and from there to a back alley, where the coroner's driver was waiting.

When, two hours later, Detective Jimmy Littlemore arrived—not in uniform—he was flummoxed. It had taken some time for the mayor's messenger boys to find Littlemore; the detective had been in the basement of the new police headquarters still under construction on Centre Street, trying out the pistol range. Littlemore's orders were to make a thorough inspection of the murder scene. Not only did he find no murder scene, he found no murderee. Mr. Banwell would not speak with him. The staff also proved surprisingly untalkative.

And there was one person whom Detective Littlemore did not even get a chance to interview: the maid who had found the body. After Coroner Hugel left but before the detective arrived, the manager had called the young woman to his office and handed her an envelope with her month's pay—minus one day, of course, since it was only August 30. He informed the girl he was letting her go. "I'm sorry, Betty," he said to her. "I'm really sorry."

❧

BEFORE ANYONE ELSE was up, I examined the Monday morning newspapers in the opulent rotunda of the Hotel Manhattan, where Clark University was housing Freud, Jung, Ferenczi, and myself for the week. (Brill, who lived in New York, did not require a room.) Not one of the papers carried a story about Freud or his upcoming lectures at Clark. Only the New Yorker Staats-Zeitung ran anything at all, and this was a notice announcing the arrival of a "Dr. Freund from Vienna."

I never intended to be a doctor. It was my father's wish, and his wishes were supposed to be our commands. When I was eighteen and still living in my parents' house in Boston, I told him I was going to be America's foremost scholar of Shakespeare. I could be America's hindmost scholar of Shakespeare, he replied, but fore or hind, if I did not intend to pursue a career in medicine, I would have to find my own means of paying Harvard's tuition.

His threat had no effect on me. I didn't care at all for the family's Harvardiana, and I would be happy, I told my father, to complete my education elsewhere. This was the last conversation of any length I ever had with him.

Ironically, I was to obey my father's wish only after he no longer had any money to withhold from me. The collapse of Colonel Winslow's banking house in November 1903 was nothing compared to the panic in New York four years later, but it was good enough for my father. He lost everything, including my mother's bit. His face aged ten years in a single night; deep creases appeared unannounced on his brow. My mother said I must take pity on him, but I never did. At his funeral—which compassionate Boston avoided in droves—I knew for the first time I would go on in medicine, if able to continue my studies at all. Whether it was a newfound practicality that drove my decision or something else, I hesitate to say.

It was I, as things fell out, on whom pity had to be taken, and Harvard that took it. After my father's funeral, I notified the university that I would be withdrawing at year's end, the two-hundred-dollar tuition being now far beyond my means. President Eliot, however, waived the fee. Probably he concluded that Harvard's long-term interests would be better served not by giving the boot to the third Stratham Younger to trudge through the Yard, but by forgiving the demi-orphan his tuition in expectation of future rewards. Whatever the motivation, I will be forever grateful to Harvard for letting me stay on.

Only at Harvard could I have attended Professor Putnam's famous lectures on neurology. I was a medical student by then, having won a scholarship, but was proving an uninspired doctor-to-be. One spring morning, in an otherwise dust-dry account of nervous diseases, Putnam referred to Sigmund Freud's "sexual theory" as the only interesting work being done on the subject of the hysterical and obsessional neuroses. After class, I asked for readings. Putnam pointed me to Havelock Ellis, who accepted Freud's two most radical discoveries: the existence of what Freud called "the unconscious" and the sexual aetiology of neurosis. Putnam also introduced me to Morton Prince, who was then just starting his journal on abnormal psychology. Dr. Prince had an extensive collection of foreign publications; it turned out he had known my father. Prince took me on as a proofreader. Through him, I got my hands on almost everything Freud had published, from *The Interpretation of Dreams* to the groundbreaking *Three Essays*. My German was good, and I found myself consuming Freud's work with an avidity I had not felt for years. Freud's erudition was breathtaking. His writing was like filigree. His ideas, if correct, would change the world.

The hook was sunk for good, however, when I came across Freud's solution to *Hamlet*. It was, for Freud, a throwaway, a two-hundred-word digression in the middle of his treatise on dreams. Yet there it was: a brand-new answer to the most famous riddle in Western literature.

Shakespeare's *Hamlet* has been performed thousands upon thousands of times, more than any other play in any language. It is the most written-about work in all of literature. (I do not count the Bible, of course.) Yet there is a strange void or vacuum at the core of the drama: all the action is founded on the inability of its hero to act. The play consists of a series of evasions and excuses seized on by the melancholy Hamlet to justify postponing his revenge on his father's murderer (his uncle, Claudius, now King of Denmark and wed to Hamlet's mother), punctuated by anguished soliloquies in which he vilifies himself for his own paralysis, the most famous of them all beginning, of course, *To be*. Only after his delays and missteps have brought about ruin—Ophelia's suicide; the murder of his mother, who drinks a poison Claudius prepared for Hamlet; and his own receipt of a fatal cut from Laertes' envenomed sword—does Hamlet at last, in the play's final scene, take his uncle's triply forfeited life.

Why doesn't Hamlet act? Not for lack of opportunity: Shakespeare gives Hamlet the most propitious possible circumstances for killing Claudius. Hamlet even acknowledges this (*Now might I do it*), yet still he turns away. What stops him? And why should this inexplicable faltering—this seeming weakness, this almost cowardice—be capable of riveting audiences around the world for three centuries? The greatest literary minds of our era, Goethe and Coleridge, tried but failed to pull the sword from this stone, and hundreds of lesser lights have broken their heads on it.

I didn't like Freud's Oedipal answer. In fact, I was disgusted by it. I didn't want to believe it, any more than I wanted to believe in the Oedipus complex itself. I needed to disprove Freud's shocking theories, I needed to find their flaw, but I could not. My back against a tree, I sat in the Yard day after day for hours at a time, poring over Freud and Shakespeare. Freud's diagnosis of *Hamlet* came to seem increasingly irresistible to me, not only yielding the first complete solution to the riddle of the play, but explaining why no one else had been able to solve it, and at the same time making lucid the tragedy's mesmerizing, universal grip. Here was a scientist applying his discoveries to Shakespeare. Here was medicine making contact with the soul.

When I read those two pages of Dr. Freud's *The Interpretation of Dreams,* my future was determined. If I could not refute Freud's psychology, I would devote my life to it.

❦

CORONER CHARLES HUGEL had not liked the peculiar noise that came from the walls of Miss Riverford's bedroom, like an immured spirit wailing for its life. The coroner could not get that sound out of his head. Moreover, something had been missing from the room; he was sure of it. Back downtown, Hugel rang for a messenger boy and sent him running up the street for Detective Littlemore.

Yet another thing Hugel did not like was the location of his own office. The coroner had not been invited to move into the resplendent new police headquarters or the new First Precinct house being built on Old Slip, both of which would be equipped with telephones. The judges had got their Parthenon not long ago. Yet he, not only the city's chief medical examiner but a magistrate by law, and far more in need of modern utilities, had been left behind in the crumbling Van den Heuvel building, with its chipping plaster, its mold, and, worst of all, its water-stained ceilings. He abhorred the sight of those stains, with their brownish-yellow jagged edges. He particularly abhorred them today; he felt the stains were larger, and he wondered if the ceiling might crack open and fall down on him. Of course a coroner had to be attached to a morgue; he understood that. But he emphatically did not understand why a new and modern morgue could not have been built into the new police headquarters.

Littlemore ambled into the coroner's office. The detective was twenty-five. Neither tall nor short, Jimmy Littlemore wasn't bad-looking, but he wasn't quite good-looking either. His close-cropped hair was neither dark nor fair; if anything, it was closer to red. He had a distinctly American face, open and friendly, which, apart from a few freckles, was not particularly memorable. If you passed him in the street, you were not likely to recall him later. You might, however, remember the ready smile or the red bow tie he liked to sport below his straw boater.

The coroner ordered Littlemore to tell him what he had found out about the Riverford case, trying his best to sound commanding and peremptory. Only in the most exceptional matters was the coroner placed directly in charge of an investigation. He meant Littlemore to understand that serious consequences would follow if the detective did not produce results.

The coroner's magisterial tone evidently failed to impress the detective. Although Littlemore had never worked on a case with the coroner, he doubtless knew, as did everyone else on the force, that Hugel was disliked by the new commissioner, that his nickname was "the ghoul" because of the eagerness with which he performed his postmortems, and that he had no real power in the department. But Littlemore, being a fellow of excellent good nature, conveyed no disrespect to the coroner.

"What do I know about the Riverford case?" he answered. "Why, nothing at all, Mr. Hugel, except that the killer is over fifty, five-foot-nine, unmarried, familiar with the sight of blood, lives below Canal Street, and visited the harbor within the last two days."

Hugel's jaw dropped. "How do you know all that?"

"I'm joking, Mr. Hugel. I don't know Shinola about the murderer. I don't even know why they bothered sending me over. You didn't happen to lift any prints, did you, sir?"

"Fingerprints?" asked the coroner. "Certainly not. The courts will never admit fingerprint evidence."

"Well, it was too late by the time I got there. The whole place was already cleaned out. All the girl's things were gone."

Hugel was incensed. He called it tampering with evidence. "But you must have learned something about the Riverford girl," he added.

"She was new," said Littlemore. "She only lived there a month or two."

"They opened in June, Littlemore. *Everyone* has lived there only a month or two."

"Oh."

"Is that all?"

"Well, she was a real quiet type. Kept to herself."

"Was anyone seen with her yesterday?" asked the coroner.

"She came in around eight o'clock. Nobody with her. No guests later. Went to her apartment and never came out, as far as anybody knows."

"Did she have any regular visitors?"

"Nope. Nobody remembers anybody ever visiting her."

"Why was she living alone in New York City—at her age and in so large an apartment?"

"That's what I wanted to know," said Littlemore. "But they clammed up on me pretty good at the Balmoral, every one of them. I was serious about the harbor though, Mr. Hugel. I found some clay on the floor of Miss Riverford's bedroom. Pretty fresh too. I think it came from the harbor."

"Clay? What color clay?" asked Hugel.

"Red. Cakey, kind of."

"That wasn't clay, Littlemore," said the coroner, rolling his eyes, "that was my chalk."

The detective frowned. "I wondered why there was a whole circle of it."

"To keep people away from the body, you nitwit!"

"I'm just joking, Mr. Hugel. It wasn't your chalk. I saw your chalk. The clay was by the fireplace. A couple of small traces. Needed my magnifying glass before I saw it. I took it home to compare with my samples; I got a whole collection. It's a lot like the red clay all over the piers at the harbor."

Hugel took this in. He was considering whether to be impressed. "Is the clay in the harbor unique? Could it come from somewhere else—the Central Park, for example?"

"Not the park," said the detective. "This is river clay, Mr. Hugel. No rivers in the park."

"What about the Hudson Valley?"

"Could be."

"Or Fort Tryon, uptown, where Billings has just turned over so much earth?"

"You think there's clay up there?"

"I congratulate you, Littlemore, on your outstanding detective work."

"Thanks, Mr. Hugel."

"Would you be interested in a description of the murderer, by any chance?"

"I sure would."

"He is middle-aged, wealthy, and right-handed. His hair: graying, but formerly dark brown. His height: six foot to six-foot-one. And I believe he was acquainted with his victim—well acquainted."

Littlemore looked amazed. "How—?"

"Here are three hairs I collected from the girl's person." The coroner pointed to a small double-paned rectangle of glass on his desk, next to a microscope: sandwiched between the panes of glass were three hairs. "They are dark but striated with gray, indicating a man of middle age. On the girl's neck were threads of white silk—most probably a man's tie, evidently used to strangle her. The silk was of the highest quality. Thus our man has money. Of his dexterity, there can be no doubt; the wounds all proceed from right to left."

"His dexterity?"

"His right-handedness, Detective."

"But how do you know he knew her?"

"I do not *know*. I suspect. Answer me this: in what posture was Miss Riverford when she was whipped?"

"I never saw her," the detective complained. "I don't even know cause of death."

"Ligature strangulation, confirmed by the fracture of the hyoid bone, as I saw when I opened her chest. A lovely break, if I may say, like a perfectly split wishbone. Indeed, a lovely female chest altogether: the ribs perfectly formed, the lungs and heart, once removed, the very picture of healthy asphyxiated tissue. It was a pleasure to hold them in one's hands. But to the point: Miss Riverford was standing when she was whipped. This we know from the simple fact that the blood dripped straight down from her lacerations. Her hands were undoubtedly tied above her head by a heavy-gauge rope of some kind, almost certainly attached to the fixture in the ceiling. I saw rope threads on that fixture. Did you? No? Well, go back and look for them. Question: why would a man who has a good sturdy rope strangle his victim with a delicate silk? Inference, Mr. Littlemore: he did not want to put something so coarse around the girl's neck. And why was that? Hypothesis, Mr. Littlemore: because he had feelings for her. Now, as to the man's height, we are back to certainties. Miss Riverford was five-foot-five. Judging from her wounds, the whipping was administered by someone seven to eight inches above her. Thus the murderer's height was between six foot and six-foot-one."

"Unless he was standing on something," said Littlemore.

"What?"

"On a stool or something."

"On a stool?" repeated the coroner.

"It's possible," said Littlemore.

"A man does not stand on a stool while whipping a girl, Detective."

"Why not?"

"Because it's ridiculous. He would fall off."

"Not if he had something to hold on to," said the detective. "A lamp, maybe, or a hat rack."

"A hat rack?" said Hugel. "Why would he do that, Detective?"

"To make us think he was taller."

"How many homicide cases have you investigated?" asked the coroner.

"This is my first," said Littlemore, with undisguised excitement, "as a detective."

Hugel nodded. "You spoke with the maid at least, I suppose?"

"The maid?"

"Yes, the maid. Miss Riverford's maid. Did you ask her if she noticed anything unusual?"

"I don't think I—"

"I don't want you to think," snapped the coroner. "I want you to detect. Go back to the Balmoral and talk to that maid again. She was the first one in the room. Ask her to describe to you exactly what she saw when she went in. Get the details, do you hear me?"

❧

ON THE CORNER of Fifth Avenue and Fifty-third Street, in a room no woman had ever entered, not even to dust or beat the curtains, a butler poured from a sparkling decanter into three etched-crystal goblets. The bowls of these goblets were intricately carved and so deep they could hold an entire bottle of claret. The butler poured a quarter inch of red wine into each.

These glasses he offered to the Triumvirate.

The three men sat in deep leather armchairs arranged around a central fireplace. The room was a library containing more than thirty-seven hundred volumes, most of which were in Greek, Latin, or German. On one side of the unlit fireplace stood a bust of Aristotle atop a jade-green marble pedestal. On the other was a bust of an ancient Hindu. Over the mantel was an entablature: it displayed a large snake curled into a sine wave, against a background of flames. The word CHARAKA was engraved in capital letters underneath.

Smoke from the men's pipes caressed the ceiling high above them. The man in the center of the three made a barely perceptible motion with his right hand, on which he wore a large and unusual silver ring. He was in his late fifties, elegant, gaunt in the face, and wiry in build, with dark eyes, black eyebrows below his silver hair, and the hands of a pianist.

In response to his sign, the butler put a spark to the hearth, causing a thick set of papers therein to catch and burn. The fireplace glowed and crackled with dancing orange flames. "Be sure to preserve the ashes," said the master to his servant.

Nodding his assent, the butler silently withdrew, closing the door behind him.

"There is only one way to fight fire," continued the man with pianist's hands. He raised his goblet. "Gentlemen."

As the two other men raised their crystal glasses, an observer might have noticed that they also wore a similar silver ring on their right hands. One of these other two gentlemen was portly and red-cheeked, with muttonchop sideburns. He completed the elegant man's toast—"With fire"—and drained his glass.

The third gentleman was balding, sharp-eyed, and thin. He said not a word but merely sipped his wine, a Château Lafite of the 1870 vintage.

"Do you know the Baron?" asked the elegant man, turning to this balding gentleman. "I suppose you are related to him."

"Rothschild?" the balding man replied blandly. "I've never met him. Our ties are with the English branch."

CHAPTER THREE

FOR FREUD'S FIRST destination in America, Brill chose Coney Island, of all places. We set off by foot for the Grand Central Station, just down the block from our hotel. The sky was cloudless, the sun already hot, the streets clogged with Monday morning traffic. Motorcars accelerated impatiently around horse-drawn delivery wagons. Conversation was impossible. Across from the hotel, on Forty-second Street, a colossal scaffold had been erected where a new building was going up, and the pneumatic drills set up a deafening clatter.

Inside the terminal, it was suddenly quiet. Freud and Ferenczi stopped in awe. We were in a fabulous glass and steel tunnel, six hundred fifty feet long and a hundred feet high, with massive gas-fueled chandeliers running the entire length of its curved ceiling. It was a feat of engineering far surpassing Mr. Eiffel's tower in Paris. Only Jung seemed unimpressed. I wondered if he was well; he looked a little pale and distracted. Freud was shocked, as I had been, to learn they were about to tear the station down. But it was built for the old steam locomotives, and the era of steam had come to an end.

As we descended the stair to the IRT, Freud's mood blackened. "He is terrified of your underground trains," Ferenczi whispered in my ear. "A bit of unanalyzed neurosis. He told me so last night."

Freud's humor did not improve when our train lurched to a violent halt in a tunnel between stations, its lights flickering out, plunging us into a pitch, hot darkness. "Buildings in the sky, trains in the earth," said Freud, sounding irritated. "It is Virgil with you Americans: if you cannot bring the heavens down, you are determined to raise hell."

"That is *your* epigraph, no?" asked Ferenczi.

"Yes, but it was not supposed to be my epi*taph*," answered Freud.

"Gentlemen!" Brill cried out without warning. "You still haven't heard Younger's analysis of the paralyzed hand."

"A case history?" said Ferenczi enthusiastically. "We must hear it, by all means."

"No, no. It was incomplete," I said.

"Nonsense," Brill upbraided me. "It's one of the most perfect analyses I've ever heard. It confirms every tenet of psychoanalysis."

Having little choice, I recounted my small success, as we waited in the stifling dark for the train to return to life.

❧

I GRADUATED FROM Harvard in 1908, with a degree not only in medicine but also in psychology. My professors, impressed by my industry, brought me to the attention of G. Stanley Hall, the first man ever to receive a Harvard psychology degree, a founder of the American Psychological Association, and now the president of Clark University in Worcester. Hall's ambition was to make the upstart, fabulously endowed Clark the leading institution of scientific research in the country. When he offered me a position as an assistant lecturer in psychology, with the ability to begin my medical practice— and get out of Boston—I accepted at once.

One month later, I had my first analytic patient: a girl, whom I shall call Priscilla, sixteen years old, delivered to my office by her distraught mother. Hall was responsible for the family's decision to bring her to me. More than that I can't say without revealing the girl's identity.

Priscilla was short and heavy but had a pleasing face and an uncomplaining character. For a year she had been suffering from bouts of acute shortness of breath, occasional incapacitating headache, and a total paralysis of her left hand—all of which baffled and embarrassed her. Hysteria was plainly indicated by the paralysis, which afflicted the whole of her hand, including the wrist. As Freud had pointed out, paralyses of this kind do not conform to any genuine dermatone innervation and hence can claim no real physiological basis. For example, genuine neurological damage might cause certain fingers to be incapacitated, but not the wrist. Or the use of the thumb might be lost, leaving the other digits unaffected. But when a paralysis seizes an entire body part across all its differentiated neural reticulations, it is not physiology but psychology that must be consulted, for this kind of seizure corresponds solely to an idea, a mental image—in Priscilla's case, the image of her left hand.

The girl's doctor had naturally found no organic basis for her complaints. Nor had the chirologist, brought in from New York; his prescription had been rest and a complete withdrawal from active endeavors, which had almost certainly exacerbated her condition. They had even called in an osteopath, who of course accomplished nothing.

After ruling out the various neurological and orthopaedic possibilities—palsy, Kienböck's lunate disease, and so on—I decided to attempt psychoanalysis. At first I made no headway. The reason was the presence of the girl's mother. No hints were sufficient to induce this good woman to leave doctor and patient to the privacy psychoanalysis requires. After the third visit, I informed the mother that I would not be able to help Priscilla, or indeed to receive her in future as my patient, unless she—the mother—absented herself. Even then I could not at first make Priscilla talk. Following Freud's most recent therapeutic advances, I had her lie down with her eyes closed. I instructed her to think of her paralyzed hand and to say whatever came into her mind in association with this symptom, giving voice to any thoughts that entered her head, no matter what they were, no matter how seemingly irrelevant, inappropriate, or even impolite. Invariably, Priscilla responded only by repeating the most superficial description of the onset of her sufferings.

The critical day, as she always told the story, had been August 10, 1907. She remembered the exact date because it was the day after the funeral of her adored elder sister, Mary, who had been living in Boston with her husband, Bradley. That summer, Mary died of influenza, leaving Bradley with two infant children to take care of. On the day after the funeral, Priscilla had been charged by her mother with writing acknowledgments to the many friends and relatives who had expressed their condolences. That evening, she experienced sharp pains in her left hand—her writing hand. She saw nothing unusual in this, both because she had written so many letters and because she had felt occasional pain in that hand for the last several years. That night, however, she awoke unable to breathe. When the dyspnea subsided, she tried to go back to sleep but could not. By morning, she was suffering the first of the headaches that would plague her for the next year. Worse, she found her left hand completely paralyzed. And in that condition it had remained, hanging uselessly from her wrist.

These and other such facts she would constantly repeat to me. Long silences would follow. No matter how forcefully I assured her that there was more she wanted to tell me—that it was quite impossible for there to be nothing in her head at all—she steadfastly insisted that she could think of nothing else to say.

I was tempted to hypnotize her. She was plainly a suggestible girl. But Freud had unequivocally rejected hypnosis. It used to be a favored technique, in the early period when he was still working with Breuer, but Freud had discovered that hypnosis was neither lasting in effect nor productive of reliable memory. I decided, however, that I might safely attempt the same technique Freud deployed after abandoning hypnosis. That is what led to the breakthrough.

I told Priscilla that I was going to place my hand on her forehead. I assured her there was a memory that wanted to come out, a memory of central importance to everything she had told me, without which we would understand nothing. I told her that she knew this memory very well, even if she did not know she knew it, and that it would emerge the moment I laid my hand on her forehead.

I did the deed with some trepidation, for I had put my authority at risk. If nothing came of it, I would be in a worse position than I had been before. But in fact the memory did emerge, just as Freud's papers suggested it would, at the very moment Priscilla felt the pressure of my hand against her head.

"Oh, Dr. Younger," she cried out, "I saw it!"

"What?"

"Mary's hand."

"*Mary's* hand?"

"In the coffin. It was terrible. They made us look at her."

"Go on," I said.

Priscilla said nothing.

"Was there something wrong with Mary's hand?" I asked.

"Oh no, Doctor. It was perfect. She always had perfect hands. She could play the piano beautifully, not like me." Priscilla was struggling with some emotion I could not decipher. The color of her cheeks and forehead alarmed me; they were almost scarlet. "She was still so beautiful. Even the coffin was beautiful, all velvet and white wood. She looked like Sleeping Beauty. But I knew she wasn't asleep."

"What was it about Mary's hand?"

"Her hand?"

"Yes, her hand, Priscilla."

"Please don't make me tell you," she said. "I'm too ashamed."

"You have nothing to be ashamed of. We are not responsible for our feelings; therefore no feeling can cause us shame."

"Really, Dr. Younger?"

"Really."

"But it was so wrong of me."

"It was Mary's left hand, wasn't it?" I said at a venture.

She nodded as if confessing a crime.

"Tell me about her left hand, Priscilla."

"The ring," she whispered, in the faintest voice.

"Yes," I said. "The ring." This *yes* was a lie. I hoped it would make Priscilla think I already understood everything, when in reality I understood nothing. This act of deception was the only aspect of the entire business that I regretted. But I have found myself repeating the same deception, in one form or another, in every psychoanalysis I have ever attempted.

She went on. "It was the gold ring Brad gave her. And I thought, What a waste. What a waste to bury it with her."

"There is no shame in that. Practicality is a virtue, not a vice," I assured her with my usual acuity.

"You don't understand," she said. "I wanted it for myself."

"Yes."

"I wanted to *wear* it, Doctor," she practically shouted. "I wanted Brad to marry *me*. Couldn't I have taken care of the poor little babies? Couldn't I have made him happy?" She buried her head in her hands and sobbed. "I was glad she was dead, Dr. Younger. I was *glad*. Because now he was free to take me."

"Priscilla," I said, "I can't see your face."

"I'm sorry."

"I mean I can't see your face because your left hand is covering it."

She gasped. It was true: she was using her left hand to wipe away her tears. The hysterical symptom had disappeared the instant she regained the memory whose repression caused it. A year has now passed, and the paralysis never recurred, nor the dyspnea, nor the headaches.

Reconstructing the story was simple enough. Priscilla had been in love with Bradley since he first came to call on Mary. Priscilla was then thirteen. I will shock no one, I hope, by observing that a thirteen-year-old girl's love for a young man can include sexual desires, even if not fully understood as such. Priscilla had never admitted to these desires, or to the jealousy she felt toward her sister as a consequence, which irresistibly led in the child's mind to the dreadful but opportunistic thought that, if only Mary were dead, the way would be open for her. All these feelings Priscilla repressed, even from her own consciousness. This repression was doubtless the original source of the occasional pains she felt in her left hand, which probably commenced on the day of the wedding itself, when she first saw the golden ring slipped onto her sister's finger. Two years later, the sight of the ring on Mary's hand in the coffin excited the same thoughts, which very nearly emerged—or perhaps, for a moment, did emerge—into Priscilla's consciousness. But now, in addition to these forbidden feelings of desire and jealousy, there was the utterly impermissible satisfaction she took in her sister's untimely death. The result was a fresh demand for repression, infinitely stronger than the first.

The role played by the thank-you letters is more complex. One can only imagine how Priscilla must have suffered at the sight of her bare left hand, ungraced by a wedding ring, repeatedly conjoined with the act of expressing sorrow at her sister's demise. Possibly this was a contradiction Priscilla could not bear. At the same time, the laborious writing may have provided a physiological underpinning for what followed. In any event, her left hand became an offense to her, reminding her of both her unmarried state and her unacceptable wishes.

The role played by the thank-you letters is more complex. One can only imagine how Priscilla must have suffered at the sight of her bare left hand, ungraced by a wedding ring, repeatedly conjoined with the act of expressing sorrow at her sister's demise. Possibly this was a contradiction Priscilla could not bear. At the same time, the laborious writing may have provided a physiological underpinning for what followed. In any event, her left hand became an offense to her, reminding her of both her unmarried state and her unacceptable wishes.

Three objectives therefore became paramount. First, she must not have such a hand; she must rid herself of a hand that had no wedding ring where a wedding ring should be. Second, she had to punish herself for her wish to replace Mary as Bradley's wife. Third, she had to make the consummation of this wish impossible. Every one of these objectives was accomplished through her hysterical symptoms; the economy with which the unconscious mind performs its work is marvelous. Symbolically speaking, Priscilla rid herself of the offending hand, simultaneously fulfilling her wish and punishing herself for having it. By making herself an invalid, she also ensured that she could no longer take care of Bradley's children or otherwise, as she so tactfully put it, "make him happy."

Priscilla's treatment, from start to finish, took all of two weeks. After I reassured her that her wishes were perfectly natural and beyond her control, she not only shed her symptoms but became fairly radiant. News of the invalid's cure spread through Worcester as if the Savior had brought sight to one of Isaiah's blind men. The story people told was this: Priscilla had fallen ill from love, and I had cured her. My placing a palm on her forehead was imbued with all sorts of quasi-mystic powers. While this made my reputation and caused my medical practice to thrive, there were less comfortable consequences too. There came a rush of thirty or forty would-be pyschoanalytic patients to my office, each of whom claimed to be suffering from symptoms disturbingly similar to Priscilla's and all of whom expected a diagnosis of unrequited love and a cure through the laying on of hands.

❧

THE TRAIN WAS pulling into City Hall station when I finished. We had to change there for the BRT at Park Row, where an elevated would take us all the way to Coney. No one commented on Priscilla's case, and I began to think I must have made a fool of myself. Brill saved me. He told Freud I deserved to know what "the Master" thought of my analysis.

Freud turned to me with, I hardly dared to believe it, a twinkle in his eyes. He said that, a few minor points aside, the analysis could not have been improved on. He called it brilliant and asked my permission to refer to it in subsequent work. Brill clapped me on the back; Ferenczi, smiling, shook my hand. This was not the most gratifying moment of my professional life; it was the most gratifying moment of my *entire* life.

I had never realized how splendid City Hall station was, with its crystal chandeliers, inlaid murals, and vaulted arches. Everyone remarked on it—with the exception of Jung, who suddenly announced that he was not coming with us. Jung had made no comments either during or after my case history. Now he said he needed to get to bed.

"Bed?" Brill asked. "You went to bed last night at nine." While the rest of us had retired well past midnight after dining together in the hotel, Jung had gone to his room as soon as we arrived and had not come down.

Freud asked Jung whether he was all right. When Jung replied that it was only his head again, Freud instructed me to take him back to the hotel. But Jung declined assistance, insisting he could easily retrace our steps. Hence Jung took the train back uptown; the rest of us went on without him.

❧

WHEN DETECTIVE JIMMY LITTLEMORE returned to the Balmoral Monday evening, one of the doormen had just come on duty. This man, Clifford, had worked the graveyard shift the night before. Littlemore asked if he knew the deceased Miss Riverford.

Apparently Clifford had not received the order to hold his tongue. "Sure, I remember her," he said. "What a looker."

"Talk to her?" asked Littlemore.

"She didn't talk much—not to me, anyway."

"Anything special you remember about her?"

"I opened the door for her some mornings," said Clifford.

"What's special about that?"

"I'm off at six. The only girls you see at that hour are working girls, and Miss Riverford didn't look like a working girl, if you know what I mean. She would have been going out at, I don't know, maybe five, five-thirty?"

"Where was she going?" asked Littlemore.

"Beats me."

"What about last night? Did you notice anybody or anything unusual?"

"What do you mean unusual?" asked Clifford.

"Anything different, anybody you had never seen before."

"There was this one fella," said Clifford. "Left about midnight. In a big hurry. Did you see that fella, Mac? Didn't look right, if you ask me."

The doorman addressed as Mac shook his head.

"Smoke?" said Littlemore to Clifford, who accepted the cigarette, pocketing it since he wasn't permitted to indulge on duty. "Why didn't he look right?"

"Just didn't. Foreigner, maybe." Clifford was unable to articulate his suspicion with any greater specificity, but he asserted positively that the man did not live in the building. Littlemore took a description: black hair, tall, lean, well dressed, high forehead, mid- to late thirties, wearing glasses, carrying a black case of some kind. The man climbed into a hackney cab outside the Balmoral, heading downtown. Littlemore questioned the doormen for another ten minutes—none remembered Clifford's black-haired man entering the building, but he might well have gone up unremarked with a resident—and then asked where he could find the Balmoral's chambermaids. They pointed him downstairs.

In the basement, Littlemore came to a hot low-ceilinged room with pipes running along its walls and a clutch of maids folding linen. All knew who Miss Riverford's girl was: Betty Longobardi. In whispers, they confided to the detective that he wouldn't find Betty anywhere in the building. She was gone. Betty had left early without saying good-bye to anyone. They didn't know why. Betty was a handful but such a nice girl. She didn't take any lip, not even from the wing manager, the women told Littlemore. Maybe she'd had another fight with him. One of the maids knew where Betty lived. With this information secured, Littlemore turned to go. It was then that he noticed the Chinaman.

Clad in a white undershirt and dark shorts, the man had come into the room carrying a wicker basket overflowing with freshly cleaned sheets. Having deposited the contents of this basket onto a table filled with like items, he was walking out again when he attracted the detective's attention. Littlemore stared at the retreating man's thick calves and sandals. These were not in themselves particularly interesting; nor was his gait, which involved the sliding of one foot after the other. The result, however, was arresting. Two wet stripes were left on the floor in the man's wake, and these stripes were flecked with a glistening dark-red clay.

"Hey—you there!" cried Littlemore.

The man froze, his back to the detective, shoulders hunched. But the next moment he started off again at a run, disappearing around a corner, still carrying his basket. The detective sprang after him, turning the corner just in time to see the man pushing through a pair of swinging doors at the end of a long corridor. Littlemore ran down the corridor, passed through the doors—and gazed out at the Balmoral's cavernous and noisy laundry, where men were laboring at ironing boards, washboards, steam presses, and hand-cranked washing machines. There were Negroes and whites, Italians and Irish, faces of all kinds—but no Chinamen. An empty wicker basket lay on its side next to an ironing board, rocking gently as if recently set down. The floor was thoroughly wet, disguising any tracks. Littlemore pushed up the brim of his boater and shook his head.

❦

GRAMERCY PARK, at the foot of Lexington Avenue, was Manhattan's sole private park. Only the owners of the houses opposite the park's delicate wrought-iron fence had the right to enter. Each house came with a key to the park gates, offering access to the small paradise of flower and greenery within.

To the girl emerging from one of those houses early Monday evening, August 30, that key had always been a magical object, gold and black, delicate yet unbreakable. When she was a little girl, old Mrs. Biggs, their servant, used to let her carry the key in her tiny white purse on their way across the street. She was too small to turn the key by herself, but Mrs. Biggs would guide her hand and help her do it. When the iron gate released, it was as if the world itself were opening up before her.

The park had grown much smaller as she grew up. Now, at seventeen, she could of course turn the key without assistance—and did so this evening, letting herself in and walking slowly to her bench, the one she always sat on. She was carrying an armload of textbooks and her secret copy of *The House of Mirth*. She still loved her bench, even though the park had somehow become, as she got older, more an attachment to her parents' house than a refuge from it. Her mother and father were away. They had repaired to the country five weeks earlier, leaving the girl behind with Mrs. Biggs and her husband. She had been delighted to see them go.

The day was still oppressively hot, but her bench lay in the cool shade of a willow and chestnut canopy. The books sat unopened beside her. The day after tomorrow, it would be September, a month she had been looking forward to for what seemed an eternity. Next weekend, she would turn eighteen. Three weeks after that, she would matriculate at Barnard College. She was one of those girls who, despite a fervent wish to be living another life, had staved off womanhood as long as she could, through the ages of thirteen, fourteen, and fifteen, clinging to her stuffed animals even while school friends were already discussing stockings, lipstick, and invitations. At sixteen, the stuffed animals had finally been relegated to the upper reaches of a closet. At seventeen, she was lithe, blue-eyed, and heart-stoppingly beautiful. She wore her long blond hair tied with a ribbon in the back.

When the bells of Calvary Church struck six, she saw Mr. and Mrs. Biggs hurrying down the front stoop, rushing off to the shops before they closed. They waved to the girl, and she to them. A few minutes later, brushing tears from her eyes, she set off slowly toward home, clutching her textbooks to her chest, looking at the grass and the clover and the hovering bees. Had she turned to her left, she might have seen, on the far side of the park, a man watching her from outside the wrought-iron fence.

This man had been watching her a long time. He carried a black case in his right hand and was dressed in black—overdressed, in fact, given the heat. He never took his eyes from the girl as she crossed the street and climbed the stairs to her townhouse, a handsome limestone affair with two miniature stone lions mounting an ineffectual guard on either side of the front door. He saw the girl open the door without having to unlock it.

The man had observed the two old servants leaving the house. Glancing left, right, and over his shoulder, he started off. Quickly he approached the house, ascended the steps, tried the door, and found it still unlocked.

A half hour later, the summer-evening silence of Gramercy Park was ruptured by a scream, a girl's scream. It carried from one end of the street to the other, hanging in the air, persisting longer than one would have thought physically possible. Shortly thereafter, the man burst out the back door of the girl's house. A metal object no larger than a small coin flew from his hands as he stumbled down the rear steps. It hit a slate flagstone and bounced surprisingly high into the air. The man nearly fell to the ground himself, but he recovered, fled past the garden potting shed, and escaped from the garden down the back alley.

Mr. and Mrs. Biggs heard the scream. They were just returning, laden with bags of groceries and flowers. Horrified, they trundled into the house and up the stairs as quickly as they were able. On the second floor, the master bedroom door was open, which it should not have been. Inside that room, they found her. The shopping bags fell from Mr. Biggs's hands. A pound of flour spread out around his old black shoes, raising a little cloud of white dust, and a yellow onion rolled all the way to the girl's bare feet.

She stood in the center of her parents' bedroom, clad only in a slip and other undergarments not meant for servants' eyes. Her legs were naked. Her long slender arms were outstretched above her head, the wrists bound by a thick rope, which was secured in turn to a ceiling fixture from which a small chandelier depended. The girl's fingers nearly touched its crystal prisms. Her slip was torn, both front and back, as if rent by the lashes of a whip or cane. A man's long white tie or scarf was wound tightly around her neck and between her lips.

She was not, however, dead. Her eyes were wild, staring, unseeing. She looked on the familiar old servants not with relief but with a kind of terror, as if they might be murderers or demons. Her whole frame shivered, despite the heat. She made to scream again, but no sound came out, as if she had expended all her voice.

Mrs. Biggs came to her senses first and ordered her husband out of the room, telling him to fetch the doctor and a policeman. Gingerly she went to the girl, trying to calm her, unwinding the tie. When her mouth was freed, the girl made all the motions that normally accompany speech, but still no sound came out, no words at all, not even a whisper. When the police arrived, they were dismayed to learn that she could not speak. A still greater surprise lay in store for them as well. Paper and pencil were brought to the girl; the police asked her to tell them in writing what happened. *I can't*, she wrote. Why not? they asked. Her reply: *I can't remember.*

CHAPTER FOUR

IT WAS ALMOST seven on Monday evening when Freud, Ferenczi, and I returned to the hotel. Brill had gone home, tired and happy. I believe Coney Island is Brill's favorite place in America. He once told me that when he first arrived in this country at the age of fifteen, penniless and alone, he used to spend entire days on the boardwalk and sometimes nights beneath it. All the same, it wasn't obvious to me that Freud's first taste of New York should have included the Live Premature Incubator Babies show or Jolly Trixie, the 685-pound lady, advertised under the rapturous slogan HOLY SMOKE — SHE'S FAT! SHE'S AWFUL FAT.

But Freud seemed delighted, comparing it to Vienna's Prater — "only on a gigantic scale," he said. Brill even persuaded him to rent a bathing costume and join us in the enormous saltwater swimming pool inside Steeplechase Park. Freud proved a stronger swimmer than either Brill or Ferenczi, but in the afternoon he had an attack of prostatic discomfort. We sat down, therefore, at a boardwalk café, where, punctuated by the clattering roar of the roller coasters and the steadier pounding of surf, we had a conversation I will never forget.

Brill had been ridiculing the treatment of hysterical women practiced by American physicians: massage cures, vibrating cures, water cures. "It is half quackery and half sex industry," he said. He described an enormous vibrating machine recently purchased — for four hundred dollars — by a doctor he knew, a professor at Columbia no less. "Do you know what these doctors are actually doing? No one admits it, but they are inducing climax in their women patients."

"You sound surprised," replied Freud. "Avicenna practiced the same treatment in Persia nine hundred years ago."

"Did he make himself rich from it?" asked Brill, with a note of bitterness. "Thousands a month, some of them. But the worst of it is their hypocrisy. I once pointed out to this august physician, who just happens to be my superior at work, that if his treatment worked it was a proof of psychoanalysis, establishing the link between sexuality and hysteria. You should have seen the look on his face. There was nothing sexual in his treatment, he said, nothing at all. He was simply allowing patients to discharge their excess neural stimulation. If I thought otherwise, what it proved was the corrupting effect of Freud's theories. I'm lucky he didn't fire me."

Freud merely smiled. He had none of Brill's bitter edge, none of his defensiveness. One could not blame the ignorant, he said. In addition to the inherent difficulty of uncovering the truth about hysteria, there were powerful repressions, accumulated over millennia, which we could not expect to vanquish in a day. "It is the same with every disease," said Freud. "Only when we understand the cause can we claim to understand the sickness, and only then can we treat it. For now the cause remains hidden from them, so they remain in the Dark Ages, bleeding their patients and calling it medicine."

It was then that the conversation took its remarkable turn. Freud asked if we would like to hear one of his recent cases, about a patient obsessed with rats. Naturally we said yes.

I had never heard a man speak as Freud did. He recounted the case with such fluency, erudition, and insight that he held us rapt for over three straight hours. Brill, Ferenczi, and I would periodically interrupt, challenging his inferences with objections or questions. Freud would answer the challenge before the questioner had even got the words out of his mouth. I felt more alive in those three hours than at any other moment in my life. Amid the barkers, screaming children, and thrill seekers of Coney Island, the four of us, I felt, were tracing the very edge of man's self-knowledge, breaking ground in undiscovered country, forging uncharted paths the world would some day follow. Everything man thought he knew about himself—his dreams, his consciousness, his most secret desires—would be changed forever.

Back at the hotel, Freud and Ferenczi were preparing to go to Brill's for dinner. Unfortunately, I was committed to dine elsewhere.

Jung was meant to go with them but was nowhere to be found. Freud had me knock on Jung's door, to no avail. They waited until eight, then set off for Brill's without him. I changed hurriedly but irritably into evening dress. Under any circumstances, I would have been annoyed by the prospect of a ball, but to miss dinner with Freud as a result was vexing beyond description.

❧

NEW YORK SOCIETY in the Gilded Age was essentially the creation of two very rich women, Mrs. William B. Astor and Mrs. William K. Vanderbilt, and of the titanic clash between them in the 1880s.

Mrs. Astor, née Schermerhorn, was highborn; Mrs. Vanderbilt, née Smith, was not. The Astors could trace their wealth and lineage to New York's Dutch aristocracy of the eighteenth century. To be sure, the term *aristocracy* in this usage is a bit of a stretch, since Netherlandish fur traders in the New World were not exactly princes in the Old. European ladies and gentlemen may not have read their Tocqueville, but the one difference between the United States and Europe on which they all agreed was that America, to its misfortune, lacked an aristocracy. Nevertheless, by the late nineteenth century, the fabulously monied Astors would be received at the Court of St. James and would soon have their aristocratic claims confirmed by English titles of nobility, which were far superior to Dutch ones, had there been any Dutch ones.

By contrast, a Vanderbilt was a nobody. Cornelius "Commodore" Vanderbilt was merely the richest man in America—indeed, the richest man in the world. Being worth a million dollars made one a man of fortune in the mid-nineteenth century; Cornelius Vanderbilt was worth a hundred million when he died in 1877, and his son was worth twice that a decade later. But the Commodore was still a vulgar steamship and rail magnate who owed his wealth to industry, and Mrs. Astor would call on neither him nor his relations.

In particular, Mrs. Astor would not set foot in the home of the young Mrs. William K. Vanderbilt, wife to the Commodore's grandson. She would not even leave her card. It was thus established that the Vanderbilts were not to be received in the best Manhattan houses. Mrs. Astor let it be known that there were only four hundred men and women in all New York City fit to enter a ballroom—that number being, as it happened, the quantity of guests who fit comfortably into Mrs. Astor's own ballroom. The Vanderbilts were not among the Four Hundred.

Mrs. Vanderbilt was not vindictive, but she was intelligent and indomitable. No penny would be spared to break the Astor ban. Her first measure, achieved with a liberal dose of her husband's largesse, was to procure an invitation to the Patriarchs' Ball, a significant event in New York's social calendar, attended by the city's most influential citizens. But she was still excluded from Mrs. Astor's more rarefied circle.

Her second step was to have her husband build a new house. It would be located on the corner of Fifth Avenue and Fifty-second Street and like no house yet seen in New York City. Designed by Richard Morris Hunt—not only the most famous American architect of the time but a welcome guest of the Astors—660 Fifth Avenue became a white limestone French château in the style of the Loire Valley. Its stone entry foyer was sixty feet long, with a double-height vaulted ceiling, at the end of which rose a magnificent carved Caen stairwell. Among its thirty-seven rooms were a soaring dining hall lit by stained-glass windows, an enormous third-and-fourth-floor gymnasium for her children, and a ballroom capable of holding eight hundred guests. Throughout the house were Rembrandts, Gainsboroughs, Reynoldses, Gobelin tapestries, and furniture that once belonged to Marie Antoinette.

As the mansion neared completion in 1883, Mrs. Vanderbilt announced a housewarming party, on which she would eventually spend some $250,000. The cleverest use of her wealth, by far, lay in securing in advance the attendance of a few notable but purchasable guests not beholden to Mrs. Astor's rules, including several English ladies, a smattering of Teutonic barons, a coterie of Italian counts, and one former United States president. Dropping hints of these advance bookings, as well as of sumptuous and unheard-of entertainments, Mrs. Vanderbilt issued a total of twelve hundred invitations. Her anticipated ball became the talk of the town.

One especially eager little partygoer happened to be Carrie Astor, Mrs. Astor's favorite daughter, who all summer long had been preparing with her friends a Star Quadrille for Mrs. Vanderbilt's ball. But of those twelve hundred invitations, not one had gone to Carrie Astor. All Carrie's friends had been invited—they were already excitedly planning the gowns they would wear for their quadrille—but not the tearful Carrie herself. To everyone who would listen, Mrs. Vanderbilt expressed sympathy for the poor girl's plight, but how *could* she invite Carrie, the hostess asked the world, when she had never been introduced to the girl's mother?

So it happened that Mrs. William Backhouse Astor took to her carriage one afternoon in the winter season of 1883 and had her footman, clad in blue livery, present her engraved card at 660 Fifth Avenue. This gave Mrs. Vanderbilt an unprecedented opportunity to snub the great Caroline Astor, an opportunity that would have been irresistible to a less farsighted woman. But Mrs Vanderbilt immediately responded by delivering to the Astor residence an invitation to her ball, as a result of which Carrie was able to attend after all, accompanied by her mother—in a diamond bodice that cost $200,000 — and the rest of Mrs. Astor's Four Hundred.

By the turn of the century, New York society had been transformed from Knickerbocker bastion into a volatile amalgam of power, money, and celebrity. Anyone worth a hundred million could buy his way in. Society gentlemen mixed with showgirls. Society ladies left their husbands. Even Mrs. Vanderbilt was Mrs. Vanderbilt no longer: she had obtained a shocking divorce in 1895 in order to become Mrs. Oliver H. P. Belmont. Mrs. Astor's own daughter Charlotte, the mother of four children, ran away to England with another man. Three sons and one grandson of the multimillionaire Jay Gould took actresses for wives. James Roosevelt Roosevelt married a prostitute. Even the occasional murderer could be lionized, provided he was of the right breed. Harry Thaw, heir though he was to a modest Pittsburgh mining fortune, would never have achieved celebrity in New York had he not killed the renowned architect Stanford White on the rooftop of Madison Square Garden in 1906. Although Thaw shot the seated White full in the face in plain view of a hundred diners, a jury acquitted him—by reason of insanity—two years later. Some observers said that no American jury would convict a man for murdering the scoundrel who had bedded his wife, although, to be fair to White, his liaison with the young lady in question occurred when she was only a sixteen-year-old unmarried showgirl rather than the respectable Mrs. Harry Thaw. Others opined that this jury was especially disinclined to convict, having received too great a sum from Thaw's attorney to feel free, in conscience, to reject his closing plea.

In the summers, Manhattan's rich repaired to marble palaces in Newport and Saratoga, where yachting, horsing, and cardplaying were the principal occupations. In those days, the leading families could still demonstrate why they were their country's finest. Young Harold Vanderbilt, who grew up at 660 Fifth Avenue, would successfully defend the America's Cup three times against British assault. He also invented contract bridge.

As September approached in 1909, a new season was about to begin. Everyone agreed that the crop of debutantes that year was among the choicest in recent memory. Miss Josephine Crosby, the *Times* observed, was a particularly handsome girl, gifted with a beautiful singing voice. The shapely Miss Mildred Carter had returned with her father from London, where she had danced with the king. Miss Hyde, the heiress, was also to debut, as were Miss Chapin and Miss Rutherford, who was last seen as a bridesmaid to her cousin, the former Miss White, at the latter's marriage to Count Sheer-Thoss.

The inaugural event of the season was a charitable ball, thrown by Mrs. Stuyvesant Fish on Monday night, August 30, to raise funds for the city's new Free Hospital for Children. It had become fashionable at that time to hold parties at the city's grand hotels. Mrs. Fish's party was to take place at the Waldorf-Astoria.

That hotel on Fifth Avenue and Thirty-fourth Street stood on the spot where Mrs. Astor had lived a quarter century earlier, when she was bested by Mrs. Vanderbilt. By comparison with the gleaming Vanderbilt mansion, the Astors' fine old brick townhouse had suddenly looked small and drab. Therefore Mrs. Astor unceremoniously razed it and built herself a double-sized French château—not in the Loire style but in the more dignified Second Empire fashion—thirty blocks north, with a ballroom big enough for twelve hundred. On the land vacated by Mrs. Astor, her son erected the world's largest and the city's most luxurious hotel.

Society entered the Waldorf-Astoria through a wide, three-hundred-foot-long corridor off Thirty-fourth Street, known as Peacock Alley. On the occasion of a fancy ball, blue-stockinged doormen would greet the carriages as they drew up, and Peacock Alley would be lined with hundreds and hundreds of spectators, an audience of groundlings for the procession of wealth and importance making its stately way inside. The Palm Garden was the Waldorf's massive domed and gilded restaurant, walled in glass to ensure continuing visibility to the outside world and paneled everywhere with full-length mirrors to ensure that the ladies and gentlemen of the inner world saw even more of themselves than outsiders could. To accommodate her party, Mrs. Stuyvesant Fish had booked not only the Palm Garden but also the Empire Room, the outdoor Myrtle Room, and the entire orchestra and company of the Metropolitan Opera.

It was the strains of this music that greeted Stratham Younger as he strolled the length of Peacock Alley, his arm in the grasp of his cousin Miss Belva Dula, a half hour after his European guests had departed for their dinner at the Brills'.

❧

MY MOTHER WAS a Schermerhorn. Her sister married a Fish. These two majestic genealogical facts got me invited to every royal ball in Manhattan.

Living in Worcester, Massachusetts, supplied an excuse sufficient to dodge most of these engagements. But I had to make an exception for parties thrown by my outré Aunt Mamie—Mrs. Stuyvesant Fish—who, though not really my aunt, has insisted on my calling her so since I was little, when I used to spend summers in her Newport house. After my father died, it was Aunt Mamie who made sure my mother was comfortable and did not have to vacate the Back Bay house where she had lived throughout her marriage. As a result, I could never say no when Aunt Mamie asked me to one of her galas. On top of this obligation, there was also cousin Belva, whom I had agreed to escort down the alley.

"What is that again?" Belva asked me, referring to the music, as we made our way down the endless hallway with throngs of onlookers on either side of us.

"It is Mr. Verdi's *Aïda*," I answered, "and we are the marching animals."

She pointed to a rotund woman escorted by her husband not far ahead of us. "Oh, look, the Arthur Scott Burdens. I have never seen Mrs. Burden in a huge crimson turban before. Perhaps we are meant to think of elephants."

"Belva."

"And there are the Condé Nasts. Her Directoire hat is much more suitable, don't you think? Her gardenias I approve as well, but I'm less sure about the ostrich feathers. It may incline people to bury their heads in the sand when she passes."

"Heel, Belva."

"Do you realize there must be a thousand people watching us right now?" Belva was manifestly relishing the attention. "I'll bet you have nothing like this in Boston."

"We are sadly behind in Boston," I said.

"The one with the perfect mass of jewels in her hair is the Baroness von Haefton, who excluded me from her party last winter for the Marquis de Charette. Those are the John Jacob Astors—they say he's been seen everywhere with Maddie Forge, who is not a day older than sixteen—and our hosts, the Stuyvesant Fishes."

"Fish."

"I beg your pardon?"

"The plural of Stuyvesant Fish," I explained, "is Stuyvesant Fish. One says 'the Fish,' not 'the Fishes.'" It was rare that I could even pretend to correct Belva on a point of New York etiquette.

"I don't believe that for a moment," she replied. "However, Mrs. Fish is looking almost plural herself this evening."

"Not a word against my aunt, Belva." Cousin Belva was my age almost exactly, and I had known her since infancy. But the poor, scrawny, ungainly thing had come out almost ten years ago, and no one had taken the bait. At twenty-seven, she was, I'm afraid, quite desperate, the world already consigning her to spinsterhood. "At least," I added, "Aunt Mamie hasn't brought her dog tonight."

Aunt Mamie had once thrown a ball in Newport for a new French poodle, which made its entrance prancing down a red carpet in a diamond-encrusted collar.

"But look, she *has* brought her dog," replied Belva pleasantly, "and still wearing the diamond collar." Belva was pointing to Marion Fish, Aunt Mamie's youngest daughter, to whose stunning debut Belva had not been invited.

"That's it, cousin. You're on your own." Having come to the end of the corridor, I discharged Belva, or rather Aunt Mamie prized me from her, pairing me off instead with a Miss Hyde, who was plainly rich but had few other charms. I danced with several other misses as well, including the tall and balletic Eleanor Sears, who was quite amiable, although I was obliged constantly to duck her hat, which was shaped like a sombrero. And of course I took a turn with poor Belva.

After the requisite oyster cocktail, we were fed—according to the gilt-edged menu—a *buffet russe,* roast mountain sheep with chestnut purée and asparagus, champagne sherbet, diamondback Maryland terrapin, and ruddy duck with an orange salad. This was only the first of two suppers, the second to be served after midnight. After the second supper, the cotillion would get under way, with the formal dances—probably a Mirror, if I knew Aunt Mamie—starting around one-thirty in the morning.

I really didn't mind the occasional party in New York. I had stopped attending social functions in Boston, where I could not escape the whispers and sidelong glances owing to the circumstances of my father's death. The difference between Boston and New York society was this: the goal in Boston was to do nothing but what had always been done; in New York it was to outdo anything that had ever been done. But the sheer spectacle of a New York party—and one was of course supposed to be part of that spectacle—was a thing my Boston blood could never quite grow used to. The debutantes in particular, while far more plentiful than their Bostonian counterparts, and far better-looking, were too sparkly for my taste. They were an efflorescence of diamond and pearl—on their corsages, around their necks, dangling from their ears, draped on their shoulders, nested in their hair—and though all these articles were doubtless genuine, I could not help the feeling that I was looking at paste.

"Here you are, Stratham!" cried Aunt Mamie. "Oh, why must you be cousins with my Marion? I would have married you off to her years ago. Now listen to me. Miss Crosby is asking everyone who you are. She is eighteen this year, the second handsomest girl in New York, and you are still the single handsomest man—I mean the handsomest single man. You must dance with her."

"I have danced with her," I replied, "and I have it on good authority that she means to marry Mr. de Menocal."

"But I don't want her to marry de Menocal," answered Aunt Mamie. "I wanted de Menocal to marry Franz and Ellie Sigel's granddaughter Elsie. She, however, has run away to Washington. It was my understanding that people ran away *from* Washington. What can the girl have been thinking? One might as well elope to the Congo. Have you said hello to Stuyvie yet?"

Stuyvie was, of course, her husband, Stuyvesant. As I had not yet exchanged greetings with Uncle Fish, Aunt Mamie conducted me toward him. He was engaged in close conversation with two men. Next to Uncle Fish, I recognized Louis J. de G. Milhau, whom I knew as a fellow undergraduate at Harvard. The other man, perhaps forty-five years old, looked familiar, but I couldn't place him. He had closely cropped dark hair, intelligent eyes, no beard, and an air of authority. Aunt Mamie solved my difficulty when she added, under her breath, "The mayor. I shall introduce you."

Mayor McClellan, it turned out, was just departing. Aunt Mamie cried out in protest, objecting that he would miss Caruso. Aunt Mamie detested opera, but she knew the rest of the world considered it the pinnacle of taste. McClellan apologized, thanking her cordially for her beneficence to the city of New York, and swore he would never leave at such an hour, were it not for a very serious matter demanding his immediate attention. Aunt Mamie objected even more strenuously, this time to the use of the term "very serious matter" in her presence. She did not want to hear about any very serious matters, she said, fleeing us in a cloud of chiffon.

To my surprise, Milhau then said to the mayor, "Younger here is a doctor. Why don't you tell him about it?"

"By gad," exclaimed Uncle Fish, "that's right. A Harvard doctor. Younger will know the man for the job. Tell him about it, McClellan."

The mayor surveyed me, made some sort of internal decision, and put a question. "Do you know Acton, Younger?"

"Lord Acton?" I responded.

"No, Harcourt Acton of Gramercy Park. It's about his daughter."

Miss Acton had apparently been the victim of a brutal assault earlier this evening, in her family's house, while her parents were away. The criminal had not been apprehended, nor had he even been seen by anyone else. Mayor McClellan, who knew the family, desperately wanted from Miss Acton a description of the criminal, but the girl could neither speak nor even remember what had happened to her. The mayor was returning to police headquarters this instant; the girl was still there, attended by her family doctor, who had professed himself mystified by her condition. He could find no physical injuries capable of producing her symptoms.

"The girl is hysterical," I said. "She is suffering from crypto-amnesia."

"Crypto-amnesia?" repeated Milhau.

"Loss of memory brought on by repression of a traumatic episode. The term was coined by Dr. Freud of Vienna. The condition is essentially hysterical and can be found with aphonia—speech loss—as well."

"By gad," said Uncle Fish again. "Speech loss, did you say? That's it!"

"Dr. Freud," I went on, "has a book on speech dysfunction." Freud's monograph on the aphasias was read in America long before his psychological writings became known. "He is probably the world's leading authority on the subject and has specifically shown an association with hysterical trauma—especially sexual trauma."

"Pity your Dr. Freud is in Vienna," said the mayor.

CHAPTER FIVE

I HAMMERED ON Brill's door until at last his wife, Rose, answered. I was bursting to tell them not only that I had arranged
Freud's first American consultation but that a motorcar and driver
were waiting downstairs to take him there, sent by the mayor of New
York himself. The scene into which I intruded, however, was so full
of good spirit and conviviality that I could not immediately see my
way to breaking it up.

Brill's place was on the fifth floor of a six-story apartment house
on Central Park West. And it was tiny—just three rooms, each
smaller than my chamber at the Manhattan. But it looked out directly on the park, and nearly every inch of it was crammed with
books. A homey smell of cooked onions hung in the air.

Jung was there, as well as Brill, Ferenczi, and Freud, all crowded
around a small dining table in the middle of the main room, which
served as kitchen, dining area, and parlor all at once. Brill shouted
out that I must sit down and have some of Rose's brisket; wine was
poured for me before I could reply. Brill and Ferenczi were in the
middle of a story about being analyzed by Freud, with Brill acting the
part of the Master. Everyone was laughing, even Jung, whose eyes, I
noticed, lingered on Brill's wife.

"But come, my friends," said Freud, "that does not answer the
question: why America?"

"The question, Younger," Brill clarified for my benefit, "is this.
Psychoanalysis is excommunicated everywhere in Europe. Yet here,
in puritanical America, Freud is to receive his first honorary degree
and is asked to lecture at a prestigious university. How can that be?"

"Jung says," Ferenczi added, "it is because you Americans don't understand Freud's sexual theories. Once you do, he says, you will drop psychoanalysis like hot apple."

"I don't think so," I said. "I think it will spread like wildfire."

"Why?" asked Jung.

"Precisely because of our puritanism," I answered. "But there is something I—"

"That is opposite," said Ferenczi. "A puritan society should ban us."

"It *will* ban you," said Jung, laughing out loud, "as soon as it figures out what we are saying."

"America puritan?" Brill put in. "The devil was more puritan."

"Quiet, all of you," said Rose Brill, a dark-haired woman with firm, no-nonsense eyes. "Let Dr. Younger explain what he meant."

"No, wait," said Freud. "There is something else Younger wants to say. What is it, my boy?"

❧

WE TRUNDLED DOWN the four flights of stairs as quickly as we could. The more he heard of the affair, the more intrigued Freud became, and when he learned of the mayor's personal involvement, he was as excited as I to get downtown, notwithstanding the hour. The motorcar being a four-seater, there was one extra place, so Freud decided Ferenczi would accompany us. Freud had first invited Jung, who seemed strangely uninterested and declined; he had not even come down to the street.

Just before we drove off, Brill said, "I don't like your leaving Jung here. Let me go get him; you can squeeze him in and drop him at the hotel."

"Abraham," Freud replied with surprising severity, "I have told you repeatedly how I feel about this. You must overcome your hostility to Jung. He is more important than the rest of us put together."

"It's not that, for heaven's sake," protested Brill. "I've just given the man dinner in my own home, haven't I? It's his—*condition*—I'm talking about."

"What condition?" asked Freud.

"He's not right. He's flushed, overly excited. Hot one minute, cold the next. Surely you noticed. Some of what he says makes no sense at all."

"He's been drinking your wine."

"That's another thing," said Brill. "Jung never touches alcohol."

"That was Bleuler's influence," Freud remarked. "I've cured him of it. You don't object to Jung's drinking, Abraham?"

"Certainly not. Anything is better than Jung sober. Let's keep him drunk all the time. But there's something unsettling about him. From the moment he came in. Did you hear him ask why my floor was so soft—my wood floor?"

"You are imagining things," said Freud. "And behind the imagination there is always a wish. Jung is merely unused to alcohol. Just make sure he gets back to the hotel safely."

"Very well." Brill bade us good luck. As we pulled away, he called out, "But there can also be a wish *not* to imagine."

❧

IN THE OPEN-ROOFED CAR, rattling down Broadway, Ferenczi asked me if it was normal in America to eat a melange of apples, nuts, celery, and mayonnaise. Rose Brill had evidently served her guests a Waldorf salad.

Freud had fallen silent. He appeared to be brooding. I wondered if Brill's comments were troubling him; I myself had begun to think something might be wrong with Jung. I also wondered what Freud meant when he said that Jung was more important than the rest of us put together.

"Brill is a paranoiac," Ferenczi said abruptly, addressing Freud. "It is nothing."

"The paranoid is never entirely mistaken," Freud replied. "Did you hear Jung's slip?"

"What slip?" said Ferenczi.

"His slip of the tongue," answered Freud. "He said, 'America will ban you'—not *us* but *you*."

Freud relapsed into silence. We took Broadway all the way down to Union Square, then Fourth Avenue to the Bowery Road through the Lower East Side. As we passed the closed stalls of the Hester Street market, we had to slow down. Although it was nearly eleven, Jewish men crowded the streets, wearing their long beards and peculiar outfits, black from head to foot. Perhaps it was too hot to sleep in the airless, crammed tenements in which so many of the city's immigrants lived. The Jews walked arm in arm or gathered in small circles, with much gesturing and loud disputation. The sound of their mongrel low German, which the Hebrews call Yiddish, was everywhere.

"So this is the New World," Freud observed from the front seat, not favorably. "Why on earth would they come so far, only to re-create what they left behind?"

I hazarded a question: "Are you not a religious man, Dr. Freud?"

It was infelicitous. At first I thought he hadn't heard me. Ferenczi answered instead: "It depends on what is meant by *religious*. If, for example, religious means believing God is gigantic illusion inspired by collective Oedipal complex, Freud is very religious."

Freud now fixed on me for the first time the piercing gaze I had seen on the quay. "I will tell you your thought process in asking me that," he said. "I asked why these Jews had come here. It occurred to you to say *They came for religious freedom,* but you reconsidered, because it seemed too obvious. You then reflected that if I, a Jew, could not see that they came for religious freedom, it must be that religion does not signify much for me—indeed, so little that I failed to see how important it is for them. Hence your question. Do I have it right?"

"Completely," I replied.

"Not to worry," interposed Ferenczi. "He does this to everyone."

"So. You ask me a direct question," said Freud; "I will give you a direct answer. I am the deepest of unbelievers. Every neurosis is a religion to its owner, and religion is the universal neurosis of mankind. This much is beyond doubt: the characteristics we attribute to God reflect the fears and wishes we first feel as infants and then as small children. Anyone who does not see that much cannot have understood the first thing about human psychology. If it is religion you are looking for, do not follow me."

"Freud, you are being unfair," said Ferenczi. "Younger did not say he was looking for religion."

"The boy has taken an interest in my ideas; he may as well know their implications." Freud scrutinized me. All at once, the severity disappeared, and he gave me an almost fatherly look. "And as I may possibly take an interest in *his,* I return the question: are you a religious man, Younger?"

To my embarrassment, I did not know how to respond. "My father was," I said.

"You answer a question," Ferenczi replied, "different from the one that was put."

"But I understand him," said Freud. "He means: because his father believed, he is inclined to doubt."

"That's true," I said.

"But he also wonders," Freud added, "whether a doubt so founded is a good doubt. Which inclines him to believe."

I could only stare. Ferenczi asked my question. "How can you possibly know that?"

"It all follows," answered Freud, "from what he told us last night: that going into medicine was his father's wish, not his own. And besides," he added, taking a satisfied pull at his cigar, "I felt the same way when I was younger."

❧

WITH ITS GRAND marble façade, Greek pediments, and fantastic dome, softly lit by streetlamps, the new police headquarters at 240 Centre Street looked more like a palace than a municipal building. Passing through a pair of massive oak doors, we found a uniformed man behind a semicircular desk raised up to chest level. Electrical lights cast a yellow glow around him. He cranked up a telephonic device, and soon enough we were greeted by Mayor McClellan, together with an older, worried-looking, potbellied gentleman named Higginson, who turned out to be the Actons' family doctor.

Shaking each of us by the hand, McClellan apologized to Freud profusely for causing him so dreadful an inconvenience. "Younger tells me you are also an expert on ancient Rome. I will give you my book on Venice. But I must take you upstairs. Miss Acton is in the most lamentable condition."

The mayor led us up a marble staircase. Dr. Higginson talked a good deal about the measures he had taken—none of which sounded harmful, so we had some luck there. We entered a large office in the classic style, with leather chairs, a good deal of brass, and an imposing desk. Behind this desk, looking much too small for it, a girl was seated, wrapped in a light blanket, with a policeman on either side of her.

McClellan was correct: she was in a pitiable state. She had been crying hard; her face was horribly red and swollen from it. Her long blond hair was loose and matted. She looked up at us with the largest, most fearful eyes I have ever seen—fearful and distrustful.

"We've been at it every which way," McClellan declared. "She is able to tell us, by writing, everything that happened before and after. But as to the—ah—incident itself, she remembers nothing." Next to the girl were sheets of paper and a pen.

The mayor introduced us. The girl's name was Nora. He explained that we were special doctors who, he hoped, would be able to help her recover her voice and her memory. He spoke to her as if she were a child of seven, perhaps confusing her speaking difficulty with a difficulty in understanding, although one could tell instantly from her eyes that she had no impairment on that score. Predictably, the entrance of three more strange new men had the effect of overwhelming the girl Tears came to her eyes, but she held them back. She actually wrote an apology to us, as if she were at fault for her amnesia.

"Please proceed, gentlemen," said McClellan.

Freud wanted first to rule out a physiological basis for her symptoms. "Miss Acton," he said, "I would like to be sure you have not suffered an injury to your head. Will you permit me?" The girl nodded. After making a thorough inspection, Freud concluded, "There is no cranial injury of any kind."

"Damage to the larynx could cause aphonia," I remarked, referring to the girl's loss of voice.

Freud nodded and invited me, by gesture, to examine the girl myself.

Approaching Miss Acton, I felt inexplicably nervous. I could not identify the source of this anxiety; I seemed to be afraid that I would appear to Freud as inexperienced, yet I had performed examinations infinitely more complicated—and these in front of my professors at Harvard—without any such unease. I explained to Miss Acton that it was important to determine whether a physical injury might be causing her inability to speak. I asked if she would take my hand and place it on her neck in such a way as to minimize her own discomfort. I held my hand out, two fingers extended. Reluctantly, she conducted it toward her throat, placing my fingers, however, on her collarbone. I asked her to lift her head. She complied, and as I ran my fingers up her throat to the larynx, I noticed, despite her injuries, the soft, perfect lines of her neck and chin, which might have been carved in marble by Bernini. When I applied pressure to various points, she squinted but did not draw back. "There is no evidence of laryngeal trauma," I reported.

Miss Acton looked even more mistrustful now than when we first came in. I didn't blame her. It can be more upsetting for a person to find out there isn't anything physically wrong with her than to find out there is. At the same time, she was without her family, surrounded by strange men. She seemed to be assessing us all, one by one.

"My dear," Freud said to her, "you are anxious about the loss of your memory and your voice. You need not be. Amnesia after such an incident is not uncommon, and I have seen loss of speech many times. Where there is no permanent physical injury—and you have none—I have always succeeded in eliminating both conditions. Now: I am going to ask you some questions, but none about what happened to you today. I want you to tell me only how you are at this moment. Would you care for something to drink?" She nodded gratefully; McClellan sent out one of the officers, who returned shortly with a cup of tea. In the meantime, Freud engaged the girl in conversation—he speaking, she writing—but only on the most general of facts, such as, for example, that she was to be a freshwoman at Barnard starting next month. In the end, she wrote that she was sorry she could not answer the policemen's questions, and she wanted to go home.

Freud indicated that he wished to speak with us outside the girl's hearing. This prompted a grave trooping of men—Freud, Mayor McClellan, Ferenczi, Dr. Higginson, and me—to the far corner of the spacious office, where Freud asked, in a very low voice, "Was she violated?"

"No, thank God," whispered McClellan.

"But her wounds," said Higginson, "are conspicuously concentrated around her—private parts." He cleared his throat. "Apart from her back, it seems she was whipped repeatedly about her buttocks and—ah—pelvis. In addition, she was cut once on each of her thighs with a sharp knife or razor."

"What kind of monster does such a thing?" McClellan asked.

"The question is why it doesn't happen more often," replied Freud quietly. "Satisfying a savage instinct is incomparably more pleasurable than satisfying a civilized one. In any event, the best course of action tonight is certainly inaction. I am not convinced her amnesia is hysterical. Severe asphyxiation could bring about the same effect. On the other hand, she is plainly suffering from some deep self-reproach. She should sleep. She may wake up asymptomatic. If her symptoms persist, analysis will be in order."

"Self-reproach?" asked McClellan.

"Guilt," said Ferenczi. "The girl is suffering not only from attack but from guilt she feels in connection with it."

"Why on earth would she feel guilt?" asked the mayor.

"There are many possible reasons," said Freud. "But an element of self-reproach is almost invariable in cases of sexual assault on the young. She has already twice apologized to us for her memory loss. Her voice loss is more puzzling."

"Sodomized, perhaps?" asked Ferenczi in a whisper. "*Per os?*"

"Great God," McClellan interjected, also whispering. "Is that possible?"

"It is possible," Freud answered, "but not likely. If an oral penetration were the source of her symptoms, her inability to use her mouth would be expected to extend to taking *in*. But you will notice she drank her tea without difficulty. Indeed, that is why I asked if she was thirsty."

We contemplated this momentarily. McClellan spoke again, no longer whispering. "Dr. Freud, forgive my ignorance, but does her memory of the event still exist, or has it been, so to speak, wiped out?"

"Assuming hysterical amnesia, the memory certainly exists," Freud answered. "It is the cause."

"The memory is the cause of the amnesia?" McClellan asked.

"The memory of the attack—along with the deeper recollections rekindled by it—is unacceptable. Therefore she has repressed it, producing the appearance of an amnesia."

"Deeper recollections?" repeated the mayor. "I don't follow you."

"An episode of the kind this girl has undergone," said Freud, "however brutal, however terrible, will not at her age ordinarily cause amnesia. The victim remembers, provided she is otherwise healthy. But where the victim has suffered another, earlier traumatic episode— so traumatic the memory of it had to be wholly suppressed from consciousness—an attack can bring about amnesia, because the fresh attack cannot be remembered without also triggering recollections of the older episode, which her consciousness cannot allow."

"Good Lord," said the mayor.

"What is to be done?" asked Higginson.

"Can you cure her?" the mayor cut in. "She is the only one who can give us a description of her assailant."

"Hypnosis?" Ferenczi suggested.

"I advise strongly against it," said Freud. "It would not help her, and memories yielded under hypnosis are not reliable."

"What of this—this *analysis,* as you call it?" the mayor asked.

"We could begin as early as tomorrow," Freud replied. "But I should warn you: psychoanalysis is an intensive treatment. The patient must be seen daily, for at least an hour each day."

"I see no difficulty there," declared McClellan. "The question is what to do with Miss Acton tonight." The girl's parents, summering at their house in the Berkshire country, could not be reached. Higginson suggested calling on some friends of the family, but the mayor said it wouldn't do. "Acton will not want word of the episode to get out. People might believe the girl has been permanently injured."

Miss Acton almost certainly overheard the last comment. I saw her now writing a new note for us. I went to her and received it; *I want to go home,* it said. *Now.*

McClellan immediately told the girl he could not allow it. Criminals had been known, he warned her, to return to the scene of their crime. The assailant might be keeping watch over her house even now. Fearing that she could identify him, he might believe his only hope of escaping justice was to take her life. Returning to Gramercy Park was therefore out of the question, at least until her father was back in town to assure her safety. At this, Miss Acton's face changed again and she made a gesture with her hands, expressing an emotion I could not identify.

"I have it," McClellan announced. Miss Acton, he said, would be taken to the Hotel Manhattan, where we were staying. The mayor himself would pay for her rooms. She would be settled there along with Mrs. Biggs, the old housekeeper, who could see to it that proper attire and other necessaries were sent up from Gramercy Park. Miss Acton would stay at the hotel until her parents returned from the country. This arrangement would be not only the safest but the most convenient for purposes of commencing her treatment.

"There is a further difficulty," said Freud. "Psychoanalysis requires from the doctor a substantial commitment of time. Obviously I cannot make such a commitment. Neither can my colleague Dr. Ferenczi. What about you, Younger? Will you take her on?"

Freud saw by my hesitation that I wished to respond privately to him. He drew me aside.

"It should be Brill," I said, "not me."

Freud fixed me again with the look that could bore into rock. He replied quietly, "I have no doubt of your abilities, my boy; your case history proves them. I want you to take her on."

It was simultaneously an order I could not disobey and an expression of confidence whose effect on me I cannot describe. I agreed.

"Good," he said aloud. "She is yours. I will supervise as long as I remain in America, but Dr. Younger will perform the analysis. Assuming, of course," he added, turning toward Miss Acton, "that our patient is as willing as we are."

PART

II

CORONER HUGEL'S SUNKEN CHEEKS, Detective Little-
more noticed on Tuesday morning, were looking even hollower than
usual. The pouches below his eyes had pouches of their own, the
dark circles their own circles. Littlemore felt sure his discoveries
would boost the coroner's spirits.

"Okay, Mr. Hugel," said the detective, "I went back to the Balmoral. Wait till you hear what I got."

"You spoke with the maid?" Hugel asked immediately.

"Doesn't work there anymore," answered the detective. "She was
fired."

"I knew it!" the coroner exclaimed. "Did you get her address?"

"Oh, I found her all right. But here's the first thing: I went back
to Miss Riverford's bedroom to look at that molding on the ceiling—
you know, the bowling-ball thing you said she was tied up to? You
were right. There were rope threads on it."

"Good. You secured them, I trust?" said Hugel.

"I got 'em. And the whole ball too," said Littlemore, provoking an
unpleasant look of foreboding on the coroner's face. The detective
continued: "I didn't think it looked very strong, so I got up on the bed
and gave it a good yank, and it broke right off."

"You didn't think the ceiling looked very strong," the coroner repeated, "so you gave it a yank, and it broke. Excellent work, Detective."

"Thanks, Mr. Hugel."

"Perhaps you could destroy the whole room next time. Is there
any other evidence you damaged?"

"No," answered Littlemore. "I just don't get the way it broke off
so easy. How could it hold her up?"

"Well, it obviously did."

"There's more, Mr. Hugel, something big. Two things." Little-more described the unknown man who left the Balmoral around midnight on Sunday carrying a black case. "How about that, Mr. Hugel?" asked the detective proudly. "It could be him, right?"

"They're certain he wasn't a resident?"

"Positive. Never saw him before."

"Carrying a bag, you say?" asked Hugel. "In what hand?"

"Clifford didn't know."

"You asked?"

"Sure did," said Littlemore. "Had to check the guy's dexterity."

Hugel grunted dismissively. "Well, it's not our man anyway."

"Why not?"

"Because, Littlemore, our man has graying hair, and our man lives in that building." The coroner grew animated. "We know Miss Riverford had no regular visitors. We know she had no visitors from outside the building on Sunday night. How then did the murderer get into her apartment? The door was not forced. There is only one possibility. He knocked; she answered. Now, would a girl, living alone, open her door to just anyone? In the nighttime? To a stranger? I doubt it very much. But she would open it to a neighbor, someone who lived in the building—someone she was expecting, perhaps, someone to whom she had opened her door before."

"A laundry guy!" said Littlemore.

The coroner stared at the detective.

"That's the other thing, Mr. Hugel. Listen to this. I'm down in the basement of the Balmoral when I see this Chinaman tracking clay—red clay. I took a sample; it's the same clay I saw up in Miss Riverford's room, I'm sure of it. Maybe *he's* the killer."

"A Chinaman," said the coroner.

"I tried to stop him, but he got away. Laundry worker. Maybe this guy makes a laundry delivery to Miss Riverford on Sunday night. She opens the door for him, and he kills her. Then he goes back down to the laundry, and nobody's the wiser."

"Littlemore," said the coroner, taking a deep breath, "the murderer was not a Chinese laundry boy. He is a wealthy man. We know that."

"No, Mr. Hugel, you figured he was wealthy because he strangled her with a fancy silk tie, but if you work in a laundry you clean silk ties all the time. Maybe this Chinaman steals one from there and kills Miss Riverford with it."

"With what motive?" asked the coroner.

"I don't know. Maybe he likes killing girls, like that guy in Chicago. Say, Miss Riverford comes from Chicago. You don't think—?"

"No, Detective, I don't. Nor do I think your Chinaman has anything to do with Miss Riverford's murder."

"But the clay—"

"Forget the clay."

"But the Chinaman ran when—"

"No Chinaman! Do you hear me, Littlemore? No Chinaman figures in any way in this murder. The killer is at least six feet tall. He is white: the hairs I found on her body are Caucasian. The maid—the maid is the key. What did she tell you?"

༄

I GOT TO breakfast with about fifteen minutes to spare before I was to call on Miss Acton. Freud was just sitting down. Brill and Ferenczi were already at table, Brill with three empty plates in front of him and at work on a fourth. I had told him yesterday that Clark would pay for his breakfast. He was evidently making up for lost time.

"Now *this* is America," he said to Freud. "You begin with toasted oats in sugar and cream, then hot leg of lamb with French-fried potatoes, a basket of raised biscuits with fresh butter, and finally buckwheat cakes with syrup tapped from Vermont maples. I am in heaven."

"I am not," Freud replied. He was apparently in some digestive distress. Our food, he said, was too heavy for him.

"For me too," complained Ferenczi, who had nothing but a cup of tea before him. He added unhappily, "I think it was mayonnaise salad."

"Where is Jung?" asked Freud.

"I haven't any idea," answered Brill. "But I do know where he went Sunday night."

"Sunday night? He went to bed Sunday night," said Freud.

"Oh, no, he didn't," Brill replied, in what was evidently meant to be a tantalizing tone. "And I know whom he was with. Here, I'll show you. Look at this."

From below his seat, Brill withdrew a thick sheaf of papers, wrapped in rubber bands, perhaps three hundred pages. The top page read, *Selected Papers on Hysteria and Other Psychoneuroses* by Sigmund Freud, translation and preface by A. A. Brill. "Your first book in English," said Brill, handing the manuscript to Freud with a glowing pride I had never seen him reveal before. "It will be a sensation, you'll see."

"I am overjoyed, Abraham," said Freud, returning the manuscript. "Really I am. But you were telling us about Jung."

Brill's face fell. He rose from his seat, lifted his chin, and declared haughtily, "So that is how you treat my life's work of the last twelve months. Some dreams do not require interpretation; they require action. Good-bye."

Then he sat down again.

"Sorry, don't know what came over me," he said. "Thought I was Jung for a moment." Brill's rendition of Jung—which had been remarkable—put Ferenczi in stitches but left Freud unmoved. Clearing his throat, Brill directed our attention to the name of his publisher, Smith Ely Jelliffe, on the manuscript's title page. "Jelliffe runs the *Journal of Nervous Disease*," said Brill. "He's a doctor, rich as Croesus, very well connected, and another convert to the cause, thanks to me. By God, I will make this Gomorrah a very Eden for psychoanalysis; you'll see. Anyway, our friend Jung had a secret rendezvous with Jelliffe on Sunday night."

It turned out that Jelliffe, when Brill picked up the manuscript from him this morning, had mentioned having Jung to dinner at his apartment on Sunday night. Jung had told us nothing about such a meeting. "Apparently their chief topic of conversation was the location of Manhattan's best brothels, but listen to this," Brill continued. "Jelliffe has asked Jung to give a series of lectures on psychoanalysis next week at Fordham University, the Jesuit school."

"But that is excellent news!" Freud exclaimed.

"Is it?" asked Brill. "Why Jung, rather than you?"

"Abraham, I am giving a lecture every day in Massachusetts beginning Tuesday of next week. I couldn't possibly lecture in New York at the same time."

"But why the secrecy? Why conceal his meeting with Jelliffe?"

To this question, none of us had an answer. Freud, however, was unconcerned, commenting that there was undoubtedly a good reason for Jung's reticence.

All this time, I had been holding Brill's thick manuscript. Having read the first couple of pages, I turned to the next and was surprised by the sight of an almost completely blank sheet. On it were only five lines of print: centered, italicized, capitalized. It was a biblical verse of some kind.

"What's this?" I asked, displaying the page.

Ferenczi took the page from my hand and read as follows:

TAKE AWAY THE FORESKINS OF YOUR HEART,

YE MEN OF JERUSALEM:

LEST MY FURY COME FORTH LIKE FIRE,

AND BURN THAT NONE CAN QUENCH IT,

BECAUSE OF THE EVIL OF YOUR DOINGS.

"Jeremiah, no?" Ferenczi added, demonstrating a knowledge of scripture considerably superior to my own. "What is Jeremiah doing in your hysteria book?"

Odder still, at the bottom of the page—which Ferenczi now placed in the center of our table—was the ink-stamped image of a face. It was a wizened Oriental sage of some kind, with a turban on his head, a long nose, a longer beard, and wide-open, mesmerizing eyes.

"A Hindoo?" asked Ferenczi.

"Or an Arab?" I suggested.

Oddest of all, the next page of the manuscript was just the same—blank but for the biblical passage in the center—although there was no wide-eyed, turbaned face stamped on it. I riffled through the remaining pages. All were the same, minus the face.

"Is this a joke, Brill?" said Freud.

Judging by the look on Brill's face, it was not.

❧

DETECTIVE LITTLEMORE WAS sorely disappointed by the coroner's dismissal of his discoveries, but he allowed Hugel to change the subject back to Miss Riverford's maid, who had also provided interesting information.

"She's real bad off, Mr. Hugel; I wish I could do something for her," said the detective. In fact, he had: finding Betty reluctant to speak with him at first, Littlemore had taken her to a soda fountain. When he told her he knew she had been let go, she burst out about how unfair it was. Why had they fired her? She hadn't done anything. Some of the other girls stole from the apartments—why didn't they fire one of them? And what would she do now? It turned out that Betty's father had passed away the year before. For the last two months, Betty had been supporting her whole family—her mother and three little brothers—with her wages from the Balmoral.

"What did she tell you, Detective?" asked the coroner, biting his lip.

"Betty says she didn't like going into Miss Riverford's apartment. She said it was haunted. Twice she was sure she heard a baby crying, but there wasn't any baby; the apartment would be empty. She says Miss Riverford was strange. Just shows up one day about four weeks ago. No moving trucks; no nothing. The apartment was furnished before she got there. Real quiet type, very private. Never any mess. Always made her own bed and kept her things just so—one of her closets was always locked. She tried to give Betty a pair of earrings once. Betty asked were they real—real diamonds, that is—and when Miss Riverford said yes, Betty wouldn't take them. But Betty almost never saw her. Betty worked nights for a while, and she saw Miss Riverford a couple of times then. Otherwise she was always up and out of the apartment before seven, when Betty got there. One of the doormen told me Miss Riverford left the building a couple of times before six. What's that mean, Mr. Hugel?"

"It means," answered the coroner, "you are going to send a man to Chicago."

"To talk to the family?"

"Correct. What did the maid tell you about the bedroom when she first discovered the body?"

"The thing is, Betty doesn't remember that part too well. All she can remember is Miss Riverford's face."

"Did she see anything near the dead girl or lying on top of her?"

"I asked her, Mr. Hugel. She can't remember."

"Nothing?"

"She just remembers Miss Riverford's eyes, open and staring."

"Weak little idiot."

Littlemore was taken aback. "You wouldn't say that if you talked to her," he said. "How do you figure something changing anyway?"

"What?"

"You're saying something in the room changed from when Betty first went in to when you got there. But I thought they locked the apartment right away and put that butler guy in the hall to keep everybody out until you got there."

"I thought so too," the coroner replied, pacing the short length of his cramped office. "That's what we were told."

"So why do you think someone got in the room?"

"Why?" repeated Hugel, scowling. "You want to know why? Very well, Mr. Littlemore. Follow me."

The coroner strode out the door. The detective followed him—down three flights of old stairs and through a maze of peeling corridors, eventually emerging in the morgue. The coroner unlocked a vaulted door. When he opened it, Littlemore felt the blast of stale, freezing air, then saw rows of cadavers on wooden shelves, some naked and stretched out for all to see, others covered by sheets. He could not help looking at their privates, which repulsed him.

"No one else," announced the coroner, "would have examined her body closely enough to see this clue. No one." He strode to the back of the chamber where a body lay on the farthest shelf. A white sheet covered it, on which was written *Riverford, E.: 29.8.09.* "Now look at her carefully, Detective, and tell me exactly what you see."

The coroner threw back the sheet with a flourish. Littlemore's eyes went wide, but Hugel looked even more astonished than the detective. Beneath the sheet lay not Elizabeth Riverford's corpse, but that of a black-toothed, slack-skinned old man.

❧

I took the elevator to Miss Acton's floor—and then remembered that I had to go back to my own first, to get paper and pens. The bizarre biblical passage in his manuscript had affected Brill deeply. He seemed actually frightened. He said he was going straight back to Jelliffe, his publisher, for an explanation; I felt there might be something he wasn't telling us.

I had expected Freud to be present at my initial sessions with Miss Acton. Instead, he instructed me to report to him afterward. His presence, he felt, would disrupt the transference.

The transference is a psychoanalytic phenomenon. Freud discovered it by accident, and much to his surprise. Patient after patient reacted to analysis by worshiping him—or occasionally by hating him. At first he tried to ignore these feelings, viewing them as unwelcome and unruly intrusions into the therapeutic relationship. Over time, however, he discovered how crucial they were, to both the patient's illness and the cure. The patient was reenacting, inside the analyst's office, the very same unconscious conflicts that caused the symptoms, *transferring* to the doctor the suppressed desires that lay at the heart of the illness. This was not fortuitous: the entire disease of hysteria, Freud had found, consisted of an individual's transferring to new persons, or sometimes even to objects, a set of buried wishes and emotions formed in childhood but never discharged. By dissecting this phenomenon with the patient—by bringing the transference to light and working it through—analysis makes the unconscious conscious and removes the cause of the illness.

Thus the transference turned out to be one of Freud's most important discoveries. Would I ever have an idea of comparable importance? Ten years ago, I thought I already had. On December 31, 1899, I excitedly announced it to my father, actually interrupting him in his study a few hours before the guests would arrive for the New Year's Eve dinner party my mother always threw. He was quite surprised and, I suppose, irritated that I would bother him at his work, although of course he didn't say so. I told him I had made a discovery of potentially great moment and asked permission to inform him. He tilted his head. "Proceed," he said.

Since the dawn of the modern age, I argued, a peculiar fact held true of all man's supreme revolutionary bursts of genius, whether in art or in science. Every one of them had occurred at the turn of a century and—more specifically still—in the first decade of the new century.

In painting, poetry, sculpture, natural science, drama, literature, music, physics—in each one of these fields—which man and which work, above all others, has the best claim to world-altering genius, the kind of genius that changes the course of history? In painting, the cognoscenti uniformly point to the Scrovegni Chapel, where Giotto reintroduced three-dimensional figuration to the modern world. He painted those frescoes between 1303 and 1305. In verse, surely the crown belongs to Dante's *Inferno,* the first great work written in the vernacular, begun soon after the poet's banishment from Florence in 1302. In sculpture, there is only one possibility, Michelangelo's *David,* carved from a single block of marble in 1501. That same year marked the fundamental revolution of modern science, for it was then that a certain Nicolaus of Torún traveled to Padua, ostensibly to study medicine but secretly to continue the astronomical observations from which he had glimpsed a forbidden truth; we know him today as Copernicus. In literature, the choice has to be the grandsire of all novels, *Don Quixote,* who first tilted at windmills in 1604. In music, none will dispute Beethoven's pathbreaking symphonic genius; he composed his First in 1800, the defiant Eroica in 1803, the Fifth by 1807.

This was the case I made to my father. It was juvenile, I know, but I was seventeen. I supposed it a great thing to be alive at the turn of a century. I predicted a wave of groundbreaking works and ideas in the next few years. And what would one not give to be alive at the turn of the millennium a hundred years hence!

"You are certainly—enthusiastic" was my father's phlegmatic reply. His only reply. I had made the mistake of showing excitement. *Enthusiastic* was for my father a term of utmost deprecation.

But my enthusiasm was vindicated. In 1905, an unknown Swiss patent agent of German-Jewish extraction produced a theory he called relativity. Within twelve months, my professors at Harvard were saying that this Einstein had changed our ideas of space and time forever. In art, I concede, nothing happened. In 1903, the crowd at St. Botolph's made a great fuss over a Frenchman's water lilies, but these proved to be the work of an artist who was merely losing his eyesight. When it came, however, to man's understanding of himself, my predictions were again fulfilled. Sigmund Freud published his *Interpretation of Dreams* in 1900. My father would have scoffed, but I am convinced that Freud too will have changed our thinking forever. After Freud, we will never look at ourselves or others in the same way again.

My mother was always "protecting" us from my father. This was an irritant to me; I didn't need it. My elder brother did, but her protection in his case was quite ineffectual. What an advantage to come second: I saw it all. Not that I was favored, but by the time my father came around to me, I had learned to be impenetrable, and he could do no serious damage. I did have an Achilles' heel, however, which he eventually found. It was Shakespeare.

My father never said aloud that my fascination with Shakespeare was excessive, but he made his opinion clear: there was something unwholesome about my taking a greater interest in a fiction, especially *Hamlet,* than in reality itself, and something arrogant as well. Once only did he give voice to this sentiment. When I was thirteen, thinking no one home, I delivered Hamlet's *What's Hecuba to him, or he to Hecuba, that he should weep for her?* Possibly I sawed the air a little hard on *bloody, bawdy villain*; conceivably I was a little earsplitting on *Oh vengeance!* or *Fie upon 't! Foh!* My father, unbeknownst to me, witnessed the whole thing. When I was done, he cleared his throat and asked what Hamlet was to me, or I to Hamlet, that I should weep for him?

Needless to say, I had not wept. I have never cried at all, in conscious memory. My father's point, if not solely to embarrass me, was that my devotion to *Hamlet* could mean nothing in the scope of things: nothing in my future, nothing in the world. He wanted to make me understand this early on. He succeeded and, what's more, I knew he was right.

Yet that knowledge did not impair my devotion to Shakespeare. It will have been noticed that I left the poet of Avon off my list of world-changing geniuses. I also left him off the list when I made the case to my father in 1899. The omission was strategic. I wanted to see if my father might take the bait. It would have appealed to him to use my "beloved Shakespeare," as my father used to refer to him, against me. He was far too subtle to cite a Dickens or a Tolstoy: he would have seen at once that I would call them classic mid-century giants, masters of existing forms rather than inventors of new ones. But he also would have known that I could never deny the title of revolutionary genius to Shakespeare, who might thus have been presented as an instant, devastating rebuttal of my argument.

Perhaps my father smelled the trap. Perhaps he knew his history better than I expected. At any rate he didn't ask, so I didn't get to tell him that *Hamlet* was written in 1600.

Nor did I get a chance to point out that I was hardly the only one impassioned about Shakespeare. Men were once ready to die over *Hamlet*. My father did not know it—indeed, nearly everyone has forgotten it—but there was once a riot over *Hamlet* even here in the uncultured United States. Only sixty years ago, the storied American actor Edwin Forrest toured England, where he saw the famous William Macready, the aristocratic British tragedian, playing the Prince of Denmark. Forrest volubly expressed his disgust. According to Forrest, who was of muscular build and hailed from an impoverished, democratic upbringing, Macready's Hamlet pranced across the stage in effete, mincing steps absurd in themselves and degrading to the noble prince.

So began a public and escalating quarrel between these two international celebrities. Forrest was driven from the boards in England, and when Macready came to America the favor was returned. Eggs of doubtful purity, old shoes, copper coins, and even chairs were catapulted from audience to stage. The culmination of the quarrel took place in front of the old Astor Place Opera House in Manhattan on May 7, 1849, when fifteen thousand belligerents gathered to disrupt a Macready performance. The inexperienced mayor of New York, who had taken office only the week before, called up the militia, and the order was eventually given to open fire on the crowd. Some twenty or thirty men died that night.

And all for nothing, my father would have said: for Hamlet. But that is how it always is. Men care most about that which is least real. Medicine, to me, stood for reality. Nothing I did before medical school seems real any longer; it was all play. That is why fathers have to die: to make the world real for their sons.

It is the same with the transference: the patient forms an attachment to the doctor of the most strenuously emotional nature. A female patient will weep for her doctor; she will offer herself to him; she will be ready to die for him. But it is all a fiction, a chimera. In reality, her feelings have nothing to do with the doctor, onto whose person she is projecting some violent, roiling affect properly directed elsewhere. The grossest blunder an analyst can make is to mistake these artifactual feelings, whether seductive or hateful, for reality. So I steeled myself as I strode down the corridor to Miss Acton's room.

CHAPTER SEVEN

THE OLD WOMAN let me in to Miss Acton's suite, calling out, "Young doctor's here!"

The girl was perched on a sofa under the window, one leg tucked beneath her, reading what appeared to be a mathematics textbook. She looked up but did not greet me—understandable, since she could not speak. A chandelier hung from the ceiling, its teardrop crystals trembling slightly, perhaps an effect of the underground trains rumbling far below us.

Miss Acton was simply attired in a white dress with blue trim. She wore no jewelry. Around her neck, just above a delicate clavicle, was a scarf the color of the sky. Given the summer heat, there could be only one explanation for the scarf: the bruises on her throat would still have been visible, and she wished to conceal them.

Her appearance was so different from the night before that I might have failed to recognize her. Her long hair, a tangle last night, was now perfectly smooth and shining, gathered in a long braid. Shivering uncontrollably yesterday, she was today a picture of grace, her chin held high over her long neck. Only her lips remained slightly swollen where she had been struck.

From my black bag I removed several notebooks, along with a variety of pens and inks. These were not for myself but for Miss Acton, so she could communicate with me by writing. Following Freud's advice, I never took notes during an analytic session but transcribed the conversation from memory afterward.

"Good morning, Miss Acton," I said. "These are for you."

"Thank you," she said. "Which one shall I use?"

"Whichever is—" I began, before the obvious fact took hold. "You can speak."

"Mrs. Biggs," she said, "will you pour the doctor some tea?"

I declined the tea. To the annoyance I felt at having been taken by surprise was now added the realization that I was a doctor capable of resenting a patient for improving without my assistance. "Have you also recovered your memory?" I asked.

"No. But your friend, the old doctor, said it would all come back naturally, didn't he?"

"Dr. Freud said your *voice* was likely to come back naturally, Miss Acton, not your memory." This was a strange thing for me to say, given that I wasn't at all sure I had it right.

"I hate Shakespeare," she replied.

She kept her eyes on mine, but I saw what had prompted this inconsequent remark. My copy of *Hamlet* was poking out of the stack of notebooks I had offered her. I retrieved the play, putting it back in my bag. I was tempted to ask why she hated Shakespeare but thought better of it. "Shall we begin your treatment, Miss Acton?"

Sighing like a patient who had seen too many doctors, she turned and looked out the window, offering her back to me. Evidently the girl thought I was going to use my stethoscope on her or perhaps examine her wounds. I informed her that we were only going to talk.

She exchanged a skeptical glance with Mrs. Biggs. "What sort of treatment is that, Doctor?" she asked.

"It is called psychoanalysis. It's very simple. I must ask your servant to excuse us. Then, if you will be so good as to lie down, Miss Acton, I will ask you questions. You need only say whatever comes into your mind in response. Please don't be concerned if what occurs to you seems irrelevant or unresponsive or even impolite. Just say the first thing that comes to mind, whatever it is."

She blinked at me. "You are joking."

"Not at all." It took several minutes to overcome the girl's hesitation—and then several more to overcome her servant's declaration that she had never heard of such a thing—but at last Mrs. Biggs was persuaded to go and Miss Acton to recline on her sofa. She adjusted her scarf, straightened the skirt of her dress, and looked appropriately uncomfortable. I asked if the injuries to her back troubled her; she said no. Positioning myself on a chair out of her sight, I began. "Can you tell me what you dreamt last night?"

"I beg your pardon?"

"I am sure you heard me, Miss Acton."

"I don't see what my dreams have to do with it."

"Our dreams," I explained, "are composed of fragments from the previous day's experiences. Any dream you recall may help us recover your memory."

"What if I don't want to?" she asked.

"You had a dream you would prefer not to describe?"

"I didn't say that," she said. "What if I don't want to remember? You all assume I want to remember."

"I assume you *don't* want to remember. If you wanted to remember, you would."

"What is that supposed to mean?" She sat up, glaring at me with undisguised hostility. As a rule, I am not often hated by people I have only recently met; this case appeared to be an exception. "You think I am pretending?"

"Not pretending, Miss Acton. Sometimes we don't want to remember events because they are too painful. So we shut them out, especially childhood memories."

"I am not a child."

"I know that," I said. "I meant you may have memories from years ago that you are keeping out of your consciousness."

"What are you talking about? I was attacked yesterday, not years ago."

"Yes, and that is why I have asked you about your dreams last night."

She looked at me suspiciously, but with considerable cajoling I induced her to lie down again. Gazing at the ceiling, she said, "Do you ask your other female patients to describe their dreams, Doctor?"

"Yes."

"How entertaining that must be," she remarked. "But what if their dreams are very dull? Do they invent more interesting ones?"

"Please don't be concerned about that."

"About what?"

"About your dreams being dull," I answered.

"I didn't have any dreams. You must adore Ophelia."

"I'm sorry?"

"For her docility. All of Shakespeare's women are fools, but Ophelia is the worst."

This took me aback. I suppose I always have adored Ophelia. In fact, everything I know of women, I feel I learned from Shakespeare. Miss Acton was obviously changing the subject, and while one can of course be waylaid, it is sometimes useful in analysis to play along with these evasions, since they often lead back to the crux of the matter. "What is your objection to Ophelia?" I asked.

"She kills herself because her father died—her stupid, pointless father. Would you kill yourself if your father died?"

"My father did die."

Her hand shot to her mouth. "Forgive me."

"And I did kill myself," I added. "I don't see what's so unusual about it."

She smiled.

"When you think about yesterday's events, Miss Acton, what comes to mind?"

"Nothing comes to mind," she said. "I believe that's what it means to have amnesia."

The girl's resistance did not surprise me. The one piece of advice Freud had given me was not to be put off too easily. In hysterical amnesia, some deeply forbidden and long-forgotten episode from the patient's past, stirred into life by a recent event, presses at her consciousness, which in turn fights back with all its strength to keep out the inadmissible memory. Psychoanalysis takes the side of memory against the forces of suppression; it therefore provokes immediate and sometimes intense hostility.

"There is never nothing in one's mind," I said. "What is in yours, at this moment?"

"Right now?"

"Yes: don't reflect; just speak it."

"All right. Your father didn't die. He committed suicide."

There was a momentary silence. "How did you know that?"

"Clara Banwell told me."

"Who?"

"George Banwell's wife," she said. "Do you know Mr. Banwell?"

"No."

"He is a friend of my father's. Clara took me to the horse show last year. We saw you there. Were you at Mrs. Fish's ball last night?"

I acknowledged the fact.

"You are wondering if my family was invited," she said, "but you are afraid to ask, for fear that we were not."

"No, Miss Acton. I was wondering how Mrs. Banwell knew the circumstances of my father's death."

"Is it awkward when people know?"

"Are you trying to make things awkward?"

"Clara says all the girls find it fascinating—your having a father who killed himself. They think it gives you soul. The answer is that we *were* invited, but that I would never go to one of your balls in a thousand years."

"Really?"

"Yes, really. They are sickening."

"Why?"

"Because they are so—so tiresome."

"They are sickeningly tiresome?"

"Do you know what a debutante is made to do, Doctor? First, together with her mother, she must call on all her mother's acquaintance—perhaps a hundred houses. I doubt you can imagine how excruciating that is. In every house, the women invariably comment on how 'grown up' you look, by which they mean something—quite disgusting. When the grand day arrives, you are exhibited like a talking animal on whom conversational open season has been declared. Then you are forced to endure a cotillion at which every man believes he has a right to make love to you, no matter who he is, no matter how old, no matter how bad his breath. And I haven't even gotten to having to dance with them. I'm starting college this month; I will never come out."

I chose not to respond to this disquisition, which on the whole seemed quite persuasive. Instead I said, "Tell me what happens when you try to remember."

"What do you mean, 'what happens'?"

"I want you to tell me whatever thought or image or feeling comes to you when you try to remember what happened yesterday."

She took a deep breath. "Where the memory should be, there is a darkness instead. I don't know how else to describe it."

"Are you there, in the darkness?"

"Am I there?" Her voice quieted. "I think so."

"Is anything else there?"

"A presence." She shuddered. "A man."

"What does the man make you think of?"

"I don't know. It makes my heart beat faster."

"As if you had something to fear?"

She swallowed. "To fear? Let me think. I have been attacked in my own house. The man who attacked me has not been caught. They do not even know who it was. They believe he may yet be watching my house, planning to kill me if I return. And your penetrating question is whether I have something to fear?"

I should have been more sympathetic, but I decided to loose the one arrow I had. "This was not the first time you lost your voice, Miss Acton."

She frowned. I noticed, for some reason, the graceful oblique lines of her chin and profile. "Who told you that?"

"Mrs. Biggs told the police yesterday."

"That was three years ago," she replied, coloring slightly. "It is absolutely unconnected to anything."

"You have nothing to be ashamed of, Miss Acton."

"*I* have nothing to be ashamed of?"

I heard the emphasis on *I* but could not decipher it. "We are not responsible for our feelings," I replied. "Therefore no feeling can cause us shame."

"That is the least perceptive remark I have ever heard in my life."

"Oh, really?" I answered. "What about when I asked if you had something to fear?"

"Of course feelings can cause people shame. It happens all the time."

"Are you ashamed of what happened when you lost your voice the first time?"

"You have no idea what happened," she said. Although she didn't sound it, she seemed suddenly fragile.

"That is why I am asking."

"Well, I am not going to tell you," she replied, and rose from the sofa. "This is not medicine. It is—it is *prying*." She raised her voice. "Mrs. Biggs? Mrs. Biggs, are you there?" The door flew open, and Mrs. Biggs bustled in. She must have been in the corridor all along, no doubt with her ear to the keyhole. "Dr. Younger," Miss Acton addressed me, "I am going out to buy a few things, since no one seems to know how long I shall be staying here. I'm sure you can find your way back to your own room."

❧

THE MAYOR MADE Coroner Hugel wait an hour in his anteroom. Impatient under ordinary conditions, Hugel looked irate now. "It is obstruction in the first degree," he cried out, when finally admitted into Mayor McClellan's office. "I demand an investigation."

George Brinton McClellan, Jr.—son of the famous Civil War general—was the most intellectually accomplished and forward-thinking man ever to have held the office of mayor of New York City. In 1909, only a handful of Americans were recognized as authorities on Italian history; McClellan was one of them. At forty-three, he had already been a newspaper editor, lawyer, author, congressman, lecturer on European history at Princeton University, honorary member of the American Society of Architects, and mayor of the nation's largest city. When the aldermen of New York City passed a measure in 1908 prohibiting women from smoking in public, McClellan vetoed it.

His hold on the mayoralty, however, was tenuous. The next election was less than nine weeks away, and although the candidates had not been officially named, McClellan still had no offer of nomination from any major party or syndicate. He had made two potentially fatal political mistakes. The first was having in 1905 narrowly defeated William Randolph Hearst, who ever since had filled his newspapers with sensational accounts of McClellan's shameless corruption. The second was having broken with Tammany Hall, which hated him for his incorruptibility. Tammany Hall ran the Democratic Party in New York City, and the Democrats ran the city. It was a rewarding arrangement: the Tammany leadership had unburdened the city of at least $500 million over the years. McClellan had originally been a Tammany nominee, but once elected he refused to make the brazen patronage appointments demanded of him. He ousted the most notoriously corrupt officials and brought charges against many others. He hoped to wrest control of the party from Tammany, but in this goal he had not yet succeeded.

On the mayor's walnut desk, in addition to a copy of all fifteen of the city's major newspapers, was a set of blueprints. These depicted a soaring suspension bridge, anchored by two gigantic but marvelously thin towers. Streetcars were shown traversing an upper deck, while below were six lanes of horse, automobile, and rail traffic. "Do you know, Hugel," said the mayor, "you are the fifth person today who has demanded an investigation of one thing or another?"

"Where did the body go?" Hugel replied. "Did it get up and walk away on its two feet?"

"Look at this," the mayor replied, gazing at the blueprints. "This is the Manhattan Bridge. It has cost thirty millions to build. I will open it this year, if it is the last thing I do in office. This arch on the New York side is a perfect replica of the St. Denis portal in Paris, only twice the size. A century from now, this bridge—"

"Mayor McClellan, the Riverford girl—"

"I *know* about the Riverford girl," McClellan said with sudden authority. He looked Hugel full in the face: "What am I supposed to tell Banwell? What is he to tell the girl's wretched family? Answer me that. Of course there should have been an investigation; you should have completed it long ago."

"I?" asked the coroner. "Long ago?"

"How many bodies have we lost in the past six months, Hugel, including the two unaccounted for after we repaired the leak? Twenty? You know as well as I do where they are going."

"You are not suggesting that I—"

"Of course not," said the mayor. "But someone on your staff is selling our cadavers to the medical schools. I am told they are worth five dollars a head."

"Am I to blame," responded Hugel, "with the conditions I am given—no protection, no guards, the corpses piling up, no room for them all, sometimes rotting before they can be disposed of? Every month I have reported on the humiliating conditions at the morgue. But you leave me in that rabbit warren."

"I am sorry for the state of the morgue," said McClellan. "No one could have managed half so well as you have, given the resources. But you have turned a blind eye to this stealing of cadavers, and I am about to pay the price for it. You will interrogate every member of your staff. You will contact every medical school in the city. I want that body found."

"This body is not at a medical school," the coroner objected. "I had already performed the autopsy. I had ventilated the lungs, for God's sake, to confirm asphyxiation."

"What of it?"

"No medical school wants a cadaver after an autopsy. You want your body intact."

"So the thieves made a mistake."

"There was no mistake," said the coroner vehemently. "The man who murdered her stole her body."

"Control yourself, Hugel," said the mayor. "You are wild."

"I am in perfect control."

"I don't take your meaning. You are saying that Miss Riverford's murderer broke into the morgue last night and absconded with his victim's corpse?"

"Precisely," said Hugel.

"Why?"

"Because there is evidence on the girl, on her body, evidence he did not want us to have."

"What evidence?"

The coroner's jaws were working so hard his temples had turned a shade of plum. "The evidence is—it is—I am not yet sure what it is. That is why we must get the body back!"

"Hugel," said the mayor, "you have locks on the morgue, do you not?"

"Certainly."

"Good. Was the lock broken this morning? Was there any evidence of a burglary?"

"No," Hugel allowed grudgingly. "But anyone with a decent skeleton key—"

"Mr. Coroner," said McClellan, "here is what you will do. Make it known to your people immediately that there will be a fifteen-dollar reward to whoever 'finds' the Riverford girl at one of the medical schools. Twenty-five dollars if they find her today. That will bring her back. Now: you will excuse me; I'm very busy. Good day." As Hugel reluctantly turned to leave, the mayor suddenly looked up from his desk. "Wait a moment. Wait a moment. Did you say the Riverford girl was asphyxiated?"

"Yes," said the coroner. "Why?"

"How asphyxiated?"

"By ligature."

"She was garroted?" asked McClellan.

"Yes. Why?"

The mayor ignored the coroner's question for a second time. "Were there any other wounds on her body?"

"It was all in my report," answered the aggrieved Hugel, to whom the knowledge that the mayor had not read his report was a fresh indignity. "The girl was whipped. There were lacerations on the posterior, spine, and chest. In addition, she was cut twice, by an extremely sharp blade, at the intersection of the S-two and L-two dermatomes."

"Where? In English, Hugel."

"On the upper inner thigh of each leg."

"In the name of God," replied the mayor.

❧

I WENT DOWN for a late breakfast, trying to sort out my encounter with Miss Acton. Jung was there, reading an American newspaper. I joined him. The others had set off for the Metropolitan Museum. Jung stayed behind, he explained, because he was going to pay a call this morning on Dr. Onuf, a neuropsychiatrist at Ellis Island.

It was my first time alone with Jung. He appeared to be in one of his animated, outgoing moods. He had slept all yesterday afternoon, he said, and the long nap had done him a world of good. Indeed, the pallor that had worried me yesterday was visibly improved. His opinion of America, he told me, was also improving. "Americans merely lack literature," he said, "not all culture."

Jung meant this, I think, as a compliment. Nevertheless, wanting to show that Americans were not entirely illiterate, I described to him the story of the Astor Place Shakespeare riot.

"So the Americans wanted a muscular American Hamlet," Jung

mused, shaking his head. "Your story confirms my point. A masculine Hamlet is a contradiction in terms. As my great-grandfather used to say, Hamlet represents man's feminine side: the intellectual, the inward soul, sensitive enough to see the spiritual world but not strong enough to bear the burden it imposes. The challenge is to do both: to hear the voices of the other world but live in this one—to be a man of action."

I was puzzled by the "voices" Jung referred to—perhaps the unconscious?—but delighted to find he had an opinion about Hamlet. "You are describing Hamlet almost exactly as Goethe did," I said. "That was Goethe's explanation of Hamlet's inability to act."

"I believe I said it was my great-grandfather's view," Jung replied, sipping his coffee.

It took me a moment. "Goethe was your great-grandfather?"

"Freud prizes Goethe above all poets," was Jung's reply. "Jones, by contrast, calls him a *dithyrambist*. Can you imagine? Only an Englishman. I cannot understand what Freud sees in him." The Jones to whom Jung referred was surely Ernest Jones, Freud's British follower, now living in Canada and expected to join our party tomorrow. I had concluded that Jung meant to avoid my question, but then he added, "Yes, I am Carl Gustav Jung the third; the first, my grandfather, was Goethe's son. It is well known. The allegations of murder were of course ridiculous."

"I didn't know Goethe was accused of murder."

"Goethe—certainly not," Jung answered indignantly. "My grandfather. Evidently I resemble him in every way. They arrested him for murder, but it was a pretext. He wrote a murder novel, though, *The Suspect*—quite good—about an innocent man charged with murder; or at least one supposes him innocent. That was before von Humboldt took him under his protection. You know, Younger, I could almost wish your university had not bestowed equal honors on Freud and myself. He is very sensitive on such matters."

I could not well reply to this abrupt turn in Jung's conversation. Clark was not bestowing equal honors on Freud and Jung. As everyone knew, Freud was the centerpiece of Clark's celebration, the keynote speaker, delivering five full lectures, while Jung was a last-minute substitute for a panelist who had canceled.

But Jung did not wait for an answer. "I understand you asked Freud yesterday if he was a believer. A perceptive question, Younger." This was another first: Jung had not previously shown a favorable reaction to anything I said. "No doubt he told you he was not. He is a genius, but his insight has endangered him. One who spends his whole life examining the pathological, stunted, and base may lose sight of the pure, the high, the spirit. I for one don't believe the soul is essentially carnal. Do you?"

"I am not sure, Dr. Jung."

"But you are not drawn to the idea. It is not inherently appealing to you. To them, it is."

I had to ask him to whom he was now referring.

"All of them," Jung answered. "Brill, Ferenczi, Adler, Abraham, Stekel—the lot. He surrounds himself with this—this kind. They all want to tear down whatever is high, to reduce it to genitalia and excrement. The soul is not reducible to the body. Even Einstein, one of their own, does not believe that God can be eliminated."

"Albert Einstein?"

"He is a frequent dinner guest at my house," replied Jung. "But he too has this same inclination to reduce. He would reduce the entire universe to mathematical laws. It is clearly a characteristic of the Jewish mind. The Jewish male, that is. The Jewish female is simply aggressive. Brill's wife is typical of the race. Intelligent, not unattractive, but so very aggressive."

"I believe Rose is not Jewish, Dr. Jung," I said.

"Rose Brill?" Jung laughed. "A woman with that name can be of only one religion."

I made no reply. Jung had evidently forgotten that Rose's name had not always been Brill.

"The Aryan," Jung went on, "is mythic by nature. He does not try to bring everything down to man's level. Here in America, there is a similar tendency to reduce, but it is different. Everything here is made for children. All is made simple enough for children to understand: the signs, the advertisements, everything. Even the gait with which people walk is childlike: swinging the arms, like so. I suspect it is the result of your intermingling with the Negro. They are a good-natured race and very religious, but so very simpleminded. They ex-

ercise a tremendous influence on you; I notice your Southerners actually speak with the Negro's accent. This is also the explanation of
your country's matriarchy. Woman is undoubtedly the dominant figure in America. You American men are sheep, and your women play
the ravening wolves."

I did not like the color in Jung's face. At first I had deemed it an
improvement; now he seemed too flushed. The workings of his mind
worried me too, for several different reasons. His conversation was
disjointed, his logic faulty, his insinuations disturbing. On top of all
this, I thought Jung considered himself remarkably well-informed
about America for someone who had been in the country two days—
particularly on the subject of American women. I changed the subject, informing him that I had just completed my first session with
Miss Acton.

Jung's voice went cold. "What?"

"She has taken rooms upstairs."

"You are analyzing the girl—you, here, in the hotel?"

"Yes, Dr. Jung."

"I see." He wished me luck, not very convincingly, and rose to
leave. I asked him to convey my regards to Dr. Onuf. For a moment,
he looked as if I were speaking jibberish. Then he said he would be
happy to oblige me.

CHAPTER EIGHT

ON THE EASTERN bank of the Hudson River, sixty miles north of New York City, stood a massive, sprawling, red-brick Victorian institution built in the late nineteenth century, with six wings, small windows, and a central turret. This was the Matteawan State Hospital for the Criminally Insane.

The Matteawan asylum had relatively little security. After all, the 550 inmates were not criminals. They were merely criminally insane. Many had not been charged with a crime at all, and those who were had been found not guilty.

Medical knowledge of insanity in 1909 was not a perfected science. At Matteawan, some 10 percent of the occupants were determined to have been driven insane solely as a result of masturbation. Most others were found to suffer from hereditary lunacy. For a substantial number of inmates, however, the hospital's doctors were hard-pressed to say what had made them mad or, indeed, if they were mad at all.

The violent and raving were packed into overcrowded rooms with padded walls and barred windows. The others were hardly watched. No medication was on offer, no "talking cures." The organizing medical idea was mental hygiene. Hence the treatment consisted of early rising, followed by mild but time-consuming labor (principally planting and tending vegetables on the thousand-acre farm surrounding the hospital), prayer service on Sundays, a punctual but vapid supper in the refectory at five, checkers or other wholesome diversions in the evening, and an early bedtime.

The patient in room 3121 passed his days in a different fashion. This patient also had rooms 3122–24. He slept not on a cot, like the other inmates, but on a double bed. And he slept late. Not a reader of books, he received by post several of the New York dailies and all the weekly magazines, which he read over poached eggs while his fellow patients were marched en masse out to the farm for their morning labor. He met with his lawyers several times a week. Best of all, a chef from Delmonico's came up by rail on Friday evenings to prepare his supper, which he took in his own dining room. His champagne and liquor, he liberally shared with the small staff of Matteawan guards, with whom he also played poker at night. When he lost at poker, he tended to break things: bottles, windows, occasionally a chair. So the guards saw to it he did not lose much: the few nickels they sacrificed at cards were more than made up for by the payments he made them to ensure his exemption from the hospital's rules. And they pocketed what was for them a small fortune when they brought in girls for his recreation.

This was not, however, so easy to do. Getting the girls in was not the problem. But the patient in 3121 had definite tastes. He liked his girls young and pretty. This requirement alone made the guards' job a hard one. Worse still, when they found a satisfactory girl, she would never last more than a couple of visits, notwithstanding the lavish remuneration. After a mere twelve months, the guards had well nigh exhausted their supply.

The two gentlemen emerging from room 3121 at one o'clock on Tuesday, the last day of August 1909, had given considerable thought to this difficulty—and had resolved it, at least to their satisfaction. They were not guards. One was a corpulent man wearing a highly self-satisfied expression under his bowler hat. The other was an elegant older gentleman with a watch chain draped from his vest pocket, a gaunt face, and a pianist's hands.

❧

MAYOR MCCLELLAN'S DESCRIPTION of the events at the Acton residence left the coroner sputtering.

"What's the matter with you, Hugel?" asked the mayor.

"I was not informed. Why wasn't I told?"

"Because you are a coroner," said McClellan. "No one was killed."

"But the crimes are virtually identical," Hugel objected.

"I didn't know that," said the mayor.

"If you had read my report, you would have!"

"For God's sake, calm down, Hugel." McClellan ordered the coroner to take a seat. After the two men reviewed the crimes in more detail, Hugel declared that there could be no doubt: Elizabeth Riverford's murderer and Nora Acton's attacker had been one and the same man.

"Great God," said the mayor quietly. "Must I issue a warning?"

Hugel laughed dismissively. "That a killer of society girls is haunting our streets?"

McClellan was puzzled by the coroner's tone. "Well, yes, I suppose, or words to that effect."

"Men do not attack young women arbitrarily," Hugel declared. "Crimes have motives. Scotland Yard never caught the Ripper because they never found the link between the victims. They never looked. The moment they decided they were dealing with a madman, the case was lost."

"Great God, man, you're not suggesting the Ripper is here?"

"No, no, no," replied the coroner, throwing up his hands in exasperation. "I'm saying that the two attacks are not random. Something connects them. When we find the connection, we will have our man. You don't need a public warning, you need to protect that girl. He already wanted her dead, and now she is the only person who can identify him in court. Don't forget: he doesn't know she lost her memory. He will undoubtedly try to finish the job."

"Thank heavens I moved her into the hotel," said McClellan.

"Does anyone else know where she is?"

"The doctors, of course."

"Did you tell any friends of the family?" asked Hugel.

"Certainly not," said McClellan.

"Good. Then she is safe for now. Has she remembered anything today?"

"I don't know," said McClellan gravely. "I haven't been able to get through to Dr. Younger." The mayor considered his options. He wished he could have called up old General Bingham, his longtime police commissioner, but McClellan had pushed Bingham into retirement only last month. Bingham had refused to reform the police, but he was himself incorruptible and would have known what to do.

The mayor also wished Baker, the new commissioner, had not already proved so inept. Baker's only subject of conversation was baseball and how much money could be made in it. Hugel, the mayor reflected, was one of the most experienced men on the force. No: in homicides, he was *the* most experienced. If he didn't consider a warning necessary, he was probably right. The papers would certainly make hay of it, sowing as much hysteria as they possibly could and heaping scorn on the mayor as soon as they learned, as they certainly would, of the loss of the first victim's body. Then too, McClellan had assured Banwell that the police would try to solve the case without publicity. George Banwell was one of the few friends the mayor had left. The mayor decided to follow Hugel's advice.

"Very well," said McClellan. "No warning for now. You had better be right, Mr. Hugel. Find me the man. Go to Acton's at once; you will supervise the investigation there. And tell Littlemore I want to see him immediately."

Hugel protested. Cleaning his spectacles, he reminded the mayor that it was no part of a coroner's duties to gallivant up and down the city like an ordinary detective. McClellan swallowed his irritation. He assured the coroner that only he could be trusted with a case of such delicacy and importance, that his eyes were famously the sharpest on the force. Hugel, blinking in a way that appeared to express perfect agreement with these assertions, consented to go to the Actons'.

Directly Hugel left his office, McClellan summoned his secretary. "Ring George Banwell," he instructed her. The secretary informed the mayor that Mr. Banwell had been calling all morning. "What did he want?" asked the mayor.

"He was rather blunt, Your Honor," she replied.

"It's all right, Mrs. Neville. What did he want?"

Mrs. Neville read from her shorthand notes. "To know 'who the devil murdered the Riverford girl, what was taking the blasted coroner so long to finish the autopsy, and where his money was.'"

The mayor sighed deeply. "Who, what, and where. He's only missing when." McClellan looked at his watch. The *when* was running short for him as well. In two weeks at most, the candidates for mayor had to be announced. He had no hope of the Tammany nomination now. His only chance was as an independent or fusion candidate, but that kind of campaign required money. It also required good press, not news of a spree of unsolved attacks on society girls. "Ring Banwell back," he added to Mrs. Neville. "Leave word for him to meet me in an hour and a half at the Hotel Manhattan. He won't object; he has a job near there he'll want a look at in any event. And get me Littlemore."

A half hour later, the detective introduced his head into the mayor's office. "You wanted to see me, Your Honor?"

"Mr. Littlemore," said the mayor, "you are aware we have had another attack?"

"Yes, sir. Mr. Hugel told me, sir."

"Good. This case is of special importance to me, Detective. I know Acton, and George Banwell is an old friend of mine. I want to be kept abreast of every development. And I want the utmost discretion. Go to the Hotel Manhattan on the double. Find Dr. Younger and see if any progress has been made. If there is any new information, call here at once. And Detective, make yourself inconspicuous. Word must not get out that we have a potential murder witness at the hotel. The girl's life may depend on it. Do you understand?"

"Yes, sir, Mr. Mayor," Littlemore replied. "Do I report to you, sir, or to Captain Carey at Homicide?"

"You will report to Mr. Hugel," said the mayor, "and to me. I need this case solved, Littlemore. At any price. You have the coroner's description of the killer?"

"Yes, sir." Littlemore hesitated. "Um, one question, sir? What if the coroner's description of the killer is wrong?"

"Do you have reason to think it wrong?"

"I think—" said Littlemore. "I think a Chinaman might be involved."

"A Chinaman?" the mayor repeated. "Have you told Mr. Hugel?"

"He doesn't agree, sir."

"I see. Well, I would advise you to trust Mr. Hugel. I know he is—sensitive—on some points, Detective, but you must bear in mind how hard it is for an honest man to do his work in relative obscurity, while dishonest men attain wealth and renown. That is why corruption is so pernicious. It breaks the will of good men. Hugel is extremely capable. And he thinks highly of you, Detective. He asked specifically that you be assigned to this case."

"He did, sir?"

"He did. Now get going, Mr. Littlemore."

✑

I WAS LEAVING the hotel when I ran into the girl and her servant, Mrs. Biggs, about to do their shopping. A cab was just pulling up for them. Because the street bed, rutted with dirt and dry mud, was unfit, I lifted Miss Acton into the carriage. As I did, I noticed uncomfortably that her tiny waist almost fit into my two hands. I sought to assist Mrs. Biggs as well, but the good woman would have none of it.

To Miss Acton, I said I looked forward to seeing her tomorrow morning. She asked what I meant. I was referring, I explained, to her next psychoanalytic session. My hand was resting on the open door of her cab; she yanked the door shut, dislodging me. "I don't know what is wrong with all of you," she said. "I don't want any more of your sessions. I will remember everything by myself. Just leave me alone."

The cab drove off. It is hard to describe my feelings as I watched it rattle away. Disappointed would not quite be adequate. I wished my too-solid body might break up and disperse into the dirt of the street. Brill should have been the analyst. A medical journeyman, a town general practitioner, would have been better, so abysmally had I imitated a psychoanalyst.

I had failed before even beginning. The girl had rejected analysis, and I had been unable to change her mind. No: I had caused the rejection, pressing too hard before the groundwork had been laid. The truth was that I had been unprepared to find she could speak. I had forgotten Freud's own speculation that she might recover her voice overnight. Her voice ought to have been a boon to the treatment, the luckiest possible development. Instead, it disrupted me. I had pictured myself as the patient and infinitely accommodating doctor. Instead, I had dealt with her resistance defensively, like a blundering amateur.

What would I say to Freud?

✑

ENTERING THE HOTEL MANHATTAN, Detective Littlemore passed a young gentleman helping a young lady into a cab. The two figures represented, for Littlemore, a world to which he had no access. They were both easy on the eyes, decked out in the kind of fin-

ery that only the better set could afford. The young gentleman was
tall, dark-haired, and cheekbony, the young lady more like an angel
than Littlemore thought possible on earth. And the gentleman had a
way of moving, a fluidity when he swung the young lady into the carriage, that Littlemore knew he himself did not possess.

None of this bothered the detective in the least. He did not re-
sent the young gentleman, and he liked Betty, the maid, better than
he liked the angelic young lady. But he decided he was going to learn
to move the way the gentleman did. That was something he could figure out and copy. He pictured himself hoisting Betty into a cab just
like that—if he ever got to take a cab, much less take one with Betty.

A minute later, after a quick exchange with the reception clerk,
Littlemore hustled back outside toward the same young man, who
had not moved an inch. Hands clasped behind his back, he was staring at the receding carriage with such ferocious concentration that
Littlemore thought there might be something wrong with him.

"You're Dr. Younger, aren't you?" asked the detective. There was
no reply. "You okay, pal?"

"Excuse me?" replied the young gentleman.

"You're Younger, right?"

"Unfortunately."

"I'm Detective Littlemore. The mayor sent me. Was that Miss
Acton in the cab?" The detective could see that his interlocutor was
not listening.

"I beg your pardon," replied Younger. "Who did you say you
were?"

Littlemore identified himself again. He explained that Miss Acton's assailant had murdered a girl last Sunday night, but that the
police still had no witnesses. "Has the Miss remembered anything,
Doc?"

Younger shook his head. "Miss Acton has her voice back, but still
no memory of the incident."

"The whole thing seems pretty weird to me," said the detective.
"Do people lose their memory a lot?"

"No," Younger answered, "but it does happen, especially after
episodes like the one Miss Acton went through."

"Hey, they're coming back."

It was so: Miss Acton's carriage had turned around at the end of the block and was drawing near the hotel once again. As it pulled up, Miss Acton explained to Younger that Mrs. Biggs had forgotten to return their room key to the clerk.

"Give it to me," said Younger, extending his hand. "I'll take it in for you."

"Thank you, but I am quite able," replied Miss Acton, hopping out of the cab unaided and sweeping past Younger without a glance in his direction. Younger showed nothing, but Littlemore knew a feminine rebuff when he saw one, and he sympathized with the doctor. Then a different thought occurred to him.

"Say, Doc," he said, "do you let Miss Acton go around the hotel like that—by herself, I mean?"

"I have little say in the matter, Detective. None, actually. But no, I think she's been with her servant or the police at almost every moment until now. Why? Is there any danger?"

"Shouldn't be," said Littlemore. Mr. Hugel had told him that the murderer did not know Miss Acton's location. Still, the detective was uncomfortable. The whole case was out of whack: a dead girl nobody knew anything about, people losing their memory, Chinamen running away, bodies disappearing from the morgue. "Can't hurt to have a look around, though."

The detective reentered the hotel, Younger beside him. Littlemore lit a cigarette as they watched the diminutive Miss Acton cross the colonnaded, circular lobby. A man returning his room key would simply have dropped it on the desk and left, but Miss Acton stood patiently at the counter, waiting to be helped. The place was crowded with travelers, families, and businessmen. Half the men there, the detective noticed, could conceivably have met the coroner's description.

One man, however, drew Littlemore's attention. He was waiting for an elevator: tall, black-haired, wearing glasses, a newspaper in his hands. Littlemore didn't have a good angle on his face, but there was something vaguely foreign in the cut of his suit. It was the newspaper that attracted the detective's attention. The man held it slightly higher than was normal. Was he trying to cover his face? Miss Acton had returned her key; she was now walking back. The man threw a quick glance in her direction—or was it toward the detective himself?—and then buried his head in the paper again. An elevator opened; the man went in, by himself.

Miss Acton did not acknowledge the presence of the doctor or the detective as she passed them on her way out. Nevertheless, Younger followed her outside, seeing her back to her carriage.

Littlemore stayed behind. It was nothing, he told himself. Nearly every man in the lobby had looked up at Miss Acton as she walked unaccompanied across the marble floor. All the same, Littlemore kept his eye on the arrow above the elevator into which the man had stepped. The arrow moved slowly, jerking up toward the higher numbers. Littlemore did not, however, see the arrow's final resting place. It was still moving when he heard a piercing cry outside.

❦

THE CRY WAS NOT HUMAN. It was the shrill neighing of a horse in pain. The horse in question belonged to a carriage that had just emerged from a construction site on Forty-second Street, where the steel skeleton of a new nine-story commercial building was being raised. The man driving this carriage was superbly attired, with a top hat and a fine cane across his knees. It was Mr. George Banwell.

In 1909, the horse was still doing battle with the automobile on every major avenue of New York City. In fact, the battle was already lost. The jerking, honking motorcars were faster and more nimble than a buggy; more than this, the automobile put an end to pollution—a term referring at that time to horse manure, which by midday fouled the air and made the busier thoroughfares almost impassable. Although George Banwell liked his motorcars as much as the next gentleman, he was at heart a horseman. He had grown up with the horse and was not ready to give it up. In fact he insisted on driving his own carriage, making his coachman sit awkwardly beside him.

Banwell had spent most of the morning at his Canal Street site, where he was supervising a vastly larger project. At eleven-thirty, he had driven uptown to Forty-second Street between Fifth and Madison avenues, less than half a block from the Hotel Manhattan. Having completed a quick inspection of his men's work there, Banwell was now making for the hotel to meet the mayor. But a moment after taking the reins, he had given them a fierce and abrupt yank, driving the bit into the unfortunate horse's mouth, causing her to halt and cry out. This cry had no effect on Banwell. He seemed not even to hear it. Staring transfixed at a point less than a block ahead of him, he kept the bit digging ever deeper into his horse's jaw, to the appalled dismay of his coachman.

The horse threw her head side to side, trying in vain to loose the cutting bit. Finally the creature reared up on her hind legs and let out the extraordinary, anguished cry heard by Littlemore and everyone else up and down the street. She returned to earth but immediately reared again, this time even more wildly, and the entire carriage began to topple. Banwell and his coachman spilled out like sailors from a capsized boat. The carriage tumbled to the ground with an enormous clatter, dragging the horse down with it.

The coachman was first to his feet. He tried to help his master, but Banwell pushed him away violently, brushing the dirt from his knees and elbows. A crowd had gathered about them. Impatient motorists were already blowing their horns. The spell on Banwell was apparently broken. He was not the kind of man who tolerated being thrown by a horse; to be thrown from a carriage was unthinkable. His eyes were furious—at the motorists, at the gawking crowd, and above all at the confused, prostrate horse, which was struggling unsuccessfully to right herself. "My gun," he said to his coachman coldly. "Get me my gun."

"You can't destroy her, sir," objected the coachman, who was crouching by the side of the horse, extricating her hoofs from a brace of twisted ropes. "Nothing's broken. She's just tangled up. There she is. There you are"—this he said to the horse, as he helped her upright—"it wasn't your fault."

Doubtless the coachman meant well, but he could not have chosen more ill-favored words. "Not her fault, eh?" said Banwell. "She rears like an unbroken jade, and it's not her fault?" He seized the bit and roughly twisted the horse's neck, looking her in the eye. "I can see," he said to the coachman, his voice still cold, "you never taught her to keep her head down. Well, I will."

Yanking the carriage rods out of her bridle, Banwell seized the reins and mounted the horse bareback. He drove her back into the construction site and there wheeled about until he came to the great dangling hook of the crane that loomed sky-high in the middle of the plot of ground. Taking that hook in both hands, Banwell fixed it under the horse's halter, which was in turn secured firmly around her underbelly. He leaped off the horse and shouted to the crane man, "You there, take her up. You in the crane: take her up, I say. Can't you hear me? Take her up!"

The astonished crane man was slow to respond. At last he engaged the gears of the hulking machine. Its long cable went taut; its hook clenched at the saddle. The horse stirred and pawed at the uncomfortable sensation. For a moment nothing more happened.

"Lift, you bugger," Banwell cried to his crane operator, "lift or go home to your wife tonight without a job!"

The crane man manipulated the levers again. With a lurch, the horse lifted up off the ground. The moment her feet left the earth, uncomprehending panic fell upon the animal. She screamed and thrashed about, succeeding only in making herself twist wildly in the air, suspended by the crane's thick hook.

"Let her go!" a girl's voice, angry and stricken, cried out. It was Miss Acton. Watching the spectacle unfold, she had hurried across Forty-second Street and was now at the front of the crowd. Younger was right next to her, and Littlemore several rows behind. She called out again, "Let her down. Someone, make him stop!"

"Up," Banwell ordered. He heard the girl's voice. For a moment, he looked right at her. Then he returned his attention to the horse. "Higher."

The crane man did as he was bid, hoisting the creature higher and higher: twenty, thirty, forty feet above the ground. Philosophers say it cannot be known whether animals feel emotions comparable to a human's, but anyone who has seen sheer terror in a horse's eyes can never doubt it again.

Because all human eyes were on the helpless, dangling, thrashing animal, no one in the crowd noticed the stirring of the steel girder three stories up the scaffolding. This girder was secured to a rope, which was in turn connected to the crane hook. Until now that rope had been slack, the steel beam lying harmlessly in place on the scaffold. But as the hook rose, this rope too eventually pulled taut, and now, without warning, the steel girder rolled off the wooden planks. From there it swung freely. Being attached to the crane's hook, it naturally swung in the direction of the hook—which is to say, in the direction of George Banwell.

Banwell never saw the deadly girder hurtling at him, gathering speed as it swung. The beam turned inexorably in the air, so that it came at him dead on, like a gigantic spear aimed at his stomach. Had it struck, it would certainly have killed him. As it happened, it missed him by a foot. This was a stroke of excellent and not atypical good fortune for Banwell, but its consequence was that the beam flew on, now heading for the crowd, several members of whom screamed in fright, a good dozen men diving to the dirt to protect themselves.

There was only one among them, however, who should have dived away. That was Miss Nora Acton, since the twelve-foot steel girder was swinging straight toward her. Miss Acton, however, neither screamed nor moved. Whether it was because the onrushing beam held her somehow in thrall or because it was difficult to know which way to go, Miss Acton stood rooted to her spot, aghast and about to die.

Younger seized the girl by her long blond braid, pulling her hard—and not very chivalrously—into his arms. The hurtling girder whistled by them, so close the two could feel its wind, and flew high into the air behind them.

"Ow!" said Miss Acton.

"Sorry," said Younger. Then he drew her by the hair a second time, pulling her now in the other direction.

"Ow!" said Miss Acton again, more emphatically, as the steel beam, making its return trip, flew past them once more, this time just missing the back of her head.

Banwell eyed the sailing girder dispassionately as it shot by. With disgust, he watched it soar up and slam into the scaffold from which its journey had begun, destroying that structure as if it had been made of toothpicks, sending men, tools, and wooden planks flying in all directions. When the dust cleared, only the horse was still making noise, neighing and spinning helplessly above their heads. Banwell signaled the crane man to bring her down and, with a cold rage, issued orders to his men to clear the debris.

"Take me back to my room, please," Miss Acton said to Younger.

❧

THE CROWD MILLED ABOUT for a long while, admiring the damage and replaying the events. The horse was returned to the coachman, whom Detective Littlemore now approached. The detective had recognized George Banwell. "Say, how's she doing, the poor thing?" Littlemore asked the coachman. "What is she, a Perch?"

"Half Perch," replied the driver, trying as best he could to calm the still trembling animal. "They call her a Cream."

"She's a beauty, that's for sure."

"That she is," said the coachman, stroking the horse's nose.

"Gee, I wonder what made her rear up like that. Something she saw, probably."

"Something *he* saw, more like."

"How's that?"

"It wasn't her at all," grumbled the coachman. "It was him. He was trying to back her up. You can't back up a carriage horse." He spoke to the mare. "Tried to make you back up, that's what he did. Because he was scared."

"Scared? Of what?"

"Ask him, why don't you? He don't scare easy, not him. Scared like he saw the devil himself."

"How do you like that?" said Littlemore, before heading back to the hotel.

❧

AT THE SAME MOMENT, on the top floor of the Hotel Manhattan, Carl Jung stood on his balcony, surveying the scene below. He had seen the extraordinary events in the construction site. Those events had not only frightened him; they filled him with a profound, swelling elation—of a kind he had felt only once or twice in his entire life. He withdrew into his room, where he sat numbly on the floor, his back against the bed, seeing faces no one else could see, hearing voices no one else could hear.

CHAPTER NINE

WHEN WE GOT BACK to Miss Acton's rooms, Mrs. Biggs was frantic. She ordered Miss Acton first to lie down, then to sit up, then to move about in order to "get her color back." Miss Acton paid no mind to any of these commands. She headed straight to the little kitchen with which her suite was equipped and began preparing a pot of tea. Mrs. Biggs threw up her arms in protest, declaring that *she* should be fixing tea. The old woman would not be quiet until Miss Acton sat her down and kissed her hands.

The girl had an uncanny capacity either to regain her composure after the most overwhelming events or to affect a composure she did not feel. She finished the tea and handed a steaming cup to Mrs. Biggs.

"You would have been killed, Miss Nora," said the old woman. "You would have been killed if not for the young doctor."

Miss Acton placed her hand on top of the woman's, urging her to take her tea. When Mrs. Biggs had done so, the girl told her she would have to leave us because she needed to speak privately with me. After a good deal more importuning, Mrs. Biggs was persuaded to go.

When we were alone, Miss Acton thanked me.

"Why have you made your servant leave?" I asked.

"I did not 'make' her leave," replied the girl. "You wanted to know the circumstances in which I lost my voice three years ago. I wish to tell you."

The teapot now began to shake in her hands. Attempting to pour, she missed the cup altogether. She put the pot down and clasped her fingers together. "That poor horse. How could he do such a thing?"

"You are not to blame, Miss Acton."

"What is the matter with you?" She looked at me furiously. "Why would I be to blame?"

"There is no reason. But you sound as if you are blaming yourself."

Miss Acton went to the window. She parted the curtain, revealing a balcony behind a pair of French doors and opening up a panoramic view of the city below. "Do you know who that was?"

"No."

"That was George Banwell, Clara's husband. My father's friend." The girl's breathing became unsteady. "It was by the lake at his summerhouse. He proposed to me."

"Please lie down, Miss Acton."

"Why?"

"It is part of the treatment."

"Oh, very well."

When she was on the couch again, I resumed. "Mr. Banwell asked you to marry him—when you were fourteen?"

"I was sixteen, Doctor, and he did not propose marriage."

"What did he propose?"

"To have—to have—" She stopped.

"To have intercourse with you?" It is always delicate to refer to sexual activity with young female patients, because one cannot be sure how much they know of biology. But it is worse to let an excess of delicacy reinforce the pernicious sense of shame that a girl may attach to such an experience.

"Yes," she answered. "We were staying at his country house, my whole family. He and I were walking along the path around their pond. He said he had purchased another cottage nearby, where we could go, with a lovely large bed, where the two of us could be alone and no one would know."

"What did you do?"

"I slapped him in the face and ran," said Miss Acton. "I told my father—who did not take my side."

"He didn't believe you?" I asked.

"He acted as if I were the wrongdoer. I insisted he confront Mr. Banwell. A week later, he told me he had. Mr. Banwell denied the charge, according to my father, with great indignation. I am sure he wore very much the same look you saw just now. He only conceded mentioning his new cottage to me. He maintained that I had drawn the wicked inference myself, because of—because of the kind of books I read. My father chose to believe Mr. Banwell. I hate him."

"Mr. Banwell?"

"My father."

"Miss Acton, you lost your voice three years ago. But you are describing an event that occurred last year."

"Three years ago, he kissed me."

"Your father?"

"No, how disgusting," said Miss Acton. "Mr. Banwell."

"You were fourteen?" I asked.

"Were mathematics difficult for you at school, Dr. Younger?"

"Go on, Miss Acton."

"It was Independence Day," she said. "My parents had met the Banwells only a few months earlier, but already my father and Mr. Banwell were the best of friends. Mr. Banwell's people were rebuilding our house. We had just spent three weeks with them in the country while they finished all the construction. Clara was so kind to me. She is the strongest, most intelligent woman I have ever met, Dr. Younger. And the most beautiful. Did you see Lina Cavalieri's Salomé?"

"No," I answered. The famously beautiful Miss Cavalieri had performed the role at the Manhattan Opera House last winter, but I had been unable to get down from Worcester to see it.

"Clara looks just like her. She was on stage too, years ago. Mr. Gibson did a picture of her. In any event, Mr. Banwell had one of those enormous buildings of his going up downtown—the Hanover, I think. We were planning to go to the roof of that building to watch the fireworks. But my mother took ill—she always takes ill—so she remained behind. Somehow, at the last moment, my father couldn't come downtown either. I don't know why. I think he was also ill; there was a fever that summer. In any event, Mr. Banwell volunteered to take me to the rooftop, since I had been looking forward to it so very much."

"Just the two of you?"

"Yes. He drove me in his carriage. It was night. He made the horses canter down Broadway. I remember the hot wind in my face. We rode up in the elevator together. I was very nervous; it was the first time I had ever been in an elevator. I couldn't wait for the fireworks, but when the first cannons burst out, they scared me terribly. I may have screamed. The next thing I knew he had clasped me in both arms. I can still feel him pulling my—my upper body—against him. Then he pressed his mouth upon my lips." The girl grimaced, as if she wanted to spit.

"And then?" I asked.

"I tore myself from him, but there was nowhere to go. I didn't know how to escape from his roof. He motioned me to calm down, to be quiet. He told me it would be our secret and said we would just watch the fireworks now. Which is what we did."

"Did you tell anyone?"

"No. That is when I lost my voice: that night. Everyone thought I had caught the fever. Perhaps I had. My voice came back to me the next morning, just as it did this time. But I have told no one until this day. After that, I would not consent to be alone with Mr. Banwell again."

A long silence ensued. The girl had evidently come to the end of her immediately conscious memories. "Think of yesterday, Miss Acton. Do you remember anything?"

"No," she said quietly. "I'm sorry."

I asked her permission to convey what she had said to Dr. Freud. She agreed. I then informed her that we should resume our conversation tomorrow.

She seemed surprised: "What else do we have to converse about, Doctor? I have told you everything."

"Something more may occur to you."

"Why do you say that?"

"Because you are still suffering your amnesia. When we have uncovered everything connected with this event, I believe your memory will come back to you."

"You think I am concealing something?"

"It is not concealment, Miss Acton. Or rather, it is something you are concealing from yourself."

"I don't know what you are talking about," the girl replied. When I was a step from the door, she stopped me with her clear, soft voice. "Dr. Younger?"

"Miss Acton?"

Her blue eyes had tears in them. She held her chin high. "He did kiss me. He did—propose to me by the lake."

I hadn't realized how anxious she was over the possibility that I too, like her father, might not credit what she told me. There was something indescribably endearing in the way she used "propose" instead of "proposition." "Miss Acton," I replied, "I believe every word you say."

She burst into tears. I left her, wishing Mrs. Biggs a good afternoon as I passed her in the hallway.

IN A PRIVATE CORNER of the saloon at the Hotel Manhattan, George Banwell sat with Mayor McClellan. The mayor remarked that Banwell looked as if he had been in a fistfight. Banwell shrugged. "A little problem with a filly," he said.

The mayor withdrew an envelope from his breast pocket and handed it to Banwell. "Here's your check. I advise you to go to your bank this afternoon. It's very large. And it's the last one. There won't be any more, no matter what. Do we understand each other?"

Banwell nodded. "If there are additional costs, I'll bear them myself."

The mayor then explained that Miss Riverford's murderer had apparently struck again. Did Banwell know Harcourt Acton?

"Of course I know Acton," Banwell replied. "He and his wife are at my summerhouse now. They joined Clara there yesterday."

"So that's why we have not been able to reach them," said McClellan.

"What about Acton?" asked Banwell.

"The second victim was his daughter."

"Nora? Nora Acton? I just saw her on the street, not one hour ago."

"Yes, thank God she survived," answered the mayor.

"What happened?" asked Banwell. "Did she tell you who did it?"

"No. She's lost her voice and can't remember a thing. She doesn't know who did it, and neither do we. Some specialists are looking at her now. She's here, in fact. I've put her up at the Manhattan until Acton gets back."

Banwell took this in. "A good-looking girl."

"She certainly is," agreed the mayor.

"Raped?"

"No, thank heavens."

"Thank heavens."

I FOUND THE OTHERS in the halls of Roman and Greek antiquity at the Metropolitan Museum. While Freud was engrossed in conversation with the guide—Freud's knowledge was quite astounding—I fell behind with Brill. He was feeling better about his manuscript. His publisher, Jelliffe, had at first been as mystified as we had been, but then recalled that he lent his press the previous week to a church minister, who was publishing a series of edifying biblical pamphlets. Somehow the two jobs must have been merged together.

"Did you know," I asked Brill, "that Goethe was Jung's great-grandfather?"

"Rot," said Brill, who had lived in Zurich for a year, working under Jung. "Self-glorifying family legends. Did he get to von Humboldt too?"

"Yes, actually," I replied.

"You would think it would be enough for a man to marry into a fortune without having to invent a lineage for himself."

"Unless that's why he invents it," I said.

Brill grunted noncommittally. Then, with a strange lightness, he pulled back a forelock of his hair, revealing a wicked scrape on his brow. "You see that? Rose did that last night, after you had all left. She threw a frying pan at me."

"Good Lord," I said. "Why?"

"Because of Jung."

"What?"

"I told Rose about the remarks I made to Freud concerning Jung," said Brill. "It sent her into a rage. She told me I was jealous of Jung, that Freud values him, and that I was a fool because Freud would see through my envy and think worse of me for it. To which I replied that I had good reason to be jealous of Jung, given the way she was looking at him all night. In retrospect that may have been a false note, since it was Jung who was looking at her. Do you know she has the same medical training I do? But she can't get a job as a doctor, and I can't support her, with my four patients."

"She threw a frying pan at you?" I asked.

"Oh, don't give me that diagnostic look. Women throw things. All of them, sooner or later. You'll learn. All except Emma, Jung's wife. Emma merely hands Carl a fortune, mothers his children, and smiles when he cheats on her. Serves his mistresses dinner when he brings them into the house. The man is a sorcerer. No, if I hear another word about Goethe and von Humboldt, I just may kill him."

Before we left the museum, there was nearly a crisis. Freud suddenly required a urinal, just as he had at Coney Island, and the guide sent us to the basement. On the way downstairs, Freud remarked, "Don't tell me. I will have to go through endless miles of corridor, and at the end there will be a marble palace." He was right on both counts. We only reached the palace in the nick of time.

CORONER HUGEL DID NOT get back to his office until Tuesday evening. He had spent the afternoon at the Acton house on Gramercy Park. He knew what he would write in his report: that physical evidence—hairs, silk threads, shreds of rope—now proved beyond doubt that the same man who killed Elizabeth Riverford attacked Nora Acton. But the coroner cursed himself for what he had *not* found. He had scoured the master bedroom. He had pored over the rear garden. He had even crawled through it on hands and knees. As he knew he would, he found broken branches, trampled flowers, and plenty of other signs of flight, but nowhere the proof he sought, the one piece of hard evidence with which he could expose the perpetrator's identity.

He was exhausted when he reached his office. Despite the mayor's command, Hugel hadn't circulated to his staff the offer of a reward to anyone who found the Riverford girl's body. But he could hardly be blamed for that, Hugel told himself. It had been the mayor who ordered him to go directly to the Actons' house rather than back to the morgue.

In the hall, he found Detective Littlemore waiting. Littlemore reported that one of the barracks boys, Gitlow, was on a train to Chicago. He would be there by tomorrow night. In his usual chipper spirits, Littlemore also recounted the strange episode of Mr. Banwell and the horse. Hugel listened intently and then exclaimed, "Banwell!

He must have seen the Acton girl outside the hotel. That's what scared him!"

"Miss Acton's not exactly what I'd call scary, Mr. Hugel," said Littlemore.

"You fool," was the coroner's response. "Of course—he thought she was dead!"

"Why would he think she was dead?"

"Use your head, Detective."

"If Banwell's the guy, Mr. Hugel, he knows she's alive."

"What?"

"You're saying Banwell's the guy, right? But whoever attacked Miss Acton knows she's alive. So if Banwell's the guy, he doesn't think she's dead."

"What? Nonsense. He might have thought he had finished her. Or—or he may have been afraid she would recognize him. Either way, he would have panicked when he saw her."

"Why do you think he's the guy?"

"Littlemore, he is over six foot tall. He is middle-aged. He is rich. His hair was dark but now is graying. He is right-handed. He lived in the same building as the first victim, and he panicked at the sight of the second."

"How do you know that?"

"From you. You said his driver told you he took fright. What other explanation is there?"

"No, I meant how do you know he's right-handed?"

"Because I met him yesterday, Detective, and I make use of my eyes."

"Gee, you're something, Mr. Hugel. What am I, right-handed or left-handed?" The detective put his hands behind his back.

"Will you stop it, Littlemore!"

"I don't know, Mr. Hugel. You should have seen him after it was all over. He was cool as a cucumber, giving orders, cleaning everything up."

"Nonsense. A good actor, in addition to a murderer. We have our man, Detective."

"We don't exactly have him."

"You're right," mused the coroner. "I still have no hard evidence. We need something more."

CHAPTER TEN

LEAVING THE METROPOLITAN, we took a carriage across the park to Columbia University's new campus, with its stupendous library. I had not been there since 1897, when I was fifteen and my mother dragged us to the dedication of the Schermerhorn building. Brill, fortunately, did not know of my marginal connection to that clan, or he doubtless would have mentioned it to Freud.

We visited the psychiatric clinic, where Brill had an office. Afterward, Freud announced that he wished to hear about my session with Miss Acton. So, while Brill and Ferenczi remained behind, discussing therapeutic technique, Freud and I took a stroll on Riverside Drive, whose broad promenade afforded a fine lookout on the Palisades, the wild and broken New Jersey cliffs across the Hudson River.

I left out nothing, describing to Freud both my first session with Miss Acton, ending in failure, and the second, ending in her revelations concerning her father's friend, Mr. Banwell. He questioned me closely, wanting every detail, no matter how seemingly irrelevant, and insisting that I mustn't paraphrase but relay her exact words. At the close, Freud stubbed out his cigar on the sidewalk and asked whether I thought the episode on the rooftop three years ago was the cause of Miss Acton's loss of voice at the time.

"It would seem so," I answered. "There was involvement of the mouth and an injunction not to tell. Something unspeakable had been done to her; therefore she made herself unable to speak."

"Good. So the fourteen-year-old's shameful kiss on the roof made her hysterical?" said Freud, measuring my reaction.

I understood: he meant the opposite of what he was saying. The episode on the roof, as Freud saw things, could not be the cause of

Miss Acton's hysteria. That episode was not from her childhood, nor was it Oedipal. Only childhood traumas lead to neurosis, although a later event is typically the trigger that awakens the memory of the long-repressed conflict, producing hysterical symptoms. "Dr. Freud," I asked, "isn't it possible in this one case that an adolescent trauma caused hysteria?"

"It's possible, my boy, except for one thing: the girl's behavior on the roof was already entirely and completely hysterical." Freud drew another cigar from his pocket, thought better of it, and put it back. "Let me offer you a definition of the hysteric: one in whom an occasion for sexual pleasure elicits feelings largely or wholly unpleasurable."

"She was only fourteen."

"And how old was Juliet on her nuptial night?"

"Thirteen," I acknowledged.

"A robust, fully mature man—of whom we know nothing other than that he is strong, tall, successful, well-made—kisses a girl on the lips," said Freud. "He is obviously in a state of sexual arousal. Indeed, I think we may be confident that Nora had a direct sensation of this arousal. When she says she can still feel this Banwell pulling her body against his, I have little doubt what part of the man's body she felt. All this, in a healthy girl of fourteen, would certainly have produced a pleasurable genital stimulation. Instead, Nora was overcome by the unpleasurable feeling proper to the back of the throat or gorge—that is, by disgust. In other words, she was already hysterical long before that kiss."

"But mightn't Banwell's advances have been—unwelcome?"

"I very much doubt they were. You disagree with me, Younger."

I did disagree—strenuously—although I had been trying not to show it.

Freud went on. "You imagine Mr. Banwell thrusting himself on an unwilling and innocent victim. But perhaps it was she who seduced him: a handsome man, her father's best friend. The conquest would have appealed to a girl her age; it would likely have inspired jealousy in her father."

"She rejected him," I said.

"Did she?" asked Freud. "After the kiss, she kept his secret, even after regaining her voice. Correct?"

"Yes."

"Is that more consistent with fearing repetition of the event—or desiring it?"

I saw Freud's logic, but the innocent explanation of the girl's behavior did not yet seem refuted. "She refused to be alone with him afterward," I countered.

"On the contrary," rejoined Freud. "She walked with him alone, two years later, by the shore of a lake, a romantic location if ever there was one."

"But she rejected him there again."

"She slapped him," said Freud. "That is not necessarily a rejection. A girl, like an analytic patient, is required to say no before she says yes."

"She complained to her father."

"When?"

"Immediately," I stated, a little too immediately. Then I reflected. "Actually, I don't know that. I didn't ask."

"Perhaps she was waiting for Mr. Banwell to make another attempt on her, and, when he did not, she told her father out of pique." I did not say anything, but Freud could see I was not entirely persuaded. He added, "In this, my boy, you must bear in mind that you are not disinterested."

"I don't follow you, sir," I said.

"Yes, you do."

I considered. "You mean I *wish* Miss Acton to have found Banwell's advances unwelcome?"

"You have been defending Nora's honor."

I was conscious that I continued to call Miss Acton "Miss Acton," whereas Freud called her by her first name. I was also conscious of a rush of blood to my face. "That is only because I'm in love with her," I said.

Freud said nothing.

"You must take over the analysis, Dr. Freud. Or Brill. It should have been Brill in the first place."

"Nonsense. She is yours, Younger. You are doing very well. But you must not take these feelings of yours so seriously. They are unavoidable in psychoanalysis. They are part of the treatment. Nora is very probably coming under the influence of the transference, as you are of the counter-transference. You must treat these feelings as data; you must deploy them. They are fictitious. They have no more reality than the feelings an actor generates onstage. A good Hamlet will feel rage toward his uncle, but he will not mistakenly suppose he is actually angry at his fellow tragedian. It is the same with analysis."

For a time, neither of us spoke. Then I asked, "Have you ever had—feelings for a patient, Dr. Freud?"

"There have been times," Freud replied slowly, "when I welcomed such feelings; they reminded me that I was not altogether past desire. Yes, I have had some narrow escapes. But you must remember: I came to psychoanalysis when I was already much older than you, which made it easier for me. In addition, I am married. To the knowledge that these feelings are factitious, there is added, in my case, a moral obligation I could not violate." It will seem ridiculous, but the only thought in my head after Freud finished was this: how could *factitious* be synonymous with *fictitious*?

Freud continued. "Enough. For now the chief task is to discover the preexisting trauma that caused the girl's hysterical reaction on the roof. Tell me this: why didn't Nora tell the police where her parents were?"

I had asked myself the same thing. Miss Acton had told me that her parents were at George Banwell's country house, yet she had never mentioned this fact to the police, allowing them instead to send message after message to her own family's summer cottage, where no one was home. To me, however, this reticence was not mysterious. I have always envied those able to receive genuine comfort from their parents in times of crisis; there must be no comfort equal to it. But that was never my lot. "Perhaps," I answered Freud, "she didn't care to have her parents nearby after the attack?"

"Perhaps," he said. "I concealed my worst self-doubts from my father for the whole of his lifetime. Like you." Freud made the latter observation as if it were well known; in fact, I had not said a word about it to him. "But there is always a neurotic ingredient in such concealment. Start on this point with Nora tomorrow, Younger. That is my advice. There is something in that country house. Undoubtedly it will be connected to the girl's unconscious desire for her father. I wonder." He stopped walking and shut his eyes. A long moment passed. Then, opening his eyes, he said, "I have it."

"What?" I asked.

"Well, I have a suspicion, Younger, but I am not going to tell you what it is. I don't want to plant ideas in your head—or hers. Find out if she has a memory connected with this country house, a memory predating the episode on the roof. Remember, be opaque with her. You must be like a mirror, showing her nothing but what she shows you. Perhaps she saw something she should not have seen. She may not want to tell you. Don't let her off."

❧

ON TUESDAY, in the late afternoon, the Triumvirate were reassembled in the library. They had a great deal to discuss. One of the three gentlemen turned over, in his fine long hands, a report he had recently received and had shared with the others. The report included, among other things, a set of letters. "These," he said, "we do not burn."

"I told you: they are degenerates, all of them," added the portly, ruddy-complexioned man next to him, with the muttonchop side-burns. "We must wipe them out. One by one."

"Oh, we will," said the first. "We are. But we will make use of them first."

There was a brief silence. Then the third man, the balding one, spoke. "What of the evidence?"

"There will be no evidence," replied the first, "except what we choose to leave behind."

❧

DETECTIVE JIMMY LITTLEMORE exited the subway at Seventy-second Street and Broadway, the stop closest to the Balmoral. Mr. Hugel might have his money on Banwell, but Littlemore hadn't given up on his own leads.

The evening before, when the Chinaman had disappeared, Littlemore had not been able to find out anything about him. The other laundry workers knew him as Chong, but that was all they knew about him. An assistant had told him to come back in the daytime and ask for Mayhew, the bookkeeper.

Littlemore found Mayhew recording figures in a back office. The detective asked the bookkeeper about the Chinaman who worked in the laundry.

"Just penciling in his name now," said Mayhew, without looking up.

"Because he didn't show up for work today?" asked Littlemore.

"How did you know that?"

"Lucky guess," said the detective. Mayhew had the information he wanted. The Chinaman's full name was Chong Sing. His address was 782 Eighth Avenue, in Midtown. Littlemore asked if Mr. Chong ever made laundry deliveries to the Alabaster Wing—more specifically, to Miss Riverford.

Mayhew looked amused. "You can't be serious," he said.

"Why not?"

"The man's Chinese."

"So?"

"This is a first-class building, Detective. Normally we don't even hire Chinese. Chong was not allowed out of the basement. He was lucky to have a job here at all."

"Bet he was real grateful," said Littlemore. "Why'd you hire him?"

Mayhew shrugged. "I haven't any idea. Mr. Banwell asked us to find work for him, and that is what we did. Evidently, he didn't realize how fortunate he was."

Littlemore's next task was to find the cabbie who picked up the black-haired man Sunday night. The doormen told the detective to try the stables on Amsterdam Avenue, where all the hacks got their horses. But they said he shouldn't bother going until later. The night drivers didn't come on until nine-thirty or ten.

The interval suited Littlemore just fine. It gave him a chance first to take another look at Miss Riverford's apartment and then to drop in on Betty. She was in a much better mood. Agreeing to come out to a nickelodeon, Betty introduced the detective to her mother and gave a good-bye hug to each of her little brothers—who gaped when the detective showed them his gun and who were delighted when he let them play with his badge and handcuffs. Betty, it turned out, had a new job. She had spent a luckless morning presenting herself at the large hotels, hoping vainly to find a spot for an experienced maid. But at a shirtwaist factory near Washington Square, she got an interview with the owner, a Mr. Harris, who hired her on the spot. She would start tomorrow.

The hours of Betty's new job were not so nice: seven in the morning to eight at night. Nor was she enthusiastic about the pay. "At least it's by the piece," she said. "Mr. Harris says some of the girls make two dollars a day."

About half past nine, Littlemore went to the stable on Amsterdam Avenue near 100th Street. Over the next two hours, a good dozen hackney drivers came in to drop off or pick up a horse. Littlemore talked with every one of them but drew a blank. When the last stall was empty, the stableboy told Littlemore to wait for one more old-timer who kept his own horse. Sure enough, a little before twelve, an old nag came slow-stepping in, piloted by an ancient driver. At first the old man wouldn't answer the detective, but when Littlemore began flipping a quarter in the air, he found his tongue. He had indeed picked up a black-haired man in front of the Balmoral two nights ago. Did he remember where they went? He did: the Hotel Manhattan.

Littlemore was speechless, but the old driver had more to say. "Know what he does when we get there? Climbs straight into another cab, one of those red and green gasoline jobs, right in front of my face. Taking money from my pocket, that's what I calls it, and putting it in somebody else's."

❧

FREUD CUT OUR conversation short, abruptly declaring that he had to return to the hotel at once. I understood what was happening. Luckily, a carriage was right at hand.

The instant Freud and I set foot in the hotel, Jung accosted us. He must have been waiting for Freud to return. With inexplicable ardor, he planted himself right in front of Freud, blocking our way, insisting on speaking with him without delay. The moment was the least propitious possible. Freud had just informed me, with evident embarrassment, how pressing was his need.

"Great heavens, Jung," said Freud, "let me through. I have to get to my room."

"Why? Are you having the—the problem again?"

"Lower your voice," Freud said. "Yes. Now let me pass. It is urgent."

"I knew it. Your enuresis," said Jung, using the medical term for involuntary micturition, "is psychogenic."

"Jung, it is—"

"It is a neurosis. I can help you!"

"It is—" Freud stopped in mid-sentence. His voice changed altogether. He spoke evenly and very quietly, looking straight at Jung. "It is now too late."

An extremely awkward pause ensued. Then Freud went on. "Do not look down, either of you. Jung, you will turn around and walk just in front of me. Younger, you will be on my left. No, on my *left*. Walk directly to the elevator. Go."

Thus arranged, we made a stiff procession to the elevators. One of the clerks stared at us; it was irritating, but I don't think he suspected. To my astonishment, Jung would not stop talking. "Your Count Thun dream—it is the key to everything. Will you let me analyze it?"

"I am hardly in a position to refuse," was Freud's reply.

Freud's dream of Count Thun, the former Austrian prime minister, was known to everyone who had read his work. Reaching the elevator bank, I tried to leave them. To my surprise, Jung stopped me. He said he needed me. We let one car go; the next we had to ourselves.

Inside the elevator, Jung went on. "Count Thun represented *me*. Thun: Jung—it could not be clearer. Both names have four letters. Both share the *un,* whose meaning is obvious. His family was originally German but obliged to emigrate; so was mine. He is of higher birth than you; so am I. He is the picture of arrogance; I am accused of arrogance. In your dream, he is your enemy but also a member of your inner circle; someone you lead, but someone who threatens you—and an Aryan, decidedly an Aryan. The conclusion is inescapable: you were dreaming of *me,* but you had to distort it, because you did not want to acknowledge that you regard me as a threat."

"Carl," said Freud slowly, "I dreamt of Count Thun in 1898. That was more than a decade ago. You and I did not meet until 1907."

The doors opened. The corridor was empty. Freud walked briskly out; we followed. I could not imagine what Jung was thinking or what his response would be. It was this: "I know it! We dream what is to come as well as what has passed. Younger," he exclaimed, his eyes unnaturally bright, "you can confirm it!"

"I?"

"Yes, of course you. You were there. You saw the whole thing." Suddenly Jung seemed to change his mind and addressed Freud again. "Never mind. Your enuresis signifies ambition. It is a means of drawing attention to yourself—as you did just now, in the lobby. It appears whenever you feel you have an enemy, an opposite number, an *un* you must overcome. I am now that *un*. Hence your problem has reappeared."

We reached Freud's room. He fished in his pocket for the key—a task uncomfortable for him at present. In the end, the key dropped to the floor. No one moved. Then Freud picked it up. When upright again, he said to Jung, "I doubt very much I enjoy Joseph's gift of prophecy, but I can tell you this: you are my heir. You will inherit psychoanalysis when I die, and you will become its leader even before that. I will see to it. I *am* seeing to it. I have said all this to you before. I have told the others; I say it now again. There is no one else, Carl. Do not doubt it."

"Then tell me the rest of your Count Thun dream!" cried Jung. "You have always said there was a part of that dream you did not reveal. If I am your heir, tell me. It will confirm my analysis; I am certain of it. What was it?"

Freud shook his head. I think he was smiling—ruefully, perhaps. "My boy," he said to Jung, "there are some things even I cannot divulge. I should never have any authority again. Now leave me, both of you. I will join you in the dining room in half an hour."

Jung turned without a word and strode away.

❧

THE MANHATTAN BRIDGE, nearing completion in the summer of 1909, was the last of the three great suspension bridges built across the East River to connect the island of Manhattan with what had been, until 1898, the City of Brooklyn. These bridges—the Brooklyn, the Williamsburg, the Manhattan—were, when constructed, the longest single spans in existence, extolled by *Scientific American* as the greatest engineering feats the world had ever known. Together with the invention of spun-steel cable, one particular technological innovation made them possible: the ingenious conceit of the pneumatic caisson.

The problem to which the caisson responded was this. The massive support towers for these bridges, necessary to hold up their suspension cables, had to rest on foundations built underwater, almost a hundred feet beneath the surface. These foundations could not be laid directly on the soft riverbed. Instead, layer upon layer of sand, silt, shale, clay, and boulder had to be dredged, broken, and sometimes dynamited until one reached bedrock. To perform such excavation underwater was universally regarded as impossible—until the idea of the pneumatic caisson was hit upon.

The caisson was basically an enormous wooden box. The Manhattan Bridge caisson, on the New York City side, had an area of seventeen thousand square feet. Its walls were made from countless planks of yellow pine lumber, bolted together to a thickness of over twenty feet and caulked with a million barrels of oakum, hot pitch, and varnish. The lower three feet of the caisson were reinforced with boiler plate, inside and out. The weight of the whole: over sixty million pounds.

A caisson had a ceiling but no man-made floor. Its floor was the riverbed itself. In essence, the pneumatic caisson was the largest diving bell ever built.

In 1907, the Manhattan Bridge caisson was sunk to the river bottom, water filling its internal compartments. On land, enormous steam engines were fired up, which, running day and night, pumped air through iron pipes down into the great box. The forced air, building up to enormous pressure, drove out all the water through boreholes drilled in the caisson's walls. An elevator shaft connected the caisson to a pier. Men would take this elevator down into the caisson, where they could breathe the pumped, compressed air. There they had direct access to the riverbed and hence were able to perform the underwater construction work previously considered impossible: hammering the rock, shoveling the mud, dynamiting the boulders, laying the concrete. Debris was discharged through ingeniously devised compartments called windows, although one could not see through them. Three hundred men could work in the caisson at one time.

An invisible danger lay in wait for them there. The men who emerged from a day's work in the very first pneumatic caisson—employed for the Brooklyn Bridge—frequently began to feel a strange light-headedness. This was followed by a stiffening of their joints, then by a paralysis of the elbows and knees, then by an unendurable pain throughout the entire body. Doctors called the mysterious condition *caisson disease*. Workmen called it "the bends," because of the contorted posture into which its sufferers were driven. Thousands of workers had their health ruined by it, hundreds endured paralysis, and many died before it was discovered that slowing the climb back to the surface—forcing the men to spend time at intermediate stages as they ascended the shaft—prevented the disorder.

By 1909, the science of decompression had advanced impressively. Tables had been drawn up prescribing exactly how long a man needed to decompress, which depended on how much time he had spent down in the caisson. From these tables, the man preparing to enter the caisson just after midnight on August 31, 1909, knew he could spend fifteen minutes down below without requiring any decompression at all. He had no fear of the underwater descent. He had made the trip many times. This trip, however, would be different in one respect. He would be alone.

He had driven one of his automobiles almost down to the river itself, navigating around machinery, lumber, tilting corrugated tin shacks, fifty-foot rounds of steel cable, and piles of broken stone. The construction site was deserted; the night watchman had completed his final rounds, and the first crews of workmen would not arrive until dawn. The tower of the bridge, virtually finished, cast a shadow over his car in the moonlight, making him all but invisible from the street. The steam engines were still roaring, pumping air down to the caisson a hundred feet below and masking all other sound.

From the back of his car, he removed a large black trunk, which he carried onto the pier to the mouth of the caisson shaft. Another man would not have been able to manage the feat, but this man was strong, tall, and athletic. He knew how to hoist a heavy trunk over his back. It made an incongruous sight, since the man was wearing black tie and tails.

He unlocked the elevator and entered it, dragging the trunk in with him. Two jets of blue flame provided light. As the elevator made its journey downward, the roar of the steam engines became a distant throbbing. The darkness became cooler. There was a deep, dank smell of earth and salt. The man felt the pressure building in his inner ear. He negotiated the air lock without difficulty, opened the caisson hatch, forced the trunk down a ramp—it echoed monstrously as it fell—and descended to the wooden planks below.

Blue-flame gaslights also illuminated the caisson. They burned pure oxygen, providing enough light to work by while emitting neither smoke nor odor. In their unsteady glow, catlike shadows shifted on the ground and in the rafters. The man looked at his watch, went directly to one of the so-called windows, opened its inner hatch, and with a grunt pushed the trunk inside it. Resealing the window, he operated two pull chains hanging from the wall. The first opened the window's outer hatch. The second caused the window's compartment to rotate, dumping its contents—in this case, one heavy black trunk—into the river. With a different set of chains, he closed the outer hatch and activated an air pipe that flushed the river water from the compartment, making the window ready for the next user.

He was done. He looked at his watch: only five minutes had elapsed since he entered the caisson. Then he heard a piece of wood creaking.

Among the various sounds one can hear indoors in the nighttime, some are instantly recognizable. There is, for example, the unmistakable pattering of a small animal. There is the banging of a door in the wind. Then there is the sound of an adult human being shifting his weight or taking a step on a wooden floor: this was the sound the man had just heard.

He spun around and called out, "Who's there?"

"It's only me, sir," answered a voice, sounding falsely distant in the compressed air.

"Who is *me*?" said the man in black tie and tails.

"Malley, sir." Out from the shadows where two joists intersected stepped a redheaded man, short but with the girth of a bear, muddy, unkempt, and smiling.

"Seamus Malley?"

"The one and only," answered Malley. "You won't fire me, will you, sir?"

"What the devil are you doing down here?" replied the taller man. "Who else is with you?"

"Not a soul. It's just they have me working twelve hours of a Tuesday, sir, and then the morning shift on Wednesday."

"You're spending the night here?"

"What's the point of going up at all, I ask, when by the time you're up it's only time to come down again?" Malley was a favorite among the workmen, known for his fine tenor, which he liked to exercise in the echoing chambers of the caisson, and his seemingly unlimited capacity to consume alcoholic potables of any kind. The latter talent had caused him trouble around the Malley household the day before yesterday, which, being a Sunday, was a time when no alcohol ought to have been consumed at all. His incensed wife told him not to show his face until he could show it sober the next Sunday. It was this injunction that, in truth, had obliged Malley to make his bed in the caisson. "So I say to myself, Malley, just kip down here for the night, why don't you, and none the worse or the wiser."

"Been watching me all this time, have you, Seamus?" asked the man.

"Never in life, sir. I was sleeping all the while," said Malley, who shivered like a man who had been sleeping in a cold, damp place.

The man in black tie doubted this assertion very much, although it happened to be true. But true or not, it made no difference, because Malley had seen him now. "Shame on me, Seamus," he said, "if I'm the man to fire you for such a thing. Don't you know my mother, God rest her soul, was Irish?"

"I didn't know it, sir."

"Why, didn't she take me by the hand thirty years ago to see Parnell himself come off the ship, practically right above our heads, where we're standing at this moment?"

"You're a lucky man, sir," Malley answered.

"I'll tell you what you need, Seamus, and that's a fifth of good

Irish whiskey to keep you company down here, which I happen to have in my car. Why don't you come up with me and I'll give it to you, provided you share a drop first. Then you can come back and make yourself comfortable."

"You're too good, sir, too good," said Malley.

"Oh, stop your gabbing and come on then." Ushering Malley up the ramp to the elevator, the man in black tie pulled the lever to begin their ascent. "I'll be needing to charge you rent, don't you know. It's only fair."

"Why, I'd pay anything at all for the view alone," replied Malley. "We're going to miss the first holding stage, sir. You need to stop."

"Not a bit of it," said the taller man. "You're coming straight back down in five minutes, Seamus. No need to stop if you go straight back down."

"Is that it, sir?"

"That's it. It's all in the tables." And the man in black tie actually pulled a copy of the decompression tables from his vest, waving them before Malley. It was quite true: a man in the caisson could make a quick trip up and down without illness, provided he spent no more than a few minutes on the surface. "All right: ready to hold your breath?"

"My breath?" Malley asked.

The man in black tie yanked down the elevator brake, jerking the cabin to a sudden stop. "What are you thinking, man?" he cried. "We're going straight up, I tell you. You've got to hold your breath from here clear to the top. You want to die of the bends?" They were about a third of the way up the shaft, some sixty-five feet below the surface. "How long have you been down, fifteen hours?"

"Closer on to twenty, sir."

"Twenty hours down, Seamus—you'd be paralyzed sure, if you lived at all. I'll tell you what it is. You take a deep breath, like me, and you hold it for dear life. Don't let go. You'll feel a little pressure, but don't let go, no matter what. Are you ready?"

Malley nodded. The two men each swallowed an immense lungful of air. Then the man in black tie started the elevator once more. As they rose, Malley felt an increasing burden in his chest. The man in black tie felt no such pressure, because he was only pretending to hold his breath. In actuality, he was steadily but invisibly exhaling as the elevator made its way to the surface. Over the throbbing din of the steam engines, the sound of his breath escaping could not be heard.

Malley's chest began to ache. To indicate his discomfort, and his difficulty keeping in his breath, he pointed at his chest and mouth. The man in black tie shook his head and waved his forefinger, emphasizing how important it was that Malley not exhale. He beckoned Malley toward him, put his large hand over Malley's mouth and nose, closing off those passageways completely. He raised his eyebrows as if to ask Malley whether that was better. Malley nodded, grimacing. His face turned redder, his eyes began to bulge, and just as the elevator reached its terminus, he coughed involuntarily into the hand of the man with black tie. That hand was now covered with blood.

The human lung is surprisingly inelastic. It cannot stretch. At sixty-five feet below the earth's surface, when Malley took his last breath, the ambient pressure is approximately three atmospheres, which means that Malley took into his lungs three times the normal quantity of air. As the elevator ascended, this air expanded. His lungs quickly inflated beyond their capacity, like overstretched balloons. Soon the pleura in Malley's lungs—the tiny sacs that hold the air—began to burst, rapid-fire, one after the other. The released air invaded his pleural cavity—the space between chest and lung—causing a condition called pneumothorax, in which one of his lungs collapsed.

"Seamus, Seamus, you didn't exhale, did you?" They had reached the top, but the man in black tie made no move to open the elevator door.

"I swear I didn't," Malley gasped. "Mother of God. What's wrong with me?"

"You've lost a lung, is all," replied the tall man. "That won't kill you."

"I need"—Malley collapsed to his knees—"to lie down."

"Lie down? No, man: we have to keep you standing, do you hear me?" The taller man seized Malley under the shoulders, hauled him upright, and propped him against the elevator wall. "That's better."

Like most gases trapped in a liquid, air bubbles in a man's bloodstream rise straight upward. Keeping Malley vertical ensured that the air bubbles still in Malley's lungs, forcing their way through his ruptured pleural capillaries, would proceed directly to his heart and from there to his coronary and carotid arteries.

"Thanks," whispered Malley. "Will I be all right?"

"We'll know any minute now," said the man.

Malley gripped his head, which began to swim. The veins in his cheeks were showing blue. "What's happening to me?" he asked.

"Well, I'd say you're having a stroke, Seamus."

"Am I going to die?"

"I'll be honest with you, man: if I took us straight back down, right now, all the way down, I might just save you." This was true. Recompression was the only way to save a man dying from decompression. "But do you know what it is?" The man in black tie took his time, cleaning the blood from his hand with a fresh handkerchief before finishing: "My mother wasn't Irish."

Malley's mouth opened as if to speak. He looked at the man who had killed him. Then his head jerked back, his eyes glazed over, and he moved no more. The man in black tie calmly opened the elevator door. No one was there. He returned to his car, found a bottle of whiskey in the back, and returned to the elevator, where he placed the bottle next to the slumped body. Poor Malley's corpse would be discovered in a few hours, to be mourned as yet another victim of the caisson. A good man, his friends would agree, but a fool to have been spending nights down there, in a place unfit for man or beast. Why, some wondered, had he tried to come out in the middle of the night, and how could he have forgotten to stop at the holding stages? Must have been spooked as well as drunk. On the pier, no one would notice the red clay footprints left by the murderer. All the caisson men tracked the same stuff, and the outlines of the man's elegant shoes were soon obliterated by the random treading of a thousand heavy boots.

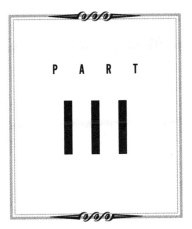

PART

III

I WOKE AT SIX on Wednesday morning. I hadn't dreamt of Nora Acton—so far as I knew—but as I opened my eyes in the wainscoted white box of my hotel room, I was thinking of her all the same. Could sexual desire for her father really underlie Miss Acton's symptoms? That was plainly the thrust of Freud's thinking. I didn't want to believe it; the thought repulsed me.

I never liked Oedipus. I didn't like the play, I didn't like the man, and I didn't like Freud's eponymous theory. It was the one piece of psychoanalysis I never embraced. That we have an unconscious mental life, that we are constantly suppressing forbidden sexual desires and the aggressions that arise in their wake, that these suppressed wishes manifest themselves in our dreams, our slips of the tongue, our neuroses—all this I believed. But that men want sex with their mothers, and girls with their fathers—this I did not accept. Freud would say, of course, that my skepticism was "resistance." He would say I did not want the Oedipus theory to be true. No doubt that was so. But resistance, whatever else it is, surely does not prove the truth of the idea resisted.

Which is why I kept coming back to *Hamlet* and to Freud's irresistible but infuriating solution to its riddle. In two sentences, Freud had demolished the long-standing notion that Hamlet was, as Jung's "great-grandfather" Goethe had it, the overly intellectual aesthete, constitutionally incapable of resolute action. As Freud pointed out, Hamlet repeatedly takes decisive action. He kills Polonius. He plans and executes his play-within-a-play, tricking Claudius into revealing his guilt. He sends Rosencrantz and Guildenstern to their deaths. Apparently there is just one thing he cannot do: take vengeance on the villain who killed his father and bedded his mother.

And the reason, Freud says, the real reason, is simple. Hamlet sees in his uncle's deeds his own secret wishes realized: his Oedipal wishes.

Claudius has done only what Hamlet himself wanted to do. "Thus the loathing which should drive him on to revenge"—to quote Freud—"is replaced in him by self-reproaches, by scruples of conscience." That Hamlet suffers from self-reproach is undeniable. Over and over, he castigates himself—excessively, almost irrationally. He even contemplates suicide. Or at least that is how the *To be, or not to be* speech is always interpreted. Hamlet is wondering whether to take his own life. Why? Why does Hamlet feel guilty and suicidal when he thinks of avenging his father? No one in three hundred years had ever been able to explain the most famous soliloquy of all drama—until Freud.

According to Freud, Hamlet knows—unconsciously—that he himself wished to kill his father and that he himself wished to replace his father in his mother's bed, just as Claudius has done. Claudius is, therefore, the embodiment of Hamlet's own secret wishes; he is a mirror of Hamlet himself. Hamlet's thoughts run straight from revenge to guilt and suicide because he sees himself in his uncle. Killing Claudius would be both a reenactment of his own Oedipal desires and a kind of self-slaughter. That is why Hamlet is paralyzed. That is why he cannot take action. He is an hysteric, suffering from the overwhelming guilt of Oedipal desires he has not successfully repressed.

And yet, I felt, there must be some other explanation. There must be another meaning of *To be, or not to be*. If I could only solve that soliloquy, I somehow imagined it would vindicate my objection to the entire Oedipus theory. But I never had.

At breakfast, I found Brill and Ferenczi at the same table they had occupied yesterday. Brill was manfully assaulting a plate of steak and eggs. Ferenczi was not so hale: he insisted he was not going to touch a crumb all day. Both seemed a little forced in their conversation with me; I think I had interrupted them in private talk. "The waiters," said Ferenczi, "they are all Negro. Is that common in America?"

"Only in the better establishments," replied Brill. "New Yorkers opposed emancipation, don't forget, until they realized what it meant: they would get to keep their blacks as servants, only it would cost them less."

"New York did not oppose emancipation," I put in.

"A riot is not opposition?" asked Brill.

Ferenczi said, "You must ignore him, Younger, really you must."

"Yes, ignore me," Brill responded. "Everyone does. Instead, we must attend solely to Jung, because he is 'more important than the rest of us put together.'"

I saw that Jung had been their topic before I appeared. I asked if they could give me a clearer sense of Jung's relationship to Freud. They did.

Quite recently, over the last two years, Freud had attracted a new set of Swiss followers. Jung was the most prominent. The Zurichers were resented by Freud's original Viennese disciples, whose jealousy had intensified when Freud made Jung editor in chief of the *Psychoanalytical Yearbook,* the first periodical in the world devoted to the new psychology. In this position, Jung had the power to rule on the merits of everyone else's work. The Viennese objected that Jung had not genuinely embraced the "sexual aetiology"—Freud's core discovery that repressed sexual wishes lie behind hysteria and other mental illnesses. They felt Jung's elevation demonstrated favoritism on Freud's part. Here, Brill told me, the Viennese were righter than they knew. Freud not only favored Jung but had already selected him as his "crown prince" and "heir"—the man who would take over the movement.

I didn't mention having already heard Freud make this very statement to Jung last night, principally because I would then have had to describe Freud's mishap. Instead, I observed that Jung seemed highly sensitive to Freud's opinion of him.

"Oh, we all are," Ferenczi answered. "But, not to question, Freud and Jung have very father-son relations. I saw them myself on the ship. Hence Jung is very sensitive to any rebuke. It enrages him. Especially about the transference. Jung has—how shall I say?—a different philosophy when it comes to transference."

"Really? Has he published it?" I asked.

Ferenczi exchanged a look with Brill. "Not exactly. I am speaking of his approach to his patients. His—ah—female patients. You understand."

I was beginning to.

Brill whispered, "He sleeps with them. He is notorious."

"Myself, I have never," said Ferenczi. "But I have not yet faced too many temptations, so congratulations in my case are sadly premature."

"Does Dr. Freud know?"

This time Ferenczi whispered, "One of Jung's patients wrote to Freud, most upset, describing everything. Freud showed me letters on the ship. There is even a letter from Jung to the girl's mother—very peculiar. Freud consulted me for guidance." Ferenczi was distinctly proud of this. "I told him he should not take the girl's word as proof. Of course I already knew all about it. Everyone does. A beautiful girl—Jewish—a student. They say Jung did not treat her well."

"Oh, no," said Brill, looking at the entryway to the breakfast room. Freud was on his way in, but not by himself. He was accompanied by another man, whom I had met in New Haven at the psychoanalytic congress there a few months ago. It was Ernest Jones, Freud's British follower.

Jones had come to New York to join our party for the week. He would then travel up to Clark with us on Saturday. About forty, Jones was as short as Brill but a little stouter, with an exceedingly white face, dark well-oiled hair, almost no chin, and a tight, thin-lipped smile more suggestive of self-satisfaction than amiability. He had the peculiar habit of looking away from a person while addressing him. Freud, who was joking with Jones as they approached our table, was plainly delighted to see him. Neither Ferenczi nor Brill appeared to share this sentiment.

"Sándor Ferenczi," said Jones. "What a surprise, old fellow. But you weren't invited, were you? By Hall, I mean, to give a paper at Clark?"

"No," answered Ferenczi, "but—"

"And Abraham Brill," Jones went on, casting his eyes about the room as if expecting to find others he knew. "How are we getting on? Still only three patients?"

"Four," said Brill.

"Well, count yourself lucky, old man," replied Jones. "I am so crawling with patients in Toronto I don't have a minute to put pen to paper. No, all I have in the pipeline is my handwriting piece for *Neu-*

rology, a little thing for *Insanity,* and the lecture I gave at New Haven, which Prince wants to publish. What about you, Brill, anything coming out?"

Jones's remarks had produced an atmosphere less than convivial. Brill assumed an expression of feigned disappointment. "Only Freud's hysteria book, I'm afraid," he said.

Jones's lips worked, but nothing came out.

"Yes, only my translation of Freud," Brill went on. "My German was rustier than I would ever have believed, but it's done."

Relief filled Jones's countenance. "Freud doesn't need translating into German, you sod," he said, laughing out loud. "Freud writes in German. He needs an *English* translator."

"I *am* the English translator," said Brill.

Jones looked dumbfounded. To Freud he said, "You—you don't—you're letting Brill translate you?" And to Brill, "But is your English quite up to it, old man? You *are* an immigrant, after all."

"Ernest," said Freud, "you are displaying jealousy."

"Me?" answered Jones. "Jealous of Brill? How could I be?"

At that moment, a boy carrying a silver platter called out Brill's name. The platter had an envelope on it. With a self-important air, Brill tipped the boy a dime. "I've always wanted to receive a telegram in a hotel," he said cheerily. "I nearly sent one to myself yesterday, just to see how it felt."

When, however, Brill pulled the message from its envelope, his features froze. Ferenczi seized the missive from his hands and showed it to us. The telegram read:

THEN THE LORD RAINED UPON SODOM BRIMSTONE AND FIRE STOP AND LO THE SMOKE OF THE COUNTRY WENT UP AS THE SMOKE OF A FURNACE STOP BUT HIS WIFE LOOKED BACK FROM BEHIND HIM AND SHE BECAME A PILLAR OF SALT STOP BEFORE IT IS TOO LATE STOP

"Again," Brill whispered.

"I say," Jones responded, "there's no reason to look as if one had seen a ghost. It is plainly from some religious fanatic. America is full of them."

"How did they know I would be here?" Brill replied, unreassured.

❦

MAYOR GEORGE McCLELLAN lived on the Row, in one of the stately Greek Revival townhouses lining Washington Square North. Leaving his house early Wednesday morning, McClellan was startled to see Coroner Hugel rushing toward him from the park across the street. The two gentlemen met between the Corinthian columns framing the mayor's front door.

"Hugel," said McClellan, "what are you doing here? Good Lord, man, you look like you haven't slept in days."

"I had to be sure of finding you," exclaimed the winded coroner. "Banwell did it."

"What?"

"George Banwell killed the Riverford girl," said Hugel.

"Don't be ridiculous," replied the mayor. "I've known Banwell for twenty years."

"From the moment I entered her apartment," said Hugel, "he tried to obstruct the investigation. He threatened to have me removed from the case. He tried to prevent the autopsy."

"He knows the girl's father, for God's sake."

"Why should that prevent an autopsy?"

"Most men, Hugel, would not relish the sight of their daughter's corpse sawed open."

If the mayor intended a hint concerning Hugel's sensibilities, the coroner did not take it. "He fits the description of the murderer in every respect. He lived in her building; he was a friend of the family, to whom she would have opened her door; and he had her entire apartment cleared out before Littlemore could search it."

"You had already searched it," the mayor rejoined.

"Not at all," said Hugel. "I only inspected the bedroom. Littlemore was to search the rest of the apartment."

"Did Banwell know Littlemore was coming? Did you tell him?"

"No," the coroner grumbled. "But how do you explain his terror at the sight of Miss Acton on the street yesterday?" He relayed to the mayor the account of the previous day's events reported to him by

Littlemore. "Banwell was trying to flee because he thought she would identify him as her attacker."

"Nonsense," was the mayor's response. "He met me in the hotel directly afterward. Are you aware that the Banwells and Actons are the closest of friends? Harcourt and Mildred Acton are at George's summer cottage now."

"You mean he knows the Actons?" Hugel demanded. "Why, that proves it! He is the only one who knew both victims."

The mayor regarded the coroner dispassionately. "What's that on your jacket, Hugel? It looks like egg."

"It *is* egg." Hugel wiped at his lapel with a yellowed handkerchief. "Those hooligans on the other side of your park threw it at me. We must arrest Banwell at once."

The mayor shook his head. The south side of Washington Square was not genteel, and McClellan had not been able to rid the southwest corner of the park of a gang of boys for whom proximity to the mayor's house must have been an additional inducement to their prankstering. McClellan strode past the coroner to the horse-drawn carriage awaiting him. "I'm surprised at you, Hugel. Speculation piled on top of speculation."

"It will not be speculation when you have another murder on your hands."

"George Banwell did not kill Miss Riverford," said the mayor.

"How do you know?"

"I *know*," answered McClellan definitively. "I won't hear another word of this ludicrous slander. Now go home. You are not fit to be in your office in this state. Get some rest. That's an order."

❧

THE BUILDING LITTLEMORE found at 782 Eighth Avenue— where Chong Sing supposedly lived in apartment 4C—was a five-story tenement, dirty, grimy, with fragrant shanks of red-roasted pork and dripping carcasses of duck hanging in the second-floor windows, behind which was a Chinese restaurant. Below the restaurant, at street level, was a dingy bicycle shop, the proprietor of which was white. All the other people in and around the building—the old women bustling in and out the front door, the man smoking a long

pipe on the stoop, the faces peering out the upper-story windows—
were Chinese.

When the detective began mounting the third flight of unlit
stairs, a small man in a long tunic appeared out of the shadows,
blocking his way. This man had a wispy beard, a queue hanging down
his back, and teeth the color of fresh rust. Littlemore stopped. "You
go wrong way," the Chinese said, without introduction. "Restaurant
back there. Second floor."

"I'm not looking for the restaurant," the detective replied. "I'm
looking for Mr. Chong Sing. Lives on the fourth floor. You know him?"

"No." The Chinese man continued to bar Littlemore's way. "No
Chong Sing upstair."

"You mean he's out, or he doesn't live here?"

"No Chong Sing upstair," the Chinese man repeated. He pushed
his fingertips against Littlemore's chest. "You go way."

Littlemore pushed past the man and continued up the narrow
stairway, which creaked under his feet. The fatty smell of meat accompanied him. As he trod the smoky corridor of the fourth floor—
windowless and dark, though it was a bright morning—he saw eyes
watching him from doorways barely cracked open. No one answered
at apartment 4C. Littlemore thought he heard someone hurrying
down a back stairway. At first, the aroma of roasted meat had stimulated the detective's appetite; now, in the airless upper floors, mixing
with curls of opium smoke, it nauseated him.

✴

WHEN THE MAYOR arrived at City Hall, Mrs. Neville informed
him that Mr. Banwell was calling. McClellan told her to put him
through.

"George," said George Banwell, "it's George."

"By George, it is," said George McClellan, completing an exchange they had initiated almost twenty years ago as fledgling members of the Manhattan Club.

"Just wanted you to know I got through to Acton last night," said
Banwell. "Told him the ghastly news. He's driving in post haste this
morning. He should be at the hotel by noon. I'm meeting him there."

"Excellent," said McClellan. "I'll join you."

"Has Nora remembered anything?"

"No," said the mayor. "The coroner has a suspect, however. You."

"Me?" exclaimed Banwell. "I didn't like that little weasel the moment I saw him."

"Apparently the feeling was mutual."

"What did you tell him?"

"I told him you didn't do it," said the mayor.

"What about Elizabeth's body?" asked Banwell. "Riverford's wiring me about it every other minute."

"The body has been stolen, George," said the mayor.

"What?"

"You know the troubles I've had with the morgue. I hope to get it back. Can you put Riverford off for one more day?"

"Put him off?" repeated Banwell. "His daughter's been murdered."

"Can you try?" asked the mayor.

"The devil," said Banwell. "I'll see what I can do. By the way, who are these—these *specialists* looking at Nora?"

"Didn't I tell you?" answered the mayor. "They are therapeutists. Apparently they can cure amnesia just by talking. Fascinating business, actually. They get the patient to tell them all kinds of things."

"What kinds of things?" asked Banwell.

"*All* kinds," answered McClellan.

❧

CORONER HUGEL, obeying the mayor's orders, went back to his home, the top two floors of a small wood-frame house on Warren Street. There he lay down on his lumpy bed but didn't sleep. The light was too bright, and the shouts of the teamsters were too loud, even with a pillow over his head.

The house in which Hugel lived was at the outer edge of the Market District in lower Manhattan. When he first rented his rooms, the district was a pleasant residential neighborhood; by 1909, it was overrun by produce warehouses and manufacturing buildings. Hugel had never moved. On a coroner's pay, he could not afford two full floors of a house in a more fashionable part of the city.

Hugel hated his rooms. The ceilings had the same disgusting brown-edged water stains he had to endure at his office. Hugel swore bitterly to himself. He was the coroner of New York City. Why did he have to live in such undignified quarters? Why did his suit have to be so shabby compared to the brushed and tailored cut of George Banwell's jacket?

The evidence against Banwell was easily sufficient to arrest him. Why couldn't the mayor see that? He wished he could arrest Banwell himself. The coroner had no power to make an arrest; he wished he did. Hugel went over everything again. There had to be something more. There had to be a way to make the whole story fit together. If Elizabeth Riverford's murderer had stolen her body from the morgue because there was evidence on that body, what could the evidence be? Suddenly he had an inspiration: he had forgotten the photographs he took in Miss Riverford's apartment. Wasn't it possible for one of his photographs to reveal the missing clue?

Hugel climbed out of bed and dressed hurriedly. He could develop them himself: although he rarely used it, he had his own darkroom adjacent to the morgue. No, it would be safer if Louis Riviere, the police department's photographic expert, did the work.

❧

AT NINE I WENT to Miss Acton's room. No one was there. By chance I inquired at the front desk, where I found a message waiting for me, in which Miss Acton informed me that she would be back in her room at eleven: I might call on her then, if I wished.

This was all wrong, analytically. First, I was not "calling" on Miss Acton. Second, it was not the patient, but the doctor, who ought to control the timing.

In the event, I did call on Miss Acton at eleven. She was perched comfortably on her sofa, just as she had been yesterday morning, taking tea, framed by the French doors opening out to the balcony. Without looking up, Miss Acton invited me to take a seat. This irritated me as well. She was too comfortable. The analytic setting ought to have been an office—my office—and I ought to have been in command of it.

Then she did look up, and I was entirely taken aback. She was tremulous and full of agitation. "Whom did you tell?" she asked, not accusingly but anxiously. "About what—what Mr. Banwell did to me?"

"Only Dr. Freud. Why? What's happened?"

She made eye contact with Mrs. Biggs, who produced a piece of paper, folded in two, which the old woman handed to me. On the note was written, in pen, *Hold your tongue.*

"A boy," said Miss Acton fretfully, "out in the street—he put that in my hands and ran off. Do you think Mr. Banwell attacked me?"

"Do you?"

"I don't know, I don't know. Why can't I remember? Can't you make me remember?" she beseeched me. "What if he's out there, watching me? Please, Doctor, can't you help me?"

I had not seen Miss Acton like this. It was the first time she had actually asked for my help. It was also the first time since coming to the hotel that she seemed genuinely afraid. "I can try," I answered.

Mrs. Biggs knew enough to leave the room of her own accord this time. I put the threatening message on the coffee table and made the girl lie down, although she plainly did not like it. She was so agitated she could hardly keep still.

"Miss Acton," I resumed, "think back to three years ago, before the incident on the rooftop. You were with your family, at the Banwells' country house."

"Why are you asking me about that?" she burst out. "I want to remember what happened two days ago, not three years ago."

"You don't want to remember what happened three years ago?"

"That's not what I meant."

"It's what you said. Dr. Freud believes you may have seen something then—something you've forgotten—something that's keeping you from remembering now."

"I have not forgotten anything," she retorted.

"Then you did see something."

She was silent.

"You have nothing to be ashamed of, Miss Acton."

"Stop saying that!" the girl cried out, with a fury entirely unexpected. "What would *I* have to be ashamed of?"

"I don't know."

"Go away," she said.

"Miss Acton."

"Go away. I don't like you. You are not clever."

I did not budge. "What did you see?" As she made no reply but stared determinedly in another direction, I stood and took a chance. "I'm sorry, Miss Acton, I can't help you. I wish I could."

She took a deep breath. "I saw my father with Clara Banwell."

"Can you describe what you saw?"

"Oh, all right."

I took my seat.

"There is a large library on the first floor," she said. "I often couldn't sleep, and when I couldn't, that's where I would go. I could read by moonlight there, without even lighting a candle. One night, the door to the library was ajar. I could tell someone was inside. I put my eye to the crack. My father was sitting on Mr. Banwell's chair, facing me, the same chair I always sat in. I could see him in the moonlight, but his head was thrown back in a disgusting way. Clara was on her knees before him. Her dress was unfastened. It had fallen down past her waist. Her back was entirely bare. She has a lovely back, Doctor, perfectly white, unblemished, the same pure white skin that you see in . . . in . . . and shaped just like an hourglass, or a cello. She was—I don't know how to describe it—undulating. Her head rose and fell in a slow rhythm. I could not see her hands; I believe they were in front of her. Once or twice, she threw her hair over her shoulder, but she kept rising and falling. It was mesmerizing. I did not, of course, understand at that time what I was witnessing. I found her movement beautiful, like a gentle wave lapping at a shore. But I knew very well they were doing something wrong."

"Go on."

"Then my father began making a repulsive, rasping noise of some kind. I wondered how Clara could stand that sound. But she not only stood it. It seemed to make her undulation grow faster, more determined. He clutched the armrests of his chair. She rose and fell more and more quickly. I'm sure I was fascinated, but I did not want to watch anymore. I tiptoed upstairs, back to my bedroom."

"And then?"

"There is no more. That was the end." We looked at each other. "I hope your curiosity is satisfied, Dr. Younger, because I don't believe my amnesia has been cured."

I tried to think through, psychoanalytically, the episode Miss Acton had just described. It had the form of a trauma, but there was one difficulty. Miss Acton did not seem to have been traumatized. "Did you experience any physical difficulties afterward?" I asked her. "Loss of voice?"

"No."

"A paralysis of any part of your body? A cold?"

"No."

"Did your father find out you saw him?"

"He is too stupid."

I took this in. "When you think of your amnesia, right now, what comes to mind?"

"Nothing," she said.

"There is never nothing in one's mind."

"You said that last time!" she exclaimed angrily, then fell silent. She fixed me with her blue eyes. "Only one thing you have ever done," she said, "even began to make me think you could help me, and that had nothing to do with all your questions."

"What was that?"

She dropped her gaze. "I do not know if I should tell you."

"Why?"

"Oh, never mind why. It was in the police station."

"I examined your neck."

She spoke quietly, her head averted. "Yes. When you first touched my throat, for one second I almost saw something—some picture, some memory. I don't know what it was."

This news was unexpected but not illogical. Freud himself had discovered that a physical touch could release suppressed memories. I had employed that very technique with Priscilla. Possibly, Miss Acton's amnesia was susceptible to this form of treatment as well. "Are you willing to try something similar again?" I asked her.

"It frightened me," she said.

"It probably will again."

She nodded. I went to her and extended my palm. She began to remove her scarf. I told her she needn't; I would touch her forehead, not her neck. She was surprised. I explained that touching the brow was one of Dr. Freud's standard methods for eliciting memory. She did not look satisfied but said I should proceed. Slowly I placed my palm to her forehead. There was no reaction. I asked if any thought had come to her.

"Only that your hand is very cold, Doctor," she replied.

"I'm sorry, Miss Acton, but it seems we must resume talking. The touching has not succeeded." I took my seat again. She looked almost cross. "Can you tell me one thing?" I went on. "You said that Mrs. Banwell's back—her bare back—was as white as something you had seen before. But you did not say what."

"And you would like to know?"

"That is why I asked."

"Get out," she said, sitting up.

"I beg your pardon?"

"Get out!" she cried and flung the bowl of sugar cubes at me. Then she stood and did the same with her saucer and cup. Or, rather, these she did not fling; she threw them overhand, as hard as she could. Fortunately, the two objects skewed off in opposite directions, the saucer flying to my left, the cup sailing high and to my right, breaking into several pieces when it hit the wall. Miss Acton picked up the teapot.

"Don't do that," I said.

"I hate you."

I stood as well. "You don't hate me, Miss Acton. You hate your father for trading you to Banwell—in exchange for his wife."

If I thought the girl's reaction to this would be to collapse in tears on her sofa, I was mistaken. She pounced like a feral cat, swinging the teapot at me. It hit me on my left shoulder. The force was impressive; she had tremendous strength for such a small thing. The top of the pot flew off. Boiling-hot water spilled onto my arm. It hurt, actually, considerably—the scalding water, not the pot—but I neither moved nor showed any reaction. This, I guess, incensed her. She swung the pot at me again, this time at my head.

I was so much taller than she that all I had to do was draw back slightly. The teapot missed its target, and I caught Miss Acton by the arm. Her momentum carried her around, so that her back was to me. I held her arms tightly against her waist, pinning her to me.

"Let me go," she said. "Let me go or I will scream."

"And then? Will you tell them I attacked you?"

"I am counting to three," she replied fiercely. "Let me go or I will scream. One, two, th—"

I seized her throat, stopping the word in her mouth. I should not have done so, but my blood was up. It stifled any possibility of her screaming but produced an unexpected side effect as well. All the tension in her body drained away. She dropped the teapot. Her eyes opened wide, disoriented, her sapphire irises darting rapidly back and forth. I didn't know what was stranger: her assault on me or this sudden transformation. I released my hold on her immediately.

"I saw him," she whispered.

"Can you remember?" I asked.

"I saw him," she repeated. "Now it's gone. I think I was tied up. I couldn't move. Oh, why can't I remember?" She turned at once to face me. "Do it again."

"What?"

"What you just did. I will remember, I'm sure of it."

Slowly, never taking her eyes off mine, she undid her scarf, revealing her still-bruised neck. She clutched my right hand in her delicate fingers and drew it toward her neck, just as she had the first time I saw her. I touched the soft skin under her chin, careful to avoid the ugly bruises.

"Is there anything?" I asked.

"No," she whispered. "You have to do what you did before."

I made no reply. I didn't know if she meant what I had done in the police station or what I had done a moment ago.

"Choke me," she said.

I did nothing.

"Please," she said. "Choke me."

I put my finger and thumb to the place on her neck where the reddish marks were. She bit her lip; it must have hurt. With these bruises covered, there was no sign of her previous attack. There was only her exquisitely turned neck. I squeezed her throat. Instantly her eyes closed.

"Harder," she said softly.

With my left hand, I held the small of her back. With my right, I choked her. Her back arched, her head fell back. She gripped my hand tightly but did not try to pull it away. "Do you see anything?" I asked. She shook her head faintly, her eyes still closed. I drew her in more firmly, pressing harder at her neck. Her breath caught in her throat, then stopped altogether. Her lips, vermilion, parted.

It is not easy for me to confess to the wholly improper reactions that came upon me. I had never seen a mouth so perfect. Her lips, slightly swollen, were trembling. Her skin was the purest cream. Her long hair was sparkling, like falling water turned gold by sunlight. I drew her still closer to me. One of her hands was resting on my chest. I don't know when or how it got there.

Suddenly I became aware of her blue eyes looking up into mine. When had they opened? She was mouthing a word. I hadn't realized. The word was *stop*.

I let go her throat, expecting her to gasp desperately for breath. She did not. Rather, she said, so softly I could barely hear it, "Kiss me."

I am obliged to admit I don't know what I would have done with this invitation. But there came, at that moment, a sudden loud rapping at the door, followed by the rattling of a key being worked frantically in the lock. I released her immediately. In the space of a second, she retrieved the teapot from the floor and placed it on the table, from which she also seized the note I'd left there. We both faced the door.

"*I remember*," she whispered urgently to me, as the knob turned. "*I know who did it.*"

CHAPTER TWELVE

AT NOON THE SAME DAY, September 1, Carl Jung was taken
to lunch by Smith Ely Jelliffe—publisher, doctor, and professor of
mental diseases at Fordham University—at a club on Fifty-third
Street overlooking the park. Freud was not invited; neither was Ferenczi, nor Brill, nor Younger. Their exclusion did not perturb Jung. It
was another mark, he felt, of his rising international stature. A less
magnanimous man would have been crowing about such a thing,
rubbing the invitation in the others' noses. But he, Jung, took his duty
of charity seriously, so he concealed.

It was painful, however, to have to hide so much. It had started
the very first day out of Bremen. Jung had not actually lied, of course.
That, he told himself, he would never do. But it was not his fault;
they drove him to dissemble.

For example, Freud and Ferenczi had booked second-class
berths on the *George Washington*. Was he to blame? Not wanting to
shame them, he had been obliged to say that, by the time he bought
his ticket, only first-class cabins were available. Then there had been
his dream the first night on board. Its true message was obvious—
that he was surpassing Freud in insight and reputation—so, out of
solicitude for Freud's sensitive pride, he asserted that the bones he
discovered in the dream belonged to his wife, rather than to Freud.
In fact, he had cleverly added that the bones belonged not only to his
wife but also his wife's sister: he wanted to see how Freud would react to that, given the skeletons in Freud's own closet. These were
trivialities, but they had laid the groundwork for the far greater dis-
simulation that had become necessary since his arrival in America.

The lunch at Jelliffe's club was most gratifying. Nine or ten men sat at the oval table. Intermixed with knowledgeable scientific conversation and an excellent claret was a goodly dose of ribald humor, which Jung always enjoyed. The women's suffrage movement bore the brunt of the raillery. One of the men asked whether anyone had ever met a suffragette he could imagine bedding. The unanimous answer was no. Someone ought to notify these ladies, another gentleman said, that even if they got the vote it didn't mean anyone would sleep with them. All agreed that the best cure for a woman demanding the suffrage was a good healthy servicing; that treatment, however, was so unappetizing one might as well give them the vote instead.

Jung was in his element. For once, there was no need to pretend to be less wealthy than one was. There was no obligation to deny one's ancestry. After the meal, the members repaired to a smoking room, where the conversation continued over cognac. Their ranks gradually thinned until Jung was left with only Jelliffe and three older men. One of these gentlemen now made a subtle signal; Jelliffe instantly rose to leave. Jung stood as well, assuming that Jelliffe's departure indicated his own. But Jelliffe informed him that the three gentlemen wanted the briefest of words with him alone and that a carriage would be waiting when they had done.

In actual fact, Jelliffe was not a member of this club at all. He yearned to belong to it. The men with authority over the society and its membership were those now remaining with him. It was they who had told Jelliffe to bring Jung to them today.

"Do sit down, Dr. Jung," said the man who had dismissed Jelliffe, gesturing toward a comfortable armchair with one of his elegant hands.

Jung tried to remember the gentleman's name, but he had met so many, and was so unused to wine at lunch, he could not.

"It's Dana," the man said helpfully, his dark eyebrows setting off his silver hair. "Charles Dana. I was just speaking of you, Jung, with my good friend Ochs over at the *Times*. He wants to do a story about you."

"A story?" asked Jung. "I don't understand."

"In connection with the lectures we've arranged for you at Fordham next week. He wants an interview with you. He proposes a short biography—two full broadsheet pages. You'll be quite famous. I didn't know if you'd agree. I told him I'd ask."

"Why," answered Jung, "I—I don't—"

"There is just one obstacle. Ochs"—Dana pronounced it *Oaks*— "is afraid you are a Freudian. Doesn't want his paper associated with a—with a— Well, you know what they say about Freud."

"A sex-crazed degenerate," said the portly man to the right, smoothing his muttonchop whiskers.

"Does Freud actually believe what he writes?" asked the third gentleman, a balding fellow. "That every girl he treats attempts to seduce him? Or what he says about feces—feces, for God's sake. Or about fastidious men wanting sex through the anus?"

"What about boys wanting to penetrate their own mothers?" rejoined the portly man, with an expression of utmost disgust.

"What about God?" asked Dana, tamping the tobacco from his pipe. "Must be hard on you, Jung."

Jung was uncertain exactly what was being referred to. He didn't answer.

"I know you, Jung," said Dana. "I know what you are. A Swiss. A Christian. A man of science, like us. And a man of passion. One who acts on his desires. A man who needs more than one woman to thrive. There is no need to hide such things here. These so-called men who don't act, who let their desires fester like sores, whose fathers were peddlers, who have always felt inferior to us—only they could dream up such vile, bestial fantasies, theorizing God and man into the sewer. It must be hard on you to be associated with that."

Jung was finding it increasingly difficult to absorb the flow of words. The alcohol must have gone to his head. This gentleman did seem to know him, but how? "Sometimes it is," Jung answered slowly.

"I am not in the least anti-Semitic. You need only ask Sachs here." He indicated the balding man on his left. "On the contrary, I admire the Jews. Their secret is racial purity, a principle they have understood far better than we. It is what has made them the great race they are." The man referred to as Sachs gave away nothing; the portly man merely pursed his fleshy lips. Dana continued: "But last Sunday, when I looked up at our bleeding Savior and imagined this

Viennese Jew saying our passion for Him is sexual, I found it difficult to pray. Very. I should think you might have encountered similar difficulties. Or are Freud's disciples required to give up the church?"

"I go to church" was Jung's awkward reply.

"For myself," said Dana, "I can't say I see it: this rage for psychotherapeutics. The Emmanuels, the New Thought, mesmerism, Dr. Quackenbos—"

"Quackenbos," harrumphed the muttonchops.

"Eddyism," Dana went on, "psychoanalysis—they are all cults, to my thinking. But half the women in America are running around demanding it, and it's best they don't drink from the wrong well. They'll be drinking from yours, believe me, after they read about you in the *Times*. Well, the long and short of it is this: we can make you the most famous psychiatrist in America, but Ochs can't write you up unless you make clear in your lectures at Fordham—unmistakably clear—that you don't go in for the Freudian obscenities. Good afternoon, Dr. Jung."

&

THE RAPPING ON the door of Miss Acton's hotel room continued as the doorknob turned this way and that. At last the door flew open, and in rushed five persons, three of whom I recognized: Mayor McClellan, Detective Littlemore, and George Banwell. The other two were a gentleman and lady of evident wealth.

The man looked to be in his late forties, fair in complexion but sunburned and peeling, with a pointy chin, deeply receding hairline, and a white gauze bandage over most of his left eye. It was instantly clear that he was Miss Acton's father, although the long limbs that were so graceful on her frame looked effete on him, and the features so softly feminine in her case conveyed diffidence in his. The woman, whom I took to be Miss Acton's mother, was at most five feet tall. She was of greater girth than her husband, had a deal of jewelry and paint on her face, and wore shoes with dangerously high heels, presumably to add a few inches to her height. Possibly she had been attractive once. It was she who spoke first, crying out, "Nora, you piteous, unlucky girl! I have been in agony since I heard the monstrous news. We have been riding for hours. Harcourt, are you just going to stand there?"

THE INTERPRETATION OF MURDER | 151

Nora's father apologized to the stout woman, extended his arm to her, and conducted her safely to a chair, into which she dropped with a great cry of exhaustion. The mayor introduced me to Acton and his wife, Mildred. It turned out their party had just arrived in the lobby when someone called down to the front desk complaining about noises in Miss Acton's room. I assured them we were quite safe, rather wishing the teacup was not lying in pieces against the far wall. Their backs were to it; I think they didn't see.

"Everything's going to be all right now, Nora," said Mr. Acton. "The mayor tells me there has been nothing in the press, thank goodness."

"Why did I listen to you?" Mildred Acton asked her daughter. "I said we should never have left you behind in New York. Didn't I say so, Harcourt? Do you see what has happened? I thought I would die when I heard. Biggs! Where is that Biggs? She will pack for you. We must get you out of here, Nora, at once. I do believe the rapist is here in this hotel. I have a sense for these things. The moment I walked in, I felt his eyes on me."

"On you, my dear?" asked Acton.

I cannot say I observed in Miss Acton the warm affection or the sense of protection you might wish to see in a girl greeting her parents after a prolonged and eventful separation. Nor could I blame her, given the tenor of the remarks made to her so far. The odd thing was that Miss Acton had not yet said a word. She had made several starts at speaking, but none of these efforts had eventuated in speech. A furious influx of blood now came to her cheeks. Then I realized: the girl had lost her voice again. Or so I thought, until Miss Acton said, quietly and evenly, "I have not been raped, Mama."

"Hush, Nora," her father replied. "That word is not spoken."

"You cannot know, poor thing!" her mother exclaimed. "You have no memory of the crime. You will never know."

Now was the moment when, if she were going to, Miss Acton would have said that she had recovered her memory. She did not do so. Instead, the girl replied, "I will stay here in the hotel to continue my treatment. I don't want to go home."

"Do you hear her?" cried her mother.

"I will not feel safe at home," said Miss Acton. "The man who attacked me may be watching for me there. Mr. McClellan, you said so yourself on Sunday."

"The girl is right," the mayor replied. "She is much safer in the hotel. The murderer does not know she is here."

I knew this to be false, because of the note Miss Acton received in the street. Miss Acton obviously knew the same. In fact, at the mayor's words I saw her right hand clench; a corner of the note was sticking out from her fist. Yet she said nothing. Instead, she looked from McClellan to her parents, as if he had quite vindicated her position. It came to me that she was avoiding Mr. Banwell's scrutiny.

Banwell had been eyeing Nora with a peculiar expression. Physically, he dominated the others. He was taller than anyone else in the room with the exception of myself and had a barrel chest. His dark hair was smoothed back with an unguent of some kind and graying handsomely at the temples. His gaze was fixed on Nora. It will seem preposterous, and another observer would no doubt have denied it, but the best way I can describe his expression is to say that, to me, he looked like he wished to do her violence. He now spoke, but his voice betrayed no such feeling. "Surely the best thing is to get Nora out of the city," he said with what sounded like gruff but genuine concern for her safety. "Why not my country place? Clara can take her."

"I prefer to stay here," said Nora, looking down.

"Really?" replied Banwell. "Your mother thinks the murderer is in the hotel. How can you be sure he isn't keeping watch on you even now?"

Miss Acton's face reddened as Banwell spoke to her. Her whole body, to me, seemed tense with fear.

I announced that I would be leaving. Miss Acton looked up at me anxiously. I added, as if just recalling something, "Oh, Miss Acton, your prescription—for the sedative I mentioned. Here it is." I withdrew a scrip from my pocket, quickly filled it out, and handed it to her. On it was written, *Was it Banwell?*

She saw my message. She nodded to me, slightly but definitively.

"Why don't you give that to me?" asked Banwell, narrowing his eyes on me. "My man downstairs can run to the pharmacy right now."

"Very well," I replied. From Miss Acton's hand, I took both my scrip and the anonymous note. I handed the latter to him. "See if your man can fill that."

Banwell read it. I half expected him to crush it and glare at me menacingly, revealing himself like the villain in some cheap romance. Instead, he exclaimed, "What the devil is this—*Hold your tongue?* You'd better have an explanation, young man."

"This is a warning Miss Acton received on the street this morning," I said, "as you well know, Mr. Banwell, since you wrote it." A stunned silence followed. "Mr. Mayor, Mr. Littlemore: this man is the criminal you are looking for. Miss Acton remembered the attack on her just minutes before you came in. I advise you to arrest him at once."

"How dare you?" said Banwell.

"What is this—this person?" asked Mildred Acton, referring to me. "Where does he come from?"

"Dr. Younger," said Mayor McClellan, "you do not appreciate the gravity of a false accusation. Withdraw it. If Miss Acton has told you this, her memory is playing a trick on her."

"Mr. Mayor, sir—" began Detective Littlemore.

"Not now, Littlemore," the mayor said calmly. "Doctor, you will withdraw your accusation, offer Mr. Banwell an apology, and tell us what Miss Acton has said to you."

"But Your Honor—" said the detective.

"Littlemore!" the mayor barked so furiously it drove Littlemore back a step. "Didn't you hear me?"

"Mayor McClellan," I broke in, "I don't understand. I have just told you Miss Acton remembers the attack. Your own detective seems to have something confirmatory to add. Miss Acton has positively identified Mr. Banwell as her assailant."

"We have only your word for that, Doctor—if that's what you are," said Banwell. He looked hard at Miss Acton; it seemed to me he was laboring strenuously to restrain a powerful emotion. "Nora, you know perfectly well I have done nothing to you. Tell them, Nora."

"Nora," said the girl's mother, "tell this young man he is under a misimpression."

"Nora dear?" said her father.

"Tell him, Nora," said Banwell.

"I won't tell him," answered the girl, but that is all she said.

"Mr. Mayor," I said, "you cannot allow Miss Acton to be cross-questioned by the man who attacked her—a man who has already murdered another girl."

"Younger, I am convinced you mean well," replied the mayor, "but you are wrong. George Banwell and I were together Sunday night, when Elizabeth Riverford was murdered. He was with me—do you hear it, *with me*—all that evening and night and well into Monday morning as well. Two hundred fifty miles out of town. He could not have killed anyone."

IN THE LIBRARY, after Jung's departure, curling tails of smoke wafted up to the ceiling. A servant removed glasses, replaced ashtrays, then quietly withdrew.

"Do we have him?" asked the balding man, who had been referred to as Sachs.

"Without doubt," answered Dana. "He is even weaker than I had imagined. And we have more than sufficient to destroy him in any event. Does Ochs have your remarks, Allen?"

"Oh, yes," answered the portly, sideburned gentleman with the thick lips. "He will publish mine the same day he interviews the Swiss."

"What about Matteawan?" asked Sachs.

"Leave that to me," Dana replied. "What remains is to block their other means of dissemination. Which, by tomorrow, we will have done."

EVEN AFTER HEARING the mayor exculpate him, I could not accept Banwell's innocence. Subjectively, that is. Objectively, I had no grounds for disbelief or protest.

Nora refused to go home. Her father pleaded. Her mother was indignant at what she called the girl's obstinacy. The mayor resolved the situation. Now that he had seen the note, he said, it was clear the hotel was no longer safe. But the Actons' home could be secured. Indeed, it could be made safer than could a large hotel with its many entrances. He would station policemen outside the house, front and back, day and night. Moreover, he reminded Miss Acton, she was still a minor: under the law, he would be obliged to effectuate her father's wishes, even against her will.

I thought Miss Acton would burst out in some way. Instead she gave in, but only on the condition that she be permitted to continue her medical treatment tomorrow morning. "Especially," she added, "now that I know my memory is not to be trusted." This she said with apparent sincerity, but it was impossible to say whether she was faulting the trustworthiness of her memory or rebuking those who refused to trust it.

She did not look at me after that, not even once. The silent ride down the elevator was excruciating, but Miss Acton held herself with a dignity lacking in her mother, who appeared to regard everything she encountered as a personal affront. An appointment was made for me to visit their house on Gramercy Park early the next day, and they set off in an automobile downtown. McClellan did the same. Banwell, casting a last glance in my direction, by no means benevolent, departed in a horse-drawn carriage, leaving Detective Littlemore and me on the sidewalk.

He turned to me. "She told you it was Banwell?"

"Yes," I said.

"And you believe her, don't you?"

"I do."

"Can I ask you something?" said Littlemore. "Say a girl loses her memory. Just comes up empty. Then her memory comes back. Can you put money on it, when it comes back? Can you bank on it?"

"No," I replied. "It could be false. It could be fantasy, mistaken for memory."

"But you believe her?"

"Yes."

"So what are you saying, Doc?"

"I don't know what I'm saying," I said. "Can I ask *you* something, Detective? What were you going to tell the mayor in Miss Acton's room?"

"I just wanted to remind him that Coroner Hugel—he's in charge of the case—thought Banwell was the killer too."

"Thought so?" I asked. "You mean he doesn't anymore?"

"Well, he can't anymore, not after what the mayor just said," Littlemore replied.

"Couldn't Banwell have attacked Miss Acton even if someone else killed the other girl?"

"Nope," answered the detective. "We've got proof. It was the same guy both times."

I went back inside, unsure of myself, my patient, my situation. Was it conceivable that McClellan was covering for Banwell? Would Nora be safe at her house? The front clerk called out my name. There was a letter for me, just delivered. It proved to be from G. Stanley Hall, president of Clark University. The letter was long— and deeply disturbing.

❧

OUTSIDE THE HOTEL MANHATTAN, Detective Littlemore made for the cabstand.

From the old hack last night, Littlemore knew that the black-haired man—the one who left the Balmoral at midnight on Sunday—had climbed into a red and green gas-powered taxi in front of the Hotel Manhattan. That piece of information told the detective a good deal. Only a decade previously, every taxi in Manhattan had been horse-drawn. By 1900, a hundred motorized taxis tooled around the city, but these were electrically powered. Weighed down by their eight-hundred-pound batteries, the electric taxis were popular but ponderous; passengers occasionally had to get out and help push when going up the rare steep incline. In 1907, the New York Taxicab Company launched the first fleet of gasoline cars for hire, equipped with meters so that riders could see the fare. These cabs were instant hits—hits, that is, with the better class, who alone could afford the fifty-cents-per-mile charge—and quickly came to outnumber all other cabs, electric and horse, in the city. You always knew a New York Taxicab when you saw one, because of its distinctive red and green paneling.

Several of these vehicles were parked at the Hotel Manhattan cabstand. The drivers told Littlemore to try the Allen garage on Fifty-seventh Street, between Eleventh and Twelfth avenues, where New York Taxicab had its main office and where he could easily find out who had been working the graveyard shift on Sunday. The detective's luck was good. Two hours later, he had answers. A driver named Luria had picked up a black-haired man in front of the Hotel Manhattan after midnight last Sunday. Luria remembered it distinctly, because the man had come not out of the hotel but out of a hackney. Littlemore also learned where the black-haired man had gone, and the detective went to that destination—a private house—himself. There his luck ran out.

The house was on Fortieth just off Broadway. It was a two-story affair, with a gaudy knocker and thick red curtains on its windows. Littlemore had to knock five or six times before an attractive young woman answered. The girl was considerably underdressed for the middle of the afternoon. When Littlemore explained that he was a police detective, she rolled her eyes and told him to wait.

He was shown to a parlor with thick Oriental carpets on the floor, a dazzling array of mirrors on the walls, and a smother of purple velour on the furniture. The odor of tobacco and alcohol clung to the folds of the curtains. A baby was crying upstairs. Five minutes later, another woman, older and quite fat, came down the red-carpeted stairs in a claret-colored robe.

"You've got a lot of nerve," said this woman, who introduced herself as Susan Merrill—Mrs. Susan Merrill. From a wall safe concealed behind a mirror, she withdrew a carved iron strongbox, which she opened with a key. She counted out fifty dollars. "Here. Now get out. I'm already late."

"I don't want your money, ma'am," said Littlemore.

"Oh, don't tell me. You make me sick, all of you. Greta, get back in here." The underdressed girl lounged in, yawning. Although it was a quarter past three, she had in fact been asleep until Littlemore knocked at the door. "Greta, the detective doesn't want our money. Take him to the green room. Make it quick, mister."

"I'm not here for that either, ma'am," said Littlemore. "I just want to ask you a question. There was a guy who came here late Sunday night. I'm trying to find him."

Mrs. Merrill eyed the detective dubiously. "Oh, so now you want my customers? What are you going to do, shake them down too?"

"You must know some bad policemen," said Littlemore.

"Is there any other kind?"

"A girl was killed Sunday night," Littlemore answered. "The guy who did it whipped her. Tied her up, cut her up pretty good too. Then he strangled her. I want that guy. That's it."

The woman drew her burgundy robe around her shoulders. She restored her money to the strongbox and shut it. "Was she a street-walker?"

"No," said the detective. "Rich girl. Really rich. Lived in a fancy building uptown."

"Well, isn't that a shame. What's it got to do with me?"

"This guy who came here," Littlemore answered. "We think he might be the killer."

"Do you have any idea, Detective, how many men come through here on a Sunday night?"

"This guy would have been by himself. Tall, black hair, carrying a black case or bag or something."

"Greta, do you remember anybody like that?"

"Let me think," mused the dreamy Greta. "No. Nobody."

"Well, what do you want from me?" said Mrs. Merrill. "You heard her."

"But the guy came here, ma'am. The cabbie left him off right out-side your door."

"Left him off? That doesn't mean he came in. I'm not the only house on the block."

Littlemore nodded slowly. It seemed to him that Greta was a lit-tle too blasé, and Mrs. Merrill a little too eager to see him leave.

CHAPTER THIRTEEN

SHE HAD ASKED me to kiss her.

I was walking across town on Forty-second Street, but in my mind's eye I kept seeing Nora Acton's parted lips. I kept feeling her soft throat in my hands. I heard her whisper those two words.

President Hall's letter was in my vest pocket. I should have had only one thought in my head: how to deal with the potential ruination not only of next week's conference at Clark but of Dr. Freud's entire reputation, at least in America. All I could see, however, was Miss Acton's mouth and closed eyes.

I didn't fool myself. I knew what her feelings for me were. I had seen it before, too many times. One of my Worcester patients, a girl named Rachel, used to insist on disrobing down to her waist at every analytic session. Each time she offered a new reason: an irregular heartbeat, a rib she feared broken, a throbbing pain in her lower back. And Rachel was just one of many. In all these cases I had never resisted temptation—because I had never been tempted. On the contrary, the emergence of seductive machinations in my analysands struck me as macabre.

Had my patients been more attractive, I doubt their behavior would have inspired in me the same feelings of unwholesomeness. I have no particular virtue. But these women weren't attractive. Most of them were old enough to be my mother. Their desire repulsed me. Rachel was different. She was appealing: long legs, dark eyes—a little close-set, to be sure—and a figure that would have been called good, or better than good. But she was aggressively neurotic, which has never enticed me.

I used to imagine other girls, prettier ones, consulting me. I used to imagine indescribable—but not impossible—events in my office. Thus it came to pass that whenever a new psychoanalytic patient first called on me, I found myself assessing her comeliness. As a result, I began to repulse myself, to the point where I wondered if I ought to continue holding myself out as an analyst. I hadn't taken on a new analytic patient all this summer—until Miss Acton.

And now she had invited me to kiss her. There was no hiding, from myself, what I wanted to do with her. I had never experienced so violent a desire to overpower, to possess. I very much doubted I was in the throes of the counter-transference. To be candid, I had felt the same desire practically the first instant I laid eyes on Miss Acton. But for her the case was clearly different. She was not just recovering from the trauma of a physical attack. More than this, the girl was suffering a transference of the most virulent strain.

She had shown every sign of disliking me until the moment when she felt her suppressed memories flooding back, released by the physical pressure I had applied to her neck. At that moment, I became for her some kind of masterful figure. Before then, dislike was too mild a term. She hated me; she said so. After that moment, she wanted to give herself to me—or so she thought. For it was plain as newsprint, sorry though I was to admit it, that this love she felt, if love it could be called, was an artifact, a fiction created by the intensity of the analytic encounter.

Although I have no memory of crossing Sixth or Seventh Avenue, I found myself abruptly in the middle of Times Square. I went to the roof garden at Hammerstein's Victoria, where I was to have met Freud and the others for lunch. The roof garden was a theater in its own right, with a raised stage, terraces, box seats, and a roof of its own fifty feet overhead. The show, a high-wire act, was still going. The tightrope artist was a bonneted French girl, clad in a sky-blue dress and blue stockings. Each time she threw out her parasol for balance, the well-dressed women in the audience would scream in unison. I have never understood why audiences react that way: surely the person on the high wire is only pretending to be in danger.

I couldn't find the others. I was obviously too late; they must have gone on. So I went back up to Brill's building on Central Park West, where I knew they would eventually return. No one answered the buzzer. I crossed the street and took a seat on a bench, quite by myself, Central Park behind me. From my briefcase I pulled out Hall's letter. After rereading it at least a half dozen times, I finally put it away and took out some other reading matter—I need hardly say what it was.

✑

"You have them?" Coroner Hugel demanded of Louis Riviere, head of photographic facilities, in the basement of police headquarters.

"I am varnishing now," called out Riviere, standing over a sink in his darkroom.

"But I left the plates for you at seven this morning," Hugel protested. "Surely they're ready."

"Be tranquil, if you please," said Riviere, switching on a light. "Come in. You can look at them."

Hugel entered the darkroom and pored over the pictures with nervous excitement. He went through the plates rapidly, one by one, casting aside those in which he was not interested. Then he stopped, gazing at a close-up of the girl's neck, showing a prominent circular mark.

"What's this, here, on the girl's throat?" he asked.

"A bruise, no?" said Riviere.

"No ordinary bruise would be so perfectly circular," the coroner replied, taking off his glasses and bringing the picture within an inch of his face. The photograph showed a grainy, round black spot against an almost white neck. "Louis, where is your glass?"

Riviere produced what looked like an inverted shot glass. The coroner snatched it from his hands, placed it on the photograph where the dark spot was, and put his eye to it. "I have him!" he cried. "I have him!"

From outside the darkroom came Detective Littlemore's voice. "What is it, Mr. Hugel?"

"Littlemore," said Hugel, "you're here. Excellent."

"You asked me to come, Mr. Hugel."

"Yes, and now you'll see why," said the coroner, gesturing for Littlemore to look through Riviere's magnifying glass. The detective complied. Under magnification, the grainy lines inside the black circle resolved into a more distinct figuring.

"Say," said Littlemore, "are those letters?"

"They are indeed," replied the coroner triumphantly. "Two letters."

"There's something funny about them," Littlemore went on. "They don't look right. The second one could be a J. The first one—I don't know."

"They don't look right because they are backward, Mr. Littlemore," said the coroner. "Louis, explain to the detective why the letters are backward."

Riviere looked through the glass. "I see them: two letters, interlocking. If they are backward, then the one on the right, which Monsieur Littlemore called J, is not J but G."

"Correct," said the coroner.

"But why," Riviere asked, "should the writing be backward?"

"Because, gentlemen, it is an imprint left on the girl's neck by the murderer's tiepin." Hugel paused for dramatic effect. "Recall that the murderer used his own silk tie to strangle Miss Riverford. He was clever enough to remove that tie from the murder scene. But he made one mistake. On his tie, when he committed the act, was his pin—a pin embossed with his own monogram. By chance, the pin was in direct contact with the soft, sensitive skin of the girl's throat. Because of the extreme and lengthy pressure, the monogram left an impression on her neck, just as a tight ring will leave an indentation on the finger. This imprint, gentlemen, records the murderer's initials as definitively as if he had left us a calling card, except in mirror image. The letter on the right is a reverse G, because G is the first initial of the man who killed Elizabeth Riverford. The letter on the left is a reverse B, because that man was George Banwell. Now we know why he had to steal her body from the morgue. He saw the telltale bruise on her neck and knew I would eventually decipher it. What he did not foresee was that stealing the corpse would be useless—because of this photograph!"

"Mr. Hugel, sir?" said Detective Littlemore.

The coroner heaved a sigh. "Shall I explain it again, Detective?"

"Banwell didn't do it, Mr. Hugel," Littlemore said. "He's got an alibi."

"Impossible," said Hugel. "His apartment is on the same floor of the very same building. The murder occurred between midnight and two on a Sunday. Banwell would have returned from any engagement before that."

"He's got an alibi," Littlemore repeated, "and what an alibi. He was with the mayor all Sunday night until early Monday morning—out of town."

"What?" said the coroner.

"There is another flaw in your argument," interjected Riviere. "You are not so familiar with photographs as I. You took these pictures yourself?"

"Yes," replied the coroner, frowning. "Why?"

"These are ferrotypes. Most retrograde. You are fortunate I keep a supply of iron sulfate. The image you have here differs from the reality. Left is right, and right is left."

"What?" said Hugel again.

"A reverse image. So if the mark on the girl's neck is the reverse of the true monogram, then the photograph is the reverse of the reverse."

"A double reverse?" asked Littlemore.

"A double negative," said Riviere. "And a double negative is a positive. Meaning that this picture shows the monogram as it would actually look, not a reverse of it."

"It can't be," cried Hugel, more injured than disbelieving, as if Littlemore and Riviere were deliberately trying to rob him.

"But undoubtedly it is, Monsieur Hugel," said Riviere.

"So that *was* a J," said Detective Littlemore. "The guy's named Johnson or something. What's the first letter?"

Riviere put his eye to the glass again. "It does not look like a letter at all. But it is possibly an *E*, I would like to say—or no, maybe a *C*."

"Charles Johnson," said the detective.

The coroner only stood where he was, repeating, "It can't be."

❧

AT LAST A TAXI pulled up at Brill's building, and the four men—Freud, Brill, Ferenczi, and Jones—piled out. It turned out they had gone to a moving-picture show after lunch, a cops-and-robbers affair with wild chases. Ferenczi could not stop talking about it. He had, Brill told me, actually dived out of his seat when a locomotive appeared to steam straight at the audience; it was his first motion picture.

Freud asked me if I wanted to take an hour in the park with him to report on Miss Acton. I said I would like nothing more but that something else had come up; I had received unpleasant news in the post.

"You're not the only one," said Brill. "Jones got a wire this morning from Morton Prince up in Boston. He was arrested yesterday."

"Dr. Prince?" I was shocked.

"On obscenity charges," Brill continued. "The obscenity in question: two articles he was about to publish describing cures of hysteria effected through the psychoanalytic method."

"I shouldn't worry about Prince," said Jones. "He was mayor of Boston once, you know. He'll come out right."

Morton Prince was never mayor of Boston—his father was—but Jones was so definite I didn't want to embarrass him. Instead I asked, "How could the police know what Prince was planning to publish?"

"Exactly what we have been wondering," said Ferenczi.

"I never trusted Sidis," added Brill, referring to a doctor on the editorial board of Prince's journal. "But we must remember it's Boston. They'll arrest a chicken breast sandwich there if it's not properly dressed. They arrested that Australian girl—Kellerman, the swimmer—because her bathing costume didn't cover her knees."

"I'm afraid my news is even worse, gentlemen," I said, "and it concerns Dr. Freud directly. The lectures next week are in doubt. Dr. Freud has been personally attacked—I mean, his name has been attacked—in Worcester. I cannot tell you how sorry I am to be the messenger."

I proceeded to summarize as much as I could of President Hall's letter without entering into the sordid accusations against Freud. An agent representing an exceedingly wealthy New York family met with Hall yesterday, offering a donation to Clark University that Hall described as "most handsome." The family was prepared to fund a fifty-bed hospital for mental and nervous disorders, paying for a new building as well as all the most modern equipment, nurses, staff, and salaries sufficient to attract the best neurologists from New York and Boston.

"That would cost half a million dollars," said Brill.

"Considerably more," I replied. "It would make us in one blow the leading psychiatric institute in the nation. We would surpass McLean."

"Who is the family?"

"Hall doesn't say," I replied to Brill.

"But is this permitted?" asked Ferenczi. "A private family paying a public university?"

"It is called philanthropy," answered Brill. "It is why American universities are so rich. And why they will soon overtake the greatest European universities."

"Bosh," ejaculated Jones. "Never."

"Go on, Younger," said Freud. "There is nothing amiss in what you have told us so far."

"The family has stipulated two conditions," I continued. "A member of the family is apparently a well-known physician with views about psychology. The first condition is that psychoanalysis cannot be practiced at the new hospital or taught anywhere in Clark's curriculum. The second is that Dr. Freud's lectures next week must be canceled. Otherwise the gift will go to another hospital—in New York."

Various exclamations of dismay and denunciation followed. Only Freud remained stoic. "What does Hall say he will do?" he asked.

"I'm afraid that is not all," I said. "Nor is it the worst. President Hall was given a dossier on Dr. Freud."

"Go on, for God's sake," Brill scolded me. "Don't play hide-and-seek."

I explained that this dossier purported to document instances of licentious—indeed, criminal—behavior by Freud. President Hall was told that Freud's gross misconduct would soon be reported by the New York press. The family was certain that Hall, after reading the contents, would agree that Freud's appearance at Clark must be canceled for the good of the university. "President Hall did not send the file itself," I said, "but his letter summarizes the charges. May I give you the letter, Dr. Freud? President Hall asked me specifically to say he felt you had a right to be informed of everything said against you."

"Sporting of him," remarked Brill.

I don't know why—perhaps because I was the letter's bearer—but I felt responsible for the unfolding disaster. It was as if I had personally invited Freud to Clark, only to destroy him. I was not anxious solely for Freud's sake. I had selfish reasons for not wanting to see this man brought down, on whose authority I had staked so many of my own beliefs—indeed, so much of my own life. None of us is saintly, but somehow I had formed the belief years ago that Freud was different from the rest of us. I imagined that he (unlike myself) had through psychological insight acceded to a plane above the baser temptations. I hoped to heaven the accusations in Hall's letter were false, but they had that degree of detail that imparts the ring of truth.

"There is no need for me to read the letter privately," said Freud. "Tell us what has been said against me. I have no secrets from anyone here."

I started with the least of the charges: "You are said not to be married to the woman you live with, although you hold her out to the world as your wife."

"But that's not Freud," cried Brill. "It's Jones."

"I beg your pardon," Jones replied indignantly.

"Oh, come, Jones," Brill said. "Everyone knows you're not married to Loë."

"Freud not married," said Jones, looking behind his left shoulder. "How absurd."

"What else?" asked Freud.

"That you were discharged from employment at a respected hospital," I continued, awkwardly, "because you would not stop discussing sexual fantasies with twelve- and thirteen-year-old girls, who were in the hospital for the treatment of purely physical, not nervous, conditions."

"But it's Jones they're talking about!" exclaimed Brill.

Jones had taken a sudden and minute interest in the architecture of Brill's apartment building.

"That you have been sued by the husband of one of your female patients and shot at by another," I said.

"Jones again!" Brill called out.

"That you are currently having a sexual affair," I went on, "with your teenage housekeeper."

Brill looked from Freud to me to Ferenczi to Jones, who was now gazing skyward, apparently studying the migratory patterns of Manhattan's avian species. "Ernest?" said Brill. "Surely you're not. Tell us you're not."

A series of musical throat-clearing noises came from Jones, but no verbal response.

"You're disgusting," Brill said to Jones. "Really disgusting."

"Is that the end of them, Younger?" asked Freud.

"No, sir," I answered. The final allegation was the worst of all. "There is one more: that you are currently engaged in another sexual liaison, this one with a patient of yours, a nineteen-year-old Russian girl, a medical student. Your affair is said to be so notorious that the girl's mother wrote you, begging you not to ruin her daughter. The dossier claims to reproduce the letter you wrote the mother in reply. In your letter, or what they say is your letter, you demand money from the mother in exchange for—for refraining from further sexual relations with the patient."

After I had finished, no one spoke for a considerable time. At last Ferenczi burst out, "But that one's Jung, for heaven's sake!"

"Sándor!" Freud rejoined sharply.

"Jung wrote that?" asked Brill. "To a patient's mother?"

Ferenczi threw his hand over his mouth. "Oop," he said. "But Freud, you can't let them think it's you. They are going to tell newspapers. I am imagining headlines already."

I was too: FREUD CLEARED OF ALL CHARGES.

"So," Brill mused darkly, "we are under attack in Boston, in Worcester, and New York at same time. It cannot be a coincidence."

"What is attack in New York?" asked Ferenczi.

"The Jeremiah and Sodom and Gomorrah business," Brill answered, irritably. "Those two messages weren't the only ones I've received. There have been many."

We were all surprised and asked Brill to explain.

"It began right after I started translating Freud's hysteria book," he said. "How they knew I was doing it is a mystery. But the very week I started, I received the first one, and it's been getting worse ever since. They turn up when I least expect them. I am being threatened, I feel sure of it. Every time it's some murderous biblical passage—always about Jews and lust and fire. It makes me think of a pogrom."

No one sought to obstruct Littlemore this time as he climbed the stairs at 782 Eighth Avenue. It was four o'clock—dinner preparation hour at the restaurant, from which came shrieks of Cantonese, punctuated by the sizzling hiss of chicken parts plunged into burning oil. Littlemore, who hadn't eaten since morning, wouldn't have minded some pork chop suey himself. He felt eyes upon him at every landing but saw no one. He heard someone running in a hallway above and a whispering of voices. At Apartment 4C, his knock yielded the same result it had before: nothing but the sound of hurried footfalls retreating down the back stairs.

Littlemore looked at his watch. He lit a cigarette to combat the odors wafting through the corridor, hoping he would get to Betty's in time to ask her to dinner. A few minutes later, Officer John Reardon came trooping up the stairs with a submissive, frightened Chinese man in tow. "Just like you said, Detective," said Officer Reardon. "Barreled out the back door like his pants were on fire."

Littlemore surveyed the miserable Chong Sing. "Don't want to talk to me, Mr. Chong, do you?" he asked. "Suppose we have a look around your place. Open up."

Chong Sing was much shorter than Littlemore or Reardon. He was of stocky build, with a flat, broad nose and rutted skin. He gestured helplessly, trying to indicate that he spoke no English.

"Open it," Littlemore commanded, banging on the locked door.

The Chinaman produced a key and opened the door. His one-room apartment was a model of order and cleanliness. There was not a mote of dust or a teacup out of place. Two low cots, with seedy coverings, apparently did triple duty as beds, sofas, and tables. The walls were bare. Several sets of incense sticks burned in one corner, giving an acrid tang to the hot, motionless air.

"All cleaned up for us," said Littlemore, taking it in. "Thoughtful. Missed a spot, though." With an uptick of his chin, Littlemore signaled overhead. Both Chong Sing and Officer Reardon looked up. On the low ceiling was a thick blackish smudge, almost three feet in length, over each of the two cots.

"What's that?" asked the policeman.

"Smoke stain," answered Littlemore. "Opium. Jack, you notice anything funny about that window?"

Reardon glanced at the room's one small casement window, which was closed. "No. What about it?" he asked.

"It's closed," answered Littlemore. "A hundred degrees, and the window's closed. See what's outside."

Reardon opened the window and leaned out into a narrow air-shaft. He returned with an armful of items he found on a ledge underneath: a glass-covered oil lamp, half a dozen long pipes, bowls, and a needle. Chong Sing appeared to be in complete confusion, shaking his head, looking from the detective to the police officer and back to the detective.

"You run an opium joint here, don't you, Mr. Chong?" said the detective. "You ever go up to Miss Riverford's apartment at the Balmoral?"

"Hah?" said Chong Sing, shrugging helplessly.

"How'd you get red clay on your shoes?" the detective persevered.

"Hah?"

"Jack," said Littlemore, "take Mr. Chong to the lockup at Forty-seventh. Tell Captain Post he's an opium dealer."

When Officer Reardon seized him by the arm, Chong spoke at last. "Wait. I tell you. I only live in apartment in daytime. I don't know opium. I never see opium before."

"Sure," said Littlemore. "Get him out of here, Jack."

"Hokay, hokay," said Chong. "I tell you who sells opium. Hokay?"

"Get him out of here," said the detective.

At the sight of Reardon's handcuffs, Chong cried out, "Wait! I tell you something else. I show you something. You follow me hallway. I show you what you looking for."

Chong's voice had changed. He sounded genuinely afraid now. Littlemore signaled Reardon to let Chong precede them into the dark, narrow corridor. From two flights below, the clattering of the restaurant could still be heard, and as they followed the Chinaman down the hall, past the stairwell, Littlemore began to hear the twanging, dissonant chords of Chinese string music. The smell of meat grew stronger. Every door was slivered open to allow the residents within to observe the goings-on—every door but one. The lone closed door belonged to the room at the farthest end of the corridor. Here Chong stopped. "Inside," he said. "Inside."

"Who lives here?" asked the detective.

"My cousin," said Chong. "Leon. He live here before. Now no one."

The door was locked. There was no response to Littlemore's knock, but the moment the detective got close enough to rap his knuckles, he knew the overpowering meat odor was not coming from the restaurant after all. He drew from his pocket two thin metal picks. Littlemore was adept with locked doors. He had this one open in short order.

The room, though identical in size, contrasted in every other way with Chong Sing's. Gaudy red ornaments adorned every surface. A dozen vases, large and small, were scattered about, most of them carved in the form of dragons and demons. On the windowsill was a lacquered rouge box, with a round face mirror perched behind it; on a dresser, a painted statuette of the Virgin and Child. Nearly every square inch of wall was covered with framed photographs, all depicting a Chinese man who himself offered a stark contrast to Chong Sing. The man in the photographs was tall and arrestingly handsome, with an aquiline nose and a smooth, unblemished complexion. He wore an American jacket, shirt, and tie. Nearly all the pictures showed this man with young women—different young women.

What most commanded attention, however, was a single massive object planted squarely in the center of the room: a large closed trunk. It was the kind of trunk that well-to-do travelers use, with leather sides and brass hinges. Its dimensions were these: two feet in height, two in depth, three in length. Coils of stiff awning rope bound it shut.

The air was fetid. Littlemore could hardly breathe. The Chinese music was coming from the room directly above them; the detective found it difficult to think. The trunk seemed, impossibly, to be rippling in the thick atmosphere. Littlemore opened his pocket knife. Officer Reardon had one too. Together, wordlessly, they approached the chest and began to saw at the heavy ropes. A crowd of Chinese, many with handkerchiefs pressed against their mouths, gathered at the doorway to watch.

"Put your knife away, Jack," said Littlemore to Officer Reardon. "Just keep your eye on Chong."

The detective worked at the ropes. When he severed the last coil, the lid of the trunk burst open. Reardon staggered back, either from surprise or from the explosion of rank gas that escaped from the trunk's interior. Littlemore covered his mouth with his sleeve but remained where he was. Inside the chest were three things: a ladies' hat crowned with a stuffed bird; a thick stack of letters and envelopes tied together with string; and the crumpled body of a young woman, viciously decomposed, clad only in underthings, a silver pendant on her chest and a white silk tie tightly wound around her neck.

Officer Reardon was no longer keeping an eye on Chong Sing. Instead he was close to passing out. Seeing this, Chong slipped back into the crowd of murmuring Chinese and out the open door.

⁓

WE TRUDGED SILENTLY up the four flights of stairs to Brill's apartment, each of us wondering, I assume, how to respond to the difficulties in Worcester. We had several hours to spend before a dinner party to which Smith Jelliffe, Brill's publisher, had invited us. At the fifth-floor landing, Ferenczi commented on a peculiar smell of burning leaves or paper. "Someone is maybe cremating a dead person in their kitchen?" he suggested helpfully.

Brill opened his door. What we saw inside was unexpected.

It was snowing inside Brill's apartment—or seemed to be. A fine white dust drifted about the room, swirling in the air currents created by our opening the door; the floor was covered with the stuff. All of Brill's books, together with the tables, windowsills, and chairs, were coated. The smell of fire was everywhere. Rose Brill stood in the middle of the room with broom and dustpan, covered head to foot in a white rime, sweeping up as much as she could.

"I just got here," she cried. "Shut the door, for heaven's sake. What is it?"

I gathered some in my hands. "It's ash," I said.

"You left something cooking?" Ferenczi asked her.

"Nothing," she answered, brushing the white grains from her eyes.

"Someone put it here," said Brill. He wandered about the room in a trance, his hands outstretched before him, alternately grabbing at the ash and waving it away. Suddenly he turned to Rose. "Look at her. Look at her."

"What is it?" asked Freud.

"She's a pillar of salt."

❧

WHEN CAPTAIN POST arrived with reinforcements from the West Forty-seventh Street station, he ordered—over Detective Littlemore's objections—the arrest of a half dozen Chinese men at 782 Eighth Avenue, including the manager of the restaurant and two patrons who had the misfortune to come upstairs to see what the commotion was. The body was carted off to the morgue and a double manhunt begun.

Littlemore's first thought was that he had found Elizabeth Riverford's missing corpse, but there was too much decomposition. He was no pathologist, but he doubted Miss Riverford, murdered on Sunday night, could have putrefied so thoroughly by Wednesday. Mr. Hugel, thought Littlemore, would know for sure.

Meanwhile, the detective went through the letters he had found inside the trunk. They were love letters, more than thirty of them. All began *Dearest Leon*; all were signed *Elsie*. Neighbors differed on the name of the room's inhabitant. Some called him Leon Ling; others said he went by William Leon. He managed a Chinatown restaurant, but no one had seen him for a month. He spoke excellent English and wore only American suits.

Littlemore examined the photographs hanging on the walls. The building's occupants confirmed that the man in the pictures was Leon, but they did not know or would not say who the women were. Littlemore noticed that every single woman was white. Then he noticed something else.

The detective took down one of the photographs. It showed Leon standing, smiling, between two very attractive young women. At first the detective thought he must be mistaken. When he was convinced he was not, he put the picture into his vest pocket, made an arrangement to meet Captain Post the next day, and left the building.

The late afternoon air was still uncomfortably hot and muggy, but it was like a heavenly garden compared to the chamber from which Littlemore emerged. It was just past five when he got to Betty's apartment. She wasn't home. Her mother tried frantically to make the detective understand where "Benedetta" was, but as the woman was speaking Italian, and rapidly at that, he could make neither heads nor tails of it. At last, one of Betty's little brothers came to the door and translated: Betty was in jail.

All Mrs. Longobardi knew—because a nice Jewish girl had come to tell her—was that there had been trouble at the factory where Betty started work today. Some of the girls had been taken away, including Betty. "Taken away?" asked Littlemore. "Where?"

The mother didn't know.

Littlemore ran to the Fifty-ninth Street subway station. He stood all the way downtown, too worked up to take a seat. At police headquarters, he learned that strikers had hit one of the big garment factories in Greenwich Village, picketers had started smashing windows, and the police had arrested the worst couple dozen of them to clear the streets. All the rowdies were now in jail. The men were being held in the Tombs, the girls at the Jefferson Market.

CHAPTER FOURTEEN

IN THE 1870s, a fanciful profusion of Victorian high Gothic sprang up on a triangular plot of land at the corner of Tenth Street and Sixth Avenue, contrasting incongruously with the otherwise disreputable workingman's neighborhood. The new polychromatic courthouse was a jumble of steeply sloping roofs, with gables and pinnacles jutting out at every height and angle; its watchtower was crowned by a 170-foot turret. A five-floor prison in the same style was attached to this courthouse, and to the jail was attached another grand edifice, which housed a marketplace. Collectively, the place was known as Jefferson Market; the conceit was that institutions of law and order ought not to be sequestered from those of daily life.

By day, criminal cases of great import were tried in the Jefferson Market courthouse. After hours, the same tribunal became the city's Night Court, where vice cases were processed. As a result, the Jefferson Market jail was occupied largely by prostitutes awaiting disposition and punishment. It was here, in this jail, that Littlemore found a frazzled but unhurt Betty on Wednesday evening.

She was in a large, crowded holding cell in the basement. Some twenty-five or thirty women were detained within, standing in small knots or sitting on long narrow benches against the walls.

The cell was divided between two classes of prisoner. There were about fifteen young women in working outfits like Betty's—simple dark, solid-colored skirts, down to their ankles, of course, and white long-sleeved blouses. These prisoners were from the shirtwaist factory where Betty had for half a day been an employee. A few of these girls were as young as thirteen.

Their colleagues were another dozen women, of various ages and far more colorful in their accoutrements and cosmetics. Most were loud and conspicuously at their ease, being familiar with the surroundings. One, however, was louder than the others, complaining to the guards and demanding to know how a woman in her circumstances could be kept in jail. Littlemore recognized her at once; it was Mrs. Susan Merrill. She was the only one with a chair, which the others had deferentially yielded to her. Over her shoulders was a burgundy wrap, in her arms a baby, sleeping peacefully despite the uproar.

Littlemore's badge got him inside the jailhouse, but it couldn't get Betty out. They stood only a few inches from each other, separated by the floor-to-ceiling iron bars, speaking quietly. "Your first day of work, Betty," Littlemore said, "and you went on strike?"

She had not gone on strike. When Betty arrived at the factory that morning, she went directly to the ninth floor and joined a hundred other girls sewing. There were, however, at least fifty empty stools in front of idle sewing machines. What had happened was this: the day before, a hundred fifty seamstresses had been fired for being "union sympathizers." That evening, in response, the International Ladies Garment Workers Union called a strike against Betty's factory. As the next morning wore on, a small band of laborers and unionists gathered in the street below, shouting up to the workers on the floors above.

"They called us scabs," Betty explained. "Now I know why they hired me so quick—they were replacing the union girls. I couldn't be a scab, Jimmy, could I?"

"I guess not," said Littlemore, "but what did they want to go and strike for anyway?"

"Oh, you wouldn't believe it. First of all, it's hot, like a furnace. Then they charge the girls rent—for everything: lockers, sewing machines, needles, stools to sit on. You don't get half the pay they promise you. Jimmy, there was a girl there worked seventy-two hours last week, and she made three dollars. Three dollars! That's—that's—how much is that?"

"Four cents an hour," said Littlemore. "That's bad."

"And that's not the worst thing either. They lock all the doors to keep the girls working; you can't even go to the bathroom."

"Geez, Betty, you should of just left. You didn't have to go and picket, with people smashing windows and all."

Betty was half indignant, half confused. "I didn't picket, Jimmy."

"Well, what did they arrest you for?"

"'Cause I quit. They *told* us we'd go to jail if we quit, but I didn't believe them. And nobody was smashing windows. The policemen were just beating people up."

"Those weren't policemen."

"Oh, yes, they were."

"Oh, boy," said Littlemore. "I got to get you out of here." He beckoned to one of the guards and explained to him that Betty was his girl and wasn't part of the strike at all; she was in the lockup by mistake. At the words "my girl," Betty looked down at the floor and smiled with embarrassment.

The guard, a pal of Littlemore's, answered penitently that his hands were tied. "It ain't me, Jimmy," he said. "You got to talk to Becker."

"Beck?" asked Littlemore, his eyes lighting up. "Is Beck here?"

The guard led Littlemore down the hall to a room where five men were drinking, smoking, and playing a noisy game of cards beneath a flickering electric bulb. One of them was Sergeant Charles Becker, a bullet-headed fireplug of a man with a powerful baritone. Becker, a fifteen-year veteran on the force, worked the most vice-ridden precinct in Manhattan, the Tenderloin, where the city's glittering casinos and brothels, including Susan Merrill's, mixed with the gaudiest lobster palaces and vaudevilles. Becker's presence at the jail was a stroke of good fortune for Littlemore, who had spent six months as a beat officer in Becker's squad.

"Hey, Beck," Littlemore called out.

"Littlemouse!" boomed Becker, dealing cards. "Boys, meet my little brother detective from downtown. Jimmy, this here's Gyp, Whitey, Lefty, and Dago—you remember Dago, don't you?"

"Dago," said the detective.

"Couple two-three years ago," Becker told his cronies, referring to Littlemore, "this guy solves a pump-and-jump for me. Hands me the perp"—this was pronounced *poyp*—"who's been paying the price ever since. They always pay the price, boys. What you doing here, Jimmy, birdwatching?"

Becker heard him out, nodding, never taking his eyes from the poker table. With the roar of a man who savors a grand display of magnanimity, he ordered the guards to let out the detective's bird. Littlemore thanked Becker profoundly and hurried back to the cell, where he collected Betty. On their way out, Littlemore poked his head into the card room and thanked Becker again. "Say, Beck," he said. "One more favor?"

"Name it, little brother," replied Becker.

"There's a lady in there with a baby. Any chance we could let her out too?"

Becker stubbed out a cigarette. His voice remained casual, but the jocularity of Becker's cronies suddenly came to a halt. "A lady?" asked Becker.

Littlemore knew something was wrong, but he didn't know what.

"He's talking about Susie, boss," said Gyp, whose real name was Horowitz.

"Susie? Susie Merrill's not in my jail, is she, Whitey?" said Becker.

"She's in there, boss," answered Whitey, whose real name was Seidenschner.

"You got something going with Susie, Jimmy?"

"No, Beck," said Littlemore. "I just thought—with her having a baby and all—"

"Uh-huh," said Becker.

"Forget I said it," Littlemore put in. "I mean, if she—"

Becker bellowed to the guards to let Susie out. He added to this command several choice imprecations, expressing outrage at a baby's being locked up in his jail and yelling that if there was "any more babes" in the lockup in future, they should be brought directly to him. This remark produced a gale of laughter from his crew. Littlemore decided he had better go. He thanked Becker a third time—this one generating no reply—and led Betty away.

Tenth Street was nearly deserted. A breeze stirred from the west. On the jailhouse steps, in the shadow of the massive Victorian edifice, Betty stopped. "Do you know that woman?" she asked. "The one with the baby?"

"Kind of."

"But Jimmy, she's a—she's a madam."

"I know," said Littlemore, grinning. "I've been to her place."

Betty slapped the detective across the jaw.

"Ow," said Littlemore. "I only went there to ask her some questions about the Riverford murder."

"Oh, Jimmy, why didn't you say so?" asked Betty. She put her hands to her face, then his. She smiled. "I'm sorry."

They embraced. They were still embracing a minute later, when the heavy oaken doors to the jail creaked open and a shaft of light fell on them. Susan Merrill was in the doorway, burdened with the baby and a hat of enormous proportions. Littlemore helped her out the door. Betty asked to hold the baby, whom the older woman willingly gave over.

"So you're the one who sprung me," Susie said to Littlemore. "I guess you figure I owe you something now?"

"No, ma'am."

Susie cocked her head to get a better look at the detective. Reclaiming the baby from Betty, she said, in a whisper so faint Littlemore could hardly hear it, "You're going to get yourself killed."

Neither Littlemore nor Betty responded.

"I know who you're looking for," Susie went on, the words barely audible. "March 18, 1907."

"What?"

"I know who, and I know what. You don't know, but I know. I ain't doing nothin' for free, though."

"What about March 18, 1907?"

"You find out. And you *get* him," she hissed, with a venom so violent she put a hand over the baby's face as if to protect her from it.

"What about that day?" Littlemore pressed again.

"Ask next door," whispered Susie Merrill, before disappearing into the gathering dusk.

❧

ROSE SWEPT US out of the apartment—a kindness on her part. She certainly didn't want Freud involved in cleaning up. As for Brill, he looked as numb as a soldier with DaCosta's syndrome. He would not be coming to dinner, he said, and asked us to make an excuse for him.

Jones took the subway to his hotel, which was farther downtown and less expensive than ours, while Freud, Ferenczi, and I decided to walk to the Manhattan, cutting through the park to do so. It is extraordinary how empty New York City's largest park can be in the evening. At first we traded hypotheses about the extraordinary scene in Brill's apartment; then Freud asked Ferenczi and me how he ought to reply to President Hall's letter.

Ferenczi declared that we must send a denial at once, preferably by wire, explaining that the misconduct alleged against Freud was actually committed by Jones and Jung. The only question, as Ferenczi saw it, was whether Hall would take our word for it.

"You know Hall, Younger," said Freud. "What is your opinion?"

"President Hall would accept our word," I answered, meaning that he would accept mine. "But I have been wondering, Dr. Freud, whether that might not be precisely what they want you to do."

"Who?" asked Ferenczi.

"Whoever is behind this," I said.

"I am not following," said Ferenczi.

"I see what Younger means," Freud replied. "Whoever did this must know these allegations concern Jones and Jung, not myself. So: they induce me to incriminate my friends, at which point Hall can no longer say he is confronted by mere rumor. On the contrary, I will have corroborated the accusation, and Hall will be obliged to take responsible measures. Possibly he bars Jones and Jung from speaking next week. I keep my lectures, at the expense of disgracing two of my followers—the two best placed to carry my ideas to the world."

"But you cannot say nothing," Ferenczi protested, "as if you are guilty party."

Freud considered. "We will deny the charges—but that is all we will do. I will send Hall a short letter stating the facts: I am married, I have never been dismissed from employment at any hospital, I have never been shot at, and so on. Younger, will that put you in an awkward position?"

I understood his question. He wanted to know if I would feel bound to inform Hall that while Freud was innocent of the charges, Jones and Jung were not. Naturally, I would do no such thing. "Not at all, sir," I answered.

"Good," Freud concluded. "After that, we leave it to Hall. If, for the sake of this 'handsome donation,' Hall is prepared to keep the truths of psychoanalysis from being taught at his university, then—you will forgive me, Younger—he is not an ally worth having, and America can go to the dogs."

"President Hall will never agree to their terms," I said, with greater conviction than I felt.

❧

OUTSIDE THE JEFFERSON MARKET JAIL, Betty Longobardi had five words for Jimmy Littlemore. "Let's get out of here."

Littlemore was not so eager to leave. He led Betty toward Sixth Avenue, with its river of men and women streaming north on their way home from work. At the corner, a few steps from the ornate courthouse entrance, Littlemore stopped and wouldn't budge. Over the earthshaking roar of an elevated train, he told Betty excitedly about his eventful day.

"She said you were going to get killed, Jimmy," was Betty's reply, which struck Littlemore as less appreciative of his achievements than he had hoped.

"She also said we should ask next door," he answered. "It's got to be the courthouse. Come on; we're right here."

"I don't want to."

"It's a courthouse, Betty. Nothing can happen in a courthouse."

Back inside, Littlemore showed his badge to the clerk, who told them where the records office was but expressed the opinion that nobody was likely to be there at this hour. After climbing up two flights of stairs and working their way through an empty maze of corridors, Littlemore and Betty came upon a door marked REC-ORDS. The door was locked, the room behind it dark. Breaking and entering was not the detective's ordinary modus operandi, but under the circumstances he felt justified. Betty glanced around nervously.

Littlemore jimmied the lock. Shutting the door behind them,

he switched on an electric lamp. They were in a small office with one large desk. There was a rear exit. This was unlocked; it opened onto a more capacious storeroom. Here they saw cabinet after cabinet of labeled drawers. "There are no dates," said Betty. "Only letters."

"There'll be a calendar," said Littlemore. "There's always a calendar. Wait till I find it."

It did not take him long. He returned to the desk, where there were two typewriters, blotters, inkwells—and a stack of leather-bound ledgers, each more than two feet in width. Littlemore opened the first one. Every page within represented a day in the life of the New York Supreme Court, Trial Term, Parts I through III. The pages that Littlemore flipped through all indicated dates in 1909. He opened the second ledger, which proved to be the calendar of 1908, and then the third. Leafing through its pages, he quickly came to March 18, 1907. He saw dozens of lines of case names and numbers, set down by a practiced hand in pen and ink, often crossed out or overwritten. He read aloud:

"*Ten-fifteen A.M., day calendar, Part III: Wells v. Interborough R. T. Co. Truax, J.* Okay, Wells. We've got to find Wells." He rushed past Betty back to the storeroom, where in a drawer marked *W* he found the case of *Wells v. IRT:* a paper-clipped set of three pages. He looked through them. "This is nothing," he said. "Maybe some subway accident. They never even got to court."

He went back to the ledger. "*Bernstein v. same,*" he read. "*Mensinub v. same. Selxas v. same.* Boy, there's at least twenty of these IRT cases. I guess we have to look through them all."

"Maybe those aren't what we're looking for, Jimmy. Isn't there anything else?"

"*Ten-fifteen A.M., Trial Term: Tarbles v. Tarbles.* A divorce?"

"Is that all?" asked Betty.

"*Ten-thirty A.M., Trial Term, Part I, Criminal Term (January Term continued). Fitzgerald, J. People v. Harry K. Thaw.*"

They stared at each other. Betty and Littlemore recognized the name at once, as would anyone else in New York and nearly anyone in the country at that time. "He's the one—" said Betty.

"—who murdered the architect at Madison Square Garden," Littlemore finished. Then he realized why Betty had stopped: heavy treading could be heard down the hall.

"Who is that?" she whispered.

"Turn off the light," Littlemore instructed Betty, who was standing next to the lamp. She reached under the shade and fiddled nervously with the buttons, but the result of her efforts was to switch on another bulb. The footsteps stopped. Then they resumed; they were now undoubtedly approaching the records office.

"Oh, no," said Betty. "Let's hide in the storeroom."

"I don't think so," said Littlemore.

The footsteps grew close, halting just outside their door. The knob turned, and the door swung open. It was a short man in a fedora and a cheap-looking three-piece suit, the inner breast pocket of which bulged as if he were carrying a gun. "Ain't there no men's room?" he asked.

"Second floor," said Littlemore.

"Thanks," said the man, slamming the door behind him.

"Come on," said Littlemore, heading back into the filing room. The case of *People v. Thaw* occupied a good two dozen drawers. Littlemore found the trial transcript: there were thousands of pages in four-inch sheafs, bound by rubber bands. The transcript was illegible in places, with uneven letters, no punctuation, and whole sentences of garbled words. For the date of March 18, 1907, there were only fifty or sixty pages. Littlemore, flipping through them, quickly came upon several sheets of paper that looked different from the others: cleanly typed, organized into separate paragraphs, well punctuated.

"An affidavit," he said.

"Oh, my gosh," Betty replied. "Look!" She was pointing to the words *grasped me by the throat* and *whip*.

Littlemore hurriedly turned back to the affidavit's first page. It was dated October 27, 1903, and began, *Evelyn Nesbit, being duly sworn, says—*

"That's Thaw's wife, the showgirl," said Betty. Evelyn Nesbit had been described by more than one infatuated author of the time as the most beautiful girl that ever lived. She married Harry Thaw in 1905, a year before Thaw killed Stanford White.

"Before she was his wife," said Littlemore. They kept reading:

I reside at the Savoy Hotel, Fifth Avenue and Fifty-ninth Street, in the City of New York. I am 18 years of age, having been born on Christmas Day, in the year 1884.

For several months prior to June 1903, I had been at Dr. Bell's Hospital at West Thirty-third Street, where I had an operation performed on me for appendicitis, and during the month of June went to Europe at the request of Henry Kendall Thaw. Mr. Thaw and I traveled throughout Holland, stopping at various places to catch connecting trains, and then we went to Munich, Germany. We then traveled through the Bavarian Highlands, finally going to the Austrian Tyrol. During all this time the said Thaw and myself were known as husband and wife, and were represented by the said Thaw, and known, under the name of Mr. and Mrs. Dellis.

"The snake," said Betty.
"Well, at least he married her later," said Littlemore.

After traveling together about five or six weeks, the said Thaw rented a castle in the Austrian Tyrol, situated about halfway up a very isolated mountain. This castle must have been built centuries ago, as the rooms and windows are all old-fashioned. I was assigned a bedroom for my personal use.

The first night I was very tired, and went to bed right after dinner. In the morning I had breakfast with the said Thaw. After breakfast Mr. Thaw said he wished to tell me something, and asked me to step into my bedroom. I entered the room, when the said Thaw, without any provocation, grasped me by the throat and tore the bathrobe from my body. The said Thaw was in a terrific excited condition. His eyes were glaring, and he had in his right hand a cowhide whip. He seized hold of me and threw me on the bed. I was powerless and attempted to scream, but the said Thaw placed his fingers in my mouth and tried to choke me.

He then, without any provocation, and without the slightest reason, began to inflict on me several severe and violent blows with the cowhide whip. So brutally did he assault me that my skin was cut and bruised. I besought him to desist, but he refused. He stopped every minute or so to rest, and then renewed his attack on me.

I was absolutely in fear of my life; the servants could not hear my outcries, for the reason that my voice did not penetrate through the large castle, and so could not come to my succor. The said Thaw threatened to kill me, and by reason of his brutal attack, as I have described, I was unable to move.

The following morning Thaw again came into my bedroom and administered a castigation similar to the day before. He took a cowhide whip and belabored me with it on my bare skin, cutting the skin and leaving me in a fainting condition. I swooned and did not know how long after I returned to consciousness.

"How horrible," said Betty. "But she married him—why?"

"For his dough, I guess," said Littlemore. He leafed through the affidavit again. "You think this is it? What Susie meant us to find?"

"It must be, Jimmy. It's the same thing that was done to poor Miss Riverford."

"I know," said Littlemore. "But this is an affidavit. Does Susie seem like somebody who knows about affidavits?"

"What do you mean? It can't be a coincidence."

"Why would she remember the day, the exact day, this affidavit got read in at the trial? It doesn't add up. I think there's something else." Littlemore sat down on the floor, reading the transcript. Betty sighed impatiently. Suddenly the detective called out, "Wait a minute. Here we go. Look at the Q here, Betty. That's the prosecutor, Mr. Jerome, asking questions. Now look who the witness is, giving the answers."

At the spot indicated by the detective, the transcript read as follows:

Q. *What is your name?*
A. *Susan Merrill.*
Q. *State your business, please.*
A. *I keep a rooming house for gentlemen in Forty-third Street.*

Q. *Do you know Harry K. Thaw?*

A. *I do.*

Q. *When did you first meet him?*

A. *In 1903. He called on me to engage rooms. Which he did.*

Q. *For what purpose did he say?*

A. *He said he was engaging young ladies for work on the stage.*

Q. *Did he bring visitors to his rooms?*

A. *Mostly young women of fifteen years and on. They said they wanted to get on the stage.*

Q. *Did anything unusual happen at any time when any of these girls called?*

A. *Yes. One young girl had gone into his room. A little later, I heard screams and I ran into the room. She was tied to the bedpost. He had a whip in his right hand, and he was about to strike her. There were welts all over her.*

Q. *What was she wearing?*

A. *Very little.*

Q. *What happened next?*

A. *He was wild and hurried away. She told me he had been trying to murder her.*

Q. *Can you describe the whip?*

A. *It was a dog whip. On that occasion.*

Q. *Were there other occasions?*

A. *Another time there were two girls. One of them was undressed, the other was partly dressed. He was whipping them with a lady's riding whip.*

Q. *Did you ever speak with him about it?*

A. *Yes, I did. I told him these were all young girls and he had no right to whip them.*

Q. *What explanation did he make for doing it?*

A. *He made no explanation at all. He said they needed it.*

Q. *Did you ever inform the police?*

A. *No.*

Q. *Why not?*

A. *He said if I did he'd kill me.*

CHAPTER FIFTEEN

"COME," SAID FREUD, changing the subject, as we walked through the park on our way from Brill's to the hotel. "Let us hear how you are getting along with Miss Nora."

I hesitated, but Freud assured me that I could speak as freely to Ferenczi as to himself, so I recounted the whole story at length: the illicit congress between Mr. Acton and Mrs. Banwell, glimpsed by the fourteen-year-old Nora, which Freud had somehow foreseen; the girl's tantrum in the hotel room, directed against me; the apparent recovery of her memory, identifying George Banwell as her assailant; and the sudden arrival of Banwell himself, together with the girl's parents and the mayor, who provided Banwell's alibi.

Ferenczi, after declaring his revulsion at the nature of the sexual act Mrs. Banwell performed on Harcourt Acton—a reaction I found hard to understand, coming from a psychoanalyst—asked why Banwell couldn't have attacked Nora Acton even if he had not murdered the other girl. I explained that I had quizzed the detective on the very same point and that there was apparently physical evidence proving the two attacks were carried out by the same man.

"Let us leave the forensics to the police, shall we?" said Freud. "If the analysis should help the police, well and good. If not, we shall at least help the patient. I have two questions for you, Younger. First, do you not find something strange in Nora's assertion that, when she saw Mrs. Banwell with her father, she didn't understand at the time exactly what she was witnessing?"

"Most American girls of fourteen would be ill-informed on that point, Dr. Freud."

"I appreciate that," Freud replied. "But that is not what I meant.

She implied that she *now* understood what she had witnessed, did she not?"

"Yes."

"Would you expect a girl of seventeen to be better informed than one of fourteen?"

I began to take his point.

"How," asked Freud, "does she know now what she didn't know then?"

"She suggested to me yesterday," I answered, "that she reads books explicit in content."

"Ah, yes, that's right, very good. Well, we must think more about this. But for now, my second question: tell me, Younger, why did she turn on you?"

"You mean, why did she throw her cup and saucer at me?"

"Yes," said Freud.

"And hit you with boiling tea pot," added Ferenczi.

I had no answer.

"Ferenczi, can you enlighten our friend?"

"I am also in the dark," Ferenczi replied. "She is in love with him. That much is obvious."

Freud addressed me. "Think again. What did you say to her just before she became violent with you?"

"I had just finished the touching of her forehead," I said, "which failed. I sat down. I asked her to complete an analogy she had begun earlier. She was comparing the whiteness of Mrs. Banwell's back to something else, but she broke off. I asked her to complete the thought."

"Why?" asked Freud.

"Because, Dr. Freud, you have written that whenever a patient begins a sentence, but interrupts himself and doesn't finish, a repression is at work."

"Good boy," said Freud. "And how did Nora respond?"

"She told me to get out. Without warning. And then she began throwing things at me."

"Just like that?" asked Freud.

"Yes."

"So?"

Again I had no reply.

"Did it not occur to you that Nora would be jealous of any interest you showed in Clara Banwell? Particularly in her naked back?"

"Interest in Mrs. Banwell?" I repeated. "I've never met Mrs. Banwell."

"The unconscious does not take such niceties into account," said Freud. "Consider the facts. Nora had just described Clara Banwell performing fellatio on her father, which she witnessed at the age of fourteen. That act is of course repugnant to any decent person; it fills us with the utmost disgust. But Nora does not display to you any such disgust, despite implying that she fully understands the nature of the act. She even says she found Mrs. Banwell's movements appealing. Now, it is quite impossible that Nora should have witnessed that scene without deep jealousy. A girl has a hard enough time bearing her own mother: she will never allow another woman to arouse her father's passion without bitterly resenting the intruder. Nora, therefore, envied Clara. She wanted to be the one performing fellatio on her father. The wish was repressed; she has nurtured it ever since."

A moment ago, I had inwardly chastised Ferenczi for expressing revulsion at a "deviant" sexual act—a revulsion I, for some reason, did not exactly share, despite Freud's remark about what all decent people feel. I had just been telling myself that every lesson taught by psychoanalysis undercut society's disapproval of so-called sexual deviance. Now, however, I found myself awash in a similar feeling. The wish Freud imputed to Miss Acton revolted me. Disgust is so reassuring; it feels like a moral proof. It is hard to let go of any moral sentiment anchored by disgust. We can't do it without setting our entire sense of right and wrong a-tremble, as if we were losing a plank that supported the whole fabric.

"At the same time," Freud continued, "Nora formed a plan to seduce Mr. Banwell, in order to avenge herself on her father. That is why, only a few weeks later, Nora agreed to join Banwell alone on a rooftop to watch the fireworks. That is why she also walked with him alone by the shore of a romantic lake two years later. Probably she encouraged him with hints of interest all along, as any pretty young girl can easily do. How surprised he must have been when she rejected him—not once, but twice."

"Which she did because true object of desire was her father," Ferenczi put in. "But still, why does she attack Younger?"

"Yes, why, Younger?" asked Freud.

"Because I stand in for her father?"

"Precisely. When you analyze her, you take his place. It is the predictable transferential reaction. As a result, Nora's unconscious desire is now to gratify Younger with her mouth and throat. This fantasy was preoccupying her when Younger approached her to touch her forehead. He told us, you will remember, that at that moment she began to undo her scarf. This gesture represented her invitation to Younger to take advantage of her. Here, I may add, is also the explanation of why the touching of her throat succeeded, whereas the touching of her forehead did not. But Younger rejected this invitation, telling her to retie her scarf. She felt rebuffed."

"She did look offended," I put in. "I didn't know why."

"Don't forget," Freud continued, "she is naturally vain about the injuries she has received. Otherwise she would not wear the scarf at all. So she was already sensitive about how you would react if you saw her neck or back. When you told her to keep her scarf on, you injured her. And when, shortly afterward, you brought up the subject of Clara Banwell's back, it was as if you had said to her, 'It is Clara in whom I am interested, not you. It is Clara's back I want to see, not yours.' Thus you unwittingly recapitulated her father's act of betrayal, provoking in the girl her sudden, otherwise inexplicable fury. Hence her violent attack—followed by a desire to give you her throat and mouth."

"Irrefutable," said Ferenczi, shaking his head in admiration.

❧

ENTERING THE DRAWING ROOM of their house on Gramercy Park, Nora Acton informed her mother she would not sleep in her bedroom that night. Instead she would stay in the small first-floor parlor. From there, she could see the patrolman stationed outside. Otherwise, she said, she would not feel safe.

These were the first words Nora had addressed to either of her parents since leaving the hotel. When they arrived home, she had gone straight to her room. Dr. Higginson had been called in, but

Nora refused to see him. She also refused to come to dinner, declaring that she was not hungry. This was false; in fact she had not eaten since morning, when Mrs. Biggs had prepared breakfast for her.

Mildred Acton, reclining on the drawing-room sofa and pronouncing herself exhausted, told her daughter she was being most unreasonable. With one police officer manning the front door and another the rear, how could there be any danger? In any event, Nora's spending the night in the parlor was out of the question. The neighbors would see her. What would they think? The family must do its best now to act as if there had been no disgrace.

"Mother," said Nora, "how can you say I've been disgraced?"

"Why, I said no such thing. Harcourt, did I say any such thing?"

"No, dear," said Harcourt Acton, standing over a coffee table. He had been perusing five weeks of accumulated mail. "Of course not."

"I specifically said we must act as if you *hadn't* been disgraced," her mother clarified.

"But I haven't," said the girl.

"Don't be obtuse, Nora," counseled her mother.

Nora sighed. "What is that on your eye, Father?"

"Oh—polo accident," explained Acton. "Poked myself with my own stick. Stupid of me. You remember my old detached retina? Same eye. Can't see a deuced thing out of it now. How's that for bad luck?"

No one answered this question.

"Well," said Acton, "not compared with yours, Nora, of course, I didn't mean—"

"Don't sit there!" Mrs. Acton called out to her husband, who was about to lower himself into an armchair. "No, not there either. I had the chairs done just before we left."

"But where am I to sit, dear?" asked Acton.

Nora closed her eyes. She turned to leave.

"Nora," said her mother. "What was the name of that college of yours?"

The girl stopped, her every muscle tense. "Barnard," she answered.

"Harcourt, we must contact them first thing tomorrow morning."

"Why must you contact them?" asked Nora.

"To tell them you aren't coming, of course. It's quite impossible now. Dr. Higginson says you must rest. I never approved in the first place. A college for young ladies! We never heard of such a thing in my time."

Nora flushed. "You can't."

"I beg your pardon," said Mrs. Acton.

"I am going to be educated."

"Did you hear that? She calls me uneducated," Mrs. Acton said to her husband. "Not those glasses, Harcourt, use the ones on top."

"Father?" asked Nora.

"Well, Nora," said Acton, "we must consider what is best for you."

Nora looked at her parents with undisguised fury. She ran from the room and up the stairs, not stopping on the second floor, where her own bedroom was, or the third, but continuing all the way to the fourth, with its low ceilings and small quarters. There she ran straight into Mrs. Biggs's bedroom and threw herself on the old woman's bed, burying her head in the rough pillowcase. If her father did not let her go to Barnard, she told Mrs. Biggs, she would run away.

Mrs. Biggs did her best to comfort the girl. A good night's sleep, she said, would do a power. It was almost midnight when, at last, Nora consented to go to bed. To be sure she felt safe, Mrs. Biggs saw to it that Mr. Biggs was positioned on a chair outside Nora's bedroom door, with instructions to remain there the whole night through.

The old servant never once deserted his post that night, although he nodded off before too long. The police officers likewise remained on duty. Which made it quite surprising when, in the black of night, the girl suddenly felt a man's handkerchief pressing hard against her mouth and the cold, sharp edge of a blade on her neck.

❧

NEVER HAVING BEEN to Jelliffe's home, I was unprepared for its extravagance. The word *apartment* was inapposite, unless one had in mind the phrase *royal apartments,* as for example at Versailles, which was evidently the dwelling Jelliffe intended to bring to mind. Blue Chinese porcelain, white marble statues, and exquisitely turned legs—highboy legs, davenport legs, credenza legs—were everywhere on display. If Jelliffe meant to convey to his guests an impression of personal wealth, he succeeded.

I knew Freud well enough by now to see he was repelled; the Bostonian in me had the same reaction. Ferenczi, by contrast, was unaffectedly overwhelmed by the splendor. I overheard him exchanging pleasantries with two elderly female guests in Jelliffe's living room before dinner, where servants offered us hors d'oeuvres from gold, not silver, trays. In his white suit, Ferenczi was the only man present not wearing black. It did not seem to discomfit him in the least.

"So much gold," he said admiringly to the ladies: in the high ceiling above us, heavenly plaster scenes were lined with gold leaf. "It reminds me of our Operahaz, by Ybl, in Budapest. Have you been?"

Neither of the two ladies had. Indeed, they professed confusion. Hadn't Ferenczi just told them he came from Hungary?

"Yes, yes," said Ferenczi. "Oh, look at that little cherub in the corner, with the tiny grapes hanging out of his little mouth. Isn't he adorable?"

Freud was engrossed in conversation with James Hyslop, retired professor of logic at Columbia, who sported an ear trumpet the size of the horn on a Victrola talking machine. Jelliffe had attached himself to Charles Loomis Dana, the eminent neurologist and, unlike our host, a member of the same circles as my Aunt Mamie. In Boston, the Danas are royalty: Sons of Liberty, intimates of the Adamses, and so on. I knew one of Dana's distant cousins, a Miss Draper, from Newport, where she had more than once brought down the house with her impersonation of an old Jewish tailor. Jelliffe reminded me of a glad-handing senator. He had a look of high self-worth, carrying his impressive girth as if corpulence were next to manliness.

Jelliffe pulled me into his group, whom he was regaling with stories about his famous client, Harry Thaw, apparently living like a king in the hospital where he was confined. Jelliffe went so far as to say he would trade places with Thaw at the drop of a hat. What I drew from these remarks was that Jelliffe relished the celebrity of being Thaw's psychiatrist. "Can you imagine?" he added. "A year ago he had us all attesting to his insanity, to clear him of murder. Now he wants us to swear to his sanity to get him out of the asylum! And we shall get him out!"

Jelliffe roared with laughter, his arm around Dana's shoulder. Several of his listeners joined in; Dana decidedly did not. About a dozen guests, all told, were scattered about the room, but I understood that one more was expected. Soon enough, a butler opened the doors and preceded a woman into the room.

"Mrs. Clara Banwell," he announced.

❧

"CAN YOU PSYCHOANALYZE anyone, Dr. Freud?" asked Mrs. Banwell, as the party entered Jelliffe's dining room. "Can you psychoanalyze me?"

On certain social occasions, otherwise dignified and serious men will begin behaving unconsciously like players on a stage, performing as they talk, acting as they gesticulate. The cause is invariably a woman; Clara Banwell produced that effect on Jelliffe's male guests. She was twenty-six, her skin the white of a powdered Japanese princess. Everything about her was perfectly formed. Her shape was exquisite. Her hair was forest-dark, her eyes sea-green, with the luster of a fine provoking intelligence. An iridescent Oriental pearl hung from each ear, and a single large pink conch pearl, encased in a basket of diamonds and platinum, hung below her neck on a silver thread. When she hinted at a smile—and she never more than hinted—men fell at her feet.

In 1909, the guests at a fashionable American dinner made a pairwise procession when called to table, every woman escorted on the arm of a man. Mrs. Banwell was not on Freud's arm. She had lightly dropped her fingers on Younger's wrist at the decisive moment, but still she managed to address herself to Freud, while capturing the attention of the entire party as she did so.

Only that morning, Clara Banwell had returned to town from the country, in the same car with Mr. and Mrs. Harcourt Acton. Jelliffe had run into her in the lobby of their building quite by accident. The moment he learned that her husband, Mr. George Banwell, was to be otherwise engaged, he begged Clara to attend his dinner that evening. He assured her she would find the guests most interesting. Jelliffe found Clara Banwell utterly irresistible—and her husband equally unbearable.

"What women want," Freud replied to her question, as the guests took their seats at a table shimmering with crystal, "is a mystery, as much to the analyst as to the poet. If only you could tell us, Mrs. Banwell, but you cannot. You are the problem, but you are no better able to solve it than are we poor men. Now, what *men* want is almost always apparent. Our host, for example, instead of his spoon, has picked up his knife by mistake."

All heads turned to the smiling, bulky form of Jelliffe at the head of the table. It was so: he had his knife—not his bread knife, but his dinner knife—in his right hand. "What does that signify, Dr. Freud?" asked an elderly lady.

"It signifies that Mrs. Banwell has aroused our host's aggressive impulses," said Freud. "This aggression, arising from circumstances of sexual competition readily comprehensible to everyone, led his hand to the wrong instrument, revealing wishes of which he himself was unconscious."

There was a murmur around the table.

"A touch, a touch, I do confess it," cried Jelliffe with unembarrassed good spirits, wagging his knife in Clara's direction, "except of course when he says that the wishes in question were unconscious." His civilized scandalousness elicited a burst of appreciative laughter all around.

"By contrast," Freud went on, "my good friend Ferenczi here is fastidiously securing his napkin to his collar, as a bib is tucked into a child. He is appealing to your maternal instinct, Mrs. Banwell."

Ferenczi looked about the table with good-natured perplexity: only then did he notice that he was alone in this particular use of his dinner napkin.

"You conversed at length with my husband before dinner, Dr. Freud," said Mrs. Hyslop, a grandmotherly woman seated next to Jelliffe. "What did you learn about him?"

"Professor Hyslop," replied Freud, "will you confirm something for me, sir? You did not mention to me your mother's first name, did you?"

"What's that?" said Hyslop, holding his ear trumpet high.

"We didn't speak of your mother, did we?" asked Freud.

"Speak of Mother?" repeated Hyslop. "Not at all."

"Her name was Mary," said Freud.

"How did you know that?" cried Hyslop. He looked accusingly around the table. "How did he know that? I didn't tell him Mother's name."

"You certainly did," said Freud, "without knowing it. The puzzle to me is your wife's name. Jelliffe tells me it is Alva. I confess I had predicted a variant of Mary. I felt quite certain of it. Thus I have a question for you, Mrs. Hyslop, if you will permit me. Does your husband by any chance have a pet name by which he calls you?"

"Why, my middle name is Maria," said a surprised Mrs. Hyslop, "and he has always called me Marie."

At this admission, Jelliffe let out a whoop, and Freud received a round of applause.

"I woke up with a catarrh this morning," interjected a matron across from Ferenczi. "At the end of summer, too. Does that mean anything, Dr. Freud?"

"A catarrh, madam?" Freud paused to consider. "Sometimes a catarrh, I'm afraid, is only a catarrh."

"But are women really so mysterious?" Clara Banwell resumed. "I think you are being much too forgiving of my sex. What women want is the simplest thing in the world." She turned to the exceedingly good-looking, dark-haired young man on her right, whose white bow tie was just slightly askew. He had said nothing so far. "What do you think, Dr. Younger? Can you tell us what a woman wants?"

Stratham Younger was having difficulty taking Clara Banwell's measure. Although he did not know it, he was laboring to put out of his mind a recurrent image of Mrs. Banwell's lovely bare back, undulating gently in the moonlight as she tossed her hair over her shoulder. He was also having trouble separating the idea of Mrs. George Banwell from that of Mr. George Banwell, whom Younger could not stop thinking of as a murderer, despite the mayor's exculpation of him.

Younger believed that Nora was the loveliest girl he had ever seen. Yet Clara Banwell was quite nearly as attractive, if not more so. Desire in man, says Hegel, always begins with a desire for the other's desire. It was impossible for any man to look on Clara Banwell without wanting her to single him out, favor him, want something from him. Jelliffe, for example, would gladly have dived on a sword if Clara had only seen fit to grace him with a request to do so. On their way into the dining room, when Clara's hand had rested on his arm, Younger had felt the contact throughout his person. Yet there was something about her that distanced him too. Perhaps it was his having met Harcourt Acton. Younger did not consider himself a puritan, but the idea of Mrs. Banwell gratifying so weak-looking a man insensibly provoked him.

"I'm sure, Mrs. Banwell," he replied, "that if you would enlighten us on the subject of woman, it would be far more interesting than if I tried to."

"I *could* tell you, I suppose, how women really feel about men," said Clara invitingly. "At least about the men they care for. Would you like that?" A groundswell of assent was heard around the table, at any rate among the male guests. "But I won't, not unless you men promise to say how you really feel about women." The bargain was promptly struck by general acclamation, although Younger held his tongue, as did Charles Dana at the foot of the table.

"Well, since you force me, gentlemen," said Clara, "I'll confess our secret. Women are men's inferiors. I know it is backward of me to say so, but to deny it is folly. All of mankind's riches, material and spiritual, are men's creations. Our towering cities, our science, art, and music—all built, discovered, painted, and composed by you men. Women know this. We cannot help being overmastered by stronger men, and we cannot help resenting you for it. A woman's love for a man is half animal passion and half hate. The more a woman loves a man, the more she hates him. If a man is worth having, he must be a woman's superior; if he is her superior, part of her must hate him. It is only in beauty we surpass you, and it is therefore no wonder that we worship beauty above all else. That is why a woman," she wound up, "is at her greatest peril in the presence of a beautiful man."

Her audience was mesmerized, a reaction to which Clara Banwell was not unaccustomed. Younger felt she had thrown him the most fleeting glance at the very end of her remarks—he was not the only man at table who had this impression—but he told himself he had imagined it. It also occurred to Younger that Mrs. Banwell might have just explained the wild extremes of conflicting emotion his own mother had displayed toward his father. Younger's father killed himself in 1904; his mother had not remarried. He wondered whether his mother had always both loved and hated his father, in the manner Mrs. Banwell had described.

"Envy is certainly the predominant force in women's mental lives, Mrs. Banwell," said Freud. "That is why women have so little sense of justice."

"Men are not envious?" asked Clara.

"Men are ambitious," he replied. "Their envy derives chiefly from that source. A woman's envy, by contrast, is always erotic. The difference can be seen in daydreams. All of us daydream, of course. Men, however, have two kinds: erotic and ambitious. A woman's daydreams are exclusively erotic."

"I am sure mine are not," declared the rotund woman with the catarrh.

"I think Dr. Freud is quite right," said Clara Banwell, "on all counts, but particularly about men's ambitiousness. My husband, George, for example. He is the perfect man. He is not at all beautiful. But he is handsome, twenty years older than I, successful, strong, single-minded, indomitable. For all those things, I love him. He also hasn't the slightest awareness that I exist, the moment I am out of his sight; his ambition is that strong. For that, I hate him. Nature requires me to. The happy consequence, however, is that I am free to do whatever I like—for example, being here tonight at one of Smith's delightful dinner parties—and George will never even know I left the apartment."

"Clara," responded Jelliffe, "I'm wounded. You never told me you had such freedom."

"I said I was free to do as *I* like, Smith," Clara replied, "not as *you* like." Laughter again was general. "Well, now I've confessed. What do the men say? Don't men secretly despise the bonds of marital fidelity? No, Smith, please; I know what you think. I'd like a more objective opinion. Dr. Freud, is marriage a good thing?"

"For society or for the individual?" Freud responded. "For society, marriage is undoubtedly beneficial. But the burdens of civilized morality are too heavy for many to bear. How long have you been a wife, Mrs. Banwell?"

"I married George when I was nineteen," Clara answered, and the thought of a nineteen-year-old Clara Banwell on her wedding night occupied the minds of several guests—not only of the male variety. "That makes seven years."

"In that case you will know enough," Freud went on, "if not from your own experience, then that of your friends, not to be surprised by what I say. Satisfying intercourse does not last long in most marriages. After four or five years, marriage tends to fail utterly in this respect, and when this happens it spells the end of spiritual communion too. As a result, in the great run of cases, marriage ends in disappointment, spiritual as well as physical. The man and the woman are thrown back, psychologically speaking, to their premarital state—with only one difference. They are poorer now. Poorer by the loss of an illusion."

Clara Banwell stared intently at Freud.

"What is he saying?" old Professor Hyslop called out, trying to get his ear horn nearer to Freud.

"He is justifying adultery," replied Charles Dana, speaking for the first time. "You know, Dr. Freud, apart from the parlor tricks, it is your focus on the maladies of sexual frustration that surprises me. Our problem is surely not that we place too much constraint on sexual license; it is that we place too little."

"Oh?" said Freud.

"A billion people now live on this earth. A billion. And the number is growing geometrically. How are they to live, Dr. Freud? What are they to eat? Millions flood our shores every year: the poorest, the least intelligent, the most prone to criminality. Our city is near anarchy because of them. Our jails are bursting. They breed like flies. And they steal from us. One cannot blame them; if a man is too poor to feed his children, he must steal. Yet you, Dr. Freud, if I understand your ideas, seem concerned only with the evils of sexual repression. I would think a man of science ought to be more concerned with the dangers of sexual emancipation."

"What do you propose, Charles, an end to immigration?" asked Jelliffe.

"Sterilization," replied Dana sanguinely, dabbing a napkin to his mouth. "The meanest farmer knows not to let his worst stock breed.

Men are no more created equal than cattle. If cattle were allowed to breed freely, we should have very poor meat indeed. Every immigrant to this country without means should be sterilized."

"Not involuntarily, Charles, surely?" asked Mrs. Hyslop.

"No one compels them to come here, Alva," he replied. "No one compels them to stay. How then can it be called involuntary? If they wish to reproduce, let them leave. What is involuntary is our being required to bear the charge of their unfit offspring, who end up as beggars and thieves. I make an exception, of course, for those who can pass an intelligence test. Splendid soup, Jelliffe, a true turtle, isn't it? Oh, I know, you will all say I am cruel and heartless. But I am only taking away their fertility. Dr. Freud would take away something far more important."

"What is that?" asked Clara.

"Their morality," answered Dana. "What sort of world would it be, Dr. Freud, if your views became general? I can almost picture it. The lower orders come to scorn 'civilized morality.' Gratification becomes god. All join in rejecting discipline and self-denial, without which life has no dignity. The mob will run riot; why should they not? And this mob, what will they want when the rules of civilization are lifted? Do you think they will want only sex? They will want new rules. They will want to obey some new madman. They will want blood—your blood, probably, Dr. Freud, if history is any guide. They will want to prove themselves superior, as the lowest always do. And they will kill to prove it. I picture bloodletting, great bloodletting, on a scale never seen before. You would pipe away civilized morality— the only thing that keeps man's brutality in check. What do you offer in exchange, Dr. Freud? What will you put in its place?"

"Only the truth," said Freud.

"The truth of Oedipus?" said Dana.

"Among others," said Freud.

"A great deal of good it did him."

❧

A CANDLE FLICKERED at Nora Acton's bedside. The lamplight from Gramercy Park played palely at her curtains. The illumination was insufficient even to give a silhouette to the man whose presence

Nora felt, rather than saw, inside her room. She wanted to cry out, but her mind would not operate on her body. It had somehow broken free, her mind, and was wandering off on its own. It or she seemed to float up from her own bed, rising toward the ceiling, leaving her small nightgowned body on the bed below.

Now she saw her assailant distinctly, but from above. Looking down on herself, she saw him remove the handkerchief from her face. She saw him dab a woman's red lipstick onto her sleeping, yielding mouth. Why would he put color on her lips? She liked how it looked; she had always wondered. What would the man do next? From above, Nora watched him light a cigarette in the flame of her bedside candle, place a knee against her supine form, and extinguish the glowing cigarette directly on her skin, down there, only an inch or two from her most private part.

Her body flinched against the knee that held her down. She saw it from above; she saw herself flinch. It was as if she were in pain. But she wasn't, was she? Observing everything from above, she felt nothing at all. And if she, watching herself, was not in pain, then there was no pain—there was no one else to feel it—was there?

PART

IV

I WILL HAVE to act as if I don't love her, as if I have no feelings for her at all. So I told myself while shaving Thursday morning. At ten-thirty I was to call at the Actons' to resume Nora's analysis. I knew I could have her. But that would be exploitation, manipulation, taking advantage of her therapeutic vulnerability—violating the oath of care I took when I became a doctor.

It is impossible to describe what ideas come to mind when I picture this girl, and I picture her nearly every waking moment. Well, not impossible, but inadvisable. What I literally cannot describe is the hollowness in my lungs when I am out of her presence. It is as if I were dying from the want of her.

I feel like Hamlet, paralyzed. With this difference: I feel I will die if I do not act, while Hamlet feels he will die if he does. For Hamlet, *to be* is not to act. To take action is to die; it is "not to be":

> To be, or not to be, that is the question:
> Whether 'tis nobler in the mind to suffer
> The slings and arrows of outrageous fortune,
> Or to take arms against a sea of troubles,
> And by opposing end them. To die . . .

In other words, *to be* is merely *to suffer* one's fate, do nothing and thereby live, while *not to be* is to act, *to take arms* and *die*. Because taking action means death, Hamlet says he knows why he has not acted: the fear of death, his soliloquy concludes, or of *something after death*, has made him a coward and puzzled his will.

Thus for Hamlet, *to be* is stasis, suffering, cowardice, inaction, whereas *not to be* is linked to courage, enterprise, action. Or so everyone has always understood the speech. But I wonder. Yes, in the end, when at last Hamlet acts against his uncle, he will die. Perhaps he knows this is his fate. But being cannot be equated with inaction. Life and action are too much one. *To be* cannot mean *to do nothing*. It cannot. Hamlet is paralyzed because, for him, acting has somehow been equated with not being—and this false equation, this spurious equivalence, has never been fully understood.

But because of Freud, I can no longer think of Hamlet without thinking of Oedipus, and I fear something similar has begun to afflict my feelings for Miss Acton as well. If Freud is right about Miss Acton wishing to sodomize her own father, I believe I couldn't stand it. I know: this is wholly irrational on my part. If Freud is right, everyone has such wishes. No one can help it, and no one ought to be reviled for it. Nevertheless, the moment I entertain the conjecture in Miss Acton's case, I lose my capacity to love her. I lose my hold on love entirely: how can human beings be loved if we carry within us such repugnant desires?

❦

THURSDAY MORNING BEGAN in uproar at the Acton house. Nora woke at daybreak, staggered out of bed, threw open her door, and fell headlong over Mr. Biggs, who was asleep in his chair just outside her bedroom. The news was spread, the alarm sounded: Miss Acton had been attacked in the night.

The two patrolmen posted outside bumbled up the stairs, then down, storming about, accomplishing little. Dr. Higginson was summoned once more. The well-intentioned old doctor, visibly distressed at Nora's having been victimized yet again and embarrassed by the location of her burn, gave the girl a soothing ointment she might apply as needed. He thereupon took his leave, shaking his head, assuring the family that she had suffered no other hurt. More policemen arrived on the scene. Detective Littlemore, who had fallen asleep at his desk the night before, got there at eight.

The detective found Nora and her distraught parents in the girl's bedroom. Uniformed officers were examining the carpeted floor and windows. Littlemore handed his dusting equipment to one of the

men and instructed him to see if there were any serviceable fingerprints on the doorknob, bedposts, or windowsill. Nora was perched
on a corner of her bed, the unmoving center of the whirlwind, still in
her nightgown, hair disheveled, her eyes dazed and uncomprehending. Her statement was taken again and again.

It was George Banwell, she told them every time. It was George
Banwell with a cigarette and a knife in the nighttime. Wasn't anyone
going to arrest George Banwell? That question provoked anxious
protests from Mr. and Mrs. Acton. It couldn't have been George,
they said; it couldn't possibly have been. How could Nora be absolutely sure in the middle of the night?

Littlemore had a problem. He wished he had something else on
Banwell other than the girl's evidence. After all, Miss Acton's memory was not exactly rock solid. Worse, even she admitted she couldn't
really see the man in her room last night; it had been too dark. What
she said, and Littlemore wished she hadn't put it this way, was that
she "could just tell" it was Banwell. If Littlemore had Banwell arrested, the mayor would not be happy. His Honor wouldn't like it if
Banwell were so much as picked up for questioning.

All in all, the detective figured he'd better wait for the mayor's orders. "If you wouldn't mind, Miss Acton," he said, "could I ask you a
question?"

"Go ahead," she said.

"Do you know a William Leon?"

"I'm sorry?"

"William Leon," said Littlemore. "Chinaman. Also known as
Leon Ling."

"I know no Chinamen, Detective."

"Maybe this will jog your memory, miss," said the detective.
From his vest, he withdrew a photograph and handed it to the girl. It
was the picture he had removed from Leon's apartment, showing the
Chinese man with two young women. One of them was Nora Acton.

"Where did you get this?" the girl asked.

"If you could just tell me who he is, miss," said Littlemore. "It's
real important. He may be dangerous."

"I don't know. I never knew. He insisted on having his picture
taken with Clara and me."

"Clara?"

"Clara Banwell," said Nora. "That's her there, next to him. He was one of Elsie Sigel's Chinamen."

Both these names were acutely interesting to Detective Littlemore. Unless William Leon had a penchant for Elsies, he had just identified not only the other woman in the photograph, but the author of the letters found in the trunk—and, quite possibly, the dead girl found along with them.

"Elsie Sigel," Littlemore repeated. "Could you tell me about her, miss? A Jewish girl?"

"Good heavens, no," said Nora. "Elsie did missionary work. You must have heard of the Sigels. Her grandfather was quite famous. There is a statue of him in Riverside Park."

Littlemore whistled inwardly. General Franz Sigel was indeed famous, a Civil War hero who became a popular New York politician. At his funeral in 1902, more than ten thousand New Yorkers came to pay their respects to the old man, laid out in full-dress uniform. The granddaughters of Civil War generals were not supposed to write amorous letters to the managers of Chinatown restaurants. They were not supposed to write letters to Chinamen at all. He asked how Miss Sigel was connected to William Leon.

Nora told him what little she knew. Last spring, she and Clara had volunteered their services to one of Mr. Riis's charitable associations. They had visited tenement families all over the Lower East Side, offering what help they could. One Sunday, in Chinatown, they had come across Elsie Sigel teaching a Bible class. A pupil of hers had a camera. Nora remembered him well, because he was so different from the others—much better dressed and better spoken. Nora had never learned his name, but Elsie seemed to know him well. It was because of his apparent friendship with Elsie that Clara and she felt they could not refuse his persistent requests for a photograph.

"Do you know where Miss Sigel lives, Miss Acton?" asked Littlemore.

"No, but I doubt you would find her at home anyway, Detective," said Nora. "Elsie ran away with a young man in July. To Washington, everyone says."

Littlemore nodded. He thanked Nora; then he asked Mr. Acton

if there was a telephone he could use. When he got through to head-quarters, he left instructions to track down the parents of one Elsie Sigel, granddaughter of General Franz Sigel. If the Sigels confirmed that they had not seen their daughter since July, they were to be taken down to the morgue.

Returning to Nora's bedroom, Littlemore found only Nora and Mrs. Biggs within. The last policeman was just leaving the room: he told Littlemore that he hadn't found any prints at all on the windows or bedposts. As for the doorknobs, too many people had been in and out. Mrs. Biggs was attempting to restore order to the mess the pa-trolmen had left; Nora remained exactly as she was when he had left. Littlemore studied the bedroom. "Miss Acton," he said, "how do you think the man got in here last night?"

"Well, he must have—why, I don't know."

It was, Littlemore reflected, certainly a puzzle. There were only two doors to the Acton house, the front and the back. These had been manned all night long by two sturdy patrolmen, who swore that no one had passed through either one. To be sure, old Biggs had fallen asleep at the switch. This was acknowledged by all parties. But Biggs had smartly positioned his chair right up against the girl's bed-room door; that was why she had fallen over him in the morning. It would have been very difficult for anybody to get past Biggs without disturbing him.

Could the intruder have climbed in through a window? Nora's bedroom was on the second floor. There was no obvious way the man could have scaled the house, and, because her bedroom faced the park, anyone attempting such a feat would have been in plain view of the officer stationed out front. Could he have lowered himself from the roof? It was conceivable. The roof was accessible from the adja-cent buildings. But the neighbors swore that *their* houses had not been broken into last night. Also, it seemed to Littlemore that a large man would have had a pretty hard time squeezing through one of Nora's windows.

It was during Detective Littlemore's inspection of these windows—which showed no sign of human ingress or egress—that cracks began to appear in Nora's story. The first was the discovery, by Mrs. Biggs, of an extinguished cigarette buried in Nora's wastepaper basket. The cigarette had lipstick on it. Mrs. Biggs seemed very surprised. The detective was too.

"This yours, miss?" he asked.

"Of course not," said Nora. "I don't smoke. I don't even own any lipstick."

"What's that on your lips now?" asked Littlemore.

Nora clapped her hands to her mouth. Only then did she remember seeing Banwell put lipstick on her. Somehow she had forgotten this peculiar fact before. The whole episode was so blurred, so strangely cloudy in her mind. She told the detective what Banwell had done. She said he must have put lipstick on the cigarette too and thrown it into the basket before he left. She did not mention the most peculiar feature of her memory: that she saw Banwell from above rather than below. But she did insist that she owned no makeup at all.

"Mind if I have a look around your room, Miss Acton?" asked Littlemore.

"Your men have been examining my room for the last hour," she answered.

"Would you mind, miss?"

"All right."

None of the patrolmen thus far had searched Nora's own belongings. Littlemore did so now. In the lowest drawer of her vanity, he found several cosmetic items, including face powder, a vial of perfume, and a lipstick. There was also a pack of cigarettes.

"Those aren't mine," said Nora. "I don't know where they came from."

Littlemore brought his officers back to the room to conduct a more thorough examination. A few minutes later, on an upper shelf of the girl's closet, hidden under a pile of winter sweaters, a policeman found something unexpected. It was a short, bent-handled whip. Littlemore was unfamiliar with medieval practices of scourging, but even he could see that this particular kind of whip would allow a flogging in hard-to-reach places—such as the back of the flogger.

Good thing we didn't arrest Banwell, thought Jimmy Littlemore.

The detective didn't know what to think, however, when another officer presented him with a discovery from the backyard. The patrolman had climbed the tree to see if it was possible to get from there to the roof. It wasn't possible, but on his way down, the patrolman saw what he thought was a coin: a small, shiny metal circle, glinting deep in a notch of the tree trunk about a foot off the ground. He handed the item to Littlemore: a man's round gold tiepin, monogrammed, with a thread of white silk clinging to its catch. The initials on that tiepin were *GB*.

✍

BRILL WAS LATE to breakfast for once. When he appeared, he looked dreadful: unshaven, frightened, one of his collar points sticking up. Rose, he told Freud, Ferenczi, and me, had been insomniac all night. An hour ago, he had given her some laudanum; he had hardly slept himself. He said he needed to speak with us out of public view. We therefore repaired, the four of us, to Freud's room, leaving a message downstairs for Jones and another for Jung—although none of us knew whether Jung was even in the hotel.

"I can't do it," Brill burst out, when we got to Freud's room. "I'm sorry, but I just can't. I already told Jelliffe." He was referring, apparently, to his translation of Freud's book. "If it were only me, I promise you—but I can't endanger Rose. She's all I have. You see that, don't you?"

We induced him to sit. When he calmed down enough to speak coherently, Brill tried to persuade us that the cinders in his home were connected to the biblical telegrams he had been receiving. "You saw her," he said, referring to Rose again. "They turned her into a pillar of salt. It was in the telegram, and it happened."

"Someone deliberately delivered ash to your home?" asked Ferenczi. "Why?"

"As a warning," answered Brill.

"From whom?" I asked.

"The same people who had Prince arrested in Boston. The same people who are trying to block Freud's lectures at Clark."

"They know where you live how?" said Ferenczi.

"How do they know Jones is sleeping with his maid?" was Brill's reply.

"We mustn't jump to conclusions," said Freud, "but it is certainly true that someone has acquired a great deal of private information about us."

Brill slipped an envelope from his vest, from which he withdrew a tiny jagged square of burnt paper, with typing visible on it. A *ü* (with an umlaut) was distinctly visible on it. A space or two to its right was a letter that might have been a capital *H*. Nothing else was visible.

"I found this in my living room," said Brill. "They burned my manuscript. Freud's manuscript. And they put the ashes in my apartment. They will burn the whole building down next time. It's in the telegram: a "rain of fire"; "stop before it is too late." If I publish Freud's book they're going to kill Rose and me."

Ferenczi remonstrated with him, arguing that his fears were out of all proportion to the events, but Freud interrupted. "Whatever the explanation, Abraham," he said, placing a hand on Brill's shoulder, "let us put the book aside for now. The book can wait. It is not as important to me as you are."

Brill hung his head and put his own hand over Freud's. I thought he might be about to cry. Just then a porter knocked at the door and entered with coffee and a tray of pastries, which Freud had ordered. Brill straightened up. He accepted a cup of coffee. He seemed enormously relieved by Freud's last remarks, as if a great burden had been lifted from him. Blowing his nose, he said, in an altogether different tone—his old, familiar, half-serious note—"It's not me you should be worried about anyway. What about Jung? Are you aware, Freud, that Ferenczi and I believe Jung to be psychotic? It is our considered medical opinion. Tell him, Sándor."

"Well, psychotic I would not say," Ferenczi responded. "But I do see evidence of potential breakdown."

"Nonsense," said Freud. "What evidence?'"

"He is hearing voices," Ferenczi replied. "He is complaining Brill's floor is soft under feet. Conversation is broken. And is telling everyone he meets that grandfather was falsely accused of murder."

"I can think of explanations for that other than psychosis," said Freud. I could see he had something particular in mind, but he didn't elaborate. I was wondering whether to bring up Jung's startling interpretation of Freud's Count Thun dream, but I was concerned that Freud had not divulged it to Brill and Ferenczi. I need not have been.

"And on top of that, he says you dreamt about him ten years ago!" cried Brill. "The man is mad."

Freud took a breath and replied. "Gentlemen, you know as well as I that Jung entertains certain beliefs about clairvoyance and the occult. I am glad you share my skepticism on that subject, but Jung is hardly alone in taking a broader view."

"A broader view," said Brill. "If I took that broad a view, you would tell me I was delusional. He takes a broader view of the Oedipal complex too. He no longer accepts the sexual aetiology, you know."

"You wish that to be so," replied Freud calmly, "so that I will throw him off. Jung accepts the sexual theory without reserve. In fact, he is presenting a case of infantile sexuality at Clark next week."

"Really? Have you asked him what he intends to say at Fordham?"

Freud did not answer but eyed Brill narrowly.

"Jelliffe told me that he and Jung have been talking it over, and Jung is very concerned about overemphasizing the role of sex in the psychoneuroses. That was his word: *overemphasizing.*"

"Well, certainly he does not want to overemphasize it," snapped Freud. "I don't want to overemphasize it either. Listen to me, both of you. I know you have suffered from Jung's anti-Semitism. He spares me and therefore takes it out with greater energy on you. I also know very well—I assure you—about Jung's difficulties with the sexual theory. But you must remember: it was harder for him to follow me than it was for you. It will be harder for Younger here as well. A Gentile must overcome much greater inner resistance. And Jung is not only a Christian, he is a pastor's son."

No one said anything, so I ventured an objection. "I'm sorry, Dr. Freud, but why should it matter if one is a Christian or Jew?"

"My boy," Freud responded gruffly, "you put me in mind of one of those novels by James's brother; what is his name?"

"Henry, sir?"

"Yes, Henry." If I imagined Freud was going to say more in answer to my question, I was mistaken. Instead he returned to Ferenczi and Brill. "You would prefer psychoanalysis to be a Jewish national affair? Of course it is unjust of me to promote Jung, when others have been with me longer. But we Jews must be prepared to endure a certain amount of injustice if we want to make our way in the world. There is no other choice. Had my name been Jones, you can be sure my ideas, despite everything, would have met with far less resistance. Look at Darwin. He disproved Genesis, and he is acclaimed as a hero. Only a Gentile can bring psychoanalysis to the promised land. We must hold Jung to *die Sache*. All our hopes depend on him."

The words Freud spoke in German meant *the cause*. I don't know why he didn't use English. For several minutes no one spoke. We engaged ourselves with the breakfast things. Brill, however, did not eat. He was biting his nails instead. I imagined that there would be no further discussion of Jung, but I was wrong again.

"And what about his disappearances?" asked Brill. "Jelliffe told me that Jung left the Balmoral no later than midnight Sunday, but the clerk here swears Jung didn't return to the hotel until two. That's two hours unaccounted for after midnight. The next day, Jung claims he was in his room all afternoon napping, but the clerk says he was out until evening. You knocked at Jung's door Monday afternoon, Younger. I did too, long and hard. I don't think he was there at all. Where was he?"

I interrupted. "I'm sorry. Did you just say Jung was at the Balmoral on Sunday night?"

"That's right," Brill answered. "Jelliffe's building. You were there last night."

"Oh," I said. "I didn't realize."

"Realize what?" asked Brill.

"Nothing," I said. "Just an odd coincidence."

"What coincidence?"

"The other girl—the girl who was murdered—was killed at the Balmoral." I shifted in my chair uncomfortably. "On Sunday night. Between midnight and two."

Brill and Ferenczi looked at each other.

"Gentlemen," said Freud, "don't be ridiculous."

"And Nora was attacked on Monday evening," Brill pointed out. "Where?"

"Abraham," said Freud.

"No one is accusing anyone," Brill replied innocently, but with an overexcited expression. "I'm just asking Younger where Nora's house is."

"On Gramercy Park," I answered.

"Gentlemen, I will hear no more of this," Freud declared.

Another knock on the door; Jung himself entered. We exchanged greetings with him—stiffly, as might be expected. Jung, who did not seem to notice our discomfort, spooned sugar into his coffee and inquired whether we had enjoyed our dinner at Jelliffe's.

"Oh, Jung," Brill broke in, "you were spotted on Monday."

"I beg your pardon?" Jung replied.

"You told us," chided Brill, "you spent Monday afternoon sleeping in your room. But it turns out you were spotted up and about the town."

Freud, shaking his head, went to the window. He pushed it farther open.

"I never said I was in my room all Monday afternoon," Jung answered evenly.

"Strange," said Brill. "I would have sworn you did. That reminds me, Jung, we are thinking of visiting Gramercy Park today. I don't suppose you'll join us?"

"I see," said Jung.

"See what?" asked Brill.

"Why don't you just say it?" Jung retorted.

"I can't imagine what you're talking about," was Brill's reply. He was deliberately making himself sound like a bad actor unsuccessfully feigning ignorance.

"So: I was observed at Gramercy Park," replied Jung coldly. "What are you going to do, report me to the police?" He turned to Freud. "Well, as it seems your purpose in bringing me here was to interrogate me, you will forgive me if I don't breakfast with you." He opened the door to let himself out and stared at Brill. "I am ashamed of nothing."

❧

DUE TO THE LATE General Sigel's prominence, the police had no difficulty locating his granddaughter Elsie's address. She lived with her parents on Wadsworth Avenue near 180th Street. An officer from the Washington Heights station, dispatched to the house, escorted Mr. and Mrs. Sigel, together with their niece Mabel, to the Van den Heuvel building. There, in a waiting room outside the morgue, they met Detective Littlemore.

He learned from them that the nineteen-year-old Elsie had indeed gone missing almost a month ago, never returning from a trip to visit Grandmother Ellie in Brooklyn. In the first days after her disappearance, the Sigels had received a telegram from Elsie in Washington, D.C, indicating that she was there with a young man, evidently married to him. She begged her parents not to worry about her, assured them she was fine, and promised to be home by autumn. The parents had kept this wire, which they showed to the detective. The telegram had indeed been sent from a hotel in the capital, and Elsie's name was at the bottom, but there was of course no way to verify that she was the sender. Mr. Sigel had not yet contacted the police, hoping to hear again from his daughter and anxious to avoid a scandal.

Littlemore showed the Sigels the letters from William Leon's trunk. They recognized the handwriting. The detective next showed them the silver pendant found on the dead girl and the hat with the bird on it. Neither Mr. nor Mrs. Sigel had ever seen these objects before—and indeed positively stated they did not belong to Elsie—but Mabel contradicted them. The pendant was hers; she had given it to Elsie in June.

Littlemore, drawing Mr. Sigel aside, told the father he had better have a look at the body found in Leon's apartment. Downstairs in the morgue, Mr. Sigel could not at first identify the corpse; it was too decayed. Somberly, he told the detective he would know the truth if he looked at the teeth; his daughter's left eye tooth pointed the wrong way. And so did that of the small decomposing body lying on the marble slab. "It's her," said Mr. Sigel quietly.

When the two men returned to the waiting room, Mr. Sigel cast a stony and accusing eye on his wife. The woman must have understood; she fell into convulsions. It took a long time to quiet her. Then her husband told the story.

Mrs. Sigel did the Lord's work in Chinatown. For years she had toiled to convert the heathen Chinamen to Christianity. Last December, she had begun bringing Elsie with her to the mission house. Elsie had taken to the work with a passion that delighted her mother but disturbed her father. Despite Mr. Sigel's strong disapproval, the girl was soon eagerly traveling on her own to Chinatown several times a week and teaching her own Sunday Bible classes. One of her most avid pupils, Mr. Sigel recalled bitterly, had dared to call at their house a few months ago. Mr. Sigel did not know his name. Littlemore showed him a photograph of William Leon; the father shut his eyes and nodded.

After the Sigels left the morgue, to endure as they might both their misery and their notoriety—newspapermen were already waiting outside—Detective Littlemore wondered where Mr. Hugel was. Littlemore had assumed the coroner would have wanted to conduct the autopsy himself and to hear the Sigels' evidence. But the coroner was absent. Instead, one of his assistant physicians, Dr. O'Hanlon, had examined the body. He informed Littlemore that Miss Sigel had been strangled to death, that she had been dead three to four weeks—and that Coroner Hugel was upstairs in his office, professing a complete lack of interest in the case.

CHAPTER SEVENTEEN

THE EXQUISITE CLARA BANWELL, clad in a green dress matching her eyes, was undressing the equally exquisite, near desperate Nora Acton—quieting her, comforting her, reassuring her. Arriving at the house shortly after Littlemore's departure, Clara had gracefully ushered everyone out of Nora's bedroom, police and family alike. When Nora was naked, Clara drew her a cool bath and helped her step in. Nora, sobbing, begged Clara to let her speak: so many horrible things had happened.

Clara put two fingers to Nora's lips. "Hush," she said. "Don't speak, darling. Close your eyes."

Nora obeyed. Gently Clara bathed the girl, washed her hair, and dabbed her healing wounds with a smooth wet cloth.

"They don't believe me," said Nora, holding back tears.

"I know. It's all right." Clara tried to soothe the distraught girl. She asked Mrs. Biggs, who was hovering anxiously in the hallway, to bring the ointment Dr. Higginson left.

"Clara?"

"Yes."

"Why didn't you come earlier?"

"Shh," answered Clara, cooling Nora's brow. "I'm here now."

Later, after the bathwater drained away, Nora lay in the tub, her torso now draped with a white towel, her eyes closed. "What are you doing to me, Clara?" she asked.

"Shaving you. We need to, to clean this awful burn. Besides, it will be prettier like this." Clara placed Nora's hand protectively over the girl's most delicate spot. "There," she said. "Press down, darling." Clara placed her own strong hand atop Nora's, keeping a firm pressure and shifting position every now and then, so that she could do her work. "Nora, George was with me all last night. The police asked me, and I had to tell them. You must tell them now. Otherwise they are going to take you away. They are already making arrangements with a sanatorium."

"I shouldn't mind a sanatorium," said Nora.

"Don't be silly. Wouldn't you rather come with me to the country? That is what we will do, darling. You and I, all by ourselves, just as we like. We can talk it all out there." Clara finished her razor strokes. She applied to Nora's burn the soothing balm left by the doctor. "But you must tell them."

"What must I say?"

"Why, that you did all this to yourself. You were so angry at all of us: George, your mother and father, even me. You were trying to get back at us."

"No, I could never be angry at you."

"Oh, darling, nor I at you." Clara turned her attention to the two lacerations on Nora's thighs. To these too she applied the doctor's ointment, moving her fingers in gentle circles. "But you must tell them now. Tell them how sorry you are for everything. You will feel so much easier. And then you can come away with me for as long as you want."

✺

EVEN THE CORONER, a man of mercurial temperament, rarely passed from fury to exultation to despondency as quickly as he did when listening to Detective Littlemore's report of the events at the Acton house earlier that morning.

Littlemore had tried to interest the coroner in Elsie Sigel, but Hugel brushed the subject aside. The coroner had only heard about the hue and cry at the Actons' by accident, from one of the messenger boys. Hence his anger: why had they informed Littlemore but not himself? Then, hearing Nora's story, Hugel let out whoops of "Ha!" and "Now we have him!" and "I told you, didn't I?" Finally, learning of the discovery of the lipstick, cigarettes, and whip secreted in the girl's bedroom, he slumped back into his chair.

"It's over," said Hugel quietly. His face began to darken. "The girl must be put away."

"No, wait, Mr. Hugel. Listen to this." Littlemore told the coroner about the discovery of the tiepin.

Hugel barely registered the news. "Too little, too late," he said bitterly. He grunted in disgust. "I believed everything she said. The girl must be put away, do you hear me?"

"You think she's crazy."

The coroner took a deep breath. "I congratulate you, Detective, on your razor-sharp logic. The Riverford-Acton case is now closed. Inform the mayor. I am not speaking to him."

The detective blinked uncomprehendingly. "You can't close the case, Mr. Hugel."

"There *is* no case," said the coroner. "I cannot prosecute a murder without a corpus delicti. Do you understand? No murder without a body. And I cannot prosecute an assault without an assault. Shall we indict Miss Acton for criminal assault on her own person?"

"Wait, Mr. Hugel, I didn't even tell you. Remember the black-haired man? I found out where he went. First he goes to the Hotel Manhattan—how about that?—and then he goes to a cathouse on Fortieth Street. So I go to this cathouse myself, and the lady inside tips me off to Harry Thaw, who—"

"What are you talking about, Littlemore?"

"Harry Thaw, the guy who murdered Stanford White."

"I know who Harry Thaw is," said the coroner, with considerable self-restraint.

"You're not going to believe this, Mr. Hugel, but if the Chinaman's not the killer, I think Harry Thaw might be our guy."

"Harry Thaw."

"He got off, remember? Beat the rap," said Littlemore. "Well, at his trial, there was this affidavit from his wife, and—"

"Are you going to bring Harry Houdini into it as well?"

"Houdini? Houdini's the escape artist, Mr. Hugel."

"I know who Houdini is," said the coroner, very quietly.

"Why would I bring him into it?" asked Littlemore.

"Because Harry Thaw is in a locked cell, Detective. He did not beat the rap. He is incarcerated at the Matteawan State Hospital for the Criminally Insane."

"He is? I thought he got out. But then—then he can't be the guy."

"No."

"I don't get it. This lady at the house where the black-haired man went—"

"*Forget the black-haired man!*" the coroner exploded. "No one listens to me in any event. I write a report; no one reads it. I decide on an arrest, my decision is ignored. I am closing the case."

"But the threads," Littlemore answered. "The hairs. The injuries. You said so, Mr. Hugel, you said so yourself."

"What did I say?"

"You said the same guy who killed Miss Riverford attacked Nora Acton. You said there was proof. That means Miss Acton didn't cook it all up. There *was* an assault, Mr. Hugel. There *is* a case. *Somebody* attacked Miss Acton on Monday."

"What I said, Detective, was that the physical evidence was consistent with the assailant being the same person in both cases, not that it was proof. Read my report."

"You don't think Miss Acton—you don't think she whipped herself, do you?"

The coroner stared straight ahead with his morose, sleepless eyes. "Disgusting," he said.

"But how about the tiepin? You said there was a tiepin with Banwell's initials on it. It's exactly what you were looking for, Mr. Hugel."

"Littlemore, don't you have ears? You heard Riviere. The impression on Elizabeth Riverford's neck was not *GB*. I made a mistake," Hugel muttered angrily. "I made one mistake after another."

"So what's it doing there—the pin, in the tree?"

"How should I know?" yelled Hugel. "Why don't you ask her? We have nothing. Nothing. Only that infernal girl. No jury in the country would believe her now. She probably put the pin in the tree herself. She is—she is psychopathic. They must put her away."

❧

SÁNDOR FERENCZI, smiling and nodding encouragingly, backed himself toward the door of Jung's hotel room like a courtier withdrawing from the royal presence. He had, with some trepidation, conveyed Freud's request to see Jung alone.

"Say that I will call on him in ten minutes," Jung had answered. "With pleasure."

Ferenczi had expected an implacable Swiss in high umbrage, not the serene Jung who had greeted him. Ferenczi would have to inform Freud that Jung's change of temperament struck him as peculiar. More than that, he would have to tell Freud what Jung was doing.

Hundreds of pebbles and small stones, together with an armful of broken twigs and torn-up grass, were strewn about the floor of Jung's room. Ferenczi could not imagine where it had all come from: possibly from empty lots undergoing construction, which seemed ubiquitous in New York. Jung himself was sitting cross-legged on the floor, playing with these materials. He had pushed all the hotel furniture—armchairs, lamps, coffee table—out of the way, clearing a large empty space on the floor. In this space, he had built a village of stones, with dozens of tiny houses surrounding a castle. Each house had its own little plot of tufted grass behind it: perhaps a vegetable garden or backyard. In the center of the castle, Jung was trying to implant a forked twig with long blades of grass tied to it, but he could not make this standard stay upright. That was why, Ferenczi guessed, Jung needed another ten minutes before he could come. Assuming, Ferenczi added to himself, that the delay had nothing to do with the service revolver lying on Jung's bedside table.

❧

IT IS SURELY IMPOSSIBLE for a house to wear an expression, but I would have sworn otherwise as I neared the Actons' limestone townhouse on Gramercy Park late Thursday morning. Before anyone answered the door, I knew something was amiss within.

Mrs. Biggs let me in. The woman was literally wringing her hands. In an anguished whisper, she told me it was all her fault. She was just tidying up, she said. She would never have shown it to anyone if she had known.

Gradually Mrs. Biggs calmed down, and I learned from her all the dreadful events of the previous night, including the discovery of the telltale cigarette. At least, Mrs. Biggs added with relief, Mrs. Banwell was now upstairs. It was plain that the old servant regarded Clara Banwell as capable of taking matters in hand more competently than the girl's own mother or father. Mrs. Biggs left me in the sitting room. Fifteen minutes later, Clara Banwell entered.

Mrs. Banwell was dressed to leave. She wore a simple hat with a diaphanous veil and carried a closed parasol that must have been quite expensive, judging by its iridescent handle. "Forgive me, Dr. Younger," she said. "I don't want to delay your seeing Nora. But could I have a word with you before I go?"

"Certainly, Mrs. Banwell."

As she removed her hat and veil, I could not help noticing the length and thickness of her eyelashes, behind which sparkled her knowing eyes. She was not one of Mrs. Wharton's dryads "subdued to the conventions of the drawing-room." Rather, the conventions lit her up. It was as if all our fashions had been chosen to show off her body, her ivory skin, her green eyes. I could make nothing of her expression; she managed to look both proud and vulnerable.

"I know now what Nora has told you," she said. "About me. I didn't know last night."

"I'm sorry," I replied. "It is the unenviable hazard of being a doctor."

"Do you assume your patients tell the truth?"

I said nothing.

"Well, in this case it *is* true," she said. "Nora saw me with her father, just as she described it to you. But since you know that much, I want you to know the rest. I did not act without my husband's knowledge."

"I assure you, Mrs. Banwell—"

"Please don't. You think I am trying to justify myself." She picked up a photograph from the mantel: it was of Nora at thirteen or fourteen. "I am far past self-justification, Doctor. What I wish to tell you is for Nora's sake, not my own. I remember when they moved back into this house. George rebuilt it for them. She was shockingly attractive, even then. And only fourteen. One felt the goddesses had for once put aside their differences and made her together as a present for Zeus. I am childless, Doctor."

"I see."

"Do you? I am childless because my husband will not allow me to bear. He says it would spoil my figure. We have never had—ordinary— sexual congress, my husband and I. Not once. He will not allow it."

"Perhaps he is impotent."

"George?" She looked amused at the thought.

"It is hard to believe a man would voluntarily restrain himself un-der the circumstances."

"I believe you are complimenting me, Doctor. Well, George does not restrain himself. He causes me to gratify him in—a different fashion. For ordinary congress, he has recourse to other women. My husband wants many of the young women he meets, and he gets them. He wanted Nora. As it happened, Nora's father wanted me. George saw a way, therefore, to obtain what he wanted. He obliged me to seduce Harcourt Acton. Of course I was not permitted to do with Harcourt what was forbidden with my own husband. Hence what Nora saw."

"Your husband believed he could make Acton prostitute his own daughter?"

"Harcourt was not required actually to hand Nora over, Doctor. All my husband needed was for Harcourt to feel that his own happi-ness was so dependent on me that he would be averse, deeply averse, to any rift coming between his family and ours. That way, when the time came, he would turn a blind eye and a deaf ear."

I understood. After Mrs. Banwell entered into relations with Mr. Acton, George Banwell made his first advance on Nora. His strategy evidently worked. When Nora protested to her father and begged him to send Banwell away, Mr. Acton chose to disbelieve and scold her—just as if, Nora had told me, she had done something wrong. And she had: she had threatened his precious arrangement with Mrs. Banwell.

"You must think what it is like," Mrs. Banwell added, "for a man such as Harcourt Acton to be offered what he has only dreamed of—indeed, what he never had the courage even to dream of. I truly be-lieve the man would have done anything I asked."

I felt a peculiar pressure just below my sternum. "Did your hus-band get what he wanted?"

"Are you asking for professional reasons, Doctor?"

"Of course."

"Of course. The answer, I believe, is no. Not yet, at any rate." She returned the photograph of Nora to its place on the mantel, beside a picture of the girl's parents. "In any event, Doctor, Nora is aware that I am—unhappy—in my marriage. I believe she is now trying to rescue me."

"How?"

"Nora has a very fertile imagination. You must remember: even though to your man's eyes, Nora looks like a woman, a prize ready to be possessed, she is still just a child. A child whose parents have never had the slightest understanding of her. An only child. Nora has lived almost all her life in a world of her own."

"You said she was trying to rescue you. How?"

"She may believe she can bring George down by telling the police he attacked her. She may even believe he did. Possibly we have overwhelmed the poor thing, and she is suffering from a delusion."

"Or possibly your husband did attack her."

"I don't say he is incapable of it. Far from it. My husband is capable of nearly anything. But in this case, it happens he didn't. George came home last night just after I returned from the party. It was eleven-thirty. Nora says she did not go to her room until quarter to twelve."

"Your husband might have left home in the night, Mrs. Banwell."

"Yes, I know, he might well have on another night, but last night he didn't. He was too busy, you see, having his way with me. All night long." She smiled, a very small, ironic, perfect smile, and rubbed one of her wrists unconsciously. Her long sleeves concealed her wrists, but she saw me looking. She took a deep breath. "You might as well see."

She came very near me, so near I became aware of the diamonds glinting in her earlobes and the fragrant smell of her hair. She pushed up her sleeves a little and revealed a painful rawness, of fresh origin, on both wrists. I have heard there are men who bind women for pleasure. I cannot be sure this was the meaning of the bruised skin Mrs. Banwell showed me, but certainly it was the picture that came to mind.

She laughed lightly. The sound was wry, not bitter. "I am a fallen woman, Doctor, and at the same time a virgin. Have you ever heard of such a thing?"

"Mrs. Banwell, I am not a lawyer, but I believe you have more than ample grounds for divorce. Indeed, you may not be legally married at all, since there was never consummation."

"Divorce? You don't know George. He would sooner kill me than let me go." She smiled again. I could not help imagining what it would feel like to kiss her. "And who would have me, Doctor, even if I could get away? What man would touch me, knowing what I have done?"

"Any man," I said.

"You are kind, but you are lying." She looked up at me. "You are lying cruelly. You could be touching me right now. But you never would."

I gazed down at her flawless, irredeemably charming features. "No, Mrs. Banwell, I never would. But not for the reasons you say."

At that moment, Nora Acton appeared at the door.

❧

DETECTIVE LITTLEMORE'S STRIDE, after his interview with the coroner, lacked its customary snappiness. The news that Harry Thaw was still locked up in an asylum had come as a blow to him. Ever since he read the Thaw transcript, Littlemore had imagined that this case might be bigger than anybody realized and he might be on the verge of breaking it open. Now he didn't know if there was a case at all.

The detective had formed a high opinion of Mr. Hugel, despite all his outbursts and idiosyncracies. Littlemore felt sure Hugel could solve the case. The police weren't supposed to just give up. The coroner in particular wasn't supposed to. He was too smart.

Littlemore believed in the police force. He had been on it for eight years, ever since he lied about his age in order to become a junior beat patrolman. It was the first real job he ever had, and he stuck to it. He loved living in the police barracks when he first joined up. He loved eating with the other cops, listening to their stories. He knew there were some rotten apples, but he thought they were the exceptions. If you told him, for example, that his hero Sergeant Becker shook down every brothel and casino in the Tenderloin for protection money, Littlemore would have thought you were pulling his leg. If you told him the new police commissioner wanted in on the game, he would have said you were crazy. In short, the detective looked up to his superiors on the force, and Hugel had let him down.

But Littlemore never turned against someone who disappointed him. His reaction was the opposite. He wanted to bring the coroner back on board. He needed to find something that would convince the coroner the case was still alive. Hugel had been certain that Banwell was the perpetrator from the start; maybe he was right all along.

To be sure, Littlemore believed in Mayor McClellan even more than he believed in Coroner Hugel, and the mayor had provided Banwell with a firm alibi on the night Miss Riverford was killed. But maybe Banwell had an accomplice—maybe a Chinese accomplice. Hadn't Banwell himself hired Chong Sing to work in the laundry of the Balmoral? And now it turned out that Miss Riverford's murderer might not have been Miss Acton's assailant: that's what Mr. Hugel had just told him. So maybe Banwell's accomplice killed Miss Riverford, and Banwell attacked Miss Acton. It occurred to Littlemore that, based on this theory, Hugel would still have made a mistake. But the detective, while holding an elevated view of the coroner's powers, didn't regard him as infallible. And Hugel, Littlemore figured, wouldn't mind being wrong on a detail if he was right on the whole shebang.

So the detective, regaining the spring in his step, knew he had work to do. First, he went up the street to headquarters and found Louis Riviere in his basement darkroom. Littlemore asked Riviere if he could make a reverse image of the photograph that showed the mark on Elizabeth Riverford's neck. The Frenchman told him to come back at the end of the day to pick it up. "And can you enlarge it for me too, Louie?" Littlemore asked.

"Why not?" replied Riviere. "The sun is good."

Next the detective headed uptown. He rode the train to Forty-second Street and from there strolled over to Susie Merrill's house. No one answered, so he took up a position down the block and across the street. An hour later, the hefty Susie let herself out, wearing another of her enormous hats, this one boasting a fruit medley. Littlemore followed her to a Child's Lunch Room on Broadway. She sat down at a booth alone. Littlemore waited until she was served to see if anyone else was going to show up. As Mrs. Merrill was attacking her plate of corned beef hash, Littlemore slipped into the seat across from her.

"Hello, Susie," he said. "I found it—what you wanted me to find."

"What are you doing here? Get out. I told you to keep me out of it."

"No, you didn't."

"Well, I'm telling you now," said Susie. "You want to get us both killed?"

"By who, Susie? Thaw's in a loony bin upstate."

"Oh, yeah?"

"Yeah."

"I guess he can't be your murderer then," she observed.

"I guess not."

"So there's nothing to talk about, is there?"

"Don't hold out on me, Susie."

"You want to get yourself killed, that's fine with me, but leave me out of it." Mrs. Merrill rose, putting thirty cents on the table: a nickel for her coffee, twenty cents for her hash and poached egg, another nickel for the waitress. "I've got a baby in the house," she said.

Littlemore grabbed her arm. "Think it over, Susie, I want answers, and I'll be coming back for them."

CHAPTER EIGHTEEN

CLARA BANWELL DIDN'T show any of the discomfort I felt under Nora's frozen gaze. Filling the air with an easy flow of words, she said her good-byes, acting for all the world as if she and I had not been caught standing several inches too close together. She extended her hand to me, kissed Nora on the cheek, and thoughtfully added that we need not see her to the door, she didn't want to delay Nora's treatment a moment longer. Seconds later, I heard the front door close behind her.

Nora stood in the same spot Mrs. Banwell had occupied minutes before. I had no business noticing her looks, given the harrowing events of the night before, but I couldn't help myself. It was absurd. One could walk for miles in New York City—as I had that morning—or spend a month at the Grand Central Station, and never see a single woman of surpassing physical grace. Yet in the space of five minutes, two had stood before me in the Actons' sitting room. But what a contrast between them.

Nora wore no adornments, no jewelry, no embroidered fabric. She carried no parasol; she had no veil. She wore a simple white blouse, its sleeves ending at the elbow, tucked at her impossibly narrow waist into a sky-blue pleated skirt. The top of her shirt was gently scooped, revealing the delicate structure of her collarbone and her long, lovely neck. This neck was now almost unblemished, the bruises faded. Her blond hair was pulled back as always into a braid reaching almost to her waist. She was only, as Mrs. Banwell had said, a girl. Her youth cried out from every plane and curve of her, especially in the high color of her cheeks and eyes, which radiated with youth's hope, its freshness, and, I should add, its fury.

"I hate you more than anyone else I have ever known," she said to me.

So: I was now, more than ever, hoisted into the position of her father. As if led by some inexorable fate, she had come upon me and Clara Banwell closeted in a study just as she had come upon her father and Clara Banwell consorting in another study three years ago. The signal difference—that there was nothing between Mrs. Banwell and myself—was evidently lost on her. That was unsurprising. It was not I she was staring angrily at now. It was her father, dressed in my clothes. Had I been seeking to cement the analytic transference, I could not have devised a better stratagem. Had I been hoping to bring her analysis to a climax, I could not have asked for a luckier conspiracy of events. I now had the opportunity—and the duty—to try to show Nora the erroneous transposition occurring in her mind, so that she could recognize how the rage she imagined she felt toward me was actually the misdirected anger she harbored for her father.

In other words, I was obliged to bury my own emotion. I had to conceal the least shred of feeling I had for her, no matter how genuine, no matter how overpowering. "Then I am at a disadvantage, Miss Acton," I replied, "because I love you more than anyone else I have ever known."

A perfect silence enveloped us for several heartbeats.

"You do?" she asked.

"Yes."

"But you and Clara were—"

"We weren't. I swear it."

"You weren't?"

"No."

Nora began to breathe hard. Too hard: her outer clothes were not tight, but she seemed to be wearing something underneath that was. Her respiration was entirely concentrated in the upper part of her torso. Concerned she might faint, I guided her to the front door and opened it. She needed air. Across the street was the dappled grove of Gramercy Park. Nora stepped outside. I suggested that her parents ought to know if she was going out.

"Why?" she asked me. "We could just go to the park."

We crossed the street and, at one of the wrought-iron gates, Nora produced from her purse a gold and black key. There was an awkward moment when I helped her through the gate: a decision had to be made about whether I would offer her my arm as we walked. I managed not to.

Therapeutically speaking, I was in a great deal of trouble. I did not fear for myself, although it was remarkable that my feelings for this girl seemed impervious to the fact that she might well be unstable or even mentally ill. If Nora had actually burned herself, there were two possibilities. Either she did it with full conscious deliberation and was lying to the world, or she did it in a dissociated state, hypnoid or somnambulistic, which was shut off from the rest of her consciousness. On the whole, I think I preferred the former alternative, but neither one was attractive.

I did not regret having confessed my feelings to her. The circumstances forced my hand. But while declaring my love for her might have been honorable, acting on it would be the opposite. The lowest-bred cur would not take advantage of a girl in her condition. I had to find a way to let her know this. I had to extricate myself from the role of lover into which I had just stumbled and try to become her physician again.

"Miss Acton," I said.

"Won't you call me Nora, Doctor?"

"No."

"Why?"

"Because I am still your doctor. You can't be Nora to me. You are my patient." I wasn't sure how she would take that, but I went on. "Tell me what happened last night. No, wait: you said in the hotel yesterday that your memory of Monday's attack had come back to you. Tell me first what you remember about that."

"Must I?"

"Yes."

She asked if we could sit, and we found a bench in a secluded corner. She still did not know, she said, how it all began or how she got there. That part of her memory remained missing. What she remembered was being tied up in her parents' bedroom. She was standing, bound by the wrists to something overhead. She was wearing only her slip. All the curtains and blinds were drawn.

The man was behind her. He had tied a soft piece of fabric—perhaps silk—around her throat and was pulling it so tight she couldn't breathe, much less call out. He was also hitting her with a strap or crop of some kind. It stung but it was not unbearable—more like a spanking. It was the silk around her throat that scared her; she thought he meant to kill her. But every time she was on the verge of passing out, he would relax the stranglehold ever so slightly, just enough to let her catch her breath.

He began to strike her much harder. It became so painful she thought she couldn't stand it. Then he dropped the whip, stepped behind her, so close she could feel his harsh breath on her shoulders, and put a hand on her. She didn't say where; I didn't ask. At the same time, a part of his body—"a hard part," she said—came into contact with her hip. The man made an ugly sound, and then he made a mistake; the tie around her throat suddenly went slack. She took a deep breath and screamed—screamed as hard and as long as she could. She must have passed out. The next thing she knew, Mrs. Biggs was by her side.

Nora maintained her composure while recounting all this, her hands folded in her lap. Without changing attitude, she asked, "Are you disgusted by me?"

"No," I said. "In your memory of the attack, was the man Banwell?"

"I thought so. But the mayor said—"

"The mayor said Banwell was with him Sunday night, when the *other* girl was murdered. If you remember Banwell being your attacker, you must say so."

"I don't know," said Nora plaintively. "I think so. I don't know. He was behind me the whole time."

"Tell me about last night," I said.

She poured out the story of the intruder in her bedroom. This time, she said, she was certain it was Banwell. Toward the end, however, she turned away from me once more. Was there something she wasn't saying? "I don't even own any lipstick," she concluded earnestly. "And that horrible thing they found in my closet. Where am I supposed to have gotten that?"

I made the obvious point: "You are wearing makeup now." There was the lightest hint of gloss on her lips, and the faintest blush on her cheeks.

"But this is Clara's!" she cried. "She put it on me. She said it would suit me."

We sat in silence for a time.

At last, she spoke. "You don't believe a word I've said."

"I don't believe you would lie to me."

"But I would," she answered. "I have."

"When?"

"When I said I hated you," she replied, after a long pause.

"Tell me what you're keeping back."

"What do you mean?" she asked.

"There is something else about last night—something that makes you doubt yourself."

"How do you know?" she demanded.

"Just tell me."

Reluctantly, she confessed that there was one inexplicable piece of the episode. Her vantage point, as she saw the awful event unfold, was not from her own eye level but from a place above both herself and the intruder. She actually saw herself lying on the bed as if she were an observer of the scene, not the victim. "How is that possible, Doctor?" she cried softly. "It's not possible, is it?"

I wanted to console her, but what I had to say was not likely to be comforting. "What you are describing is how we see things sometimes in dreams."

"But if I dreamt it, how did I get burned?" she whispered. "I didn't burn myself, did I? Did I?"

I could not answer. I was picturing an even worse scenario. Could she also have inflicted those terrible wounds—the first set of wounds—on herself? I tried to imagine her drawing a knife or razor along her own soft skin, making it bleed. It was impossible for me to believe.

From far downtown, a roar of human voices suddenly erupted in a great distant cheer. Nora asked what it could be. I said it was probably the strikers. A march had been promised by union leaders in the aftermath of some labor trouble downtown yesterday. A notorious firebrand called Gompers vowed a strike that would bring the city's industry to a halt.

"They have every right to strike," said Nora, clearly eager to be distracted. "The capitalists should be ashamed of themselves, employing those people without paying them enough to feed their families. Have you seen the homes in which they live?"

She described to me how, all last spring, Clara Banwell and she had visited families in the tenements of the Lower East Side. It had been Clara's idea. That was how, said Nora, she had met Elsie Sigel with the Chinaman whom Detective Littlemore had been asking about.

"Elsie Sigel?" I repeated. Aunt Mamie had mentioned Miss Sigel to me at her gala. "Who has run off to Washington?"

"Yes," said Nora. "I thought her very foolish to be doing missionary work when people are dying for want of food and shelter. And Elsie was working only with men, when it is the women and children who are really suffering." Clara, Nora explained to me, had made a special point of calling on those families where the men had run off or been killed in work accidents. Clara and Nora got to know many such families on their visits, spending hours in their homes. Nora would care for the little ones while Clara befriended the women and the more grown-up children. They started visiting these families once a week, bringing them food and necessaries. Twice they had taken babies to the hospital, saving them from serious disease or even death. Once, Nora told me more darkly, a girl had gone missing; Clara and she visited every police station and hospital downtown, finally finding the girl in the morgue. The medical examiner said the girl had been raped. The girl's mother had no one to comfort or support her; Clara did both. Nora had seen unthinkable squalor that summer, but also—or so I guessed—a warmth of familial love previously unknown to her.

When she concluded, Nora and I sat looking at each other. Without warning, she said, "Would you kiss me if I asked you?"

"Don't ask me, Miss Acton," I said.

She took my hand and drew it toward her, touching the back of my fingers to her cheek.

"*No,*" I said sharply. She let go at once. Everything was my fault. I had given her every reason to believe she could take the liberty she had just taken. Now I had pulled the rug out from under her. "You must believe me," I told her. "There is nothing I would like more. But I can't. I would be taking advantage of you."

"I want you to take advantage of me," she said.

"No."

"Because I am seventeen?"

"Because you are my patient. Listen to me. The feelings you may think you have for me—you must not believe in them. They aren't real. They are an artifact of your analysis. It happens to every single patient who is psychoanalyzed."

She looked at me as if I must be joking. "You think your stupid questions have made me *favor* you?"

"Think of it. One moment you feel indifference toward me. Then rage. Then jealousy. Then—something else. But it's not me. It's nothing I have done. It's nothing I am. How could it be? You don't know me. You don't know the first thing about me. All these feelings come from elsewhere in your life. They surface because of these stupid questions I ask you. But they belong elsewhere. They are feelings you have for someone else, not me."

"You think I am in love with someone else? Who? Not George Banwell?"

"You might have been."

"Never." She made a genuinely disgusted face. "I detest him."

I took the plunge. I hated taking it—because I expected she would henceforth regard me with revulsion—and my timing was all wrong, but it was still my obligation. "Dr. Freud has a theory, Miss Acton. It may apply to you."

"What theory?" She was growing increasingly vexed.

"I warn you, it is distasteful in the extreme. He believes that all of us, from a very early age, harbor—that we secretly wish—well, in your case, he believes that when you saw Mrs. Banwell with your father, when you saw her kneeling before your father and—a— engaging with him in—"

"You don't have to say it," she broke in.

"He believes you felt jealous."

She stared at me blankly.

I was having trouble making myself clear. "Directly, physically jealous. What I mean is, Dr. Freud believes that when you saw what Mrs. Banwell was doing to your father, you wished you were the one who—that you had fantasies of being the one who—"

"Stop!" she cried out. She put her hands over her ears.

"I'm sorry."

"How can he know that?" She was aghast. Her hands now covered her mouth.

I registered this reaction. I heard her words. But I tried to believe I hadn't. I wanted to say, *I must be hearing things; I actually thought for a moment you asked how Freud knew.*

"I never told anyone that," she whispered, turning scarlet all over. "Not anyone. How could he possibly know?"

I could only stare at her blankly, as she had stared at me a moment before.

"Oh, I am *vile!*" she cried. She ran away, back toward her house.

ᔈ

AFTER LEAVING CHILD'S, Littlemore hoofed it over to the Forty-seventh Street police station, to see if either Chong Sing or William Leon had been collared. Both men had indeed been arrested—a hundred times, Captain Post told the detective irritably. Within hours of the perpetrators' descriptions going out, dozens of calls had come in, from all over the city and even from Jersey, from people claiming to have spotted Chong. With Leon it was even worse. Every Chinaman in a suit and tie was William Leon.

"Jack Reardon's been running around town all day like his head was chopped off," said Captain Post, referring to the officer who, having been present with Littlemore when Miss Sigel's body was discovered, was the only man Post had who had actually seen the elusive Chong Sing. Reardon had been dispatched to police stations all over town, wherever another "Mr. Chong" had been picked up, and everywhere he went, Reardon discovered another false arrest. "It's no good. We locked up half of Chinatown, and we still didn't get 'em. I had to tell the boys to lay off any more arrests. Here. You want to run any of these down?"

Post threw Littlemore a record of reported but not yet acted-upon Chong Sing and William Leon sightings. The detective perused the list, running his finger down the handwritten notes. He stopped halfway down the page, where a one-line description caught his eye. It read: *Canal at River. Chinaman seen working docks. Said to meet description of suspect Chong Sing.*

"Got a car?" asked Littlemore. "I want to have a look at this one."

"Why?"

"Because there's red clay at those docks," answered the detective.

Littlemore drove Captain Post's one and only police car downtown, accompanied by a uniformed man. They turned on Canal Street and followed it all the way to the eastern edge of the city, where the immense, newly erected Manhattan Bridge rose up over the East River. Littlemore stopped at the entry to the construction site and cast his eyes over the laborers.

"There he is," said the detective, pointing. "That's him."

It would have been hard to miss Chong Sing: a lone, conspicuous Chinese among a throng of white and black workingmen. He was wheeling a barrow filled with cinder blocks.

"Walk right at him," Littlemore instructed the officer. "If he runs, I'll take him."

Chong Sing didn't run. At the sight of a police officer, he merely put his head down and kept pushing his wheelbarrow. When the officer put the arm on him, Chong submitted without a fight. Other workmen stopped and watched the uneventful arrest unfold, but no one interfered. By the time the officer returned to the police car where Detective Littlemore was waiting, the men were back at work as if nothing had happened.

"Why'd you run away yesterday, Mr. Chong?"

"I no run," said Chong. "I go to work. See? I go to work."

"I'm going to have to charge you as an accessory to murder. You understand what that means? You could hang." Littlemore made a gesture conveying the meaning of the last word he had spoken.

"I don't know anything," the Chinese man pleaded. "Leon go away. Then smell come from Leon room. That's all."

"Sure," said the detective. Littlemore had the officer take Chong Sing to the Tombs. The detective stayed behind. He wanted a closer look at the docks. The puzzle pieces were reconfiguring themselves in the detective's mind—and beginning to fit together. Littlemore knew he was going to find clay at the foot of the Manhattan Bridge, and he had a hunch that George Banwell might have stepped in that clay.

Everyone knew Banwell was building the Manhattan Bridge towers. When Mayor McClellan awarded the contract to Banwell's American Steel Company, the Hearst papers had cried corruption,

condemning the mayor for favoring an old friend and gleefully predict-
ing delays, breakdowns, and overcharges. In fact, Banwell got those
towers up not only within budget but in record time. He had personally supervised the construction—which gave Littlemore his idea.

Littlemore walked toward the river, blending into the mass of
men. He could mix with pretty much anyone, if he wanted. Littlemore was good at seeming easy because he *was* easy, especially when
things were falling into place. Chong Sing had two jobs working for
Mr. George Banwell. Wasn't that interesting?

The detective arrived at the crowded central pier just in time for
a change of shifts. Hundreds of dirty, booted men were trudging off
the pier, while a long line of others waited to take the elevator down
to the caisson. The din of the turbines, a constant mechanical throbbing, filled the air with a furious rhythm.

If you had asked Littlemore how he knew there was some trouble, some unhappiness, in the air as well, he could not have told you.
Engaging a few of the men in conversation, he quickly learned of
Seamus Malley's bad end. Poor Malley was, the men said, yet another
victim of caisson disease. When they opened the elevator door a couple of mornings ago, they found him lying dead, dried blood trailing
from his ears and mouth.

The men complained bitterly of the caisson, which they called
"the box" or "the coffin." Some thought it cursed. Almost all had ailments they ascribed to it. Most said they were glad their work was almost finished, but the older heads clucked and replied that they'd all
be missing their sandhog days soon enough—*sandhog* being the word
for a caisson worker—when their pay stopped coming in. What pay?
one of the boys replied. Was three dollars for twelve hours of work
supposed to be called pay? "Look at Malley," this one said. "He
couldn't even afford a roof over his head with our 'pay.' That's why
he's dead. They killed him. They're killing all of us." But another
replied that Malley had a roof, all right; he just also had a wife—*that*
was why he was spending nights down in the box.

Littlemore, observing tracks of red clay all over the pier, knelt to
tie his shoes and surreptitiously collected samples. He inquired if
Mr. Banwell ever came down to the pier. The answer was yes. In fact,
he was told, Mr. Banwell took at least one trip down to the coffin

every day to inspect the work. Sometimes even His Honor, the mayor himself, would go with him.

The detective asked what Banwell was like to work for. Hell, was the answer. The men agreed that Banwell didn't care how many of them died in the caisson, if the job got done faster that way. Yesterday was the first time they could remember when Banwell had ever shown any concern for their lives.

"How's that?" asked Littlemore.

"He told us to forget about Window Five."

The "windows," the men told Littlemore, were the caisson's debris chutes. Each one had a number, and Window Five had jammed up earlier this week. Normally the boss—Banwell—would have immediately ordered them to clear the blockage, a job the sandhogs hated, because it required a difficult, dangerous maneuver with at least one man inside the window when it was inundated with water. But yesterday, for the first time, Banwell told them not to bother. One man suggested the boss might be getting soft. The others denied it; they said Banwell didn't see any point taking chances with the bridge so near completion.

Littlemore chewed this information over. Then he went to the elevator.

The elevator man—a wrinkly codger with not a hair on his head—was perched on a wooden stool inside the car. The detective asked him who locked the elevator door two nights ago, the night Malley died.

"I did," said the old man, with a proprietary air.

"Was the car up here at the pier when you locked up that night, or was it down below?"

"Up here, o'course. You ain't too quick, are you, young fella? How can my elevator be down there if I'm up here?"

The question was a good one. The elevator was manually operated. Only a man inside the car could take her up or bring her down. Hence when the elevator man completed his last run of the night, the car was necessarily up at the pier. But if the elevator man had asked Littlemore a good question, the detective replied with a better one. "So how did he get up here?"

"What?"

"The dead guy," said Littlemore. "Malley. He stayed below Tuesday night, when everybody else came up?"

"That's right." The old man shook his head. "Blamed fool. Not the first time, neither. I told him he oughtn'ta. I told him."

"And they found him right here in your car, at the pier, the next morning?"

"That's right. Dead as a dead fish. You can still see his blood. I been trying to clean it off two whole days now, and I can't. Washed it with soap, washed it with soda. See it?"

"So how did he get up here?" asked the detective again.

CHAPTER NINETEEN

CARL JUNG STOOD straight and tall in the doorway to Freud's suite. He was fully, formally dressed. Nothing in his demeanor suggested a man who had just been playing with sticks and stones on the floor of his hotel room.

Freud, in vest and shirtsleeves, begged his guest to make himself comfortable. His instinct told him this interview was decisive. Jung decidedly did not look right. Freud gave no credence to Brill's accusations, but he began to agree that Jung might be spinning out of his—Freud's—orbit.

Jung was, Freud knew, more intelligent and creative than any of his other followers—the first one with the potential to break new ground. But Jung undoubtedly had a father complex. When, in one of his earliest letters, Jung begged Freud for a photograph of himself, saying he would "cherish" it, Freud was flattered. But when he explicitly asked Freud to regard him not as an equal but as a son, Freud became concerned. He told himself then he would have to take special care.

It occurred to Freud that, as far as he knew, Jung did not have any other male friends. Rather, Jung surrounded himself with women, many women—too many. That was the other difficulty. Given Hall's communication, Freud no longer could avoid a conversation with Jung about the girl who had written claiming to be Jung's patient and mistress. Freud had seen the unconscionable letter Jung sent to the girl's mother. On top of all this, there was Ferenczi's report on the state of Jung's hotel room.

The one point on which Freud had no qualms was Jung's belief in the fundamental tenets of psychoanalysis. In their private letters and in hours of private talk, Freud had tested, prodded, probed. There could be no doubt: Jung fully believed in the sexual aetiology. And he had come to his conviction in the best of all possible ways, overcoming his own skepticism after seeing Freud's hypotheses confirmed again and again in clinical practice.

"We have always spoken freely to each other," said Freud. "Can we now?"

"I should like nothing more," said Jung. "Especially now that I have freed myself from your paternal authority."

Freud tried not to appear taken aback. "Good, good. Coffee?"

"No, thank you. Yes. It happened yesterday, when you chose to keep hidden the truth of your Count Thun dream in order to preserve your authority. You see the paradox. You feared losing your authority; as a result, you lost it. You cared more for authority than truth; with me, there can be no authority other than truth. But it is better this way. Your cause will only prosper from my independence. Indeed, it already is prospering. I have solved the problem of incest!"

Out of this rush of words, Freud fastened on two. "*My* cause?"

"What?"

"You said, 'your cause,'" Freud repeated.

"I did not."

"You did. It is the second time."

"Well, it *is* yours—is it not?—yours *and* mine. It will be infinitely stronger now. Didn't you hear me? I have solved the incest problem."

"What do you mean, 'solved' it?" said Freud. "What problem?"

"We know the grown son does not actually covet his mother sexually, with her varicose veins and sagging breasts. That is obvious to anyone. Nor does the infant son, who has no inkling of penetration. Why then does the adult's neurosis revolve so frequently around the Oedipal complex, as your cases and my own confirm? The answer came to me in a dream last night. The adult conflict *reactivates the infantile material*. The neurotic's suppressed libido is forced back into its infantile channels—just as you have always said!—where it finds the mother, who was once of such special value to him. The libido fastens onto her, without the mother ever having actually been desired."

These remarks caused a curious physical reaction in Sigmund

Freud. He suffered a rush of blood to the arteries surrounding his cerebral cortex, which he experienced as a heaviness in his skull. He swallowed and said, "You are denying the Oedipal complex?"

"Not at all. How could I? I invented the term."

"The term *complex* is yours," said Freud. "You are retaining the complex but denying the *Oedipal*."

"No!" cried Jung. "I am preserving all your fundamental insights. Neurotics do have an Oedipal complex. Their neurosis causes them to believe that they sexually coveted their mother."

"You are saying there are no actual incestuous wishes. Not among the healthy."

"Not even among the neurotic! It is marvelous. The neurotic develops a mother complex because his libido is forced into its infantile channels. Thus the neurotic gives himself a delusive reason to castigate himself. He feels guilty over a wish he never had."

"I see. What then has caused his neurosis?" asked Freud.

"His present conflict. Whatever desire the neurotic is not admitting to. Whatever life task he can't bring himself to face."

"Ah, the present conflict," said Freud. His head was no longer heavy. Instead, a peculiar lightness had come to him. "So there is no reason to delve into the patient's sexual past. Or, indeed, his childhood at all."

"Exactly," said Jung. "I have never thought so. From a purely clinical perspective, the present conflict is what must be uncovered and worked through. The reactivated sexual material from childhood can be excavated, but it is a lure, a trap. It is the patient's effort to flee from his neurosis. I am writing it all up now. You will see how many more adherents psychoanalysis will gain by reducing the role of sexuality."

"Oh, eliminate it altogether—then we shall do even better," said Freud. "May I ask you a question? If incest is not actually desired, why is it taboo?"

"Taboo?"

"Yes," said Freud. "Why would there be an incest prohibition in every human society that has ever existed, if no one has ever wished it?"

"Because—because—many things are taboo that are not actually desired."

"Name one."

"Well, many things. There is a long list," said Jung.

"Name one."

"So—for example, the prehistoric animal cults, the totems, they—ah—" Jung was unable to finish his sentence.

"May I ask you one thing more?" said Freud. "You say this insight came to you through the interpretation of a dream. I wonder what the dream was. Perhaps another interpretation is possible?"

"I did not say through the interpretation of a dream," Jung replied. "I said *in* a dream. Indeed, I was not quite asleep."

"I don't understand," said Freud.

"You know the voices one hears at night, just prior to sleep. I have trained myself to attend to them. One of them speaks to me with ancient wisdom. I have seen him. He is an old man, an Egyptian Gnostic—a chimera, really—called Philemon. It was he who revealed the secret to me."

Freud did not answer.

"I am not cowed by your hints of incredulity," said Jung. "There are more things in heaven and earth, Herr Professor, than are dreamt in your psychology."

"I daresay. But to be led by a voice, Jung?"

"Perhaps I am giving you the wrong impression," Jung replied. "I do not accept Philemon's word without reasons. He made his case through an exegesis of the primitive mother cults. I assure you, I did not believe it at first. I put several objections, each of which he was able to answer."

"You converse with him?"

"Obviously you are unhappy with my theoretical innovation."

"I am concerned about its source," said Freud.

"No. You are concerned about your theories, your sexual theories," said Jung, his indignation visibly rising. "So you change the subject and try to bait me into a conversation about the supernatural. I won't be baited. I have objective reasons."

"Given to you by a spirit?"

"Just because you have never experienced such phenomena does not mean they don't exist."

"I grant that," said Freud, "but there must be evidence, Jung."

"I have seen him, I tell you!" Jung cried. "Why is that not evidence? He wept describing to me how the pharaohs scratched their fathers' names from the monumental stelae—a fact I did not even know but which I later confirmed. Who are you to say what is evidence and what is not? You assume your conclusion: he does not exist; therefore what I see and what I hear does not count as evidence."

"What *you* hear. It is not evidence, Carl, if only one person can hear it."

A strange sound began to emanate from behind the sofa on which Freud sat: a creaking or groaning, as if there were something in the wall trying to get out. "What is that?" asked Freud.

"I don't know," said Jung.

The creaking grew louder until it filled the room. When it reached what sounded like a breaking point, it gave way to a splintering crack, like a clap of thunder.

"What on earth?" said Freud.

"I know that sound," said Jung. A triumphant gleam came to his eyes. "I have heard that sound before. *There* is your evidence! That was a catalytic exteriorization."

"A what?"

"A flux within the psyche manifesting itself through an external object," explained Jung. "I caused that sound!"

"Oh, come, Jung," said Freud. "I think it may have been a gunshot."

"You are mistaken. And to prove it, I will cause it again—this instant!"

The moment Jung uttered this remarkable pronouncement, the groan began anew. In just the same fashion, it rose to an unbearable peak and then erupted with a tremendous report.

"What do you say now?" asked Jung.

Freud said nothing. He had fainted and was slipping off the sofa.

❧

DETECTIVE LITTLEMORE, hustling up from the Canal Street docks, put it all together. It was the first murder he had ever uncovered. Mr. Hugel was going to be in heaven.

It wasn't Harry Thaw at all; it was George Banwell, from beginning to end. It was Banwell who killed Miss Riverford and stole her body from the morgue. Littlemore imagined Banwell driving to the river's edge, dragging the dead body out onto the pier, and descending the elevator down to the caisson. Banwell would have had the key to unlock the elevator door. The caisson was the perfect place to dispose of a corpse.

But Banwell would have assumed he was alone in the caisson. How stunned he must have been to discover Malley. How could Banwell have explained coming down in the middle of the night with a dead body in tow? He couldn't have explained it, so he had to kill him.

The blockage in Window Five, and Banwell's reaction to it, sealed the proof. He wouldn't want anybody discovering what had jammed up Window Five, would he?

The detective saw it all as he raced breathlessly along Canal Street—all except for the big black and red car, a Stanley Steamer, slowly trailing him half a block behind. In his mind's eye, as he crossed the street, Littlemore saw his promotion to lieutenant; he saw the mayor himself decorating him; he saw Betty admiring his new uniform; but he didn't see the Steamer's sudden lurch forward. He didn't see the vehicle swerving slightly in order to hit him dead on, and of course he couldn't see himself tumbling through the air, his legs taken out by the car's fender.

The body lay sprawled out on Canal Street as the car sped away down Second Avenue. Among the horrified onlookers, a number shouted imprecations at the fleeing hit-and-run driver. One called him a murderer. A patrolman happened to be on the corner. He rushed to the fallen Littlemore, who had enough strength to whisper something in the officer's ear. The patrolman frowned, then nodded. It took ten minutes, but a horse-drawn ambulance finally appeared. They did not bother with a hospital; rather, they took the detective's body directly to the morgue.

❧

JUNG GRASPED FREUD under the shoulders and laid him down on the sofa. Freud looked to Jung suddenly old and powerless, his fearsome faculty of judgment now as limp as his dangling arms and legs. Freud came to within a few seconds. "How sweet it must be," he said, "to die."

"Are you ill?" Jung asked.

"How did you do that? That noise?"

Jung shrugged.

"I will reconsider parapsychology—you have my word," said Freud. "Brill's behavior. I'm deeply sorry. He doesn't speak for me."

"I know."

"For a year I have placed too great a demand on you to keep me informed of your doings," said Freud. "I know it. I will withdraw the excess libido, that I promise you too. But I'm worried, Carl. Ferenczi saw your—village."

"Yes, I have found a new way to rekindle the memories of childhood. Through play. I used to build whole towns when I was a boy."

"I see." Freud sat up, handkerchief to his forehead. He accepted a glass of water from Jung.

"Let me analyze you," said Jung. "I can help you."

"Analyze *me*? Ah, my fainting just now. It was neurotic, you think?"

"Of course."

"I agree," said Freud. "But I already know its cause."

"Your ambition. It has made you blind, horribly blind. As I have been."

Freud took a deep breath. "Blind, you mean, to my fear of being dethroned, my resentment of your success, my unstinting efforts to keep you down?"

Jung started. "You knew?"

"I knew what you would say," said Freud. "What have I done to warrant that charge? Have I not advanced you at every turn, referred my own patients to you, cited you, credited you? Have I not done everything in my power for you, even at the price of injuring old friends, conferring on you positions I could have retained for myself?"

"But you undervalue the most important thing: my discoveries. I have solved the incest problem. It is a revolution. Yet you belittle it."

Freud rubbed his eyelids. "I assure you I do not. I appreciate its enormity all too well. You told us a dream you had on board the *George Washington*. Do you remember? You are deep in a cellar or cave, many levels belowground. You see a skeleton. You said the bones belonged to your wife, Emma, and her sister."

"I suppose," said Jung. "Why?"

"You suppose?"

"Yes, that's right. What of it?"

"Whose bones were they really?"

"What do you mean?" asked Jung.

"You were lying."

Jung didn't reply.

"Come," said Freud, "after twenty years of seeing patients prevaricate, you think I can't tell?"

Still Jung made no answer.

"The skeleton was mine, wasn't it?" said Freud.

"What if it was?" said Jung. "The dream told me I was surpassing you. I wished to spare your feelings."

"You wished me dead, Carl. You have made me your father, and now you wish me dead."

"I see," said Jung. "I see where you are going. My theoretical innovations are an attempt to overthrow you. That's what you always say, isn't it? If anyone disagrees with you, it can only be a neurotic symptom. A resistance, an Oedipal wish, a patricide—anything but objective truth. Forgive me, I must have been infected with a desire to be understood intellectually for once. Not diagnosed, just understood. But perhaps that is not possible with psychoanalysis. Perhaps the real function of psychoanalysis is to insult and cripple others through subtle whispering about their complexes—as if that were an explanation of anything. What an abysmal theory!"

"Listen to what you are saying, Jung. Hear your voice. I ask you only to consider the possibility, just the possibility, that your 'father complex'—your own words—is at work here. It would be a terrible pity for you to make a public pronouncement of views whose true motivations you saw only later."

"You asked if we could speak honestly," said Jung. "I for one intend to. I see through you. I know your game. You ferret out everyone else's symptoms, every slip of their tongue, aiming continually at their weak spots, turning them all into children, while you stay on top, reveling in the authority of the father. No one dares tweak the Master's beard. Well, I am not in the least neurotic. I am not the one who fainted. I am not incontinent. You said one true thing today: your fainting was neurotic. Yes, I have suffered from a neurosis—

yours, not mine. I think you *hate* neurotics; I think analysis is the out-let for it. You turn us all into your sons, lying in wait for some expression of aggression from us—which you have made certain will occur—and then you spring, shouting Oedipus or death wish. Well, I don't give a damn for your diagnoses."

There was perfect silence in the room.

"Of course you will take all this as criticism," said Jung, a note of diffidence creeping into his voice, "but I speak out of friendship."

Freud took out a cigar.

"It is for your own good," said Jung. "Not mine."

Freud finished his glass of water. Without lighting his cigar, he stood and walked to the hotel room door. "We have an understanding, we analysts, among ourselves," he said. "No one need feel any embarrassment about his own bit of neurosis. But to swear that one is the picture of health, while behaving abnormally, suggests a lack of insight into one's illness. Take your freedom. Spare me your friendship. Good-bye."

Freud opened the door for Jung to pass through. As he did so, Jung had a final remark. "You will see what this means to you. The rest is silence."

❧

GRAMERCY PARK WAS unreasonably cool and peaceful. I remained on the bench a long time after she ran off, staring at her house, then at my Uncle Fish's old house around the corner, which I used to visit as a boy. Uncle Fish never let us use his key to the park. At first I had the confused idea that, since Nora went home with the key, I would not to be able to get out. Then I realized the key must be for getting in, not out.

Though it was hateful to me in every possible way, I was obliged at last to concede the truth of Freud's Oedipus theory. I had held out against it so long. To be sure, several of my patients had produced confessions onto which I could have imposed an Oedipal interpretation. But I had never had a patient admit, point-blank, without interpretive gloss, to incestuous desires.

Nora had admitted hers. I expect I admired her self-awareness. But I was irredeemably repulsed.

To a nunnery, go. I was thinking of Hamlet's repeated injunction to Ophelia, right after *to be, or not to be,* to get herself to a convent. Would she be *a breeder of sinners?* he asks her. *Be thou as chaste as ice . . . thou shalt not escape calumny.* Would she paint her face? *God hath given you one face, and you make yourselves another.*

I think my heart's reasoning was as follows: I knew I could not stand to touch Nora now. I could hardly stand to think of her—that way. But I was damned if I would stand the thought of any other man touching her either.

I know how irrational my reaction was. Nora wasn't responsible for what she felt. She didn't choose to have incestuous desires, did she? I knew this, but it changed nothing.

I rose from the bench, running my hands through my hair. I made myself concentrate on the medical aspects of the case. I was still her doctor. Clinically speaking, Nora's admission that she had witnessed last night's assault from above was much more important than her acknowledgment of her Oedipal wishes. I had told her that such experiences were common in dreaming, but when combined with the very real cigarette burn on her skin, her account sounded closer to psychosis. She probably needed more than analysis. In all likelihood, she ought to be hospitalized. Get thee to a sanatorium.

Nevertheless, I could not bring myself to believe that she had inflicted the initial set of wounds—the brutal whipping she suffered Monday—on herself. Nor was I prepared to acknowledge as a certainty that last night's attack was a hallucination. Some memory associated with medical school flashed in and out of my head.

New York University was not far downtown. As it turned out, the gate to Gramercy Park was indeed locked shut. I had to climb out—and felt, unaccountably, like a criminal as I did so.

Walking through Washington Square, I crossed under Stanford White's monumental arch and wondered at the murderousness of love. What else might the great architect have built if he hadn't been gunned down by a mad, jealous husband, the same man whom Jelliffe was trying to have released from the asylum? Down the street was New York University's excellent library.

I began with Professor James's work on nitrous oxide, which I already knew well from Harvard, but saw nothing there meeting the description. The general anaesthesiology texts were one and all use-less. So I turned to the psychical literature. The card catalog had an entry on ASTRAL PROJECTION, but it proved to be a piece of theosoph-ical raving. Then I came across a dozen entries under BILOCATION. Through these, after a couple of hours of digging, I finally found what I was looking for.

I was fortunate: Durville provided several references in his just-published book on apparitions. Bozzano had reported a highly sug-gestive case, and Osty an even clearer one in the May-June *Revue Métapsychique*. But it was a case I found in Battersby that eliminated all doubt. Battersby quoted the following account:

> I struggled violently so that two nurses and the specialist were unable to hold me. . . . The next thing I knew was some piercing screaming going on, that I was up in the air and looking down upon the bed over which the nurses and doctor were bending. I was aware that they were trying in vain to stop the screaming; in fact I heard them say: "Miss B , Miss B., don't scream like this. You are frightening the other patients." At the same time I knew very well that I was quite apart from my screaming body, which I could do noth-ing to stop.

I didn't have a telephone number for Detective Littlemore, but I knew he worked in the new police headquarters downtown. If I could not find him there in the flesh, at least I would be able to leave word.

CHAPTER TWENTY

IN THE VAN DEN HEUVEL building, a messenger boy ran up to Coroner Hugel's office to announce that an ambulance had just delivered another dead body to the morgue. Unmoved, the coroner dismissed the boy, but the youngster wouldn't go. It wasn't just any body, the boy said; it was Detective Littlemore's body. The coroner, surrounded by boxes and loose papers stacked in piles all over his floor, swore and ran down to the basement faster than the boy himself.

Littlemore's body was not in the morgue. It was in the laboratory antechamber, where Hugel did his autopsies. The detective had been wheeled in on a gurney and deposited on one of the operating tables. The ambulance men were already gone.

Hugel and the messenger boy froze at the sight of the detective's twisted body. Hugel took the boy's shoulder in too tight a grip.

"My God," said the coroner. "It's all my fault."

"No, it isn't, Mr. Hugel," said the body, opening its eyes.

The messenger boy screamed.

"Martin fucking Luther!" said Hugel.

The detective sat up and brushed off his lapels. He saw on the coroner's face a mixture, in roughly equal parts, of lingering grief and accumulating fury. "Sorry, Mr. Hugel," he said sheepishly. "I just thought we might have an ace in the hole if the guy who wanted to kill me thought he had pulled it off."

The coroner stalked away. Littlemore leapt from the table; the moment he hit the floor, he cried out in pain. His right leg was much worse than he had realized. He followed at Hugel's heels, describing his theory of the death of Seamus Malley.

"Preposterous," was Hugel's reply. He continued up the stairs, refusing even to look back at Littlemore, limping up behind him. "Why would Banwell, having killed this Malley, drag his dead body into the elevator? For company on the ride up?"

"Maybe Malley dies on the way up the elevator."

"Oh, I see," said the coroner. "Banwell kills him in the elevator, then leaves him there in order to maximize the probability of his being apprehended for two murders. Banwell is not stupid, Detective. He is a calculating man. Had he done what you claim, he would have taken the elevator straight back down to the caisson and disposed of this Malley in the same way you say he disposed of the Riverford girl."

"But the clay, Mr. Hugel, I forgot to tell you about the clay—"

"I don't want to hear it," said the coroner. They had arrived at his office. "I don't want to hear any more about it. Go to the mayor, why don't you? No doubt you'll find a ready audience with him. I told you, the case is closed."

Littlemore blinked and shook his head. He noticed the stacks of documents and the packing boxes spread out on the office floor. "Are you going somewhere, Mr. Hugel?"

"As a matter of fact, I am," said the coroner. "I'm quitting this employ."

"Quitting?"

"I cannot work under these conditions. My conclusions are not respected."

"But where will you go, Mr. Hugel?"

"You think this is the only city that requires a medical examiner?" The coroner surveyed the boxes of records strewn about his office. "I understand a position is available in Cleveland, Ohio, as a matter of fact. My opinions will be valued there. They will pay me less, of course, but that is no matter; I have a substantial sum set aside already. No one will be able to complain about my records, Detective. My successor will find a perfectly organized system—which I created. Do you know what the state of the morgue was before I came here?"

"But Mr. Hugel," said the detective.

At that moment, Louis Riviere and Stratham Younger appeared in the corridor. "Monsieur Littlemore!" cried Riviere. "He's alive!"

"Unfortunately," agreed the coroner. "Gentlemen, if you'll excuse me, I have work to do."

〜

CLARA BANWELL WAS cooling herself in a bath when she heard the front door slam shut. It was a Turkish bath, with blue inlaid Mudejar tiles from Andalusia, installed in the Banwells' apartment at Clara's special request. As her husband's voice bellowed her name from the entry hall, she wrapped herself hastily in two white bath towels, one for her torso and another around her hair.

Still dripping, she found her husband in their forty-five-foot living room, a tumbler in his hands, gazing out at the Hudson River. He was pouring himself a bourbon over ice. "Come here," said Banwell from across the room, without turning around. "You saw her?"

"Yes." Clara remained where she was.

"And?"

"The police believe she did the injury to herself. They believe she is either mad or pursuing a vendetta against you."

"What did you tell them?" he asked.

"That you were here at home all night."

Banwell grunted. "What does she say?"

"Nora's very fragile, George. I think—"

The sound of a whiskey bottle banging down on a glass-topped table interrupted her. The table didn't crack, but alcohol splashed from the bottle's mouth. George Banwell turned to face his wife. "Come here," he said again.

"I don't want to."

"Come here."

She obeyed. When she was close to him, he glanced down.

"No," she said.

"Yes."

She undid her husband's belt. While she extracted the belt from the loops of his trousers, he poured himself another drink. She handed him the black leather strop. Then she lifted up her hands, palms together. Banwell corded the belt around her wrists, threaded its buckle, pulled it tight. She winced.

He jerked her to him and tried to kiss her lips. She allowed him to kiss only the corners of her mouth, turning her cheek first one way, then the other. He buried his head in her bare neck; she took in a mouthful of air. "No," she said.

He forced her to her knees. Though bound by the belt, she could move her hands well enough to unfasten her husband's trousers. He tore the white towel from her body.

Sometime later, George Banwell sat on the davenport, fully dressed, sipping bourbon, while Clara, naked, knelt on the floor, her back to her husband.

"Tell me what she said," he instructed her, loosening his tie.

"George"—Clara turned and looked up at him—"couldn't it be over now? She is only a little girl. How can she hurt you any more?"

She sensed immediately that her words had fueled, rather than dampened, her husband's latent anger. He rose to his feet, buttoning himself. "Only a little girl," he repeated.

❧

THE FRENCHMAN MUST have had a soft spot for Detective Littlemore. He kissed him on both cheeks.

"I got to play dead more often," said Littlemore. "This is the nicest you've ever been to me, Louie."

Riviere pressed a large folder into the detective's arms. "It came out perfectly," he said. "I have surprised even myself, actually. I did not expect such detail in an enlargement. Very unusual." With this, the Frenchman withdrew, calling out that it was *au revoir*, not *adieu*.

I was now alone with the detective. "You—played dead?" I asked him.

"It was just a joke. When I came to, I was in an ambulance, and I got the idea it might be funny."

I reflected. "Was it?"

Littlemore looked around. "Pretty funny," he said. "Say, what are *you* doing here?"

I told the detective I had made a discovery potentially important to Miss Acton's case. Suddenly, however, I found I wasn't sure how to put things. Nora had experienced a form of bilocation—the phenomenon of seeming to be in two places at the same time. From my

Harvard days, I dimly remembered reading about bilocation in connection with some of the early experiments with the new anaesthet-
ics that had so altered surgical medicine. My research confirmed it: I
was now convinced that Nora had been given chloroform. By morning, there would have been no odor and no significant aftereffects.

My problem was that Nora had confessed to me that she hadn't
told Detective Littlemore anything about the strange way in which
she experienced the event. She had been afraid he wouldn't believe
her. I decided to be direct: "There was something Miss Acton didn't
tell you about last night's assault. She saw it—that is, she experienced her own participation in it and her own observation of it—as if
she were external to it." Hearing my own lucid words, I realized I had
chosen about the least accessible, least convincing explanation possible. The look on the detective's face did nothing to change that impression. I added, "As if she were floating above her own bed."

"Floating above her own bed?" Littlemore repeated.

"That's right."

"Chloroform!" he said.

I was dumbfounded. "How on earth did you know that?"

"H. G. Wells. He's my favorite. He's got this story where that exact same thing happens to a guy getting operated on after they put
him under with chloroform."

"I've just wasted an afternoon in the library."

"No, you didn't," said the detective. "You can back it up—
scientifically, I mean? The chloroform-floating thing?"

"Yes. Why?"

"Listen, file this for one second, okay? I got to check something
while we're here. Can you come with me?" Littlemore set off along
the corridor and down the stairs, limping badly. Over his shoulder, he
explained. "Hugel's got some real good microscopes down here."

In the basement, we came to a small forensic laboratory, with
four marble slab tables and medical equipment of excellent quality.
From his pockets, the detective took out three small envelopes, each
containing bits of a ruddy earth or clay. One of the samples, he explained to me, came from Elizabeth Riverford's apartment, another
from the basement of the Balmoral, and the third from the Manhattan Bridge—on a pier belonging to George Banwell. These three

samples he pressed onto separate glass slides, which he then placed under separate microscopes. He moved from one to the other rapidly. "They match," he said, "all three of them. I knew it."

Then he opened up Riviere's folder. The photograph, I could now see, showed a girl's neck marked with a dark, grainy round spot. It was, if I understood the detective correctly, which I may not have done, a reversed image of the picture of an imprint they had found on the neck of the murdered Miss Riverford. Littlemore examined this photograph carefully, comparing it to a man's gold tiepin that he withdrew from another pocket. He showed the pin to me—it bore the monogram *GB*—and invited me to compare the pin and the photograph.

I did so. With the tiepin in hand, I could see the outline of an unmistakably similar ligature insignia in the dark round spot in the photograph. "They're alike," I said.

"Yup," said Littlemore, "almost identical. Only problem is, according to Riviere, they shouldn't be alike. They should be opposites. I don't get that. Know where we found that tiepin? In the Actons' backyard. To me, that pin proves Banwell was at the Actons', climbing a tree, maybe, to get in Miss Acton's window." He sat down on a chair, his right leg evidently too sore for him to stand on. "You still think it was Banwell, right, Doc?"

"I do."

"You got to come with me to the mayor's office," said the detective.

❧

SMITH ELY JELLIFFE, lodged comfortably in a front-row seat at the Hippodrome, the world's largest indoor theater, wept quietly. So did most of his fellow playgoers. The spectacle so moving to them was the solemn march of the diving girls, sixty-four in all, into the seventeen-foot-deep lake that was part of the Hippodrome's gigantic stage. (The water in the lake was real; underwater air receptacles and subterranean corridors provided an escape route backstage.) Who could keep tears away as the lovely, dignified, bathing-suited girls disappeared into the rippling water, never to see Earth again, doomed to perform forever for the Martian king in his circus so far away from home?

Jelliffe's bereavement was alleviated by the knowledge that he would be seeing two of the girls again—and shortly. A half hour later, with a high-heeled diving girl on each arm, Jelliffe strode with considerable satisfaction into the colonnaded dining room of Murray's Roman Gardens on Forty-second Street. Behind Jelliffe trailed two long pink boas, one from each of his girls. Before him stood the Gardens' massive, leafy plaster columns, rising up to the ceiling a hundred feet overhead, where electric stars twinkled and a gibbous moon crossed the firmament at an unnaturally advanced clip. A triple-decker Pompeiian fountain discoursed in the center of the restaurant, while nude maidenly figures frolicked in the trompe-l'oeil distance on every wall.

By weight, Jelliffe was worth both his diving girls put together. He believed this middle-aged girth made him a most impressive man—to the female sex, that is. He took special pleasure in his diving girls because he was anxious to make an impression tonight. He was dining with the Triumvirate. They had never asked him to dinner before. The closest he had come to their inner circle was the occasional luncheon at their club. But his stock had plainly risen with his connections to the new psychotherapeutics.

Jelliffe did not need money. What he wanted was renown, esteem, standing, prestige—all of which the Triumvirate could give him. It was they, for example, who directed Harry Thaw's lawyers to him, giving Jelliffe his first taste of fame. The grandest day of his life was the day his portrait appeared in the Sunday papers, naming him "one of the most distinguished alienists in the state."

The Triumvirate had also taken a surprisingly close interest in his publishing house. They were obviously progressive men. At first they had barred him from accepting any articles mentioning psychoanalysis, but their attitude had changed. Roughly a year ago, they instructed Jelliffe to send them the abstracts of all submissions touching on Freud, notifying him afterward of the ones they sanctioned. It was the Triumvirate who advised him to publish Jung. It was they who encouraged him to take on Brill's translation of Freud's book when it looked like Morton Prince in Boston might publish it instead. Indeed, they had hired Jelliffe an editor to help smooth Brill's translation.

Jelliffe had carefully considered the number of girls to bring to dinner. Girls were his specialty. He had cemented more than a few social and professional connections with such mortar. He knew all the best gentlemen's establishments. When asked, he invariably recommended the Players Club in Gramercy Park. With the Triumvirate, Jelliffe had never been asked. When, however, they invited him to join them at the Roman Gardens, Jelliffe sensed the occasion was propitious. As every man-about-town knew, upstairs at the Gardens were twenty-four luxuriously appointed bachelor's apartments, each of which contained a double-sized bed, separate bath, and a bottle of champagne on ice. At first, Jelliffe had pictured four girls and four rooms, but on reflection this seemed insufficiently collegial. So he had secured two of each: the business of taking turns, he felt, would add sauce to the geese.

Jelliffe did make an impression, but not the one he intended. Shown to the private alcove where the Triumvirate had their table, the bon vivant and his ladies met with an unequivocal *froideur* from the three gentlemen seated there. None of them even stood. Jelliffe, failing to detect the cause, manfully greeted his hosts, called out to the maître d' for extra chairs, and announced that two bachelor's suites awaited them all after dinner. With a wave of an elegant hand, Dr. Charles Dana belayed the order for extra chairs. Jelliffe finally grasped the nettle and mumbled to his girls that they had better wait for him upstairs.

Shortly thereafter, the Triumvirate procured from Jelliffe the information that Abraham Brill had, without warning, indefinitely postponed publication of Freud's book. Pity, said Dana. And what of Dr. Jung's lectures at Fordham? Jelliffe reported that his plans for the Fordham lectures were proceeding apace—and that the *New York Times* had contacted him to arrange an interview with Jung.

Dana turned to the portly fellow with the muttonchop sideburns. "Starr, weren't you interviewed by the *Times* as well?"

Draining an oyster into his mouth, Starr said he bloody well had been interviewed and that he had been blunt about it too. The conversation then turned to Harry Thaw, concerning whom Jelliffe was advised in no uncertain terms that there should be no further experiments.

As the dinner drew to a close, Jelliffe feared he had not advanced his cause. Dana and Sachs did not even shake his hand as they left. But his flagging spirits improved when Starr, who had lingered behind the others, asked whether he had correctly heard Jelliffe to say that he had booked two rooms upstairs. Jelliffe confirmed it. The brace of corpulent gentlemen regarded each other, both picturing a boa-clad showgirl reclining next to an iced, unopened bottle of champagne. Starr expressed the opinion that things paid for ought not to be wasted.

❧

"HAVE YOU LOST your mind, Detective?" asked Mayor McClellan behind the closed doors of the mayor's office Thursday evening.

Littlemore had requested a crew of men to go down to the Manhattan Bridge caisson to investigate the malfunctioning window. He and I were seated across from the mayor's desk. McClellan was now standing.

"Mr. Littlemore," said McClellan, who had evidently inherited his father's military bearing, "I promised this city a subway, and I delivered it. I promised this city Times Square, and I delivered it. I promised this city the Manhattan Bridge, and by God I'm going to deliver it if it's the last damned thing I do in office. Under no circumstances is the work on that bridge to be hindered—not by one single goddamned minute. And under no circumstances is George Banwell to be interfered with. Do you hear me?"

"Yes, sir," said Littlemore.

"Elizabeth Riverford was murdered four days ago and, so far as I can tell, all you've done since is lose her blasted body."

"Actually, I found a body, Your Honor," said Littlemore meekly.

"Oh, yes, Miss Sigel," said McClellan, "who is now causing me more trouble than even Miss Riverford. Have you seen the afternoon papers? It's all over them. How can the mayor of this city allow a girl of good family to be found in a Chinaman's trunk?—as if I were personally responsible! Forget about George Banwell, Detective. Find me this William Leon."

"Your Honor, sir, with all respect," said Littlemore, "I think the Riverford and Sigel cases are connected. And I think Mr. Banwell is involved in both."

McClellan folded his arms. "You think this Leon was not Miss Sigel's killer?"

"I think it's possible, sir."

The mayor took a deep breath. "Mr. Littlemore, your Mr. Chong—the man you yourself arrested—confessed an hour ago. His cousin Leon killed Miss Sigel last month in a jealous rage, after he saw her with another Chinaman. The police have been to this other man's home, where they found more letters from Miss Sigel. Leon strangled her to death. Chong witnessed it. He even helped put the dead body into Leon's trunk. All right? Are you satisfied?"

"I'm not sure, sir," said Littlemore.

"Well, you'd better make yourself sure. I want answers. Where is Leon? Was Miss Acton attacked last night or not? Was she ever attacked at all? Do I have to do everyone's job? And let me tell you one more thing, Detective," said McClellan. "If you or anyone else comes running into my office yapping that Elizabeth Riverford was murdered by the one man I know could not have killed her, I'm going to fire the lot of you. Do I make myself clear?"

"Yes, sir, Your Honor, sir" was the detective's reply.

We were mercifully released. Out in the hallway, I said, "So at least the mayor is squarely behind us."

"*I* didn't lose Miss Riverford's body," objected Littlemore, showing uncharacteristic spleen. "What's come over everyone? I've got a tiepin, the clay, an unexplained death on the guy's site, he fits the coroner's description, he scares when he sees Miss Acton, she tells us he attacked her, and we can't even go down and see what's blocking the guy's underwater garbage chute?"

I made the obvious point that if Banwell was out of town the night Elizabeth Riverford was murdered, he couldn't have killed her.

"Yeah, but maybe he's got an accomplice who did it," replied Littlemore. "Know anything about the bends, Doc?"

"Yes. Why?"

"Because I know what I got to do," said Littlemore, whose limp had grown still worse, "but I can't do it by myself. Will you help me?"

When I heard the detective's proposal, I initially thought it the most foolhardy plan I had ever heard. On reflection, however, I began to think differently.

❧

NORA ACTON STOOD on the roof of her house. A breeze stirred the fine wisps of hair dangling over her forehead. She could see the whole of Gramercy Park, including the bench where, several hours ago, she had sat with Dr. Younger. She doubted she would ever sit there with him again.

She could not bear to be inside her house. Her father was locked in his study. Nora had an idea what he did in there. Not work: her father had no work. Years ago, she had found her father's secret cache of books. Revolting books. Outside, two patrolmen were once again guarding the front and back doors. They had left the house this morning; now they were back.

Nora wondered whether she would die if she jumped from the roof. She thought not. The girl went back into her house and down to the kitchen. She picked through a deep bottom drawer and found one of Mrs. Biggs's carving knives. She took it upstairs and placed it under her pillow.

What could she do? She couldn't tell anyone the truth, and she couldn't lie any longer. No one would believe her. No one did believe her.

Nora did not intend the kitchen knife for use on herself. She had no wish to die. She might, however, at least try to defend herself if he came again.

PART

V

LITTLEMORE WORKED THE LOCK while I stood behind him. It must have been about two in the morning. My job was to keep a lookout, but I could see nothing in the blackness. Nor could I hear anything over the mechanical roar that drowned out all other sound. I found myself looking instead at the canopy of stars above us.

He had it open in less than a minute. The elevator car was unexpectedly large. Littlemore pulled the door to, and we were enclosed in the dimly lit cabin. Two gas flames threw enough light to allow Littlemore to work the operating lever. With a lurch, the detective and I began our slow descent to the caisson.

"You sure you're okay?" Littlemore asked me. One of the two blue flames was reflected in his eyes—and the other in mine, I suppose. Nothing else was visible. The booming engines above us kept up a deep steady beat, as if we were making our way down the aortic artery of a gigantic bloodstream. "It's not too late. We could still turn back."

"You're right," I said. "Let's go back."

The elevator jerked to a halt. "You mean it?" Littlemore asked.

"No. I was joking. Come on, take us down."

"Thanks," he said.

He reminded me of someone, Littlemore, but I couldn't think whom. Then I remembered: when I was a child, my parents took us to the country every summer—not Aunt Mamie's "cottage" in Newport, but a real cottage of our own near Springfield, with no running water. I loved that little house. I had a best friend there, Tommy Nolan, who lived year-round on a nearby farm. Tommy and I used to walk for miles and miles along the wooden fences that separated the farms from one another. I hadn't thought of Tommy for a long time.

"What do you think the mayor will do to you when he finds out?" I asked.

"Fire me," said Littlemore. "You feel that in your ears? Pinch your nose and blow out. That's how you clear. My dad taught me."

I had a different trick. Among the many useless skills I possess is the knack for controlling by will the inner ear muscles that open the eustachian tubes. The pace of the elevator was agonizingly slow. We were barely moving at all. "How long to get down?" I asked.

"Five minutes, the guy told me," said the detective. "Dad could stay underwater better than two minutes."

"Sounds like you got on with him."

"My dad? Still do. Best man I know."

"How about your mother?"

"Best woman," said Littlemore. "I'd do anything for her. Boy, I used to think if I could only find a girl like Mom, I'd marry her in a heartbeat."

"Funny you should say that."

"Until I met Betty," Littlemore said. "She was Miss Riverford's maid. First time I ever saw her was—what, three days ago?—and right away I'm crazy about her. Crazy crazy. She's nothing like Mom. Italian. Kind of hot-tempered, I guess. She gave me a whack last night I can still feel."

"She hit you?"

"Yeah. Thought I was messing around," said the detective. "Three days, and already I can't mess around. Can you top that?"

"Maybe. Miss Acton hit me with a steaming teapot yesterday."

"Ouch," said Littlemore. "I saw the saucer on her floor."

A whistling noise commenced inside the car, as the elevator displaced air in the shaft. The booming of the engines on the surface was now more distant—a dull throbbing, more sensible than audible.

"I had a girl patient a long time ago," I said. "She told me—she told me—she wanted to have sex with her father."

"What?"

"You heard me," I said.

"That's disgusting."

"Isn't it?"

"That's about the most disgusting thing I ever heard," said the detective.

"Well, I—"

"Katie bar the door."

"All right." My voice came out much louder than I intended; the echo rang interminably in the elevator cabin. "Sorry," I said.

"No problem. It was my fault," Littlemore replied, although it wasn't.

It would have been inconceivable for my father to snap like that. He never revealed what he felt. My father lived by a simple principle: never willingly show pain. For a long time I thought pain must have been the only thing he felt—because if there had been anything else, I reasoned, he could have expressed it without violating his principle. Only later did I understand. All feeling is painful, one way or another. The most exquisite joy is a sting to the heart, and love—love is a crisis of the soul. Therefore, given his principles, my father couldn't show any of his feelings. Not only couldn't he show *what* he felt, he couldn't show *that* he felt.

My mother hated his uncommunicative nature—she says it killed him in the end—but it was, oddly enough, the thing about him I admired most. On the night he took his own life, his comportment at dinner was no different from what it had ever been. I too dissemble, every day of my life, reenacting by half my father's principle, although I don't play the half of him half so well as he. Long ago I made up my mind: I would speak what I feel, but never in any other way display emotion. That's what I mean by *half*. Truth to tell, I don't really believe in expressing one's feelings other than through language. All other kinds of expression are forms of acting. They're all show. They are all seeming.

Hamlet says something similar. It's practically the first thing he says in the play. His mother has asked him why he still seems so downcast by his father's death. *Seems, madam?* he replies. *I know not "seems."* He then deprecates all outward expressions of grief: the *inky cloak* and *customary suits of solemn black,* the *fruitful river in the eye.* These displays, he says, *indeed seem, for they are actions that a man might play*—

"My God!" I said in the dark. "My God. I've got it."

"Me too!" Littlemore exclaimed, just as eagerly. "I know how he killed Elizabeth Riverford, even though he was out of town. Banwell, I mean. She was *with* him. Nobody else knew. The mayor didn't know. Banwell kills her wherever they were—okay?—then he brings her body back to her apartment, ties her up, and makes it look like the murder happened there. I can't believe I didn't get it before. Is that what you were thinking?"

"No."

"No? What was yours, Doc?"

"Never mind," I said. "Just something I've been thinking about for a long time."

"What was it?"

Inexplicably, I decided to try to tell him. "You've heard of *To be, or not to be?*"

"As in *that is the question?*"

"Yes."

"Shakespeare. Everybody knows that," said Littlemore. "What's it mean? I always wanted to know."

"That's what I just figured out."

"Life or death, right? He's going to kill himself or something?"

"That's what everyone has always thought," I said. "But that's not it—at all."

It had come to me in a single instant: whole, all-illuminating, like the sun breaking out after a storm. Just then, however, the elevator reached the end of its descent, jolting to a halt. There was an air lock we had to negotiate. Littlemore knelt down to turn the pressure cocks, which were near the floor. Powerful jets of air poured in through them. The smell was peculiar: dry and musty at the same time. The air pressure became unbearable. My head began to pound. My eyes felt as though they were pressing into my brain. The detective was apparently suffering the same symptoms; he blew furiously from his nose, which he was simultaneously squeezing shut. I was afraid he was going to burst an eardrum. But he managed eventually, as I did, to become acclimated to the pressure. We opened the door to the caisson.

❧

NORA ACTON ROSE from her bed at two-thirty that morning, unmolested but unable to sleep. Through her window, she could see the policeman patrolling the sidewalk. There were three in all tonight:

one in front, one in back, and one stationed on the roof, who came on when night fell.

By candlelight, Nora composed a short letter, set down in her neat hand on a piece of white stationery. This she sealed in a little envelope, which she addressed and stamped. Then she stole downstairs and slipped the envelope through the front door mail slot, whence it dropped into the box outside. The mail came twice a day. The postman would pick up her letter before seven that morning; it would be delivered well before noon.

❧

I HAD NO IDEA how enormous it would be. Blue gas flames dotted the caisson's walls, casting webs of flickering light and shadow into the rafters above and the puddled floor below. From the elevator, we climbed down a steep ramp. Littlemore had a hard time of it, grimacing every time he had to put weight on his right leg. We were at the hub of a half dozen wooden plank walkways, leading out in all directions. Room after room could be seen in the distance.

"How long we got, Doc?" asked Littlemore.

"Twenty minutes," I said. "After that, we have to decompress on the way up."

"Okay. It's Window Five we want. The numbers should be on them. Let's split up."

The detective set off, limping badly, in one direction, I in another. At first all was silence, an eerie and cavernous silence, punctuated only by echoing drips of water and Littlemore's uneven receding footfalls. Then I became conscious of a deep bass rumble, like the growl of some enormous beast. It was coming, I think, from the river itself: the sound of deep water.

The caisson was strangely empty. I had expected machines, drills—signs of work and excavation. Instead there was only the occasional crowbar and broken shovel, lying abandoned among scattered boulders and pools of dark water. I passed into a large chamber, but it must have been an internal one, for I saw none of the debris chutes Littlemore called windows. A plank broke under my shoe as I stepped on it. The crunch was followed by what sounded like scurrying. Could there be mice down here, a hundred feet below the earth's surface?

The scurrying ceased so abruptly I wasn't sure if it had been real or in my head. I passed through to another chamber, as empty as the last. My walkway came to an end. I had now to step through puddles of water on the muddy ground, each splash amplified by echoes. In the next room, a series of three large steel plates a couple of feet up from the floor lined the farthest wall; I had found the windows. An array of chains, pull cords of some kind, hung beside and between them. The first had the number seven etched on it. The next had a six. As I bent to look at the last, a hand seized my shoulder.

"We found it, Doc," said the detective.

"Christ, Littlemore," I said.

He unlatched the plate numbered five and pulled up on its handle. It rose like a curtain, disappearing into the wooden wall above it. Inside was a coffin-sized space, two feet high and six feet wide, iron-clad on every side, littered with stones, rags, and rubble. The far wall of the compartment was clearly an outer hatch, giving out onto the river: one of the pull chains would doubtless open it.

"There's nothing here," I said.

"Not supposed to be," answered Littlemore. With considerable difficulty, he sat down and began taking off his shoes. "Okay, soon as I'm inside, you close the window and flush it. You give me one minute, Doc, exactly one minute, then—"

"Wait—you're not going in the water?"

"I sure am," he said, rolling up his trouser legs. "Her body's right outside the outer hatch. Got to be. I'm going to pull her back in. Then you'll pop me out, and we'll be home free."

"With your leg?"

"I'm okay."

"You can barely walk," I said. Swimming by itself would have been painful for him, given the condition of his leg—I feared a hairline fracture—but wrestling with debris or a dead body underwater, a hundred feet down, was out of the question. A strong current would carry him off.

"Only way," said Littlemore.

"No, it's not," I said. "I'm going."

"Not on your life," said the detective. He hunkered down to squeeze himself into the compartment, but he couldn't bend his right leg. He turned around and tried, vainly, to shimmy into the compartment backward. He looked at me helplessly.

"Oh, get out of there," I said. "You're the one who knows how to work this contraption anyway."

Thus, astonishingly, a minute later, the person squeezed inside the window was myself, stripped to the waist, shoes and socks off too. I examined the compartment as closely as I could, knowing that in a moment I would be immersed in cold water. An iron handle stuck out from the ceiling. To this I held on tightly. Rubber tubes protruded from the walls. I told myself I would venture into the water for the shortest possible time. After sixty seconds, Littlemore would reopen the window from the inside. I strongly suspected I would find no corpse to haul back in. Littlemore's theory now seemed totally implausible. The window's plates were much too heavy and strong. I didn't see how a girl's body could possibly obstruct its operation.

Littlemore called out a final check. From behind me the inner hatch fell shut with a clang. The blackness was so total it was disorienting. Somehow I had managed not to realize I would be in the dark. The rumble from the river outside was much louder now, echoing inside my cell. I heard a thump on the wall, Littlemore's signal that he was about to open—or try to open—the outer hatch.

That instant, I felt a hideous misgiving: we should have tested the window first. We knew there was something wrong with it. What if Littlemore couldn't open the window again after I was turned out into the water? I banged my fist against the wall to make Littlemore stop. But either he didn't hear or he interpreted my signal as an affirmative response to his. For there came next a grating of chains and a sudden shock of impossibly cold water. The entire compartment inverted, and I was churned out, irresistibly, into the depths of the river.

ᕲ

OUTSIDE THE WROUGHT-IRON fence enclosing Gramercy Park, a tall, dark-haired man stood in the shadows. It was three in the morning. The park was empty, sporadically illuminated by gas lamps scattered within it. Most of the surrounding houses were dark, although in one of them—the home of the Players Club—lights were shining and music playing. Calvary Church was black and silent, its steeple a mass of rising darkness.

The dark-haired man observed the police officer patrolling in front of the Actons' house. In the small circle of light thrown by a streetlamp, Carl Jung saw this officer converse with another policeman, who after several minutes walked away, turning a corner at an alley apparently leading to the back of the house. Jung considered his options. After several minutes, he turned around and, frustrated, returned to the Hotel Manhattan.

୬

LITTLEMORE HAD A sudden horrible thought. He had been told Window Five wasn't working right. A picture came to him of Younger underwater, pounding desperately on the hull of the caisson, eyes bulging, while he, Littlemore, stood within, jerking helplessly at the chains. What was he thinking not to have gone himself?

After exactly one minute, Littlemore manipulated the pulleys in rapid succession, righting the window and closing the outer hatch. The mechanism worked perfectly. He threw open the inner hatch. Gallons of water gushed out. This he expected. He did not, however, expect what he found inside the compartment: namely, nothing.

"Oh, no," said Littlemore. "Oh, no."

He slammed the window shut, opened the outer hatch, counted off ten seconds, and then reversed the process. He flung open the window. More water: no Younger. In a mad rush, Littlemore did it all again, but now with a difference. He prayed. With all his heart and might, he prayed that he would find the doctor inside the window. "Please, God," he begged. "Let him be there. Forget everything else. Just let him be there."

For the third time, Littlemore threw open the steel plate of Window Five, soaking his shoes and trouser bottoms as he did so. The compartment was now well washed. Its four metal walls were glistening. But it remained quite empty.

The detective read his watch: two and a quarter minutes had passed. His father's record had been just that—two minutes, fifteen seconds—but his father was floating, without exertion, in a warm and placid pond. Dr. Younger could never have survived so long. Littlemore knew this but could not accept it. Numbly, mechanically, he went through the motions a fourth time and a fifth, all to the same effect. He sank to his knees, staring into the empty metal compartment. He didn't notice the pain in his leg. He did notice, but never moved, when the million-ton frame of the caisson suffered a powerful concussion far above him. The concussion was followed by a scraping—a protracted metallic scraping—equally far above his head. It was as if the roof of the caisson had been struck by the bottom of a passing submarine.

When this sound ceased, however, he became aware of another. A faint sound. A tapping. Littlemore looked around; he could not identify the source. He crept to his left on hands and knees, holding his breath, not daring to hope. The taps were coming from behind the steel plate of Window Six. From his knees, Littlemore worked the pulleys, unlocked the plate, and pushed it open. Another windowful of water poured out, directly into the kneeling detective's face, and out of the window tumbled a large black trunk, which knocked him flat on his back. This was followed by Stratham Younger's head, a rubber hose in his mouth.

The incoming water did not entirely stop; it kept streaming in from the window as from an overflowing bathtub. Littlemore, with the trunk on his stomach, looked speechlessly up at the doctor. Younger spat out the hose.

"Br-breathing tubes," said the doctor, so cold he could not control his shaking. "Inside the w-windows."

"But why didn't you come back through number five?"

"C-c-couldn't," said Younger, his teeth chattering. "Outer hatch w-wouldn't open far enough. S-s-six was open."

Extricating himself from the trunk, Littlemore said, "You found it, Doc! You found it! Will you look at this!" The detective was wiping the mud from the trunk. "It's just like the one we found in Leon's room!"

"Open it," said Younger, his head still poking out of Window Six.

Littlemore was about to respond that the trunk's hasps were padlocked when another tremendous shudder ran through the caisson, followed once more by the loud metallic scraping overhead.

"What was that?" asked Younger.

"I don't know," said Littlemore, "but it's the second time. Come on. Let's get going."

"Slight problem." said Younger, who had not budged from the window, from which water was still streaming out. "My foot is stuck."

The outer hatch of Window Six had slammed shut like a bear trap on Younger's ankle. That was why water continued to stream in through the bottom of the window: the outer hatch remained ajar, and Younger's foot was protruding out into the river. With his free leg, Younger pushed at the outer hatch as hard as he could, but the hatch was unmovable.

"No sweat," said Littlemore, limping over to the pull chains on the wall. "I'll open it for you. Give me one second."

"Look out," replied Younger. "We're going to get a ton of water."

"I'll shut it again the second you get your foot in. Ready? Here goes. Uh-oh." Littlemore was tugging vainly on the chain. It wouldn't budge. "Maybe you can't open the outer hatch unless you close the inner hatch first. Get your head back in there."

Younger complied unhappily. He drew his head back into Window Six and clamped his jaw around the breathing tube, preparing himself for another deluge. But now Littlemore couldn't close the inner hatch. He pulled on the handle with all his might, but the plate would not come down. Perhaps, Younger suggested, the inner hatch was inoperable when the outer hatch was still open.

"But they're both open," said Littlemore.

"So they're both inoperable."

"Great," said the detective. Littlemore attempted to wrench Younger's ankle out. He tried yanking it out directly, and he tried twisting it out. This produced no effect except to cause the doctor several stabs of intense pain.

"Littlemore."

"What?"

"Why are the lights going out?"

An entire bank of blue gas flames, on the other side of the chamber, had diminished from torch strength to flickering match lights. Then they went out completely. "Someone's turning off the gas," said the detective, having slid out of the window.

Once more, a vicious, ugly noise of metal abrading wood came from overhead. This time, the scraping terminated in a distant clang, which was followed by a new sound. Littlemore and Younger both looked up at the dimly lit rafters; they heard what sounded like the thundering approach of a subway train. Then they saw it: a column of water, perhaps a foot in diameter, falling gracefully down from the ceiling. When it hit the ground, it make a colossal smash, exploding up in all directions. The East River was pouring into the caisson.

"Holy Toledo," said Littlemore.

"Great God," added Younger.

The East River was not only pouring into their chamber. From a half dozen apertures spread throughout the caisson, similar cataracts were crashing down. The roar was deafening.

What had happened was this: the work in the Manhattan Bridge caisson had come to an end. That was the reason Younger had seen no machinery or tools. The plan had always been to flood the caisson after work within it was completed. A short time ago, however, Mr. George Banwell had abruptly decided to hasten that event. He woke up two of his engineers with late-night orders. Following these orders, the engineers went to the Canal Street site and started up long-idle engines.

These engines operated what was essentially a sprinkler system built into the caisson's twenty-foot-thick roof. Because of the dynamiting to be done in the caisson, its designers were concerned about fire. Their precaution proved justified: the caisson had in fact caught fire once and was saved only by flooding its internal chambers. Three tiers of cut iron plate had to be opened to let water in; this was what caused the three separate scraping noises.

The flood was already shin deep and rising steadily. Younger strained harder to tear his foot free but could not. "This is unpleasant," he said. "You don't have a knife, do you?"

Littlemore scrambled for his pocket knife and eagerly handed it over. Younger cast a disapproving eye at the three-inch blade.

"This won't do it."

"Do what?" shouted the detective. They could hardly hear each other over the din of the flood.

"Thought I might cut it off," yelled Younger.

"Cut what off?" The water was now at his knees and rising ever more quickly.

"My foot," said the doctor. Still looking at Littlemore's knife, he added, "I guess I could kill myself. Better than drowning."

"Give me that," said the detective, snatching the pocket knife out of Younger's hand. The rising water was now only inches from the bottom of the window. "The breathing tube. Use it."

"Oh, right. Good thinking," said Younger, putting the hose back in his mouth. Immediately he took it out again: "Wouldn't you know it? They've shut off the air."

Littlemore grabbed another of the hoses and tested it himself. The results of his test were no different.

"Well, Detective," said Younger, propping himself up, "I think it would be a good time for you to—"

"Shut up," Littlemore replied. "Don't even say it. I'm not going anywhere."

"Don't be a fool. Take that trunk and get back on the elevator."

"I'm not going anywhere," Littlemore repeated.

Younger reached out and grabbed Littlemore by the shirt, drew him in close, and whispered fiercely into his ear. "Nora. I left her. I didn't believe her, and I left her. Now they're going to lock her up. Do you hear me? They're going to put her away—either that or Banwell will kill her."

"Doc—"

"Don't call me Doc," said Younger. "You have to save her. Listen to me. I can die. You didn't make me come down here; I wanted to see proof. You're the only one who believes her now. You have to make it out. You *have* to. Save her. And tell her—oh, never mind. Just get out!"

Younger pushed Littlemore away so hard the detective staggered back and fell into the water. He stood. The rising water had edged up over the bottom of the window. Littlemore gave the doctor a long look, then turned, and strode away, as best he could, past the cataract and through the thigh-high water. He disappeared.

"You forgot the trunk!" Younger shouted after him, but the detective didn't seem to hear him. The flooding was more than halfway up the window now. With great effort, Younger was able to hold his head an inch or two above the water. Then Littlemore reappeared. In his arms he held a five-foot length of lead pipe and a boulder.

"Littlemore!" shouted Younger. "Go back!"

"Ever hear of Archiemeeds?" said the detective. "Leverage."

He splashed over to Younger and set the boulder down in the window, which was now full almost to the brim. Plunging his head into the ever-gathering water, Littlemore wedged one end of his pipe under the outer hatch, next to Younger's trapped ankle, and positioned the rest of the pipe over the boulder, lever-style. With both hands, he pushed down on the free end of the pipe. Unfortunately, the only effect was to pop the boulder out from under the pipe. "Damn," said Littlemore, emerging from the water.

Younger's eyes were still above water, but his mouth was not. Neither was his nose. He raised an eyebrow at Littlemore.

"Oh, boy," said the detective. He took a breath and plunged in again. He repositioned his boulder and pipe in the same way and gave the pipe a downward tug. This time the boulder stayed in place, but still the outer hatch did not move. Littlemore sprang up out of the water as high as he could and came down with all his weight on the lever. But the lead pipe was badly corroded, and the force of Littlemore's weight upon it broke it clean in two. The moment before the pipe snapped, however, the window's outer hatch inched upward— just enough to free Younger's foot.

Both men came out of the water at the same time, but Littlemore was gulping air and thrashing about wildly while Younger barely stirred the water. He took a single lung-filling breath and said, "That was melodramatic, wasn't it?"

"You're welcome," replied Littlemore, straightening himself.

"How's that leg?" the doctor inquired.

"Fine. How's your foot?"

"Fine," said Younger. "What do you say we blow this hellhole?"

Dragging the trunk behind them while fighting through columns of crashing water, they made their way back to the central chamber. The steep ramp to the elevator was already half submerged. Water gushed down from the top of the elevator as well, spilling down the ramp and making a curtain around the car. Yet behind that curtain, the elevator cabin itself appeared dry.

Between the two of them, Littlemore and Younger contrived to push and pull the trunk up the ramp, heave it into the elevator, and tumble in themselves. Breathing hard, Younger shut the iron door. Things were suddenly still. The inundation of the caisson was a muffled roar outside. Within the car, the blue gas jets remained alight. Littlemore said, "I'm taking us up."

He thrust the operating stick into the ascent position—and nothing happened. He tried it again. Nothing.

"What a surprise," said Littlemore.

Younger climbed up on top of the trunk and knocked on the ceiling. "The whole shaft is flooded," he said.

"Look," said the detective, pointing up to where the doctor was standing, "there's a hatch in the ceiling."

It was true: in the center of the elevator's ceiling was a pair of large hinged panels.

"And there's what opens it," said Younger, indicating a thick chain on a wall, with a red wooden handle dangling from its end. He leapt down off the trunk and took hold of that handle. "We're going up, Detective—a little faster than we came down."

"Don't!" Littlemore shouted. "Are you crazy? You know how much all the water on top of us must weigh? The only way we won't drown is if we're crushed to death first."

"No. This is a pressurized cabin," said Younger. "Super-pressurized. The second I open this hatch, you and I will go up that shaft of water like a geyser."

"You're putting me on," said Littlemore.

"And listen to me. You have to exhale all the way up. I suggest you yell. I mean it. If you hold your breath even for a few seconds, your lungs will literally pop like balloons."

"What if we get caught in the elevator cables?"

"*Then* we drown," said Younger.

"Nice plan."

"I'm open to alternatives."

A glass aperture in the elevator door allowed Littlemore to look out into the caisson. It was almost entirely dark now. Water was pouring down everywhere. The detective swallowed. "What about the trunk?"

"We take it with us." The trunk had two leather grips. Each man took hold of one. "Don't forget to yell, Littlemore. Ready?"

"I guess."

"One, two—*three*." Younger pulled the red handle. The ceiling panels opened at once, and two men, yelling for their lives, with a large black trunk in tow, shot up through an elevator shaft full of water as if fired from a cannon.

CHAPTER TWENTY-TWO

THE GENEROUS FOYER of the Banwells' penthouse apartment in the Balmoral had a tiled marble floor, milky white with silver veins, in the center of which a rich, dark green inlay formed an interlocking *GB*. This *GB* supplied Mr. George Banwell with inordinate satisfaction every time he saw it; he liked having his initials on everything he owned. Clara Banwell detested it. Once she dared to introduce into the foyer an expensive Oriental carpet, explaining to her husband that the marble was so highly polished their guests were in danger of slipping on it. The next day, the foyer was bare. Clara never saw her carpet again, nor had it ever been referred to since, either by herself or her husband.

At ten on Friday morning, a butler in this foyer received the Banwells' mail. One envelope bore Nora Acton's pretty curvilinear hand. The addressee was Mrs. Clara Banwell. Unfortunately for Nora, George Banwell was still at home. Fortunately, it was the habit of Parker, the butler, to offer Mrs. Banwell her mail first, and he did so that Friday morning. Unfortunately, Clara still had Nora's letter in her hand when Banwell entered the bedroom.

Clara, her back to the door, felt her husband's presence behind her. She turned to greet him, holding Nora's letter behind her back. "George," she said. "You're still here."

Banwell took in every inch of his wife. "Use that on someone else," he replied.

"'That'?"

"That innocent expression. I remember it from when you were onstage."

"I thought you liked the way I looked onstage," said Clara.

"I like it all right. But I know what it means." George Banwell approached his wife, put his arms around her, and tore the letter out of her hands.

"Don't," said Clara. "George, it will only anger you."

Reading another's mail provides one with the taste of violating two persons at once, the sender and the recipient. When Banwell saw that his wife's letter was from Nora, this taste became sweeter. The moment lost its sweetness, however, as he began taking in the letter's contents.

"She knows nothing," said Clara.

Banwell kept reading, his features hardening.

"No one would believe her anyway, George."

George Banwell held the letter out for his wife.

"Why?" Clara asked quietly, taking it.

"Why what?"

"Why does she hate you so?"

❧

DAWN WAS BREAKING when Littlemore and I finally got back to the police car the detective had waiting for us a few blocks south of the Manhattan Bridge. The two of us had shot up through the elevator shaft and into the air a good ten feet before falling back into the water. We hadn't made it all the way up. We had to hang from the elevator cables, freezing and exhausted, until the water rose high enough to pull ourselves onto the pier. From there, we loaded the trunk in a rowboat—the same boat in which we had traveled to the pier the night before. Luckily, Littlemore's car was waiting at a dock about two blocks south; I don't think either of us could have rowed further. I had a feeling Littlemore had broken some rules in getting us the police car, but that was his business.

I told the detective that we had to telephone the Actons; not a moment could be lost. I had a terrible foreboding that something had happened there in the night. The detective drove us, soaking, to the station. I waited in the car while Littlemore limped in. He returned after a few minutes: all was quiet at the Acton house. Nora was fine.

From the police station, we went to Littlemore's apartment on Mulberry Street. There we put on dry clothes—the detective lent me an ill-fitting suit—and drank about a gallon of hot coffee each. We drove to the morgue. I suggested smashing the top of the locked trunk with a pickax, but Littlemore was determined to proceed by the book from this point forward. He sent a boy running for the locksmiths, and we waited, our hair still wet, pacing impatiently. Or rather I paced, having cleaned and bandaged my ankle. Littlemore sat on an operating table, resting his bad leg. The trunk lay at his feet. We were alone. Littlemore had hoped to find the coroner, whom I had met yesterday, but that gentleman was not in.

I ought to have left Littlemore. I should have checked in with Dr. Freud and my other guests at the hotel. Today, Friday, was our last full day in New York. We would all leave for Worcester tomorrow evening. But I wanted to see the trunk opened. If the Riverford girl were inside, surely that would prove Banwell was her murderer, and Littlemore could finally arrest him.

"Say, Doc," Littlemore called out, "can you tell from a cadaver whether somebody was strangled to death?" The detective led me to the morgue's cold room. He found and uncovered the partially embalmed body of Miss Elsie Sigel. Littlemore had already told me what he knew of her.

"This girl wasn't strangled," I said.

"That means Chong Sing is lying. How can you tell?"

"No edema in the neck," I replied. "And look at this little bone here; it's intact. Normally it breaks if someone is strangled to death. No evidence of any tracheal or esophageal trauma. Very unlikely. But it does look like asphyxiation."

"What's the difference?"

"She died from lack of oxygen. But not from strangulation."

Littlemore grimaced. "You mean somebody locks her up in the trunk while she's still alive, and then she suffocates?"

"Looks like it," I said. "Strange. See her fingernails?"

"They look normal to me, Doc."

"That's what's strange. They're smooth at the tips, undamaged."

Littlemore got it at once. "She never struggled," he said. "She never tried to get out."

We looked at each other.

"Chloroform," said the detective.

At that moment, there came a knock at the outer laboratory door. The locksmiths, Samuel and Isaac Friedlander, had arrived. With an instrument resembling oversized garden shears, they cut through the two padlocks on the hasps of the trunk. Littlemore had them sign an affidavit attesting to their actions and instructed them to wait so that they could further witness the contents. Taking a deep breath, he opened the lid.

There was no smell. A confused, densely packed assortment of waterlogged clothes, studded with jewelry, was all I saw at first. Then Littlemore pointed to a black matted mass of hair. "There she is," he said. "This isn't going to be pretty."

Donning a pair of gloves, Littlemore grasped the hair, lifted it up—and his hand came clean away with a fistful of sopping, tangled hair.

"He's cut her up," said one of the Friedlanders.

"Cut her to pieces," said the other.

"Geez," said Littlemore, gritting his teeth and throwing the mass of hair onto the table. Then he snatched it back up. "Wait a minute. This is a wig."

The detective began emptying the contents of the trunk, one item after another, recording each object in an inventory and placing them into bags or other containers. In addition to the wig, there were several pairs of high-heeled shoes, a considerable collection of lingerie, a half dozen evening gowns, a trove of jewelry and toiletries, a mink stole, a lightweight lady's coat—but no lady.

"What the heck?" asked Littlemore, scratching his head. "Where's the girl? There must have been another trunk. Doc, you must have missed the other trunk."

I offered the detective my thoughts on that hypothesis.

❧

LITTLEMORE ACCOMPANIED ME into the savagely bright street. I asked the detective what he would do next. His plan, he said, was to scour the trunk and everything in it for some link to Banwell or to the murdered girl. Perhaps the Riverford family in Chicago could identify some of the girl's belongings. "If I can put Elizabeth Riverford's name on just one of those necklaces, I got him," said the detective. "I mean, who but Banwell could have put her things in a trunk under the Manhattan Bridge the day after she was murdered? And why would he do it if he wasn't the murderer?"

"Why would he do it if he *was* the murderer?" I asked.

"Why would he do it if he wasn't?"

"This is a fruitful conversation," I remarked.

"Okay, I don't know why." The detective lit a cigarette. "You know, there's a lot about this case I don't get. For a while I thought the killer was Harry Thaw."

"*The* Harry Thaw?"

"Yup. I was all set for the biggest score any detective ever made. Then it turns out Thaw is locked up on a funny farm upstate."

"I wouldn't call him locked up, exactly." I explained what I knew from Jelliffe: that Thaw's conditions of confinement were lax at best. Littlemore wanted to know the source of my information. I told him that Jelliffe was one of Thaw's principal psychiatric consultants and that, from what I could tell, the Thaw family seemed to be paying off the entire hospital staff.

The detective stared. "That name—Jelliffe. I know it from somewhere. He doesn't live in the Balmoral, by any chance?"

"He does. I dined at his home two nights ago."

"Son of a bitch," said Littlemore.

"I think that's the first time I've ever heard you swear, Detective."

"I think that's the first time I ever did. So long, Doc." Moving as quickly as he was able, he gimped back into the building, thanking me again over his shoulder as he disappeared.

I realized I had no money. My wallet was in a pair of trousers hanging on a clothesline outside Littlemore's kitchen window. I found a nickel in the detective's pocket. It was a good thing I woke up when my train pulled into the Grand Central subway station; I don't know where I might have ended up otherwise.

❧

AT A TWO-STORY HOUSE on Fortieth Street, just off Broadway, Detective Littlemore banged the gaudy knocker furiously. In a moment the door was opened by a girl the detective had never seen before. "Where's Susie?" he demanded.

The girl, through a cigarette that never left her mouth, would say only that Mrs. Merrill was out. Hearing female voices down the hall, Littlemore made his way to the parlor. There were half a dozen girls in the richly mirrored room, in various states of undress, black and scarlet being the favored hues of such clothing as they had on. In the center was the one Littlemore was looking for. "Hello, Greta," he said.

She blinked at him, otherwise making no reply. She looked decidedly less dreamy than she had the other day.

"He was here last weekend, wasn't he?" the detective demanded. Greta still made no answer.

"You know who I'm talking about," said Littlemore. "Harry."

"We know a lot of Harrys," said one.

"Harry Thaw," said the detective.

Greta sniffed. Only then did Littlemore realize she had been crying. She was trying to hold it in, but she broke down and hid her face in a handkerchief. The other girls gathered around her at once, uttering words of sympathy.

"You're the one, aren't you, Greta?" said Littlemore. "You're the one he whipped. Did he do it again last Sunday?" He put the question to all the girls: "Did Thaw hurt her? Is that what happened?"

"Oh, leave her alone," said the girl with the cigarette in her mouth.

In addition to the handkerchief, Greta was clutching a pink cloth with little pink strings dangling from one end. It was a bib. The detective realized that the noise of an infant's crying, so piercing on his last visit, was absent today. "What happened to the baby?" he asked.

Greta froze.

Littlemore took a chance. "What happened to your baby, Greta?"

"Why couldn't I keep her?" Greta burst out, directing her words to no one in particular. She recommenced sobbing. The others did their best to comfort her, but she was inconsolable. "She never hurt anybody."

"Someone took her baby away?" asked Littlemore.

Greta buried her face again. One of the other girls spoke up: "Susie did it. Real mean, I call it. She got a family in Hell's Kitchen to take her. She won't even tell Greta who they are."

"She's docking Greta for it too," added another. "Three dollars a week. It ain't fair."

"And I'll bet you Susie's only paying them a dollar fifty," commented the smoker shrewdly.

"I don't care about the money," said Greta. "I just want Fannie. I want her back."

"Maybe I could get her back," said Littlemore.

"You could?" said Greta hopefully.

"I could try."

"I'll do anything you want," said Greta imploringly. "Anything."

Littlemore considered the prospect of prying information from a woman whose baby had just been taken from her. "No charge," he said, putting his hat on. "Tell Susie I'll be back."

He got as far as the front door when he heard Greta's voice behind him. "He *was* here," she said. "He came in around one in the morning."

"Thaw?" said Littlemore. "Last Sunday?"

Greta nodded. "You can ask all the girls. He looked kind of crazy. He asked for me. I always was his favorite. I told Susie I didn't want to, but she didn't care. She starts in on him for all the money he owes her for us keeping quiet, but he just laughs out loud and—"

"What money for keeping quiet?"

"The money so the rest of us wouldn't testify at the trial and tell them about all the things he did to us. Susie got hundreds. She told him it was for us, but she kept it all. We never saw a penny. But his mother stopped paying after he got sent away. That's why Susie was so mad. She told him he would have to pay double and up front before he could have me. She made him promise to be nice. But he wasn't." The faraway look came back to Greta, as if she were describing events that happened to someone else. "After he gets me undressed, he pulls the sheets off the bed and says he's going to tie me up, like he used to. I told him to get away or else. He says, 'Or else what?' and he's laughing like crazy. Then he says, 'Don't you know I'm insane? I can do anything I want. What are they going to do, lock me up?' That's when Susie comes in. She was listening the whole time, I guess."

"No, she wasn't," piped up one of the other girls, the group having assembled in the hall. "*I* was listening. I told Susie what he was up to. So Susie marches right in. He was always scared to death of her. Course she wouldn't of done nothing if Thaw had paid up front, like she wanted him to. But you should of seen him run out of there, the little rat."

"He came into my room," said another girl, "wailing and waving his arms like a little boy. Then Susie comes in and chases him out again."

The girl with the cigarette had the end of the story: "She chased him all over the house. You know where she caught him? Behind the icebox. Chewing his fingernails off. Susie pulls him up by the ear, drags him down the hall, and throws him out on the street, like the sack of garbage he is. That's why she went to jail, you know. Becker came around a couple of days later."

"Becker?" asked Littlemore.

"Yeah, Becker," was the reply. "Nothing happens without Becker gets his fingers in it."

"Will you testify that Thaw was here last Sunday?" Littlemore asked.

None of them answered until Greta said, "I will, if you find my Fannie."

Again Littlemore was about to leave, when the smoker asked, "Want to know where he went after he left?"

"How would you know?" returned the detective.

"I heard his friend tell the driver. From the upstairs window."

"What friend?"

"The one he come in with."

"I thought he was alone," said Littlemore.

"Huh-uh," she replied. "Fat man. Thought he was the Lord's gift. Ready enough with his money, though, I'll give him that. Dr. Smith, he called himself."

"Dr. Smith," repeated the detective, feeling that he had heard that name recently. "Where'd they go?"

"Gramercy Park. I heard him tell the driver loud and clear."

"Son of a bitch," said Littlemore.

❧

IT WAS PAST ten when I arrived at the hotel. Handing over my key, the clerk looked down his nose at Littlemore's threadbare jacket, which left a conspicuous gap between the ends of its sleeves and the beginnings of my hands. There had been a letter for me, I was told, but Dr. Brill received it on my behalf. The clerk gestured toward a corner of the lobby; there was Brill, sitting with Rose and Ferenczi.

"Good Lord, Younger," said Brill when I greeted them. "You look terrible. What have you been doing all night?"

"Just trying to keep my head above water, really," I said.

"Abraham," Rose chided her husband, "he is simply wearing another man's suit."

"Rose is here," Brill said to me, "to tell everyone what a coward I am."

"No," replied Rose firmly, "I am here to tell Dr. Freud that he and Abraham must go forward with the publication of Dr. Freud's book. The cowards are the ones leaving you those dreadful messages. Abraham has told me all about it, Dr. Younger, and we are not going to be intimidated. Imagine burning a book in this country. Don't they know we have freedom of the press?"

"They got into our apartment, Rosie," said Brill. "They buried it in ash."

"And you want to go hide in a mouse hole?" she answered.

"I told you," Brill said to me, raising his eyebrows helplessly.

"Well, I don't. And I won't have you hiding behind my skirts either, as if I'm the one you're protecting. Dr. Younger, you must help me. Tell Dr. Freud it will be an insult to me if concern over my safety should in any way delay his book. This is America. What did those young men die for at Gettysburg?"

"To ensure that all slavery would be wage slavery?" asked Brill.

"Be quiet," was Rose's reply. "Abraham has poured his heart into that book. It has given meaning to his life. We are not rich, but we have two things in this country that are worth more than anything else: dignity and freedom. What is left if we give in to such people?"

"Now she is running for office," commented Brill, causing Rose to mount an assault on his shoulder with her handbag. "But you see why I married her."

"I am serious," Rose continued, rearranging her hat. "Freud's book must be published. I am not leaving this hotel until I tell him so myself."

I commended Rose's bravery, whereupon Brill rebuked me, declaring that the greatest risk I had ever taken with my own safety was dancing all night with overeager debutantes. I said he was probably right and asked after Freud. Apparently he had not come down at all this morning. According to Ferenczi, who had knocked at his door, he was "undigested." Moreover, Ferenczi added in a whisper, there had been a tremendous row between Freud and Jung last night.

"There's going to be a worse one when Freud sees what Hall sent Younger this morning," said Brill, handing me the letter he had procured from the clerk.

"You have not actually opened my correspondence, Brill?" I asked.

"Isn't he awful?" said Rose, referring to her husband. "He did it without telling us. I would never have let him."

"It was from Hall, for God's sake," Brill protested. "Younger had vanished. If Hall intends to cancel Freud's lectures, don't you think we ought to know?"

"Impossible," I declared.

"Virtually certain," Brill replied. "See for yourself."

The envelope was oversized. Inside was a folded-up piece of vellum. When I straightened it out, I was looking at a full-page, seven-column article in newspaper type under the banner headline, "AMERICA FACING ITS MOST TRAGIC MOMENT"—DR. CARL JUNG. Below was a full-length photograph of a dignified, bespectacled Jung, referred to as "the famous Swiss psychiatrist." The odd thing was that the paper was too thick and of too high a quality for newsprint. More puzzlingly, the date shown at the top was Sunday, September 5, two days hence.

"It is the galley proof of an article that will appear in this Sunday's *Times*," said Brill. "Read Hall's note."

Suppressing my irritation, I followed this instruction. Hall's letter read as follows:

My Dear Younger,

I received the enclosed today from the family that has offered the University so handsome a donation. I am told it is a page from the New York Times, forthcoming Sunday. You will see what it says. The family was kind enough to give me advance notice so that I might take action now, rather than after the taint of scandal has become inevitable. Please assure Dr. Freud I have no wish to cancel his lectures, to which I have looked forward so keenly, but surely it would not serve his interests, or ours, if his presence here drew a certain kind of attention. Naturally I myself give no credence to innuendo, but I am obliged to consider what others may think. It is my fervent hope that this supposed newspaper article is not genuine and that our vigentennial will proceed unclouded and undisrupted.

Yours, etc. etc.

The letter, to my dismay, confirmed Brill's view: Hall was on the verge of canceling Freud's lectures. Who was orchestrating this campaign against him? And what did Jung have to do with it?

"Frankly," said Brill, snatching the newspaper article out of my hands, "I don't know who comes off worse from this idiotic story, Freud or Jung. Listen to this. Where is it? Ah, yes: 'American girls like the way European men make love.' That's our Jung speaking. Can you believe it? 'They prefer us because *they* sense we are a little dangerous.' All he can talk about is how much American girls want him. 'It is natural for women to want to be afraid when they love. The American woman wants to be mastered and possessed in the archaic European way. Your American man only wants to be the obedient son of his mother-wife.' This is 'America's tragedy.' He's gone completely off his chain."

"But that isn't an attack on Freud," I said.

"They have someone else pronouncing on Freud."

"Who?" I asked.

"An anonymous source," said Brill, "identified only as a doctor who speaks for the 'reputable' American medical community. Listen to what he says:

"I knew Dr. Sigmund Freud of Vienna very well some years ago. Vienna is not a moral city. Quite the contrary. Homosex-

uality, for example, is there considered the sign of an ingenious temperament. Working side by side with Freud in the
laboratory all through one winter, I learned that he enjoyed
Viennese life—enjoyed it thoroughly. He felt no compunc-
tion about cohabitation, or even about fathering children out
of wedlock. He was not a man who lived on a particularly
high plane. His scientific theory, if that is what it should be
called, is the result of this saturnalian environment and the
peculiar life he led there."

"My God," I said.

"It is purely personal attack," Ferenczi commented. "Will American paper publish such things?"

"There's your freedom of the press," said Brill, who received a
withering glance from his wife. "They've won. Hall will cancel. What
can we do?"

"Does Freud know?" I asked.

"Yes. Ferenczi told him," said Brill.

"I gave highlights of newspaper article," explained Ferenczi,
"through door. He is not so upset. He says he has heard worse."

"But Hall hasn't," I observed. Freud had endured calumny a long
time. He expected it; he was to a degree inured to it. Hall, however,
had as perfect a horror of scandal as any other New Englander of old
Puritan stock. To have Freud proclaimed a libertine in the *New York
Times* the day before the inauguration of Clark's celebrations would
be too much for him. Aloud, I said, "Does Freud have any idea who
in New York knew him in Vienna?"

"There is no one," Brill cried. "He says he never worked with any
Americans."

"What?" I said. "Why, that's our chance. Maybe the whole article
is a fake. Brill, call your friend at the *Times*. If they are really planning
to publish this, tell them it's libel. They can't publish an outright lie."

"And they are going to take my word for it?" he answered.

Before I could reply, I noticed that Ferenczi and Rose had fixed
their glance slightly behind me. I turned around to find a pair of blue
eyes looking up at me. It was Nora Acton.

CHAPTER TWENTY-THREE

I THINK MY HEART actually stopped for several seconds. Every feature of Nora Acton's person—the loose strands of hair dancing about her cheek, the imploring blue eyes, her slender arms, the white-gloved hands, the diminishing shape from her chest to her waist—all conspired against me.

Seeing Nora in the hotel lobby, I suspected I required treatment more than she. On the one hand, I doubted I would ever feel this way about anyone else; on the other, I was disgusted. In the caisson, when death loomed close at hand, I could think only of Nora. Seeing her now in the flesh, once again I could not get out of my mind the secret of her repugnant longings.

I must have stood staring a good deal longer than politeness permitted. Rose Brill came to my rescue, saying, "You must be Miss Acton. We are friends of Dr. Freud and Dr. Younger. Can we help you, my dear?"

With admirable grace, Nora shook hands, exchanged pleasantries, and let it be known, without saying so, that she wished a word with me. I knew to a certainty that the girl had to be in inner turmoil. Her poise was remarkable, and not only for a seventeen-year-old.

Away from the others, she said, "I've run away. I couldn't think of anyone else to go to. I'm sorry. I know I repulse you."

Her last words were a knife in my heart. "How could you possibly have that effect on anyone, Miss Acton?"

"I saw the look on your face. I hate your Dr. Freud. How could he know?"

"Why have you run away?"

The girl's eyes welled up. "They are planning to lock me up. They call it a sanatorium; they call it a rest treatment. My mother has been on the telephone with them since dawn. She told them I had a fantasy of being attacked in the night—and she raised her voice so that I would be sure to hear her, and Mr. and Mrs. Biggs too. Why can't I remember it more—more normally?"

"Because he gave you chloroform."

"Chloroform?"

"A surgical anaesthetic," I went on. "It produces the very effects you experienced."

"Then he *was* there. I knew it. Why would he do that?"

"So he could make it seem as if you had done it to yourself. Then no one would believe you about either attack," I said.

She looked at me and turned away.

"I've told Detective Littlemore," I said.

"Will Mr. Banwell come for me again?"

"I don't know."

"At least my parents can't send me away now."

"They can," I said. "You are their child."

"What?"

"The decision is theirs so long as you are a minor," I explained. "Your parents may not accept my word. We can't prove it. Chloroform leaves no trace."

"How old must one be before one is no longer a child?" she asked with a sudden urgency.

"Eighteen."

"I shall be eighteen this Sunday."

"Will you really?" I was going to say that she therefore had no need to fear an involuntary confinement, but a foreboding overtook me.

"What's wrong?" she asked.

"We must fend them off until Sunday. If they succeed in hospitalizing you today or tomorrow, you could not be released until your parents said so."

"Even after I turned eighteen?"

"Even after."

"I *will* run away," she said. "I know—our summer cottage. Now they have come back, it's empty. It's the last place he'll look for me.

It's the last place any of them will look. Can you see me there? It's only an hour away by ferry. The Day Line stops right in Tarry Town if you ask them. Please, Doctor. I have no one else."

I considered. Getting Nora out of town was very sensible. George Banwell had somehow gotten into her bedroom wholly unobserved; he might get to her again. And Nora could hardly take the ferry herself: it wasn't safe for a young woman, particularly of Miss Acton's allure, to travel upriver alone. Everything else could wait until this evening. Freud was stuck in bed. If Brill's efforts to contact his friend at the *New York Times* proved fruitless, the next step would be for me to go to Worcester personally to speak with Hall, but I could do that tomorrow.

"I'll take you," I said.

"Are you going to wear that suit?" she asked.

✺

A HALF HOUR AFTER the delivery of the morning post, the Banwells' maid informed Clara that a visitor—"a policeman, ma'am"—was waiting in the foyer. Clara followed her maid to the marble entry hall, where her butler was holding the hat of a small, pale man in a brown suit, with beady, almost desperate eyes, a bushy mustache, and equally bushy eyebrows.

Clara started when she saw him. "And you are—?" she asked stiffly.

"Coroner Charles Hugel," he replied, no less stiffly. "I am chief investigator of the murder of Elizabeth Riverford. I would like a word with you."

"I see," replied Clara. She turned to her butler. "Surely this is Mr. Banwell's business, Parker, not mine."

"I beg your pardon, ma'am," answered Parker. "The gentleman asked for you."

Clara turned back to the coroner. "Did you ask for me, Mr.—Mr.—?"

"Hugel," said Hugel. "I—no, I merely thought, with your husband out, Mrs. Banwell, that you—"

"My husband is not out," said Clara. "Parker, inform Mr. Banwell that we have a caller. Mr. Hugel, I am sure you will excuse me." A few minutes later, from her dressing room, Clara heard a cascade of oaths sworn in George Banwell's deep voice, followed by a slamming of the front door. Then Clara heard her husband's heavy footsteps approaching. For a moment Clara's hands—applying powder to her lovely face—began to tremble, until she willed them still.

AN HOUR AND A QUARTER LATER, Nora Acton and I were steaming north up the Hudson River past the spectacular burnt-orange cliffs of New Jersey. We had left the Hotel Manhattan through a basement door, just in case—after I had changed clothes. On the New York side of the river, an armada of three-masted wooden ships was anchored under Grant's Tomb, their white sails flapping lazily in the bright sunshine, part of the elaborate preparations for the Hudson-Fulton celebrations this fall. A few puffs of cloud floated in an otherwise unblemished sky. Miss Acton sat on a bench near the prow, her hair flowing and tousled by the breeze.

"It's lovely, isn't it?" she said.

"If you like boats," I answered.

"Don't you?"

"I'm against boats," I said. "There is first of all the wind. If people enjoy a wind in their face, they should stand in front of an electric fan. Then there are the exhaust fumes. And the infernal horn—the visibility is perfect, there's no one around for miles, and they blow that blasted horn so loud it kills entire schools of fish."

"My father withdrew me from Barnard this morning. He called the registrar. Mother made him."

"That is reversible," I said, embarrassed to have been chattering so ridiculously.

"Did your father teach you to shoot, Dr. Younger?" she asked.

The question took me by surprise. I couldn't tell what she meant by it—or if she even knew what she might have meant by it.

"What makes you think I can shoot?" I said.

"Can't all men of our social class shoot?" She uttered *social class* almost contemptuously.

"No," I answered, "unless you include shooting one's mouth off."

"Well, *you* can," she said. "I saw you."

"Where?"

"I told you: at the horse show last year. You were amusing your-self at the shooting gallery."

"Was I?"

"Yes," she said. "You seemed to be enjoying yourself a good deal."

I looked at her for a long time, trying to see how much she knew. My father's suicide had involved a gun. Not to put too fine a point on it, he had blown his brains out. "My uncle taught me," I said. "Not my father."

"Your Uncle Schermerhorn or your Uncle Fish?"

"You know more about me than I realized, Miss Acton."

"A man who lists himself in the Social Register can hardly com-plain if his relations are common knowledge."

"I did not list myself. I was listed, just as you were."

"Did you grieve when he died?"

"Who?"

"Your father."

"What is it you want to know, Miss Acton?"

"Did you?"

"No one mourns a suicide," I said.

"Really? Yes, I suppose the death of fathers is common. Your fa-ther lost a father, after all, and that father lost his too."

"I thought you hated Shakespeare."

"What is it like, Doctor, to be raised by someone you despise?"

"Wouldn't you know better than I, Miss Acton?"

"Me?" she said. "I was raised by someone I love."

"You do not usually display that emotion when speaking of your parents."

"I am not speaking of my parents," Nora replied. "I am speaking of Mrs. Biggs."

"I didn't hate my father," I said.

"I hate mine. At least I am not afraid to say so."

The wind grew stronger. Perhaps the weather was turning. Nora gazed steadfastly at the shore. What exactly she meant to make me feel, I didn't know.

"We have this much in common, Miss Acton," I said: "We both

grew up wishing not to be like our parents. Either of them. But defiance, Dr. Freud says, shows just as much attachment as obedience."

"I see: you have achieved detachment."

Some minutes later, she asked me to tell her more about Freud's theories. I did, avoiding any mention of Oedipus and his cognates. Breaching the usual professional etiquette, I described to her some of my previous analysands—anonymously, of course—hoping to illustrate the workings of the transference and its extreme effects on analytic patients. To this end I told her about Rachel, the girl who had tried to disrobe for me in virtually every session.

"Was she good-looking?" asked Nora.

"No," I lied.

"You're lying," she said. "Men always like that kind of girl. I suppose you had sex with her."

"I certainly did not," I answered, surprised by her explicitness.

"I am not in love with you, Doctor," she said, as if it were a perfectly logical reply to make. "I know that's what you think. I mistakenly supposed I had some feelings for you yesterday, but that was the product of very trying circumstances and your own declaration of affection for me."

"Miss Acton—"

"Don't be alarmed. I don't hold you to it. I understand that what you said yesterday no longer reflects your true sentiments, just as what I said yesterday no longer reflects mine. I have no feelings for you. This, this transference of yours, which you say makes patients either love or hate their doctors, has no application to me. I am your patient, as you said. That is all."

I let her words pass without response as the ferry churned upriver.

❧

A LITTLE AFTER NOON on Friday, Detective Littlemore stood outside a small, filthy cell in the massive gray detention castle known as the Tombs. There was no daylight, no window anywhere in sight. Next to Littlemore was a prison guard. The two of them were staring through a grill of iron bars at the sprawled-out body of Chong Sing, who lay unconscious on a lousy cot. His white undershirt was badly stained. His feet were bare and dirty.

"He's asleep?" asked Littlemore.

Chuckling, the guard explained that Sergeant Becker had kept Chong up all last night. Littlemore was at first surprised to hear Becker's name. Then he realized: Miss Sigel was found in the Tenderloin, so the interrogation would naturally have been given to Becker. Still, the detective was puzzled. Chong had already talked yesterday; he had admitted seeing his cousin Leon kill the girl. The mayor had said so. What did Becker want with him last night?

The prison guard was able to answer that question. It was Becker who had made Chong talk in the first place. But Chong wouldn't admit to having assisted in the killing itself. He insisted he had gone into Leon's room only after the girl was already dead.

"And Becker didn't buy it?" asked Littlemore.

The guard hummed a little tune and shook his head. "Kept at him real good. All night, like I said. Shoulda seen him."

The sleeping Chong Sing turned over on the cot, revealing his right eye, purpled and swollen to the size of a plum. Dried blood was visible under Sing's nose and below his ear. The nose may have been broken, but Littlemore could not be sure.

"Oh, boy," said the detective. "Did Chong break?"

"Huh-uh."

Littlemore had the guard open the cell. He woke the sleeping prisoner. The detective pulled up a chair, lit himself a cigarette, and offered one to the Chinese. Chong eyed his new interrogator unhappily. He took the cigarette.

"I know you understand English, Mr. Chong," said Littlemore. "I may be able to help you. Just answer a couple of questions. When did you start working at the Balmoral, end of July?"

Chong Sing nodded.

"What about down at the bridge?" asked the detective.

"Maybe same time," he said hoarsely. "Maybe few days later."

"If you weren't there, Chong, how'd you see it?" asked Littlemore.

"Hah?"

"If you went into Leon's room *after* he killed the girl, how do you know he killed her?"

"I told already," Chong replied. "I hear fighting. I look through keyhole."

Littlemore glanced at the guard, who confirmed that Chong had told the same story the day before. The detective turned back to Chong Sing. "Is that right?"

"That right."

"No, it's not. I was there, Mr. Chong, remember? I went to Leon's room. I picked the lock. I looked through that keyhole. You can't see anything through it."

Chong was silent.

"How'd you get those jobs, Chong? How'd you get two jobs working for Mr. Banwell?"

The Chinese shrugged.

"I'm trying to help you," said Littlemore.

"Leon," said Chong quietly. "He got me jobs."

"How did Leon know Banwell?"

"I don't know."

"You don't know?"

"I don't know," Chong Sing insisted. "I not murder anyone."

Littlemore rose and signaled the guard to open the cell again. "I know you didn't," he said.

❧

THE ACTONS' SUMMER COTTAGE was a cottage in the Newport sense of the word, meaning an estate aspiring to—indeed, exceeding—the standards of lower European royalty. I had intended to return to the city after seeing Nora to the door, but I found I couldn't. I didn't want to leave her alone, even here.

The servants greeted Nora warmly, throwing open doors and windows in a flurry of activity. They appeared to know nothing of her travails. Although barely speaking, Nora evidently wanted me to see everything. She led me through the first floor of the main house. A double-winged marble staircase ascended from the gallery of its two-story entry hall. To the right was a stained-glass cupola; to the left an octagonal, wood-beamed library. Marble columns and gilded plaster abounded.

In back was a tile-ceilinged veranda. A rolling sward of green grass and tall oaks descended clear down to the river far below. The girl set out into the greenery. I followed, and we arrived shortly at the stables, where the air smelled wholesomely of horse and fresh hay. It turned out the cook had already taken the liberty of sending a picnic basket down to the stable in case Miss Nora wanted to go for a ride.

She proved every bit as good a rider as I. After a quick canter, we spread a blanket in a shady spot with a magnificent view of the Hudson. Inside the picnic basket, we found a dozen clams packed on ice, cold chicken, potato croquettes, a tin full of tiny soda biscuits, and a cherry and watermelon salad. Along with a canteen of iced tea, the cook had included a half bottle of claret, evidently for "the gentleman." I had not eaten a thing since the previous evening.

When we were done, Nora asked me, "Are you honest?"

"To a fault," I said, "but only because I am such a bad actor. Will the servants call your parents to tell them you're here?"

"There's no telephone." She removed her panama hat, allowing the sun to tangle up its rays in her hair. "I am sorry for my behavior on the ferry, Doctor. I don't know why I brought up your father. Please forgive me. I feel I am in a house that's burning down and there's no way out. Clara is the only person I have been able to turn to, and now even she can't help me."

"There *is* a way out," I said. "You will stay here till Sunday. You will then be eighteen and out of your parents' control. At the same time, with any luck, Detective Littlemore will have traced the evidence we found to Banwell and arrest him."

"What evidence?"

I told her of our trip to the caisson. Even now, I explained, Detective Littlemore might have confirmed that the contents of the trunk belonged to Miss Riverford, which would be all he needed to put Mr. Banwell under arrest. Perhaps Banwell was under arrest already.

"I doubt it very much," said Nora, shutting her eyes. "Tell me something else."

"What?"

"Tell me anything so long as it does not concern George Banwell."

❧

IN THE ACTON RESIDENCE on Gramercy Park, Nora's mother was ransacking her daughter's bedroom. Nora had disappeared. Mildred Acton sent Mrs. Biggs to see if Nora was in the park, but the girl was not there. The thought of being deceived by her daughter filled Mrs. Acton with indignation. Apparently her daughter was deranged, wicked and deranged. Nothing she said could be trusted. Mrs. Acton had seen the discovery of cigarettes and cosmetics in her daughter's bedroom; what else might she be concealing there?

Mrs. Acton found nothing worth confiscating until she poked a hand beneath her daughter's pillow. She was astonished to discover a kitchen knife.

The discovery had an odd effect on Mildred Acton. For a split second, a series of bloody images flashed through her mind. Among these were memories of the birth of her only child, which in turn reminded Mrs. Acton, as it always did, that she and her husband had slept in different beds since that day. A moment later, these sanguinary images and associations were gone. Mrs. Acton had quite forgotten them, but they left her in a state. Feeling a great sense of her own propriety in protecting her daughter from herself, she returned the knife to its place in the kitchen.

Mrs. Acton wished her husband would do something. She wished he were not so hopeless, always holed up in his study in town or playing polo in the country. Harcourt spoiled Nora dreadfully. But then Harcourt was a failure at everything. If he had not inherited a small fortune from his father, the man would have ended in the poorhouse. Mildred had told him so many times.

Mrs. Acton decided she must call at once on Dr. Sachs for another electromassage treatment. True, she had just had one yesterday and the cost was outrageous, but she felt she couldn't live without another. Dr. Sachs was so good at it. It would have been nicer, she reflected, if she had found a Christian physician who was equally expert. But didn't everyone say the best doctors were Jewish?

❧

NATURALLY MY MIND went blank the moment Nora asked me to say something to distract her. Then it came to me. "Last night," I said, "I solved *To be, or not to be*."

"I didn't know a solution was required," she answered.

"Oh, people have been trying to solve it for centuries. But no one has, because everyone has always thought that *not to be* means to die."

"Doesn't it?"

"Well, there's a problem if you read it that way. The whole speech equates *not to be* with action: taking up arms, taking vengeance, and so on. So if *not to be* meant to die, then death would have the name of action on its side, when surely that title belongs to life. How did acting get on the side of not being? If we could answer that question, we would know why, for Hamlet, *to be* means not to act, and then we would have solved the real riddle: why he doesn't act, why he is paralyzed for so very long. I'm boring you, I'm sorry."

"You aren't in the least. But *not to be* can only mean death," said Nora. "Not to be means"— she shrugged—"not to be."

I had been reclining on my side. Now I sat up. "No. I mean yes. I mean, *not to be* has a second meaning. The opposite of being is not only death. Not for Hamlet. To not be is also to seem."

"To seem what?"

"Just to *seem*." I stood, pacing and, I'm ashamed to say, cracking my knuckles savagely. "The clue has been there all along, at the very beginning of the play, where Hamlet says, *Seems, madam? Nay it is. I know not 'seems.'* Think of it. Denmark is rotten. Everyone ought to be in mourning for Hamlet's father. His mother especially ought to be in mourning. He, Hamlet, ought to be king. Instead, Denmark is celebrating his mother's marriage to, of all people, his loathsome uncle, who has assumed the throne.

"And what most galls him is the feigning of grief, the *seeming,* the wearing of black by people who can't wait to feast at the marriage tables and disport themselves like animals in their beds. Hamlet wants no part of such a world. He won't pretend. He refuses to *seem*. He *is*.

"Then he learns of his father's murder. He swears revenge. But from that point on, he enters the world of seeming. His first step is to *put an antic disposition on*—to *pretend* to be mad. Next he listens in awe as an actor weeps for Hecuba. Then he actually instructs the players on how to pretend convincingly. He even writes a script for them himself, to be played that night, a scene he must pretend is anodyne, but that will actually reenact his father's murder, in order to surprise his uncle into an admission of guilt.

"He is falling into the domain of playing, of seeming. For Hamlet, *To be, or not to be* isn't 'to be, or not to *exist*.' It's 'to be, or to *seem*'; that's the decision he has to make. To seem is to act—to feign, to play a part. There's the solution to all of *Hamlet,* right there, in front of everyone's nose. Not to be is to seem, and to seem is to act. *To be,* therefore, is "not to act." Hence his paralysis! Hamlet was determined not to seem, and that meant never acting. If he holds to that determination, if he would *be,* he cannot act. But if he would take arms and avenge his father, he *must* act—he must choose to seem, rather than to be."

I looked to my audience of one. "I see," she said. "Because he must deceive to get at his uncle."

"Yes, yes, but it's also universal. All action is acting. All performing is performance. There's a reason these words have double meanings. To design means to plan, but also to deceive. To fabricate is to make with skill, but also to deceive. Art means deception. Craft—deception. There is no escaping it. If we would play a part in the world, we must act. Say a man psychoanalyzes a woman. He becomes her doctor; he assumes a role. It isn't lying, but it is acting. If he drops that role with her, he assumes another—friend, lover, husband, whatever it is. We can choose what part we play, but that's all."

Nora's brows were knit. "I've acted," she said. "With you."

It happens that way sometimes: the moment of truth erupts right in the middle of some other scene, when the action is elsewhere and the attention diverted. I knew what she must be talking about: her secret fantasy about her father, which she had confessed yesterday, but which she had naturally tried to keep secret. "It's my fault," I replied. "I didn't want to hear the truth. I felt the same way about *Hamlet* for the longest time. I didn't want to believe that Freud's view of the play could be right."

"Dr. Freud has a view about Hamlet?" she inquired.

"Yes, it's—it's what I told you. That Hamlet has a secret wish to—to have sex with his mother."

"Dr. Freud says that?" she exclaimed. "And you believe it? How repulsive."

"Well, yes, but I'm a little surprised to hear you say so."

"Why?" she asked.

"Because of what you said yesterday."

"What did I say?"

"You confessed," I said, "to the same kind of incestuous wish."

"You are insane."

I lowered my voice but spoke severely. "Miss Acton, you admitted to me in the park yesterday, very plainly, that you were jealous when you saw Clara Banwell with your father. You said you wished you were the one who—"

She flushed scarlet. "Stop it! Yes, I said I was jealous, but not of Clara! How disgusting! I was jealous of my father!"

We faced each other, both standing now, across the little woolen blanket. A pair of squirrels, which had been frolicking about a nearby tree trunk, froze in their tracks and eyed us suspiciously. "That's why you thought you were vile?" I asked.

"Yes," she whispered.

"That's not vile," I said. "At least, not by comparison."

My remark did not amuse her. I touched her cheek. She looked down. Taking her chin in my hand, I lifted her face to mine and bent toward her. She pushed me away.

"Don't," she said.

She wouldn't meet my eyes. She withdrew from me and set about the picnic things, gathering the remains, packing them in the basket, shaking the crumbs from the blanket. In silence, we rode back to the stables and returned to the house.

So: all my fine ethical scruples about taking advantage of Nora's transferential interest in me—supposing she had any—melted away when I discovered she had confessed to a Sapphic desire, not an incestuous one. I was embarrassed to discover this about myself, but there was a logic to it. The moment I understood the truth, I no longer felt Nora would be kissing her father were she to kiss me. Perhaps I ought to have concluded she would be kissing Clara, but it didn't feel that way.

The main house was quiet now, the summer afternoon air perfectly still, the large interior rooms shadowy and empty. All the windows were shuttered again—to keep the sun off the drapery and furniture, I supposed. Nora, pensive and wordless, led me into the octagonal library with the splendidly carved woodwork. She locked the doors behind us and pointed to an armchair. I was meant to sit down in it—and did. Nora knelt on the floor in front of me.

For the first time since she had turned me away, she spoke. "Do you remember when you first saw me? When I couldn't speak?"

I was unable to read her expression. She looked penitent and vir-ginal at once. "Of course," I said.

"I didn't lose my voice."

"I beg your pardon?"

"I only pretended," she said.

I tried not to reveal how dry my mouth suddenly felt. "That's why you could speak the next morning," I said.

She nodded.

"Why?" I asked.

"And my amnesia."

"What about it?"

"That wasn't real either," she said.

"You had no amnesia?"

"I was pretending."

The girl gazed up at me. I had the peculiar notion that she was someone I had never met before. I tried to reorient what I knew or thought I knew around these new facts. I tried to restructure all the various scenes of the last week, to make them cohere—but couldn't. "Why?"

She shook her head, biting her lower lip.

"You were trying to ruin Banwell?" I asked. "You were going to say he did it?"

"Yes."

"But you were lying."

"Yes. But the rest of it—almost all of it—was true."

She seemed to be pleading for sympathy. I felt none. No wonder she said the transference had no application to her. I hadn't psycho-analyzed her at all. "You made a fool of me," I said.

"I didn't mean to. I couldn't—it's so—"

"Everything you told me was a lie."

"No. He did try to take me when I was fourteen. He tried again when I was sixteen. And I did see my father with Clara. Right here, in this room."

"You told me you saw your father and Clara at the Banwells' summerhouse."

"Yes."

"Why would you lie about that?"

"I didn't."

My mind wheeled and groped. I remembered now: her parents' summerhouse was in the Berkshires, in Massachusetts. We were not at her parents' summerhouse at all. We were at the Banwells'. The servants knew her not because they were her servants, but because she had been here so often. The reality of the situation suddenly became fragile, as if it might crack. I stood. She took my hands and gazed up at me.

"You did those things to your own body," I said. "You whipped yourself. You scarred yourself. You burned yourself."

She shook her head.

A series of recollections came to my mind. First, helping Nora into a carriage outside the hotel. My hands had closed entirely around her waist, including her lower spine, yet she had not flinched. When I touched her neck, to trigger her memories—which had all been a lie—I held her by the small of the back once more. Again she didn't wince. "You have no injuries," I said. "You faked them. You painted them on, and allowed no one to touch you. You were never attacked."

"No," she said.

"No you weren't, or no you were?"

"No," she repeated.

I seized her wrists. She gasped. "I'm asking you a simple question. Were you whipped? I don't care who did it. Did any man—if not Banwell, then someone else—whip you? Yes or no. Tell me."

She shook her head. "No," she whispered. "Yes. No. Yes. So hard I thought I would die."

If it hadn't been so awful, her changing her story four times in five seconds would have been funny. "Show me your back," I said.

She shook her head. "You know it's true. Dr. Higginson told you."

"You fooled him as well." I grasped the top of her dress, tore it, and let it fall to her shoulders. She gasped but didn't move or try to stop me. Her shoulders were unhurt. I saw the top of her bosom; bare, unhurt. I turned her around. There seemed to be no wounds on her back, but I couldn't see below her shoulder blades. A white, tight-laced corset covered her from the scapula down.

"Are you going to rip my bodice as well?" she asked.

"No. I've seen enough. I'm going back to the city, and you're coming with me." She belonged, very possibly, in a sanatorium after all. If she did not, I didn't know where she belonged, but she had to be in someone's charge, and it wasn't mine. Nor was I going to be responsible for having shipped her off to the Banwells' country house. "I'm taking you home."

"Very well," she said.

"Oh, not worried anymore about being locked up in an asylum? That was another lie?"

"No. It's true. But I have to leave here."

"Do you think I'm a fool?" I asked, knowing the answer was yes. "If you were in danger of being locked up, you would refuse to leave."

"I can't stay the night here. Mr. Banwell will find out eventually. The servants may wire from town this evening."

"So what?" I asked.

"He will come to kill me," she said.

I laughed dismissively, but she merely looked up at me. I examined her lying blue eyes as deeply as I could. Either she believed what she was saying, or she was the best prevaricator I'd ever seen—which I already knew to be the case. "You are making a fool of me again," I said, "but I'm going to believe you mean what you say. Banwell knows you named him as your assailant; perhaps you have reason to fear him, even though you invented the attack. In any event, all the more reason I should take you home."

"I can't go like this," she said, looking down at her torn dress. "I'll find something of Clara's."

As she neared the doorway, I called out to her. "Why did you bring me here?"

"To tell you the truth." She opened the doors and ran up the marble stairway, clutching her dress to her chest with both hands. Fortunately, none of the help was there to see her. They would probably have called the police and reported a rape.

CHAPTER TWENTY-FOUR

"I'M NOT SAYING he killed her, Your Honor. I'm just saying he's hiding something." Detective Littlemore was speaking to Mayor McClellan in the latter's office late Friday afternoon. He was referring to George Banwell.

"What is your evidence?" asked an exasperated McClellan. "Be quick, man; I can give you no more than five minutes."

Littlemore considered telling the mayor about the trunk he and Younger had found in the caisson but decided against it, since the trunk had revealed nothing conclusive so far, and since he wasn't supposed to have gone down to the caisson in the first place. "I just heard from Gitlow, sir, in Chicago. He's checked with the police. He went through the whole city directory. He looked at the blue book. She didn't come from Chicago, sir. No one's ever heard of Elizabeth Riverford in Chicago."

McClellan looked long and hard at the detective. "I was with George Banwell Sunday night," he said. "I've told you that three times."

"I know, sir. And I'm sure Miss Riverford couldn't have been there with you, wherever you were, without your knowing it, right, sir?"

"What?"

"I'm sure Mr. Banwell didn't secretly bring Miss Riverford with him, sir, and kill her around midnight, and then bring her back with him to the city and put her in the apartment, making it look like she was killed there. If you follow me, Your Honor."

"Good Lord, Detective."

"It's just that I don't know where you were, sir, or how Mr. Banwell got there, or whether you were together the whole time."

McClellan took a deep breath. "Very well. On Sunday night,

Mr. Littlemore, I dined with Charles Murphy at the Grand View Hotel near Saranac Inn. The dinner was arranged that very day—by
George Banwell. Mr. Haffen was another of the guests."

Littlemore was startled. Boss Murphy was the head of Tammany
Hall. Louis Haffen, a Tammany man, had been borough president of
the Bronx—until last Sunday. "But you just had Haffen kicked out of
office, sir. By Governor Hughes."

"Hughes was down the road, at Mr. Colgate's, with Governor Fort."

"I don't understand, sir."

"I was there, Detective, to hear what conditions Murphy would
demand in exchange for making me Tammany's mayoral candidate."

Littlemore said nothing. The news astonished him. Everyone
knew the mayor had declared himself the enemy of Tammany Hall.
He had sworn to have no dealings with the likes of Murphy.

McClellan went on. "George persuaded me to go. He argued
that, with Haffen's dismissal, Murphy might be willing to deal. He
was. Murphy desired me to install Haffen in the office of the comp-
troller. Not right away, but in a month or two. If I agreed, Justice
Gaynor would stand down. I become the nominee, and the election
is mine. They claimed that Hughes wanted me nominated, which
rather surprised me, and they volunteered to commit themselves before the governor that very night, if only I would give them my word."

"What did you say, sir?"

"I told him that Mr. Haffen was not in need of a new post, having
already embezzled a quarter of a million dollars from the city in his
last one. George was quite disappointed. He wanted me to accept.
No doubt he has profited from our friendship, Littlemore, but he has
earned every dollar the city paid him. In fact, I gave him his last pay-
ment this week, not a penny more than his original bid. And no, I
don't see how he could have killed Miss Riverford at Saranac Inn. We
left the Grand View at nine-thirty or ten, dropped in at Colgate's, and
returned to the city together. We rode in my car, arriving in Manhattan at seven in the morning. I don't believe Banwell was out of my
sight for more than five or ten minutes at a time the entire night.
Why he would misrepresent the location of Miss Riverford's family is
a mystery to me—if he did. He may have meant that Riverford lives
in one of the surrounding towns."

"We're checking them now, sir."

"At any rate, he could not have killed her."

"I don't believe he did, Your Honor. I wanted to rule him out. But I'm close, sir. Real close. I have a good lead on the murderer."

"Good heavens, Littlemore. Why didn't you say so? Who is it?"

"If you don't mind, sir, I'll know if my lead pans out tonight. If I could just wait until then."

The mayor agreed. But before he dismissed Littlemore, he gave the detective a card with a telephone number on it. "That is the telephone in my house," he said. "Call me at once, at any hour, if you discover anything."

$\backsim$

AT EIGHT-THIRTY Friday evening, Sigmund Freud responded to a knock at his hotel room door. He was dressed in a bathrobe, with dinner trousers, white shirt, and black tie beneath it. Outside his door was a tall young man, looking both physically and morally exhausted.

"Younger, there you are," said Freud. "My goodness, you look terrible."

Stratham Younger made no reply. Freud could see immediately that something had happened to him. But Freud's store of sympathy was greatly depleted. The boy's dishevelment signified for him the general disarray into which things had descended since his arrival in New York. Must every American be involved in some kind of disaster? Couldn't at least one of them keep his shirt tucked in?

"I came to see how you were, sir," said Younger.

"Apart from having lost both my digestion and my most important follower, I am quite well, thank you," replied Freud. "The cancelation of my lectures at your university will of course also be a source of satisfaction. Altogether a most successful journey to your country."

"Did Brill go to the *Times*, sir?" asked Younger. "Did he find out if the article is genuine?"

"Yes. It is genuine," Freud said. "Jung gave the interview."

"I will go to President Hall tomorrow, Dr. Freud. I read the article. It is gossip, anonymous gossip. I am sure I can persuade Hall not to cancel. Jung says nothing against you."

"Nothing against me?" Freud laughed derisively, recollecting his last exchange with Jung. "He has repudiated Oedipus. He has rejected the sexual aetiology. He denies even that a man's childhood experiences are the source of his neuroses. As a result, your medical establishment has thrown its weight behind him, rather than me. And your President Hall apparently intends to follow suit."

The two men remained at the threshold of Freud's hotel room, one on either side. Freud did not invite Younger in. Neither spoke.

Younger broke the silence. "I was twenty-two when I first read your work, sir. The moment I read it, I knew the world would never be the same. Yours are the most important ideas of the century. America is hungry for them. I am certain of it."

Freud opened his mouth to answer, but his reply died on his lips. He softened. "You're a good boy, Younger," he said, sighing. "I'm sorry. As for hunger, I should not stake too much on it: a hungry man will eat anything. Speaking of which, we are going to Brill's again for dinner. Ferenczi is just on his way. You'll join us?"

"I can't," Younger replied. "I wouldn't be able to keep my eyes open."

"For heaven's sake, what have you been doing all this time?" asked Freud.

"It would be hard to describe my last twenty-four hours, sir. Most recently, I have been with Miss Acton."

"I see." Freud observed that Younger hoped to be asked in, but he did not feel up to it. In fact Freud felt as exhausted as Younger looked. "Well, you will tell me all about it tomorrow."

"Tomorrow—right," Younger replied, making to leave.

Perceiving Younger's disappointment, Freud added, "Ah, I meant to tell you. Clara Banwell, we must think about her."

"Sir?"

"All family life is organized around the most damaged person in it. We know that Nora has essentially substituted the Banwells for her own parents. The question then becomes which person in this constellation has suffered the greatest psychological injuries."

"You think it might be Mrs. Banwell?"

"We mustn't assume that it is Nora. Mrs. Banwell is a compelling figure, as narcissists often are, but the men in her life have undoubtedly mistreated her in some profound way. Her husband, certainly. You heard what she said."

"Yes," said Younger. "She told me more about that."

"At Jelliffe's?"

"No, sir. I spoke with her again at Miss Acton's."

"I see," said Freud, raising an eyebrow. "I expect it is to her that we can credit Nora's learning that Mrs. Banwell had performed fellatio on her father."

"I beg your pardon?"

"You remember," said Freud. He closed his eyes and, without opening them, recited the exchange he and Younger had had on this subject two days earlier, beginning with his own words: "'Do you not find anything strange in Nora's assertion that, when she saw Mrs. Banwell with her father, she didn't understand at the time exactly what she was witnessing?' 'Most American girls of fourteen are ill-informed on that point, Dr. Freud.' 'I appreciate that, but that is not what I meant. She implied that she *now* understood what she had witnessed, did she not?'"

Younger stared. "You have a phonographic memory, sir?"

"Yes. A useful skill for an analyst. You should cultivate it. I used to be able to recall conversations for months, but now it is only days. At any rate, I think you will find that it was Mrs. Banwell herself who educated Nora about the nature of the act. I suspect she has taken the girl into her confidence, enlisting her sympathy. Otherwise Nora's feelings for her are inexplicable."

"Nora's feelings for Mrs. Banwell," Younger repeated.

"Come, my boy, think of it. Instead of hating Mrs. Banwell as she ought to have done, Nora has essentially accepted her as a mother substitute. This means that Mrs. Banwell found a way to form a special bond with the girl, a remarkable achievement under the circumstances. Almost certainly, she confided her forbidden erotic secrets to Nora—a favorite means by which women achieve intimacy."

"I see," said Younger, glassily.

"Do you? It has undoubtedly made things harder for Nora. And it indicates a lack of scruple on Mrs. Banwell's part as well. A woman will not confide such things in a girl whom she intends to keep innocent. Well, I can see there is something you wish to tell me, but you are too tired. It would do no good to speak of it now. We'll talk tomorrow. Go take your rest."

~

SMITH ELY JELLIFFE sang an aria as he strolled into the Balmoral a little after eleven on Friday night. Tipping the doormen lavishly, he informed them, quite without having been asked, that he had spent the evening at the Metropolitan, in the company of a feminine creature of the best kind—the kind who knew how to occupy herself during an opera. His face shining, Jelliffe looked like a man convinced of the largeness of his own soul.

His glow was dimmed somewhat by the appearance of a young man in a threadbare suit blocking his path to the elevator. It was dimmed several shades further when the young man identified himself as a police detective.

"You're Harry Thaw's doctor, aren't you, Dr. Jelliffe?" asked Littlemore.

"Are you aware of the hour, my good man?" replied Jelliffe.

"Just answer the question."

"Mr. Thaw is under my care," Jelliffe acknowledged. "Everyone knows that. It has been widely reported."

"Was he under your care," pursued Littlemore, "here in town last weekend?"

"I don't know what you're talking about," said Jelliffe.

"Sure you don't," the detective replied, beckoning to a girl who, ostentatiously attired, was waiting on a leather sofa at the other end of the marble lobby. Greta now approached. Littlemore asked her if she recognized Jelliffe.

"It's him, all right," said Greta. "Dr. Smith. Came with Harry and left with him."

That afternoon, before calling on the mayor, the detective had returned to his office, reread the trial transcript, and found Jelliffe testifying that Thaw was insane. When he saw in the transcript that Jelliffe's first name was Smith, he put two and two together. "So, Dr. Smith," said Littlemore. "Want to come clean here—or downtown?"

The detective did not have to wait long for a confession. "It wasn't my decision at all," Jelliffe blurted out. "It was Dana's. Dana was in charge."

Littlemore told Jelliffe to take them to his apartment. When they entered Jelliffe's ornate foyer, the detective nodded appreciatively. "Boy, you got a lot to lose, Dr. Smith," Littlemore said. "So you brought Thaw into town last weekend? How'd you do it, bribe the guards?"

"Yes, but it was Dana's decision, not mine," Jelliffe insisted. He dropped heavily into a chair at his dining table. "I only did what he said we should."

Littlemore stared down at him. "Was it your idea to take him to Susie's?"

"Thaw chose the house, not me. Please, Detective. It was a medical necessity. A healthy man can be driven insane at a place like Matteawan. Surrounded by lunatics. Deprived of normal physical outlets."

"But Thaw *is* insane," said Littlemore. "That's why he's in the loony bin."

"He is not insane. He is highly strung," responded Jelliffe. "He has a nervous temperament. No good is done by shutting up such a man."

"Too bad you told them the opposite at the trial," remarked Littlemore. "This wasn't the first time you brought Thaw into town, was it? You had him here about a month ago, didn't you?"

"No, I swear it," said Jelliffe. "This was the first time."

"Sure it was," answered Littlemore. "And how did Thaw know Elsie Sigel?"

Jelliffe denied ever having heard of Elsie Sigel until he read about her in the papers yesterday afternoon.

"When you took Thaw to Susie's," Littlemore went on, "did you know what he liked to do to girls? Was that a medical necessity too?"

Jelliffe hung his head. "I had heard of his proclivities," he mumbled, "but I thought we had resolved them."

"Uh-huh," said Littlemore. The detective looked with disgust at Jelliffe's manicured fingernails gripping his immense waist. "Before you went to Susie's that night, when you had Thaw here at your apartment, how long was he out of your sight? Did you leave him by himself? Did he go out? What happened?"

"Here?" said Jelliffe, anxious and confused. "I would never have brought the man here."

"Don't play with me, Smith. I got plenty enough already to make you an accessory to murder—before the fact and after."

"Murder?" asked Jelliffe. "Dear God. It can't be. There was no murder."

"A girl was killed right here in this building last Sunday night, the same night you had Thaw in your apartment."

Jelliffe's face was pale. "No," he said. "Thaw came into the city Saturday night. I took the train to Matteawan with him myself Sunday morning. He was there Sunday and Monday as well. You can ask Dana. You can check the records at Matteawan. They'll prove it."

Jelliffe's desperation sounded sincere, but Littlemore had contradictory evidence. "Nice try, Smith," he said, "but I've got a half dozen girls who put you and Thaw at Susie's last Sunday. Isn't that right, Greta?"

"Yeah," said Greta. "Around one or two Sunday morning. Just like I told you."

Littlemore froze. "Wait a minute, wait a minute. Do you mean Saturday night or Sunday?"

"Saturday night—Sunday morning—same difference" was Greta's answer.

"Greta," said the detective, "I need to be sure about this. When did Thaw come in, Saturday night or Sunday night?"

"Saturday night," said Greta. "I don't work Sunday nights."

Littlemore was once more at a loss. The Thaw connection had loomed up again like a ten-ton sure thing. Everything pointed to it. But now Thaw was at Susie's the wrong night—the night before. "I'm going to check those hospital records," Littlemore said to Jelliffe, "and you better hope you're right. Come on, Greta. We're going."

Jelliffe, swallowing, hiked himself up in his chair. "I should think you owe me an apology, Detective," he said.

"Maybe," said Littlemore. "But if you ask me for it again, you'll do one to five at Sing Sing for conspiring in the escape of a state prisoner. Not to mention never practicing medicine again."

⤫

FOR A SECOND consecutive night, Carl Jung walked beneath Calvary Church across from Gramercy Park. This time, he carried his revolver in a pocket. Perhaps it gave him courage. Without wavering, he strode purposefully along the wrought-iron fence to Gramercy Park South, crossed the street, and walked straight toward the officer in front of the Actons' house. The policeman asked his business. Jung replied that he was looking for the theatrical club: could the officer direct him?

"The Players, that's what you want," said the policeman. "Number sixteen, four doors down."

Jung knocked at the door of number sixteen and, when he mentioned Smith Jelliffe's name, was allowed in. The air was filled with music and feminine laughter. Now he was inside, Jung could not believe what a fool he had been, to come almost to the door of the place twice before and then turn tail. Imagine: a man of his stature frightened of entering a house where women could be had for money.

The club's hat-check girl, greeting Jung in the foyer, was momentarily disconcerted when he drew his revolver. But he handed it to her with European politeness, explaining that, having seen a policeman a few doors down, he was concerned that there might be some murderer abroad. "It's okay," said the girl, smiling prettily at him. "For a second there, I thought *you* were the murderer."

As the two of them laughed and the front door was shut, a different man stepped out of a carriage in the shadows of Calvary Church. The cab drove away, leaving this man by himself in almost the very spot that Jung had occupied the night before. He was dressed in white tie. Despite the summer evening heat, he wore yet another layer of clothing, an overcoat, as well as white deerskin gloves. His hat was pulled low to cover as much of his face as possible. The man did not move. He watched from the darkness, where the policemen at the Actons' house could not see him.

⤫

AS SOON AS he heard the door shut, Smith Jelliffe went to his telephone. He asked an operator to connect him to the Matteawan

State Hospital. It took fifteen minutes, but Jelliffe at last got through to a hospital guard with whom he was on excellent terms. Jelliffe began issuing frantic commands, but he was quickly interrupted.

"You're too late," said the guard. "He's gone."

"Gone?"

"He left three hours ago."

Jelliffe put down the receiver. With nervous fingers, he dialed the number of Charles Dana's Fifth Avenue home. There was no answer. It was nearing midnight. After six rings, Jelliffe hung up.

"Dear God," he said.

ACROSS THE STREET from the Balmoral, Littlemore said goodbye to Greta under a streetlamp. The night was as hot and muggy as they came. "I can say he came in Sunday night," Greta volunteered, "if you want me to."

Littlemore had to laugh. He shook his head, hailing a passing cab.

"You aren't going to look for my Fannie now, are you?" she asked forlornly.

"No, I'm not going to look for her," Littlemore said. "I'm going to find her."

He told the driver Fortieth Street and gave the man a dollar to cover the fare. Greta stared at him. "You're a pistol, you know that?" she said. "You wouldn't want to marry me, by any chance? We're both redheads."

Littlemore laughed again. "Sorry, sugar, I'm spoken for."

Greta kissed him on the cheek. As the cab drove off, Littlemore turned around to find Betty Longobardi standing right behind him. On his way uptown, the detective had made a stop at the Longobardis', leaving word for Betty to meet him at the Balmoral as soon as she got home.

"Start explaining," said Betty, "and make it good."

Littlemore said she'd just have to trust him, then led her to his parked car. From the trunk, the detective drew out a lumpy sack. "I need to show you some things that might have belonged to Miss Riverford. You're the only one who can identify them."

Littlemore emptied the sack into the trunk of his car. The clothing was too soaked to be recognizable. The jewelry and shoes, Betty thought, looked familiar, but she couldn't be sure. Then she saw a sequined sleeve hanging from a dense tangle of fabric. She extricated the dress to which it belonged and held it out under the lamplight. "This was hers! I saw her in it."

"Wait a second," said Littlemore. "Wait a second." He rummaged through the clothing. "Is there anything here a woman could wear in the daytime?"

"Not these," said Betty, raising her eyebrows as she pieced through the lingerie. "Not these either. Not really, Jimmy. It's all evening wear."

"Evening wear," the detective repeated slowly.

"What is it?" asked Betty.

Littlemore said nothing, lost in thought.

"What, Jimmy?"

"But then Mr. Hugel . . ." Hurriedly, the detective began patting his pockets and fishing through them until at last he found an envelope containing several photographs. One of these he showed Betty. "Recognize this face?" he asked.

"Of course," she said, "but why—?"

"We're going back upstairs," Littlemore interrupted. He grabbed from his trunk a cumbersome brass object that looked like a motorcar's headlamp stuck to a candlestick. It was an electric lantern. Then he led Betty back into the Balmoral. They rode the Alabaster Wing elevator to the top floor.

"How tall was Miss Riverford?" Littlemore asked on their way up.

"A little taller than me." Betty was five-foot-two. "At least she looked taller."

"What do you mean?"

"She was always in heels," Betty explained. "Real tall heels. Wasn't used to them, though."

"How much did she weigh?"

"I don't know, Jimmy. Why?"

The hallway of the eighteenth floor was empty. Over Betty's objections, Littlemore picked the lock of Elizabeth Riverford's apartment and opened the front door. Inside, all was dark and silent. There were no overhead lights. The lamps had been taken away.

"What are we doing here?" asked Betty.

"Figuring something out." Littlemore headed down the corridor toward Miss Riverford's bedroom, shining his flickering light into the blackness.

"I don't want to go in there," said Betty, following reluctantly.

They came to the door. As Littlemore reached for the knob, his hand froze in midair. A high-pitched note suddenly pierced the air. It was coming from within the bedroom. The note grew louder, becoming a far-off wail.

Betty seized Littlemore's arm. "That's the sound I told you about, Jimmy, the sound we heard the morning Miss Elizabeth died."

The detective opened the door. The wail grew louder still.

"Don't go in," whispered Betty.

Abruptly the noise stopped. All was silent. Littlemore entered the room. Too afraid to stay where she was, Betty went in as well, clinging to his sleeve. The furniture was still in place: bed, mirror, end tables, chests of drawers. These created eerie shadows in the beam of the detective's lantern. Littlemore put his ear to a wall, rapping it with his knuckles, listening intently. He moved a few feet down and did the same thing.

"What are you doing?" whispered Betty.

Littlemore snapped his fingers. "The fireplace," he said. "I saw the clay near the fireplace."

He went to the fireplace and drew aside its iron-mesh curtain, stretching himself out on the floor. With his lantern, he lit up the chimney. At the far back wall of the hearth, Littlemore saw bricks, mortar—and three apertures arranged in a triangle, the topmost being circular in shape.

"That's it," said the detective. "That's got to be it. Now how would he—?"

Littlemore lit up the andirons hanging next to the fireplace. One instrument was a trident poker. Two of its three tines were sharply pointed; the other was circular. The three ends, together, made a triangle. Littlemore jumped up, took hold of this poker, and prodded the back of the chimney with it. When he found the apertures, the poker's three ends fit into them as if they had been specially designed to do so—as of course they had. A moment later, the entire hearth swung away on interior hinges, and a strong breeze blew into Littlemore's face.

"Will you look at that," said Littlemore. Inside, small jets of blue flame dotted the walls. "Where have I seen those before? Come on, Betty."

They stepped into the passage, Betty holding Littlemore's hand. When they passed a large, square iron grate on one of the walls, the detective put his ear to it and told Betty to do likewise. They could hear, far away, the same wailing noise that had given Betty such a fright.

"Air shaft," said Littlemore. "Some kind of forced-air system. There must be a pump. When the pump comes on, you get that sound. When the pump stops, the noise stops." They followed the passage several hundred feet, passing half a dozen similar grates and turning three or four sharp corners. Betty's fingernails were digging into Littlemore's arm. At last they came to the end. A wall barred their way, but on that wall, a small metal plate glinted below a final blue gas jet. Littlemore pushed on the plate, and the wall swung out.

In the light of the electric lantern, they could see an expensively furnished man's study. Bookshelves lined the walls, although, instead of books, the shelves were filled with a collection of scale models of bridges and buildings. In the middle of the study stood a massive desk with brass lamps on it. Littlemore switched on a lamp. Quietly, Littlemore and Betty left the study and walked down a hallway. They crossed a white marble entry foyer. Then they heard a muffled noise. Farther down the hall, past the most spacious living room either Littlemore or Betty had ever seen, a door was rattling, its knob turning back and forth. Someone was evidently behind the door and trying in vain to open it. Littlemore called out, identifying himself as a police detective.

A female voice answered. "Open the door. Let me out."

It did not take Littlemore long to do so. When the door opened, a linen closet was revealed, as was the back of a woman, pressed into a space not intended for a person, her hands tied behind her. Mrs. Clara Banwell turned around, thanked the detective, and begged him to untie her.

❧

SWEAT GLISTENED ON Henry Kendall Thaw's forehead as he eyed the policeman on the other side of Gramercy Park, patrolling back and forth under the gas streetlamp in front of the Actons' house. It dampened the back of his shirt below his dinner jacket. It trickled down his sleeves and trousers.

From his vantage point on East Twenty-first Street between Fourth and Lexington avenues, Thaw could see the entire row of imposing houses that lined Gramercy Park South. He could see the Players Club, lit up gaily on a Friday night. Indeed, he could see behind the translucent curtains of the club's first-floor windows, where well-heeled older men and bare-shouldered young women passed to and fro, drinking Duplexes and Bronx Cocktails.

Thaw's eyes were better than Jung's. He detected, three stories above the patrolman, a movement on the Actons' roof. There, against the night sky, he discerned the silhouette of another policeman and the outline of the rifle he was carrying. Thaw was a wiry man, thin almost to the point of appearing frail, with arms slightly longer than they should have been. His face was surprisingly boyish for a man in his late thirties. He might almost have been handsome, except that his small eyes were a little too deep-set and his lips a little too thick. Whether in motion or stationary, he seemed unable to catch his breath.

Thaw was now in motion. He walked east, keeping to the shadows. He pulled the brim of his hat even farther down as he crossed Lexington Avenue: he knew the house on this corner very well. He had watched it for hours at a time in the old days, waiting to see if a certain girl would come out of it, a pretty girl he wanted to hurt so much it made his skin tingle. He skirted the iron fence of the park until he came to its southeastern corner, with Irving Place separating him from the watchful policemen. The officers never saw him enter the back alley behind the houses of Gramercy Park South.

❧

TWO MILES AWAY, in his apartment on the second floor of the small house on Warren Street, Coroner Charles Hugel had packed his bags. He stood in the middle of his living room, biting his knuckles. He had delivered his letter of resignation to the mayor.

He had notified his landlord. He had gone to the bank and closed his account. All the money he possessed lay before him, stacked in neat piles on the floor. He had to decide how to carry it. He bent down and started counting the bills—for the third time—wondering whether it would be enough to establish him in another, smaller town. His hands jerked open and fifty-dollar bills flew into the air when he heard the pounding on his door.

❧

IF THE PATROLMAN in front of the Actons' house had only looked up, he might have noticed a deeper darkening at the window of Nora's bedroom. He might possibly have realized that a man had passed behind its curtains. But he didn't look up.

The intruder loosed the white silk tie that was around his neck. Silently, he drew the tie from his collar and wrapped its ends around his hands. He closed on Nora's bed. Despite the darkness, he could make out the girl's sleeping form on the bed. He could see the line where the pretty chin gave way to her soft, unprotected throat. Slipping the tie between headboard and pillow, he worked it downward, slowly downward, beneath the pillow, closer and closer to the girl's neck, infinitely slowly, until its two ends should emerge out from under the pillow. He listened all the while to her breathing, which went on softly, undisturbed.

It is a fine question whether the kitchen knife, had Mrs. Mildred Acton not removed it from beneath the girl's pillow, could have done any good. Could Nora Acton, jolted awake by a man in the night, have reached the knife? If she had reached it, could she have used it? Nora always slept on her stomach. Even if she had got her hands on the weapon, could she—with her breath choked off—have saved her life with it?

All fine questions, but all quite academic, since not only was the kitchen knife not there, neither was Nora.

"Put 'em up, Mr. Banwell," said a voice from behind the intruder at Nora's bed. An electric lantern, held by a uniformed officer standing in the doorway, suddenly lit up the room. George Banwell threw his hands before his face.

"Step away from the bed, Mr. Banwell," said Detective Littlemore, jutting the muzzle of his gun into Banwell's back. "Okay, Betty, you can get up now."

Betty Longobardi rose from the bed, fearful but defiant. As Littlemore patted down Banwell's pockets, he glanced at Nora's hearth. There, as he expected, a wall panel had swiveled open, revealing a secret passageway behind it. "Okay. Put your hands down now. Behind your back. Nice and slow."

Banwell didn't move. "What's your price?" he asked.

"More than you can pay," answered Littlemore.

"Twenty thousand," said Banwell, his hands still over his head. "I'll give each of you twenty thousand dollars."

"Hands behind your back," repeated Littlemore.

"Fifty thousand," said Banwell. Squinting into the beam of light, he could see there were two men in the doorway, one holding the lantern and another behind him, in addition to whoever had the gun sticking in his back. At the words "fifty thousand," the two men in the doorway shifted uneasily. Banwell addressed them. "Think of it, boys. You're smart; I can tell by the look of you. Where do you think Chief Byrnes got his? You know what Byrnes has in the bank? Three hundred fifty thousand. That's right. I made him rich, and I'll make you rich."

"The mayor won't like your trying to bribe us," said Littlemore, lowering one of Banwell's arms and placing a cuff around his wrist.

"Are you going to listen to this fool behind me?" Banwell shot out, still addressing the two men in the doorway, his voice strong and confident notwithstanding his predicament. "I'll break him during the trial. I'll break him, do you hear me? Be smart. You want to be poor your whole lives? Think of your wives, your children. You want them to be poor their whole lives? Don't worry about the mayor. I own the mayor."

"Do you, George?" said the man behind the officer holding the lantern. He stepped into the light. It was Mayor McClellan. "Do you really?"

Littlemore snapped the handcuffs over Banwell's other wrist, the lock catching with a satisfying click. With a quickness surprising for a man of his size, Banwell wrenched himself out of the detective's grip and, arms locked behind his back, made for the passageway. But he had to stop and duck to get in, which was his undoing. Littlemore had his gun in his hand. He had a clear shot but didn't fire. Instead he took one large step forward and brought the butt end of his gun down on Banwell's head. Banwell let out a cry and collapsed to the floor.

A few minutes later, Detective Littlemore sat the almost unconscious George Banwell at the foot of the Actons' stairs and secured him to the banister with a second pair of handcuffs, borrowed from one of the uniformed men. Blood was dripping down Banwell's face. Another policeman let a flustered Harcourt and Mildred Acton out of their bedroom.

❧

INSIDE THE PLAYERS CLUB, the hat-check girl welcomed a new guest, who also surprised her—not only because he had entered through the rear door, but also because the man was wearing an overcoat in the middle of summer. It gave Harry Thaw special pleasure to be enjoying his liberty in rooms designed by the very man he had murdered three years ago, Mr. Stanford White. He gave his name as Monroe Reid from Philadelphia. It was under that appellation that he introduced himself to another out-of-towner, a foreign gentleman he met in the small ballroom, where dancers were performing a show number on a raised stage. Harry Thaw and Carl Jung got on quite well that evening. When Jung mentioned that the club member he knew was Smith Jelliffe, Thaw exclaimed that he knew the man well, although he did not give an entirely truthful account of their acquaintance.

❧

"WELL DONE, DETECTIVE," said Mayor McClellan to Littlemore in the Actons' living room. "I would never have believed it if I hadn't seen it with my own eyes."

Mrs. Biggs was dressing the gash in Banwell's skull. Mr. Acton had poured himself a large drink. "Do you think you might tell us what's happening, McClellan?" he asked.

"I'm afraid I don't entirely know myself," answered the mayor. "I still cannot fathom how George could have killed Miss Riverford."

The doorbell rang. Mrs. Biggs looked to her employers, who in turn looked to the mayor. Littlemore said he would answer it. A moment later, everyone in the room saw Coroner Charles Hugel enter the room, firmly in the grasp of Officer John Reardon.

"Got him, Detective," said Reardon. "He was all packed just like you said he would be."

CHAPTER TWENTY-FIVE

THE TELEPHONE RANG in my hotel room, waking me. I didn't remember falling asleep; I hardly remembered returning to my room. It was the front desk on the line.

"What time is it?" I asked.

"Just before midnight, sir."

"What day?" The fog in my brain wouldn't clear.

"Still Friday, sir. Excuse me, Dr. Younger, but you asked to be informed if Miss Acton had any visitors."

"Yes?"

"A Mrs. Banwell is on her way to Miss Acton's room now."

"Mrs. Banwell?" I said. "All right. Don't let anyone else up, without calling me first."

Nora and I had taken the train back from Tarry Town. We barely spoke. When we arrived at the Grand Central, Nora begged me to take her back to the Hotel Manhattan—to see whether her room there was still booked in her name. If so, she asked, couldn't she stay there until Sunday, when she need no longer fear that her parents might have her hospitalized against her will?

Contrary to my better judgment, I agreed to take her to the hotel. I warned her, though, that tomorrow morning, no matter what, I would notify her father of her whereabouts. I felt sure—and told her as much—that she would be able to come up with some fictitious story to keep her parents at bay for a mere twenty-four hours. As it happened, she was right about her room: it had never been released. The clerk handed her the keys, and she disappeared into an elevator.

I did not consider Mrs. Banwell's midnight visit wise: her husband could have followed her. Nora must have telephoned her. But if

Nora could deceive me as thoroughly as she had, Clara could probably deceive her husband about an evening's errand.

Freud's remarks about Nora's feelings for Clara came back to me. He still believed, of course, that Nora harbored incestuous wishes. I no longer did. In fact, given my interpretation of *To be, or not to be*, I dared to think I finally had upended the whole Oedipus complex. Freud was right all along: yes, he had held the mirror up to nature, but he had seen in it a mirror image of reality.

It's the father, not the son. Yes, when a little boy enters the scene with his mother and father, one party in this trio tends to suffer a profound jealousy—the father. He may naturally feel the boy intrudes on his special, exclusive relationship with his wife. He may well half want to be rid of the suckling, puling intruder, whom the mother proclaims to be so perfect. He might even wish him dead.

The Oedipus complex is real, but the subject of all its predicates is the parent, not the child. And it only worsens as the child grows. A girl soon confronts her mother with a figure whose youth and beauty the mother cannot help resenting. A boy must eventually overtake his father, who as the son grows cannot but feel the churning of generations coming to plow him under.

But what parent will acknowledge a wish to kill his own issue? What father will admit to being jealous of his own boy? So the Oedipal complex must be *projected onto children*. A voice must whisper in the ear of Oedipus's father that it is not he—the father—who entertains a secret death wish against the son but rather Oedipus who covets the mother and compasses the father's death. The more intensely these jealousies attack the parents, the more destructively they will behave against their own children, and if this occurs they may turn their own children against them—bringing about the very situation they feared. So teaches *Oedipus* itself. Freud had misinterpreted *Oedipus*: the secret of the Oedipal wishes lies in the parent's heart, not the child's.

The pity of it was that this discovery, if such it was, now seemed so stale, so profitless to me. What good was it? What good did thinking ever do?

❧

"THIS IS AN OUTRAGE," said Coroner Hugel, with what looked like a barely controllable indignation. "I demand an explanation."

George Banwell grunted in pain as Mrs. Biggs applied a plaster to his skull. Blood remained clotted in his hair, but it was no longer running down his cheeks.

"What is the meaning of this, Littlemore?" asked the mayor.

"You want to tell him, Mr. Hugel?" was the detective's answer. "Or should I?"

"Tell me what?" asked McClellan.

"Let go of me," the coroner said to Reardon.

"Let him go, Officer," ordered the mayor. Reardon complied at once.

"Is this another of your jokes, Littlemore?" asked Hugel, straightening his suit. "Don't listen to anything he says, McClellan. This is a man who pretended to be dead on my operating table yesterday."

"Did you?" the mayor asked Littlemore.

"Yes, sir."

"You see?" said Hugel to McClellan, his voice rising. "I am no longer in the city's employ. My resignation was effective at five o'clock today; it is on your desk, McClellan, although no doubt you did not read it. I am going home. Good night."

"Don't let him go, Mr. Mayor," said Littlemore.

The coroner paid no heed. Placing his hat on his head, he began striding toward the door.

"Don't let him go, sir," Littlemore repeated.

"Mr. Hugel, remain as you are, if you please," ordered McClellan. "The detective has already shown me one thing tonight I would not have believed possible. I will hear him out."

"Thank you, Your Honor," said Littlemore. "I better begin with the photograph. Coroner Hugel took the picture, sir. It's a photograph of Miss Riverford with Mr. Banwell's initials showing on her neck."

Banwell stirred at the foot of the stairs. "What's that?" he asked.

"His initials? What are you talking about?" asked McClellan.

"I have a copy of it here, sir," said Littlemore. He handed the picture to the mayor. "It's kind of complicated, sir. You see, Mr. Hugel said Miss Riverford's body was stolen from the morgue because there was a clue on it."

"Yes, you mentioned that to me, Hugel," said the mayor.

The coroner said nothing, eyeing Littlemore warily.

"Then Riviere develops Mr. Hugel's plates," the detective continued, "and sure enough, we find this picture of Miss Riverford's neck with some kind of imprint on it. Riviere and I didn't get it, but Mr. Hugel explained it to us. The murderer strangles Miss Riverford with his tie, the tie still has his pin on it, and the pin has his monogram. So you see, Your Honor, the picture shows the murderer's initials on Miss Riverford's neck. That's what you told us, right, Mr. Hugel?"

"Astounding," said the mayor, who peered at the photograph, holding it close to his eyes. "By God, I see it: *GB*."

"Yes, sir. I've also got one of Mr. Banwell's tiepins, and you can see they're alike." Littlemore drew Banwell's tiepin from his trousers pocket and handed it to the mayor.

"Look at that," said the mayor. "Identical."

"Rubbish," said Banwell. "I'm being framed."

"Good Lord, Hugel," said the mayor, ignoring Banwell. "Why didn't you tell me, man? You had proof positive against him."

"But I don't—I can't—let me see that photograph," said Hugel.

The mayor gave the coroner the picture.

Hugel shook his head as he scrutinized it. "But my picture—"

"Mr. Hugel's never seen that photograph, Your Honor," said Littlemore.

"I don't understand," said the mayor.

"On Mr. Hugel's photograph—on his original photograph, sir— the initials on the girl's neck weren't *GB*. They were the reverse of *GB*, the mirror image."

"Well, as a matter of fact, the initials should have been in reverse, shouldn't they?" McClellan pointed out. "The monogram should have left a reverse imprint, just like the seal on an envelope."

"That's the trick of it," said Littlemore. "You got it right, Your Honor: the pin would have left a reverse imprint, so the reverse *GB* on Mr. Hugel's photograph made it look like Mr. Banwell was the killer. That's exactly what Mr. Hugel said. The only problem was that Mr. Hugel's photograph was already a reverse image. Riviere told us. That's what Mr. Hugel didn't realize, sir. His picture showed a backward *GB*—okay?—but his photograph was already a reverse image of the girl's neck. That meant the imprint left on her neck was a true *GB*, and that meant the murderer's monogram was *not* a true *GB* but a reverse *GB*."

"Say that again," said McClellan.

Littlemore did. In fact, he repeated the point several times until the mayor understood it. He also explained that he had made Riviere produce a reverse image of Hugel's picture, turning the *GB* around again, making it forward-facing, so he could compare the initials to Mr. Banwell's actual monogram. This reversed picture was the one he had just shown the mayor.

"But it still makes no sense," said the mayor irritably. "It makes no sense at all. How could the monogram shown in Hugel's original photograph be the exact reverse of George Banwell's?"

"There's only one way, Your Honor," said Littlemore. "Somebody drew it."

"What?"

"Somebody drew it. Somebody etched it right onto the dry plate before Riviere developed it. Somebody who had access both to Mr. Banwell's tiepin and to Mr. Hugel's plates. Somebody trying to make us think Mr. Banwell killed Elizabeth Riverford. Whoever did it must have worked at it real hard. They did almost everything right, but they made one mistake: they made the photograph show a mirror image when they shouldn't have. They knew the imprint on Miss Riverford's neck had to be the mirror image of the real monogram. So they figured the photograph had to show a mirror image. But what they forgot was that a ferrotype is already a mirror image. That was their big mistake. When they put a reverse *GB* into the photograph, they gave the game away."

Hugel broke in. "Why, even I can't understand what the harebrain is saying. We have a clear photograph here of the girl's neck. And it says *GB* on it—not a negative, or a double negative, or a triple negative, or whatever Littlemore is babbling about. Just a simple *GB*. It is proof that Banwell was the murderer."

There was a brief silence; the mayor broke it. "Detective," he said, "I believe I have followed your reasoning. But I must say things are turned around so many times I am at a loss to know who is in the right. Is this the only reason you have for believing that Mr. Hugel has tampered with evidence? Is it possible that Hugel is correct? That your photograph proves George Banwell to have been the murderer?"

Littlemore frowned. "Let's see," he said. "I guess there *is* a lot of evidence against Mr. Banwell, isn't there? Mr. Mayor, could I put a couple of questions to Mr. Banwell?"

"Go ahead," replied McClellan.

"Mr. Banwell, can you hear me okay, sir?"

"What do you want?" Banwell growled.

"You know, Mr. Banwell, now that I think of it, I'm pretty sure we can convict you of Miss Riverford's murder. I found the secret passageway between your apartments."

"Good for you," was Banwell's reply.

"There was clay in her apartment that matches the clay at your construction site."

"That's proof for you."

"And we found the trunk with Miss Riverford's things in it—the one you buried in the East River below the Manhattan Bridge."

"Impossible!" cried Banwell.

"Got it last night, Mr. Banwell. Just before you flooded the caisson."

"You were in the Manhattan Bridge caisson last night, Littlemore?" McClellan demanded.

"Yes, sir," said Littlemore sheepishly. "Sorry, Mr. Mayor."

"Oh, never mind," replied McClellan. "Go on."

"I'm being framed," Banwell interrupted. "McClellan, I was with you all Sunday night. At Saranac Inn. You know I couldn't have killed her."

"That's not how the prosecutor will see it," Littlemore replied. "He'll say you had someone drive Miss Riverford down to Saranac, that you snuck out of the dinner with the mayor, met her somewhere for a few minutes, and killed her. Then you had her body driven back to the Balmoral where it would look like she died there. You figured you'd use the mayor himself as your alibi. Too bad you left your initials on her neck. That's what the prosecutor will say, Mr. Banwell."

"I didn't kill her, I tell you," said Banwell. "I can prove it."

"How can you prove it, George?" asked McClellan.

"*Nobody* killed Elizabeth Riverford," said Banwell.

"What?" said the mayor. "She's still alive? Where?"

Banwell shook his head.

"For God's sake, man," said McClellan, "explain yourself."

"There *is* no Elizabeth Riverford," said Banwell.

"Never was," added Littlemore.

Banwell expelled a deep breath. Hugel took one. The mayor expostulated. "Will someone explain to me what's going on?"

"It was her weight that first got me thinking," said Littlemore. "Mr. Hugel's report said Miss Riverford was five-foot-five and weighed a hundred fifteen pounds. But the ceiling thing she was tied up to wouldn't have held a hundred-fifteen-pound girl. It would've broken right off. I tested it."

"I could have been slightly off in height and weight," said Hugel. "I have been under considerable strain."

"You weren't off, Mr. Hugel," said Littlemore. "You did it on purpose. You also didn't mention that Miss Riverford's hair wasn't really black."

"Of course it was black," said Hugel. "Everyone at the Balmoral will testify it was black."

"A wig," said Littlemore. "We found another one just like it in Banwell's trunk."

Hugel appealed to the mayor. "He's lost his mind. Someone is paying him to say these things. Why would I deliberately misrepresent Miss Riverford's physical appearance?"

"Why, Detective?" said McClellan.

"Because if he had told everyone that Elizabeth Riverford was five-foot-two, a hundred and three pounds, with long blond hair, things would have gotten real sticky when Miss Nora Acton, five-foot-two, a hundred and three pounds, with long blond hair, turned up with the identical wounds the very next day—the same day Miss Riverford's body disappeared—wouldn't they, Mr. Hugel?"

❧

NORA BURIED HERSELF in Clara's arms the moment the latter entered her hotel room.

"My darling," said Clara. "Thank heaven you're all right. I'm so glad you called."

"I'm going to tell them everything," Nora exclaimed. "I've tried to keep it secret, but I can't."

"I know," said Clara. "You said so in your letter. It's all right. Tell them everything."

"No," Nora replied, close to tears, "I mean *really* everything."

"I understand. It's all right."

"He didn't believe I'd been hurt at all," said Nora. "Doctor Younger. He thought I had painted on my wounds."

"How awful."

"I deserved it, Clara. Everything went wrong. I am so bad. It was all for nothing. It would be better if I were dead."

"Hush. We need something to calm our nerves, both of us." She went to a credenza on which stood a half-filled decanter and several glasses. "Here. Oh, what awful brandy. But I'm going to pour us a little. We'll share it."

She handed Nora a snifter with a little golden liquor swirling in its bowl. Nora had never had brandy before, but Clara helped her taste it and, after the first burning sensation had passed, to finish the glass. A little spilled onto the front of Nora's dress.

"Goodness," said Clara. "Is that my dress you have on?"

"Yes," said Nora. "I'm sorry. I went to Tarry Town today. Do you mind?"

"Of course not. It looks so well on you. My things always suit you." Clara poured another finger of brandy into the snifter and took a little for herself, closing her eyes. Then she put the glass to Nora's lips. "Do you know," she said, "I bought that dress with you in mind? These shoes were meant to go with it—these, the ones I am wearing now. Here, you try them. You have such a fine ankle. Let's put everything out of our minds and dress you up, just as we used to."

"Shall I?" said Nora, trying to smile.

ᴄᴾ

"YOU MEAN ELIZABETH RIVERFORD was Nora Acton?" an uncomprehending Mayor McClellan asked Detective Littlemore.

"I can prove it, Your Honor," said Littlemore. He gestured toward Betty as he pulled a photograph from his pocket. "Mr. Mayor, Betty here was Miss Riverford's maid at the Balmoral. This is a picture I found in Leon Ling's apartment. Betty, tell these people who this woman is."

"That's Miss Riverford on the left," said Betty. "The hair is different, but that's her."

"Mr. Acton, would you please look at the photograph now?" Littlemore handed Harcourt Acton the picture of Nora Acton, William Leon, and Clara Banwell.

"It's Nora," said Acton.

McClellan shook his head. "Nora Acton was living at the Balmoral under the name of Elizabeth Riverford? Why?"

"She wasn't living there," grumbled Banwell. "She was going to come up a few nights a week, that's all. What are you looking at? Look at Acton, why don't you?"

"You knew?" McClellan asked Mr. Acton incredulously.

"Certainly not," answered Mrs. Acton for her husband. "Nora must have done it on her own."

Harcourt Acton said nothing.

"If he didn't know, he's a damned fool," announced Banwell. "But I never touched her. It was all Clara's idea anyway."

"Clara knew too?" The mayor was even more incredulous.

"Knew? She arranged it." Banwell's voice broke off. Then he resumed. "Now let me go. I've committed no crime."

"Except for running me over yesterday," said Detective Littlemore. "Plus trying to bribe a police officer, trying to kill Miss Acton, and killing Seamus Malley. I'd say you had a pretty full week, Mr. Banwell."

At the sound of Malley's name, Banwell struggled to rise from the floor, despite the handcuffs attaching him to the railing. In the commotion, Hugel broke for the door. Both men failed to achieve their object. Banwell succeed only in injuring his wrists. The coroner was caught by Officer Reardon.

"But why, Hugel?" asked the mayor.

The coroner didn't speak.

"My God," the mayor went on, still addressing the coroner. "You knew Elizabeth Riverford was Nora. Was it you who whipped her? Dear God."

"I didn't," Hugel cried out, miserably, still in Reardon's grip. "I didn't whip anyone. I was only trying to help. I had to get him convicted. She promised me. I would never—she planned everything— she told me what to do—she promised me—"

"Nora?" asked the mayor. "What in God's name did she promise you?"

"Not Nora," said Hugel. He jerked his head toward Banwell. "His wife."

❧

NORA ACTON SLIPPED out of her own shoes and tried on Clara's. The heels were high and pointed, but the shoes were made of a lovely, soft black leather. When the girl looked up, she saw in Clara's hand an unexpected object: a small revolver, with a mother-of-pearl grip.

"It is so hot in here, my dear," said Clara. "Let's go out on your balcony."

"Why are you pointing a gun at me, Clara?"

"Because I hate you, darling. You made love with my husband."

"I didn't," Nora protested.

"But he wanted you to. Quite desperately. It's the same; no, it's worse."

"But you hate George."

"Do I? I suppose so," said Clara. "I hate both of you equally."

"Oh, no. Don't say that. I would rather die."

"Well, then."

"But Clara, you made me—"

"Yes, I made you," said Clara. "And now I will unmake you. Just consider my position, darling. How can I let you tell the police what you know? I am so close to success. All that stands in my way is— you. Up, my dear. To the balcony. Go. Don't make me shoot you."

Nora rose. She tottered. Clara's stiletto heels were much too high for her. She could barely walk. Supporting herself on the back of the sofa, then on an armchair, then on a table, she made her way to the open French doors that led to the balcony.

"That's it," said Clara. "Just a little farther."

Nora took a step onto the balcony and stumbled. She caught herself on the railing and stood up, facing out to the city. Eleven flights aboveground, a strong breeze was blowing. Nora felt this cooling breeze on her forehead and cheeks. "You put me in these shoes," she said, "so that it would be easy to push me over, didn't you?"

"No," answered Clara, "so that it will look like an accident. You were not used to the heels. You were not used to the brandy, which they will smell on your dress. A terrible accident. I don't want to push you, my darling. Won't you jump? Just let yourself go. I think you would rather."

Nora saw the clock on the Metropolitan Life tower a mile to the south. It was midnight. She saw the brilliant glow of Broadway to the west. "'To be, or not to be,'" she whispered.

"Not to, I'm afraid," said Clara.

"Can I ask one thing?"

"I don't know, my dear. What is it?"

"Will you kiss me?" Nora asked. "Just once, before I die?"

Clara Banwell considered this request. "All right," she said.

Nora turned, slowly, her arms behind her, gripping the railing, blinking away the tears in her blue eyes. She tipped her chin up, ever so slightly. Clara, keeping her revolver trained on Nora's waist, brushed a hair from Nora's mouth. Nora closed her eyes.

❧

STANDING OVER MY hotel room sink, I splashed cold water on my face. It was clear to me now that Nora had been, in her family, the target of an Oedipus complex of exactly the mirror-image kind I had just conceived. Without doubt, her mother was killingly jealous of her. But Nora's case was more complex because of the Banwells. Freud was right: the Banwells had in a sense become Nora's substitute mother and father. Banwell had wanted Nora—reverse Oedipus complex again—but Nora had apparently wanted Clara. That didn't fit. Neither, really, did Clara. Her position was the most complex of all. She had befriended Nora, as Freud pointed out, taking her into her confidence, describing her own sexual experiences. Freud believed Nora must be jealous of Clara. But by my lights, Clara should have been jealous of Nora. She should have hated her. She should have wanted to—

I leapt off my bed and ran from the room.

❧

THE MOMENT THEIR LIPS MET, Nora seized Clara's hand, the hand holding the gun. The revolver fired. Nora was unable to dislodge the gun from Clara's hands, but she had managed to direct the barrel away from her own body. The bullet flew into the air above the city.

Nora scratched at Clara's face, drawing blood above and below her eye. When Clara cried out in pain, Nora bit Clara's hand—again, the one holding the gun—as hard as she could. The revolver fell to the concrete floor of the balcony and skittered back into the hotel room.

Clara struck Nora in the face. She struck her a second time, then pulled the girl by the hair to the balcony's edge. There she bent Nora backward over the railing, Nora's long tresses hanging straight down in the direction of the street far, far below.

Nora raised one of her shoes from the floor and brought it down on Clara's foot, the stiletto heel digging into Clara's bare instep. Clara let out a fearful cry and lost her grip on Nora, who tore herself away. She made it past Clara, through the French doors, but fell to the floor, unable to run in Clara's heels. On hands and knees she went on, crawling to reach the gun. Her fingertips had actually touched the pearl handle when Clara yanked her backward by her dress. Clara cast Nora aside, leapt over her, strode to the middle of the room, and seized the pistol.

"Very good, my dear," said Clara, breathing hard. "I had no idea you had it in you."

They were interrupted by a crash. The locked door flew open, bits of wood scattering in the air, and Stratham Younger burst in.

❧

"DR. YOUNGER," SAID Clara Banwell, standing in the middle of Nora's living room and pointing a small revolver directly at my midsection, "how lovely to see you. Please close the door."

Nora lay on the floor a dozen feet away. I saw a bruise on her cheek but, thank God, no blood anywhere. "Are you hurt?" I asked her.

She shook her head.

Exhaling the breath I hadn't realized I was holding in, I closed the door. "And you, Mrs. Banwell," I said, "how are you this evening?"

The corners of Clara's mouth edged up ever so slightly. She was badly scratched above and below her left eye. "I will be better shortly," she said. "Step out onto the balcony, Doctor."

I didn't move.

"Onto the balcony, Doctor," she repeated.

"No, Mrs. Banwell."

"Really?" Clara returned. "Shall I shoot you where you stand?"

"You can't," I said. "You gave your name downstairs. If you kill me, they will hang you for murder."

"You are quite mistaken," replied Clara. "They will hang Nora, not me. I will tell them she killed you, and they will believe me. Have you forgotten? She is the psychopath. She is the one who burned herself with a cigarette. Even her parents think so."

"Mrs. Banwell, you don't hate Nora. You hate your husband. You have been his victim for seven years. Nora has been his victim too. Don't be his instrument."

Clara stared at me. I took a step in her direction.

"Stop where you are," said Clara sharply. "You are a surprisingly poor judge of character for a psychologist, Dr. Younger. And so credulous. What I told you, you think true. Do you believe everything women tell you? Or do you believe them only when you want to sleep with them?"

"I don't want to sleep with you, Mrs. Banwell."

"Every man wants to sleep with me."

"Please lower the gun," I said. "You are overwrought. You have every reason to be, but you misdirect your anger. Your husband beats you, Mrs. Banwell. He has never consummated your marriage. He has made you—made you perform acts—"

Clara laughed. "Oh, stop it. You are too comical. You will make me sick."

It was not the laughter as such, but the condescending note in it, that brought me up short.

"He never made me do anything," said Clara. "I am no one's victim, Doctor. On our wedding night, I told him he would never have me. I, not he. How easy it was. I told him he was the strongest man I had ever met. I told him I would do things he would like even better. Which I did. I told him I would bring him other girls, young girls, whom he could do with as he pleased. Which I did. I told him he could hurt me, and I would make him happy while he hurt me. Which I did."

Nora and I both stared at Clara in silence.

"And he liked it," she added, smiling.

Again there was silence. I finally broke it. "Why?"

"Because I *knew* him," Clara said. "His appetites are insatiable. He wanted me, of course, but not me alone. There were going to be others. Many, many others. Do you think I could consent to be one of many, Doctor? I hated him from the moment I laid eyes on him."

"It is not Nora," I said, "who has brought this upon you."

"It *is*," Clara snapped. "She destroyed everything."

"How?" This was Nora.

"By *existing*," answered Clara with undisguised venom, declining even to look in Nora's direction. "It—he fell in love with her. In love. Like a dog. Not a smart dog. A stupid dog. She was so spoiled and yet so unspoiled. What an enchanting contradiction. It became an obsession. So I had to get the dog his bone, didn't I? One can't live with a man slobbering like that."

"That is why you agreed to have an affair with my father?" asked Nora.

"I didn't *agree*," said Clara contemptuously, addressing Younger, not Nora. "It was my idea. The weakest, most boring man I have ever known. If there is a heaven for selfless women, I—but even then she ruined it. She rejected George. She actually rejected him." Clara took a deep breath; at last her demeanor lightened again. "I tried a great many things to cure him of it. Many different things. Really I did."

"Elsie Sigel," I said.

A minute flinch at the corner of her mouth revealed Clara's surprise, but she didn't waver. "You *do* have talent, Doctor, in the detection line. Have you considered changing careers?"

"You procured your husband another girl from a good family," I went on. "You thought it might make him forget Nora."

"*Very* good. I don't believe any woman alive could have done it, other than myself. But when I found her Chinaman, I had her. She had written him love letters—to a Chinaman! He sold them to me, and I told the poor girl it was my duty to give them to her father unless she helped me. But my dog of a husband wasn't interested. You should have seen him, going through the motions. His mind was"—now Clara cast an eye at the still-prostrate Nora—"on his bone."

"You killed her," I said. "With chloroform. The same chloroform you gave your husband to use on Nora."

Clara smiled. "I said you should be a detective. Elsie simply couldn't keep her mouth shut. And what an unpleasant voice that one had. She left me no choice. She would have told. I could see it in her eyes."

"Why didn't you just kill *me*?" Nora shot out.

"Oh, it did occur to me, darling, but that wouldn't have done at all. You have no idea what it was like to see my husband's face when he understood that you, the love of his life, were doing everything in your little power to ruin him, to destroy him. It was worth more than all his money. Well, almost more, and I am going to have his money in any event. Dr. Younger, I think you've kept me talking long enough."

"You can't kill us, Mrs. Banwell," I said. "If they find us both dead, shot by your gun, they will never believe you innocent. They will hang you. Put it down." I took another step forward.

"Stop!" cried Clara, turning her gun on Nora. "You are bold with your own life. You won't be so bold with hers. Now go to the balcony."

I stepped forward again—not toward the balcony, but toward Clara.

"Stop!" Clara repeated. "Are you mad? I'll shoot her."

"You'll shoot *at* her, Mrs. Banwell," I replied. "And you'll miss. What is that, a twenty-two single-action snub-nose? You couldn't hit a barn door with that unless you were within two feet of it. I'm within two feet of you now, Mrs. Banwell. Shoot me."

"Very well," said Clara, shooting me.

I had the distinct though unaccountable impression of seeing a bullet emerge from the cylinder of Clara's revolver, fly slowly toward me, and pierce my white shirt. I felt a twinge below my lowest left rib. Only then did I hear the shot.

The gun recoiled slightly. I seized Clara's wrists. She struggled to free herself, but couldn't. I forced her toward the balcony—I walking forward, she backward, the gun over our heads, pointed at the ceiling. Nora got up, but I shook my head. Clara kicked over an enormous table lamp in Nora's direction; it broke at her feet, sending a shower of glass onto her legs. I forced her on toward the balcony. We crossed its threshold. I pushed her roughly into the balcony railing, the gun still above our heads.

"It's a long way down, Mrs. Banwell," I whispered in the dark, wincing as the bullet worked its way among my entrails. "Let go of the gun."

"You can't do it," she said. "You can't kill me."

"Can't I?"

"No. That's the difference between us."

Suddenly my stomach felt as if a red-hot fire iron were inside it. I had been certain of my ability to prevent her from gaining the upper hand. Now I was certain no longer. I realized my strength might give way at any moment. The burning inside my ribs seized me again. I lifted her a foot off the floor, never letting go of her wrists, and landed her hard against the side wall of the balcony. We came to a standstill face-to-face, chest-to-chest, arms and hands entangled between our torsos, her back pressed to the wall, our eyes and mouths only a few inches apart. I looked down at Clara, and she up at me. Rage makes some women ugly, some more beautiful. Clara fell into the latter category.

She still had possession of the gun, her finger at the trigger, somewhere between our two bodies. "You don't know which of us the gun is pointed at, do you?" I asked, pressing her even harder against the wall, forcing a gasp from her. "Want to know? It's pointed at you. At your heart."

I could feel the blood running copiously down my shirt. Clara said nothing, her eyes holding mine.

Gathering my strength, I went on. "You're right, I might be bluffing. Why don't you pull the trigger and find out? It's your only chance. In a moment I'll overpower you. Go ahead. Pull the trigger. Pull it, Clara."

She pulled the trigger. There was a muffled blast. Her eyes opened wide. "No," she said. Her body went rigid. She looked at me, unblinking. "No," she repeated. Then she whispered: "My act."

The eyes never closed. Her body slackened. She fell, dead, to the floor.

I was now holding the gun. I went back inside the hotel room. I tried to go to Nora but didn't make it. Instead, I stumbled to the sofa. There I lowered myself, holding my stomach, the blood running out between my fingers, a large red stain expanding on my shirt. Nora ran to me.

"Heels," I said. "I like you in heels."

"Don't die," she whispered.

I didn't speak.

"Please don't die," she begged me. "Are you going to die?"

"I'm afraid so, Miss Acton." I turned my gaze to Clara's corpse, then to the balcony railing, past which I could see a few stars in the faraway night. Ever since they illuminated Broadway, the twinkling of stars had become a lost sight over Midtown. Finally, I looked once more into Nora's blue eyes. "Show me," I said.

"Show you what?"

"I don't want to die not knowing."

Nora understood. She turned her upper body, presenting her back to me, as she had on the day of our first session, in this same room. Lying back against the sofa, I reached out with one hand—my clean hand—and undid the buttons of her dress. When the back fell open, I loosened the ties of her corset and drew the eyelets apart. Behind the crisscrossing laces, below and between her graceful shoulder blades, there were several of the still-healing lacerations. I touched one. Nora cried out, then stifled her cry.

"Good," I said, standing up from the sofa. "That's settled then. Now let's call the police and get me some medical attention, don't you think?"

"But," replied Nora, gazing up at me stupefied, "you said you were going to die."

"I am," I replied. "Someday. But not from this fleabite."

CHAPTER TWENTY-SIX

THE MOMENT I WOKE UP, late Saturday morning, a nurse ushered in two visitors: Abraham Brill and Sándor Ferenczi.

Brill and Ferenczi sported wan smiles. They tried to brave it out, loudly asking how "our hero" was doing, keeping at me until I had reprised the whole story, but in the end they couldn't hide their gloom. I asked what the matter was.

"It's all over," said Brill. "Another letter from Hall."

"For you, in fact," Ferenczi added.

"Which Brill read, naturally," I concluded.

"For God's sake, Younger," Brill exclaimed, "for all we knew, you might be dead."

"Making it open season on my correspondence."

Hall's letter, it turned out, contained both good news and bad news. He had rejected the donation to Clark. He could not accept any funds, he explained, conditional on the university's relinquishing its academic freedom. But he had now made up his mind about Freud's lectures. Unless he heard positively from us by four o'clock today that the *Times* would not be publishing the article he had seen, the lectures would be canceled. He was most apologetic. Freud would of course receive the full fee promised him. Hall would issue a statement that Freud's health precluded him from speaking. Moreover, as a replacement, Hall would select the one person he was certain Freud would want to deliver the keynote lectures in his place: Carl Jung.

It was the last sentence, I think, that galled Brill most. "If we only knew who was behind it all," he said. I could practically hear his teeth gnashing.

There was a knock at the door. Littlemore poked his head in. After making introductions, I urged Brill to describe our situation to the detective. He did, in complete detail. The worst of it, Brill concluded, was not knowing whom we were up against. Who would be so determined to suppress Freud's book and block his lectures in Worcester?

"If you want my advice," said Littlemore, "we ought to go have a little chat with your friend Dr. Smith Jelliffe."

"Jelliffe?" said Brill. "That's ridiculous. He's my publisher. He can only gain from Freud's lectures going well. He's been pushing me to hurry the translation for months."

"Wrong way to think about it," answered Littlemore. "Don't try to figure it out all at once. This Jelliffe guy gets your book manuscript, and when he gives it back to you it's full of weird stuff. And he says it was put there by some pastor who borrowed his printing press? Fishiest story I ever heard. He's the guy to talk to first."

They tried to stop me, but I dressed to go with them. If I weren't such a fool, I would have asked for help tying my shoes; I nearly tore my stitches out doing it. Before Jelliffe's, we made a stop at Brill's apartment. There was one item of evidence Littlemore wanted us to take uptown.

❧

LITTLEMORE WAVED TO an officer in the lobby of the Balmoral. The police had been combing the Banwells' now-empty apartment all morning. Already a favorite among the uniformed men, Littlemore had suddenly become a figure of stature. News of his taking both Banwell and Hugel had spread all over the force.

Smith Ely Jelliffe opened his door clad in pajamas, a wet towel over his head. The sight of Drs. Younger, Brill, and Ferenczi startled him, but his surprise grew to alarm when he saw his nemesis, the detective from last night, jauntily following behind them.

"I didn't know," Jelliffe blurted out to Littlemore. "I didn't know anything about it until after you left. He was in town for only a few hours. There was no incident of any kind, I swear it. He's back at the hospital already. You can call. It won't happen again."

"You two know each other?" Brill asked.

Littlemore questioned Jelliffe about Harry Thaw for several minutes, to the general astonishment of the others. When the detective was satisfied, he asked Jelliffe why he had sent Brill anonymous threats, burned his manuscript, dumped ash in his apartment, and slandered Dr. Freud in the newspaper.

Jelliffe swore his innocence. He professed ignorance of any book-burning or threat-sending.

"Oh, yeah?" said Littlemore. "Then who put those pages into the manuscript, the ones with the Bible stuff on them?"

"I don't know," said Jelliffe. "It must have been those church people."

"Sure it was," said Littlemore. He showed Jelliffe the article of evidence we had stopped for on our way—the single sheet of paper from Brill's manuscript that bore not only a verse from Jeremiah but a small stamped image of a turbaned, bearded, scowling man—and went on. "Then how did this get there? Doesn't look very churchy to me."

Jelliffe's mouth fell open.

"What is it?" asked Brill. "You recognize it?"

"The Charaka," said Jelliffe.

"What?" asked Littlemore.

"Charaka is ancient Hindoo physician," replied Ferenczi. "I said Hindoo. You remember I said Hindoo?"

Younger spoke: "The Triumvirate."

"No," said Brill.

"Yes," Jelliffe acknowledged.

"What?" asked Ferenczi.

Younger addressed Brill: "We should have seen it all along. Who in New York is not only on the board of Morton Prince's journal, privy to everything Prince is going to publish, but also able to have a man arrested in Boston at the drop of a hat?"

"Dana," said Brill.

"And the family offering Clark the donation? Hall told us one of them was a doctor knowledgeable about psychoanalysis. There's only one family in the country rich enough to fund an entire hospital that can also boast a world-famous neurologist among its members."

"Bernard Sachs!" exclaimed Brill. "And the anonymous doctor in the *Times* is Starr. I should have recognized the pompous blowhard the minute I read it. Starr is always boasting of having studied in Charcot's laboratory decades ago. He might actually have met Freud there."

"Who?" asked Ferenczi. "What is Triumvirate?"

Taking turns, Younger and Brill explained. The men they had just named—Charles Loomis Dana, Bernard Sachs, and M. Allen Starr—were the three most powerful neurologists in the country. Collectively, they were known as the New York Triumvirate. They owed their extraordinary prestige and power to an impressive combination of accomplishment, pedigree, and money. Dana was the author of the nation's leading text on adult nervous diseases. Sachs had a worldwide reputation—particularly because of his work on a disease first described by the Englishman Warren Tay—and wrote the first textbook on children's nervous conditions. Naturally, the Sachses were not the social equals of the very best Danas; they could not participate in society at all, being of the wrong religion. But they were richer. Bernard Sachs's brother had married a Goldman; the private bank founded as a result of this alliance was on its way to becoming a Wall Street bastion. Starr, a professor at Columbia, was the least accomplished of the three.

"He's a windbag," said Brill, referring to Starr, "a puppet of Dana's."

"But why would they seek ruin of Freud?" asked Ferenczi.

"Because they are neurologists," answered Brill. "Freud terrifies them."

"I am not following."

"They belong to the somatic school," said Younger. "They believe that all nervous diseases result from neurological malfunction, not psychological causes. They don't believe in childhood trauma; they don't believe sexual repression causes mental illness. Psychoanalysis is anathema for them. They call it a cult."

"Over scientific disagreement," asked Ferenczi, "they would do these things—burn manuscripts, make threats, spread false accusations?"

"Science has nothing to do with it," Brill replied. "The neurologists control everything. They are the 'nerve specialists,' which makes them the experts in 'nervous conditions.' All the women go to them for their hysterics, their palpitations, their anxieties, their frustrations. The practice is worth millions to them. They're right to see us as the devil. We're going to put them out of business. No one's going to consult a nerve specialist once they realize that psychological illnesses are caused by psychology, not neurology."

"Dana was at your party, Jelliffe," Younger pursued. "He was as hostile to Freud as anyone I've ever heard. Did he know of Brill's book?"

"Yes," answered Jelliffe, "but he wouldn't have burned it. He approved it. He encouraged me to publish it. He even found me an editor to help prepare the copy."

"An editor?" asked Younger. "Did this editor ever take the manuscript out of your offices?"

"Certainly," Jelliffe replied. "He often took it home to work on."

"Well, now we know," said Brill. "The bastard."

"What's this Charaka business?" Littlemore asked.

"It's their club," Jelliffe replied. "One of the most exclusive in the city. Hardly anyone is let in. The members wear a signet ring with a face on it. That's the face there—the one on the page."

"It's a cabal," said Brill. "A secret society."

"But these are scientists," Ferenczi protested. "They would burn manuscript and dump ash in Brill's flat?"

"They probably burn incense and sacrifice virgins too," answered Brill.

"The question is whether they are responsible for the story on Jung in the *Times*," said Younger. "That's what we need to know."

"Are they?" Littlemore asked Jelliffe.

"Well, I—I may have heard them talking about it once," said Jelliffe. "And they did make the arrangements for Jung to speak at Fordham."

"Of course," said Brill. "They are launching Jung to bring Freud down. And Hall is falling for it. What are we going to do? We can't fight Charles Dana."

"I don't know about that," Littlemore replied. He addressed Jelliffe again. "You mentioned a Dana last night, didn't you? Same man?"

Jelliffe nodded.

❧

THE SERVANT AT the door of the small but elegant house on Fifty-third Street at Fifth Avenue informed us that Dr. Dana was not at home. "Tell him a detective wants to ask him a few questions about Harry Thaw," Littlemore replied. "And mention that I just came from Dr. Smith Jelliffe. Maybe he'll be at home after he hears that."

On the detective's advice, Littlemore and I alone had made the trip to Charles Dana's house; Brill and Ferenczi returned to the hotel. A minute later, the two of us were invited in.

Dana's house had none of the gaudiness of Jelliffe's apartment or of the other houses recently erected on Fifth Avenue—including those of certain relations of mine. Dana's was a red-brick affair. The furniture was handsome without being heavy. As Littlemore and I entered the foyer, we saw Dana emerge from a dark, well-stocked library. He closed the doors behind him and greeted us. He was surprised at my presence, I believe, but reacted with perfect aplomb. He asked after my Aunt Mamie, I after some of his cousins. He made no inquiry into my reason for accompanying Littlemore. One had to be impressed by the man's grace. He looked his age—sixty, I should have thought—but age suited him well. He showed us to another room where, I imagine, he did business and saw patients.

Our conversation with Dana was brief. Littlemore's tone changed. With Jelliffe, he had been hectoring. He made accusations and dared Jelliffe to deny them. With Dana, he was far more careful—still conveying, however, that we knew something Dana would not want us to know.

Dana displayed none of Jelliffe's cringing. He acknowledged that Thaw had retained his services in connection with the trial but noted that his role, unlike Jelliffe's, had been merely advisory. He had rendered no opinion about Thaw's mental state at any time, past or present.

"Did you render an opinion about Thaw's coming into New York last weekend?" asked Littlemore.

"Was Mr. Thaw in New York last weekend?" replied Dana.

"Jelliffe says it was your decision."

"I am not Mr. Thaw's physician, Detective. Jelliffe is. I severed my professional relationship with Mr. Thaw last year, as public records will demonstrate. Dr. Jelliffe has occasionally sought my counsel, and I have given him what advice I could. I know nothing of Jelliffe's ultimate treatment decisions, and I certainly could not be said to have made them."

"Fair enough," said Littlemore. "I guess I could arrest you for conspiring in the escape of a state prisoner, but it sounds like I couldn't convict you."

"I doubt it very much," said Dana. "But I could probably have you fired if you tried."

"And I guess," said Littlemore, "you also couldn't have made any decisions about stealing a manuscript, burning it, and putting the ashes in the home of Dr. Abraham Brill?"

For the first time, Dana appeared disconcerted.

"Nice ring you got there, Dr. Dana," Littlemore went on.

I hadn't noticed; on Dana's right hand there was a signet ring. No one spoke. Dana clasped his long fingers together—not, however, hiding the ring—and reclined in his chair. "What do you want, Mr. Littlemore?" he asked. He turned to me. "Or perhaps I should ask you that question, Dr. Younger."

I cleared my throat. "It's a tissue of lies," I said. "The accusations you have made against Dr. Freud. Every single one of them is false."

"Assume I know what you are talking about," answered Dana. "I ask you again: what do you want?"

"It's three-thirty," I replied. "In half an hour, I am going to wire G. Stanley Hall in Worcester. I am going to say that a certain story is not going to be published in the *New York Times* tomorrow. I want my telegram to be true."

Dana sat in silence, holding my stare. "Let me tell you something," he said at last. "The problem is this: our knowledge of the human brain is incomplete. We don't have medicines to change the way people think. To cure their delusions. To relieve their sexual desires while keeping them from overpopulating the world. To make them happy. It is all neurology, you know. It has to be. Psychoanalysis is going to set us back a hundred years. Its licentiousness will appeal to the masses. Its prurience will appeal to young scientific minds and even to some old ones. It will turn the masses into exhibitionists and physicians into mystics. But someday people will wake up to the fact that it is all the emperor's new clothes. We will discover drugs to change the way people think, sooner or later. To control the way they feel. The question is only whether, by then, we will still have enough of a sense of shame to be embarrassed by the fact that everyone is running around naked. Send your telegram, Dr. Younger. It will be true—for now."

❧

AFTER LEAVING DANA'S HOUSE, Littlemore drove me across town. "So, Doc," he said, "I know how you feel about Nora and all, but aren't you—I mean, why'd she do it?"

"For Clara," I answered.

"But why?"

I didn't answer.

Littlemore shook his head. "Everybody did everything for Clara."

"She procured girls for Banwell," I said.

"I know," replied Littlemore.

"You know?"

"Last night," he said, "Nora was telling Betty and me about the work she and Clara did with the immigrant families downtown, and it didn't sound kosher to me, if you see what I mean, not after everything else I'd heard. So I got some names and addresses from Nora and ran them down this morning. I found a few of the families Clara had 'helped.' Most of them wouldn't talk, but I finally got the story. I'm telling you, it's ugly. Clara would find girls with no fathers, sometimes no parents at all. Real young girls—thirteen, fourteen, fifteen. She'd pay off whoever was taking care of them and take them to Banwell."

Littlemore drove on without speaking.

"Did you find out," I asked, "how the passage into Nora's bedroom got there?"

"Yup. Banwell gave us his story today too," said the detective. "He blames the whole thing on Clara. He never suspected she was against him—not until yesterday. Three or four years ago, the Actons hired him to rebuild their house at Gramercy Park. That's when they met."

"And Banwell became obsessed with Nora," I said.

"Looks like it. She's—what, fourteen at the time, but he's got to have her. So get this: his boys are working on the house, and they find this old passage running from one of the second-floor rooms to the garden shed out back. Apparently the Actons didn't know it was there. But they're out of town, and Banwell never lets on. He has the passage fixed up so he can enter it from the back alley without ever going onto the Actons' property. And he designs the house so the room on the second floor becomes Nora's new bedroom. I asked him if his plan was just to go to Nora's bedroom one night and rape her. You know what? He laughed in my face. According to him, he never raped anybody. They all wanted it. With Nora, he figures he's going to seduce her, and he needs a way in and out of her room without her parents knowing about it. But I guess Nora didn't go for the seduction."

"She rejected him," I said.

"That's what he told us. He swears he never touched her. Never used the secret passage until this week. You know, I think it really upset him. Maybe no girl ever turned him down before."

"Could be," I said. "Maybe he was in love with her."

"You think so?"

"I think so. And Clara decided to get Nora for him."

"How would she do that?" asked Littlemore.

"I think she tried to make Nora fall in love with *her*."

"What?" he said.

I didn't respond.

"I don't know about *that*," Littlemore went on, "but I'll give you this much: Banwell says getting Nora to play Elizabeth Riverford was Clara's idea. When he builds the Balmoral, he lays down another passage, only this time connected to his own study. The apartment it goes to is going to be his bird's nest. He sets it up just the way he wants it: big brass bed, silk sheets, the works. Fills the closet with lingerie and furs. Puts a couple of his own suits there, too, in a different closet he keeps locked. A little while ago, if you can believe Banwell, Clara tells him Nora has finally said yes. The idea is that Nora's going to rent the apartment under a false name, and she's going to come up to see him whenever she can. I don't know what the truth is there. I didn't want to ask Nora about it."

I knew. Nora had told me the whole story last night, while we waited for the police.

One day in July, Clara tearfully told Nora that she could no longer bear her marriage. George flogged and raped her almost every night. She feared for her life but couldn't leave him, because he would kill her if she did.

Nora was horrified, but Clara said there was nothing anyone

could do. Only one thing could save her, but it was impossible. Clara knew a man highly placed in the police force: Hugel, obviously; Clara had met him when she and Nora were "helping" an immigrant family whose daughter had died. According to Clara, she revealed her plight to him. Hugel took pity on her but said the law was powerless, because a husband had a legal right to rape his wife. When, however, Clara added that George raped other girls too—whose families he paid off in exchange for their silence, and at least one of whom had been killed—the coroner had allegedly grown outraged. He supposedly decided there was only one thing to be done: they must stage a murder.

A girl must be found seemingly dead in the apartment that George kept for his mistresses. It must look like she died by his hand. It could be done, because he himself (the coroner) would administer the catalepsy-inducing drug and he himself would be the medical examiner. A piece of evidence left at the scene would identify Banwell as the perpetrator. Clara made Nora believe the entire scheme originated with the coroner.

Nora remembered being shocked by the audacity of the plan. She asked if Clara really thought it possible.

No, Clara said. She could never ask anyone to play the part of Banwell's mistress and victim. She (Clara) must simply endure her fate.

It was then that Nora said she would do it.

Clara reacted with apparent shock. Absolutely not, she replied. The girl who played the part of the victim would have to allow herself to be hurt. Nora asked Clara if, by hurt, she meant raped. Of course not, Clara said, but the victim would have to let herself be bound, with a cord or rope around her neck, and Clara might even have to leave a mark or two. Nora insisted that she would do it. At last Clara gave in, and they went forward with the plot. Nora was unsure exactly what happened at the Balmoral on Sunday night, undoubtedly because of the coroner's catalepsy-inducing drug. Nora did remember Clara telling her not to scream, and she remembered she kept forgetting her false name. The rest, however, was indistinct. I explained all this to Littlemore.

"I know what happened next," he said. "When Nora wakes up Monday morning, she's with Hugel in the morgue. He tells her the bad news: the tie he was supposed to find at the murder scene, the silk tie with Banwell's monogram, which was going to prove Banwell did it, wasn't there. That's because Banwell went in through the passage as soon as he found out about the 'murder.' He had to get his own clothes out of there, so we didn't connect him to Miss Riverford."

"But Banwell was out of town Sunday night, with the mayor," I said. "Hugel didn't know?"

"None of them knew. Banwell was supposed to be having dinner in the city. Banwell's thing with the mayor in Saranac came up at the last minute. All very hush-hush. There was no way for Clara to find out about it either, because there's no phone at the Banwells' country place. So Clara sneaks in from Tarry Town that night, does her business to Nora around nine or so, and drives back. She told Hugel to put the time of death between midnight and two, because Banwell was supposed to have been home by then."

"But Banwell saw his tie there the next morning and took it away before Hugel arrived."

"Right. Without the tie, Hugel's in trouble. He can't reach Clara. So he decides he's got to stage another fake attack, this one at Nora's house, where they'll leave another piece of evidence. He needs to convict Banwell, see? That's his deal with Clara. She had given him ten thousand dollars up front, and he was going to get another thirty thousand if Banwell was convicted. But something went wrong the second time too, I don't know what. Hugel clammed up."

Again, I could fill in the blanks. Nora had gone along with the second attack both because she still thought she was rescuing Clara and because she didn't know how else she would explain all the wounds she had woken up with. In the second "attack," the coroner would merely tie her up and leave her. She was not to be hurt again at all. And she wasn't. (That was why she hadn't been able to answer my questions yesterday. I asked her whether any *man* had whipped her. She was afraid to tell me the truth, because Clara had sworn that Banwell would kill her—Clara—if he ever found out.) But when the coroner tied Nora up, he had grown unstable. He kept staring at her. He was sweating and seemed to be having trouble swallowing, Nora said. He never threatened her; nor did he molest her. But he kept adjusting the rope around her wrists. He wouldn't leave. Then he brushed up against her.

"Apparently your coroner lost control of himself," I said, without further detail. "Nora screamed."

"And Hugel panicked, right?" said Littlemore. "He runs out the back way. He's got Banwell's tiepin; he meant to leave it in the bedroom. But he's so panicked he forgot. So he throws it into the garden, figuring we'll find it when we search the grounds."

After the coroner ran away, Nora didn't know what to do. The coroner was supposed to have rendered her unconscious, but he had run out without giving her the narcotic. At a loss, Nora pretended she couldn't speak or remember anything about what had happened. Her real voice loss from three years earlier, and her real—although quite limited—amnesia from the night before gave her the idea.

"Why did Banwell put the trunk in the river?" I asked.

"The guy was in a tight spot," said Littlemore. "Think about it. If he let us go through all the stuff in the apartment, he knew we'd trace it and bag him for the murder. But he couldn't just tell us that Elizabeth was Nora. Even if we believed him, he'd have a huge scandal on his hands, and he'd probably go to jail for corrupting a minor. So he told the mayor he was sending Miss Riverford's things back to Chicago. He loaded them into a trunk and took it down to the caisson. Figured it's the perfect place—until he ran into Malley."

"He almost fooled us," I said.

"With Malley?"

"No. When he—when he burned Nora." The thought of it made me feel I had killed the wrong Banwell.

"Yup," said Littlemore. "He wanted us to think Nora was crazy and did everything to herself. He figures if he can pull that off, he can beat the whole rap. Doesn't matter what Nora says; no one will believe her."

"What made him go back to kill her last night?" I asked.

"Nora sent Clara a letter," he answered. "It said she was going to tell the police about everything Banwell did to Clara and to the other girls, the immigrant girls. Apparently Banwell saw it."

"I wonder if Clara let him see it," I said.

"Could be. But then Hugel pays a visit. Banwell's in the apart-

ment when Hugel gets there, and he starts to put two and two together. That night, he ties Clara up to keep her out of the way and
heads downtown to the Actons'. That's when I stumble onto the secret passage at the Balmoral. Boy, Clara was good. She tells me her
husband's gone to kill Nora, but she made it seem like I was dragging
it out of her. I don't think she realized then that Nora wasn't in her
house at all. How did Clara find out Nora was at the hotel?"

"Nora called her," I said. "What about the Chinaman?"

"Leon? They'll never find him," Littlemore answered. "I had a
long talk today with Mr. Chong. Seems that Cousin Leon comes to
him a month ago, says there's a rich guy who will pay them to take a
trunk off his hands. That night, the two of them go to the Balmoral
and bring the trunk back to Leon's room by cab. Next day, Leon's
packing up. Where you going? Chong asks him. Washington, says
Leon, then back to China. Chong's getting nervous. What's in the
trunk? he asks. Look for yourself, says Leon. So Chong opens it, and
he sees one of Leon's girlfriends dead inside. Chong gets upset; he
says the police are going to think Leon killed her. Leon laughs and
says that's exactly what the police are supposed to think. Leon also
tells Chong to show up at the Balmoral the next day, and they'll give
him a real good job. Chong's mad about that. He figures Leon got
paid off big; otherwise he couldn't be going back to China. So, being
a Chinaman, Chong asks for two jobs as his reward, not one, and
Leon fixes it up for him."

We pulled up at the hotel, each in our own thoughts.

Littlemore said, "There's just one thing. Why does Clara work so
hard to get Nora for Banwell if Clara is so jealous of her? That
doesn't make sense."

"Oh, I don't know," I replied, getting out of the car. "Some people
feel a need to bring about the very thing that will most torment
them."

"They do?"

"Yes."

"Why?" asked Littlemore.

"I have no idea, Detective. It's an unsolved mystery."

"That reminds me: I'm not a detective anymore," he said. "The
mayor's making me a lieutenant."

A TORRENTIAL RAIN poured down on our entire party—Freud, a visibly uncomfortable Jung, Brill, Ferenczi, Jones, and myself—at the South Street harbor Saturday evening. As their luggage was loaded onto the overnight boat from New York to Fall River, Freud pulled me to one side.

"You are not coming with us?" he said to me, from the cocoon of his umbrella to the cocoon of mine.

"No, sir. The surgeon said I shouldn't travel for a day or two."

"I see," he replied skeptically. "And Nora remains here in New York, of course."

"Yes," I said.

"But there is still something more, isn't there?" Freud stroked his beard.

I preferred to change the subject. "How are things with Dr. Jung, sir, if I may ask?" I knew—and Freud knew I knew—of the extraordinary scene between Jung and Freud that had taken place the other night.

"Better," Freud replied. "Do you know, I believe he was jealous of you."

"Of me?"

"Yes," said Freud. "It finally came to me that he took my appointing you to analyze Nora as a betrayal. When I explained to him that I named you only because you live here, it improved things between us immediately." He looked out into the rain. "It won't last, however. Not very long."

"I don't understand Mrs. Banwell, Dr. Freud," I said. "I don't understand her feelings for Miss Acton."

Freud reflected. "Well, Younger, you solved the mystery. Remarkable."

"You solved it, sir. You warned me last night that they were all in Mrs. Banwell's orbit and that Clara's friendship with Miss Acton was not entirely innocent. I don't really understand Mrs. Banwell, Dr. Freud. I don't understand what moved *her*."

"If I had to guess," said Freud, "I would say that Nora was for Mrs. Banwell a mirror in which she saw herself as she was ten years ago—and in which she saw, therefore, by contrast, what she had become. Certainly this would account for her desire to corrupt Nora and to hurt her. You must bear in mind the years of punishment she endured as the willing object of a sadist."

"Yet she stayed with him." It couldn't have been only the money that kept her with Banwell. "She was a masochist?"

"There is no such thing, Younger, not in pure form. Every masochist is also a sadist. In men, at any rate, masochism is never primary—it is sadism turned on the self—and Mrs. Banwell unquestionably had a strong masculine side. She may have been plotting the destruction of her husband for some time."

I had one other question. I was unsure whether to voice it; it seemed so basic and ignorant. But I decided to go ahead. "Is homosexuality a pathology, Dr. Freud?"

"You are wondering if Nora is a homosexual," he said.

"I am so transparent?"

"No man can keep a secret," Freud answered. "If his lips are silent, he chatters with his fingertips."

I resisted the urge to glance at my fingertips.

"No need to look at your fingertips," he went on. "You are not transparent. With you, my boy, I merely ask myself how I would have felt in your place. But I will answer your question. Homosexuality is certainly no advantage, but it cannot be classified as an illness. It is no shame, no vice, no degradation at all. In women in particular, there may be a primary narcissism, a self-love, that directs their desire toward others of their sex. I would not call Nora a homosexual, though. I would say, rather, she was seduced. But I should have seen her love for Mrs. Banwell at once. It was plainly the strongest unconscious current in her mental life. You told me the first day how fondly she spoke of Mrs. Banwell, when of course she ought to have felt the fiercest jealousy toward a woman engaged in a sexual act with her father—an act she wished to be performing on him herself. Only the most powerful desire for Mrs. Banwell could have allowed her to repress that jealousy."

Naturally I could not wholly join in this observation. I only nodded in reply.

"You don't agree?" he asked.

"I don't believe Nora was jealous of Clara," I said, "in that way."

Freud raised his eyebrows. "You can't disbelieve that unless you reject Oedipus."

Again I said nothing.

"Ah," said Freud. And he repeated it: "Ah." He took a deep breath, sighed, and observed me closely. "That is why you are not coming to Clark with us."

I considered broaching with Freud my reinterpretation of the Oedipus complex. I would have liked to; I would have liked even more to discuss *Hamlet* with him. But I found I couldn't. I knew how much he had suffered from Jung's seeming defection. There would be other occasions. I would be in Worcester by Tuesday morning, in time for his first lecture.

"In that case," Freud resumed, "let me raise one possibility with you before I go. You are not the first to reject the Oedipus complex. You will not be the last. But you may have a special reason for doing so, associated with my person. You have admired me from afar, my boy. There is always a kind of father love in such relationships. Now, having met me in the flesh, and having the opportunity to complete this cathexis, you fear doing so. You fear I will take myself away from you, as your real father did. Thus you forestall my anticipated withdrawal by denying the Oedipus complex."

The rain beat down. Freud looked at me with kindly eyes. "Someone has told you," I said, "that my father committed suicide."

"Yes."

"But he didn't."

"Oh?" asked Freud.

"I killed him."

"What?"

"It was the only way," I said, "to overcome my Oedipus complex."

Freud looked at me. For a moment I was afraid he might actually take me seriously. Then he laughed aloud and shook my hand. He thanked me for helping him through his week in New York, and especially for rescuing his lectures at Clark. I accompanied him onto the boat. His face seemed much more deeply furrowed than it had been a week ago, his back slightly bent, his eyes a decade older. As I began to disembark, he called out my name. He was at the railing; I had taken a step or two down the gangway. "Let me be honest with you, my boy," he said, from under his umbrella, as the rain poured down. "This country of yours: I am suspicious of it. Be careful. It brings out the worst in people—crudeness, ambition, savagery. There is too much money. I see the prudery for which your country is famous, but it is brittle. It will shatter in the whirlwind of gratification being called forth. America, I fear, is a mistake. A gigantic mistake, to be sure, but still a mistake."

❧

THAT WAS THE LAST TIME I saw Freud in America. The same night, I took Nora to the top of the Gillender Building at the corner of Nassau and Wall, a place where vast fortunes were made and lost every day. On a Saturday night, Wall Street was deserted.

I had gone to the Actons' directly after seeing Freud off. Mrs. Biggs greeted me like an old friend. Harcourt and Mildred Acton were nowhere to be seen; they were evidently not receiving. I asked after Nora's condition. Mrs. Biggs noisily withdrew, and Nora came down presently.

Neither of us could find a word to say. Finally, I asked if she would care for a walk; I opined that it would be medically advisable. Suddenly I was sure she would decline and I would never see her again.

"All right," she said.

The rain had stopped. The smell of wet pavement, which in the city passes for freshness, rose pleasantly in the air. Downtown, the pavement turned to cobblestone, and the clip-clop of distant horses, with no motorcar or omnibus in sight, reminded me of the New York I knew as a boy. We spoke little.

The doorman at the Gillender heard we wished to see the famous view and let us in. In the dome room, nineteen stories up, four great pointed windows overlooked the city, one facing each direction of the compass. Uptown, we could see mile after mile of the ever-expanding northward march of electric Manhattan; to the south was the tip of the island, the water, and the burning torch of the Statue of Liberty.

"They are going to demolish the building any day now," I said.

The Gillender, when erected in 1897, was one of the tallest skyscrapers in Manhattan. With its slender silhouette and classical proportions, it was also one of the most widely admired. "It will be the tallest building in the history of the world to be torn down."

"Have you ever been happy?" Nora asked abruptly.

I considered. "Dr. Freud says that unhappiness is caused when we cannot let go of our memories."

"Does he say how one is supposed to let go of one's memories?"

"By remembering them."

Neither spoke.

"That does not sound quite logical, Doctor," said Nora.

"No."

Nora pointed to a rooftop about a block to the north. "Look. That's the Hanover Building, where Mr. Banwell forced himself on me three years ago."

I said nothing.

"You knew?" she asked. "You knew I would see it from here?"

Again I made no answer.

"You are still treating me," said Nora.

"I never treated you."

She gazed out. "I was so very stupid."

"Not nearly so stupid as I."

"What will you do now?" Nora asked.

"Return to Worcester," I said. "Practice medicine. The students will be coming back in a few weeks."

"My classes start the twenty-fourth," Nora replied.

"Then you are going to Barnard after all?"

"Yes. I have bought my books already. I'm leaving my parents' house. I'll be living uptown, in a dormitory called Brooks Hall."

"And what will you be studying at Barnard, Miss Acton?" I asked. "Shakespeare's women?"

"As a matter of fact," she replied airily, "I am thinking of a concentration in Elizabethan drama and psychology. Oh—and also detection."

"An absurd combination of interests. No one will take it seriously."

There was another pause.

"I guess," I said, "we ought to say good-bye then."

"I've been happy once," she answered.

"Once?"

"Last night," she said. "Good-bye, Doctor. Thank you."

I didn't answer. It was a good thing. Had I not given her the extra instant, she might not have said the words I longed to hear:

"Are you going to kiss me good-bye at least?" she asked.

"Kiss you?" I replied. "You are under age, Miss Acton. I wouldn't dream of it."

"I'm like Cinderella," she said, "only in reverse. At midnight I turn eighteen."

Midnight came. And so it fell out that I could not bring myself to leave New York City even once all the rest of that young month.

IN JULY OF 1910, George Banwell was found not guilty of murdering Seamus Malley, the judge dismissing the charge for want of evidence. Banwell was convicted, however, of the attempted murder of Nora Acton. He spent the rest of his life in prison.

Charles Hugel served eighteen months for accepting a bribe and falsifying evidence. He slept badly in prison, on some nights not at all, contracting nervous illnesses from which he never recovered.

One fine summer day in 1913, Harry Thaw walked out the front door of the Matteawan State Hospital for the Criminally Insane, stepped into a waiting car, and rode off to Canada. He was captured there and extradited back to New York, where he stood trial for escape. The prosecution was unwise. To convict Thaw, the prosecutor had to convince the jury that he was sane at the time of the escape, but if the jury found him sane, he had a legal right to escape, because a sane man cannot lawfully be confined in a lunatic asylum. By the end of the proceedings, Thaw had obtained a complete and unconditional release. Nine years later, he horsewhipped a young man and was incarcerated again.

Chong Sing was released from custody on September 9, 1909, his earlier confession deemed to have been the product of coercion. No charges were brought against him. Despite an international manhunt, William Leon was never found.

George McClellan did not run in the mayoral election of 1909 and never held elected office again. But he made good on his pledge to complete the Manhattan Bridge if it was the last thing he did in office. In those days, a mayor's term ended on the last day of the calendar year. On December 31, 1909, McClellan cut the ribbon on the Manhattan Bridge, opening it to traffic.

Jimmy Littlemore was officially promoted to lieutenant on September 15, 1909. He and Betty were married just before Christmas. Greta was one of the guests, accompanied by her baby.

Ernest Jones never learned of Freud's involvement in the investigation of the crimes of George and Clara Banwell. Freud did not want his role, such as it was, made public, and he did not trust Jones to keep the secret. Jones did, however, hear all about the Charaka society. He was especially taken with their signet ring. He resolved to have such a ring made for Freud's genuinely loyal followers, to identify themselves to one another wherever they should go. Jung, needless to say, did not get one.

&.

IN THE DECADES after Freud's lectures at Clark, it became clear that 1909 marked a watershed in American psychiatry and culture. Freud's appearance at the university was a signal success. Brill's translation of Freud's papers on hysteria came out—a little behind schedule—after the proceedings came to a close. Psychoanalysis took root in American soil and quickly rose to stunning prominence. Freud's sexual theories triumphed, and the psychotherapeutic culture began to spread its roots.

Jung's Fordham lectures, in which he openly broke with Freud, finally took place in 1912. That same year, the *Times* published both its admiring full-page story on Jung and Moses Allen Starr's allegations about Freud's "peculiar" life in Vienna. But it was too late. Jung's star never rose anywhere near as high as Freud's. His rupture with Freud precipitated in him a bout of deep depression, marked by several psychotic or quasi-psychotic episodes. He would later deride Freud's ideas as "Jewish psychology."

Psychoanalysis sundered the connection between neurology and nervous disease. Indeed, it made the term *nervous disease* obsolete, replacing it with a whole new vocabulary of repressed desire, unconscious fantasy, id, ego, superego, and of course sexuality. Psychology was reborn, and the somatic neurological treatment of mental illness would for almost a century be spurned as obsolete, backward, unenlightened.

Freud himself never took the satisfaction one would have

expected from the success of psychoanalysis in this country. Mystifying his colleagues, he called Smith Ely Jelliffe a criminal. His ideas might be famous in America, he said, but they were not understood. "My suspicion of America," Freud confided to a friend toward the end of his life, "is unconquerable."

The Interpretation of Murder is a work of fiction from beginning to end, but much is based on actual fact. Sigmund Freud did of course visit the United States in 1909, arriving aboard the steamship *George Washington* with Carl Jung and Sándor Ferenczi on the evening of August 29 (notwithstanding the fact that Ernest Jones's classic biography originally gave the date as September 27, "corrected" in later editions to the still-erroneous August 27). Freud did stay at the Hotel Manhattan in New York City for a week before traveling to Clark University to deliver his famous lectures, and he did contract a kind of horror of America. While in the United States, Freud was indeed asked to render impromptu psychoanalyses, although never, so far as we know, by the mayor of New York City.

The Manhattan of 1909 described in this book was painstakingly researched. The architecture, the city streets, high society—almost every detail, down to the color of the paneling on the taxis, is based on fact. Errors undoubtedly remain; readers who find any are encouraged to tell me about them at www.interpretationofmurder.com. All remaining errors are solely my responsibility.

I could not, however, stick to fact on every New York detail. To begin with, a few locations had to be changed. The main city morgue, for example, was at that time in Bellevue Hospital, on Twenty-sixth Street, whereas I have located Coroner Hugel—a fictional character—and his morgue downtown in an invented building. Similarly, I had to invent the Balmoral, where Elizabeth Riverford's body is found, but knowledgeable readers will recognize at once the real building—the Ansonia—on which the Balmoral, including its fountain with seals cavorting within, is based. Or again, while the Manhattan Bridge caisson is factual in most respects, it would have been filled with concrete by September 1909, and it did not have the pressurized debris-elimination chambers, opening onto the river, described as "windows" in this book. In reality, there would have been a longer pressurized debris chute, but I needed the "windows" for reasons I need not explain to those who have already read the book.

I have also moved certain historical events backward or forward in time. A small example involves Abraham Brill's reference to Theodore Roosevelt's "hyphenated Americans." History buffs will point out that Roosevelt did not give his well-known "hyphenated Americans" speech until 1915. (The disparaging term was, however, already in widespread use by 1909, and the press would have reported Roosevelt's views before 1915. Interested readers may, for example, consult the *New York Times* of February 17, 1912, page 3, which tells us that Roosevelt "excoriate[d] hyphenated Americans" in an article he had just published in Germany. Brill, conscious of his German accent throughout his life, would have been highly sensitive to this issue.) Or again, the texts Dr. Younger consults to discover the cause of Nora Acton's vision of herself lying in her own bed are real, but several were written after 1909. On the other hand, Detective Littlemore might indeed have read H. G. Wells's short story describing a similar event; that story, *Under the Knife,* first appeared around 1896.

Another slight temporal relocation concerns the strike at the Triangle Shirtwaist Company, where Betty is hired; the strike did not take place until November 1909 (the famous fire occurred in 1911). Another is Mrs. Fish's fictitious ball at the Waldorf-Astoria. In reality, the 1909 social season in Manhattan would have begun later. Incidentally, the Waldorf-Astoria described here is not the hotel we know by the same name today, located on Park Avenue north of Grand Central Terminal. The first Waldorf-Astoria stood on Fifth Avenue at Thirty-fourth Street; it was demolished in 1930 to make way for the Empire State Building.

A more significant case of time-shifting is my treatment of Jung's break with Freud, which in reality occurred over a three-year period culminating around 1912. I have telescoped the relevant events and moved some of them to America even though they took place elsewhere. Nevertheless, the scenes between Freud and Jung described in my book—amazing as they may seem—did apparently take place.

For example, a loud and mysterious report really did interrupt the two men in the middle of an argument about the occult (with Freud taking a skeptical position), and Jung really did claim to have caused the noise telekinetically through what he called a "catalytic exteriorization." When Freud scoffed, Jung predicted an immediate recurrence of the sound to prove his point, and, inexplicably, his words came true. This episode took place, however, not in a room at the Hotel Manhattan in September 1909, but rather in Freud's house in Vienna in March of that year. Moreover, Freud twice fainted in Jung's presence, including one occasion on August 20, 1909, the day before the voyagers set off for America. Freud's enuretic "mishap" in New York City was disclosed by Jung himself in 1951—although Jung may have invented the story to discredit Freud.

Jung's biographers disagree about his alleged philandering, delusions, and anti-semitism. The portrait of Jung in this book is just that—a portrait, based on his writings, his letters, and the conclusions reached by some, but not all, of those who have written about him.

Readers may wonder whether Freud and Jung would really have expressed the views I attribute to them in *The Interpretation of Murder*. The answer, in almost every case, is that they did express them. Much of Freud and Jung's dialogue is drawn from their own letters, essays, and statements reported in other published sources. For example, in my book Freud says, "Satisfying a savage instinct is incomparably more pleasurable than satisfying a civilized one." Interested readers can find the corresponding observation in Freud's 1930 *Civilization and Its Discontents*, in volume 21, page 79, of the Standard Edition of Freud's collected works.

As Freud aficionados will have instantly recognized, Nora is based on Dora, the young woman described in Freud's most controversial case history. Dora's real name was Ida Bauer; she was not American, nor was she treated by Freud in America, although she died in New York City in 1945. Nora is in no sense a carbon copy of Dora, but the basic facts of Nora's predicament—the advances made on her by her father's best friend, her father's refusal to take her side, her father's affair with this same friend's wife, and the attraction Nora herself feels toward the wife—can all be found in the Dora case. The Oedipal interpretation of Nora's hysteria that Freud offers

Younger in my book, including the oral component, is the actual interpretation that Freud offered the real-life Dora. The physical attacks, however, and the murder mystery are of course entirely imaginary.

Mayor George B. McClellan's attempt to wrest control of the city government from Tammany Hall is well known. Indeed, it is even possible that McClellan would have personally supervised an important homicide investigation in September 1909, because he had at that time practically put the entire police department under mayoral control. On the other hand, McClellan's interest in securing a nomination for another term is pure speculation. Publicly, he insisted he was not running.

Charles Loomis Dana, Bernard Sachs, and M. Allen Starr are historical figures. They were in fact known as the Triumvirate; all were bitter enemies of Freud and psychoanalysis. I want to emphasize, however, that the villainous acts implicitly imputed to them here are completely fictitious. There was no plot to derail Freud's lectures at Clark. I have also, for dramatic purposes, exaggerated Dana's wealth and his blood relationship to the more prominent family bearing the same last name. Although Charles L. Dana apparently descended from the same illustrious ancestor as the more prominent Danas, he was born in Vermont and may not even have known his exact relationship to Charles A. Dana, the other New York Danas, or the Boston Danas. Smith Ely Jelliffe is another historical figure whom I have embellished. Jelliffe was not, for example, rich; nor is there any reason to think he was a womanizer. (Incidentally, while the Players Club is real, the suggestion that prostitution went on there is pure speculation.) It is the case, however, that Jelliffe was both a chief psychiatric expert for the murderer Harry Thaw and the publisher of Freud's first book in English—the *Selected Papers on Hysteria,* translated by Abraham Brill. It is also the case that Jelliffe attended meetings of the Charaka Club, the exclusive (but not secret) society that Dana and Sachs cofounded.

The accounts of Thaw's sadistic attacks on his wife and other young women are taken almost verbatim from documentary sources. For the record, Mrs. Merrill's astonishing testimony was given not at Thaw's murder trial in 1907, but at one of Thaw's subsequent sanity hearings. Moreover, it is only an urban legend (although reported as fact countless times) that Thaw was tried at the Jefferson Market courthouse; he was arraigned there, but both his murder trials took place in the criminal courts building on Centre Street, next to the Tombs. There is no evidence that Thaw ever visited Mrs. Merrill's establishment during the period of his confinement in the Matteawan asylum. Given the ease with which he escaped, however, such an absence without leave would not have been inconceivable.

The body of Miss Elsie Sigel, granddaughter of General Franz Sigel, was indeed discovered in the summer of 1909 in a trunk in an Eighth Avenue apartment belonging to one Leon Ling. The character called Chong Sing in my book is a combination of the real life Chong Sing and another individual also involved in the case. Miss Sigel's body, however, was found about two and a half months before Freud arrived in New York, and, needless to say, the discovery was not made by Detective Jimmy Littlemore, who is an entirely imaginary character.

Equally imaginary is Dr. Stratham Younger, as is Younger's love affair with Nora.

ACKNOWLEDGMENTS

My deepest thanks to my brilliant wife, Amy Chua, whose idea this book was, and to my beloved daughters, Sophia and Louisa, who (reading a PG version) saw mistakes no one else did, starting on the very first page. I owe a great debt to Suzanne Gluck and John Sterling for believing in this novel, and to Jennifer Barth and George Hodgman for making it better. I want to thank my parents, brother, and sister for their deep insight and affection. Debby Rubenfeld, Jordan Smoller, Alexis Contant, Anne Dailey, Marina Santilli, Susan Birke Fiedler, Lisa Gray, Anne Tofflemire, and James Bundy were kind enough to provide early, invaluable critical readings. Heather Halberstadt was a tremendous fact-checker, and I am grateful to Kenn Russell for his meticulous eye.

JED RUBENFELD attended Princeton University, the Juilliard School of Drama, and Harvard Law School. Currently the Robert R. Slaughter Professor of Law at Yale University, Rubenfeld is the author of the recently published *Revolution by Judiciary: The Structure of American Constitutional Law* (Harvard University Press, 2005) and the acclaimed *Freedom in Time: A Theory of Constitutional Self-Government* (Yale University Press, 2001).